This book was awesome! It made me feel like I was there. When I started reading it, I did not want to stop. I was so anxious to see what would happen next. This book is definitely going on my favorite book list. **—Anna Ioannidis (10 years old)**

In *Raising Dragons,* Bryan Davis has infused fantasy into every teenager's normal high school experience. The result is riveting. The adventure mixes believable characters with heart-thumping suspense. Realistic heroes defeating delightfully evil rogues. Good versus evil—it doesn't get any better than this. Readers will be furiously reading late into the night. **—Donita K. Paul (Award-winning author of Dragonspell)**

It's AWESOME! I loved it! Why doesn't anyone publish cool books like this anymore? **—Ben Klopfenstein (15 years old)**

This is SO cool! It's one of my favorites! **—Michelle Klopfenstein (14 years old)**

Ben and Michelle DEVOURED the book and had a ball. You've told a gripping story with all the elements kids love—characters they can identify with, knights, dragons, and lots of action. You've written a great story! **—Connie Neumann (Author and mother of two)**

I love this story. If you like Christian fantasy you'll love *Raising Dragons,* in the Harry Potter genre but with more backbone. **—Thomas Tacker (Professor of Economics, Embry Riddle University)**

Just finished reading *Raising Dragons* with my son. We really enjoyed it, as much as the Redwall books and the Narnia series. **—Karen Whiting (Author, teacher, and educational television host).**

I couldn't put it down. **—Kistler London (Author's editor for books published by University Press of Florida and University of Georgia Press)**

It was very suspenseful. I can hardly wait for the sequel to be written. I'm glad I didn't miss reading this spectacular book. **—Sarah Orlando (15 years old)**

Raising Dragons was intriguing and thought provoking. It was easy to sympathize and identify with Billy. The plot was extremely suspenseful. I'm glad I read this in the summer, because I couldn't put it down. **—Heather Orlando (18 years old)**

It was very exciting and kept me on the edge of my seat. I read it every chance I had. I think it would make a great movie! **—Andrew Day (14 years old)**

This allegorical fantasy will thrill and keep any age in suspense. I was refreshed by this wholesome narrative and relationships. I was inspired by the metaphors of spiritual truths. **—Esther Day (Mother of Andrew)**

I love *Raising Dragons,* a modern-day fantasy where the basic virtues of life like trusting a loved one, hoping beyond hope, and good conquering evil are constantly being challenged and dramatically affirmed. I'm looking forward to the sequel. **—Olivia Allmand (18 years old)**

I enjoyed it so much I can't even tell you. The characters are awesome. Merlin's riddle in the beginning is pure genius. I've read *The Lord of the Rings* three times, so I know a great book. **—Duncan Stuart (11 years old)**

Raising Dragons

Bryan Davis

Raising Dragons

Living Ink Books published by AMG Publishers
6815 Shallowford Road
Chattanooga, Tennessee 37421

Raising Dragons is the first of four books in the youth fantasy fiction series, *Dragons in Our Midst.*

ISBN: 0–89957–170–0

First printing—July 2004

Cover designed by Daryle Beam, Market Street Design, Inc., Chattanooga, Tennessee

Interior design and typesetting by Reider Publishing Services, West Hollywood, California

Edited and Proofread by Jan Dennis, Jeannie Taylor, Becky Miller, Sharon Neal, and Warren Baker

Printed in Canada
10 09 08 07 –T– 12 11 10 9 8

Once upon a time a crazy father told his son about a dream he had. Together, they twisted that dream, broke it into pieces, and built it into a story that touched their hearts. Thank you, James, for dreaming with me.

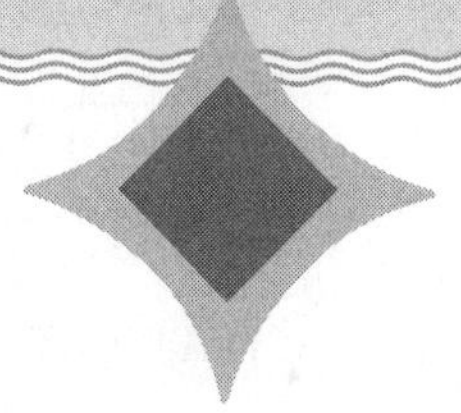

Contents

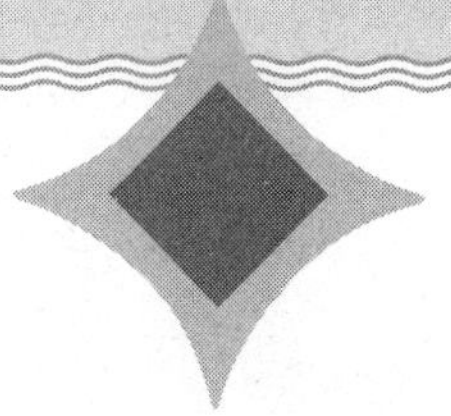

Acknowledgments

To my precious seven, my inspiration for all things fantastic, for as long as I draw breath, for as long as I am able to carry my sword and raise my shield, I will be there to protect you from the slayers. Count on it.

To my friends who worked with and for AMG to make this book possible, Dan Penwell, Warren Baker, Dale Anderson, Jeannie Taylor, and Becky Miller, thank you for dreaming BIG.

To my dear, sweet wife. . . . Thank you . . . for everything.

Merlin's Riddle

When dragons flew in days of old
With valor in their wings,
One fell prey to evil's song
And learned what Satan sings.

Goliath, stained with Satan's words,
Made other dragons flee,
For songs like leaven spread decay
Corrupting souls born free.

Now Satan's scales coat dragon lore;
He hides between the lines.
He sings foul words in books corrupt
And dances on their spines.

Are dragons vile? Are dragons tame?
Depends on whom you ask.
Do scales hide tricks of Satan when
He dons a fearful mask?

One man corrupted all his kin;
One dragon brought all shame.
One man redeemed His fallen race;
Will dragons find the same?

Yet dragons dwell in hearts of men,
From God and some from baals,
And some sing words with angels' wings
While most chant Satan's scales.

God redeems what men cannot
Forgives what e'er thou didst
Who else can save the men of earth
With dragons in our midst?

CHAPTER 1

Dragon Breath

"Halt, foul dragon!"

Billy stared at the tall stranger, a ghostly figure draped in dark chain mail. He looked like a knight of some kind, like a toy box action figure come to life. But what was he so mad about? *Could he be yelling at me?*

The knight swung a sword in his right hand. Its brilliant blade flashed in the sun, and his armor jingled all over his body, echoing his swift, skillful moves. With a wave of his shield he barked a challenge. "I fear you not, fiend, nor your hellish fire! Come to battle, and we shall see whom the Creator will protect!"

Billy opened his mouth to answer, but he couldn't talk. His throat burned like a sizzling sidewalk, and acid bubbled up from his boiling stomach. With a convulsive shudder, he belched a plume of hot, steamy gases, blistering his tongue and scorching his lips. A second later a raging river of fire blasted through his gaping mouth and hurtled toward the knight.

The warrior jerked his shield up and tucked his body behind its protective armor. The flaming torrent splashed around the shield's edges, tearing the sword from his hand and enveloping his sleeve. The knight shook his hand and flapped his blazing arm. "Cursed lizard!"

Billy clamped his hand over his mouth and tried to suck cool air between his fingers to soothe his swollen tongue. *What's going on? Did that fire come from me? Does he think I'm the dragon?* Billy looked at his hands. They were normal, eight fingers and two thumbs, no scales or claws. But something was different. A ring glittered on his right index finger. Somehow it looked . . . familiar.

In the ring's center a dark red stone stared at him like a bloody luminescent eye, the prophetic eye of a mysterious old man, a deep cauldron of swirling scarlet. Billy felt the cyclonic vision drawing him closer and closer, and his mind swam in the dizzying whirlpool. The stone reflected everything around him, even his worried face. As the eye's red glow deepened, Billy's features morphed. His ears grew long and pointed, and his mouth stretched out wide and toothy. Within seconds the transformation was complete. "I *am* a dragon!" he shouted.

The knight appeared again from behind the shield, holding his bare arm away from his body. His sleeve had been scorched to ashes. An angry, reddish brown welt on his forearm oozed curling strings of smoke like the rising fumes of a cattle brand.

"Of course you're a dragon," he bellowed. "Do you think me a fool?" He raised his sword again. This time it cast a laser-like beam through its point, shooting high into the sky, and the knight tightened his jaw with renewed strength. "I still fear you not, neither your fire from hell nor your demon wings!"

Wings? Did he say 'wings'? Billy swung his head around. Wings! He tried flapping them. They worked! He flapped them harder, and he felt his body lift from the ground. Ten feet. Twenty feet. He watched the shrinking knight wave his sword, but he could no longer understand his shouts; he squeaked like an enraged mouse, and his words scattered in the wind, becoming a ringing sound, more like an alarm clock than a bellowing knight. It slowly faded away like the sound of a tambourine in the hand of a dozing player.

Billy flew higher and higher until all light seemed to melt away, leaving him floating through a black canopy of calm. The air thinned to a bitter cold vacuum, and his wings flapped against nothingness, finding no air to grab to keep his body aloft. Without warning they collapsed and shrank to the size of butterfly wings. Billy felt like an airborne penguin, frozen and flightless, and he dropped through the vacuum like a sock full of marbles. He flailed his arms, desperately trying to grab something, anything, to stop his fall. He tried to scream, but his voice died in the hollow void. Could anyone save him? Any second he would crash into trees or rocks below, breaking every bone in his body. He closed his eyes. He was falling, falling . . .

Billy shot up to a sitting position. His eyes bulged to read the dim surroundings. He panted, his tongue hanging out like a thirsty spaniel's. Instead of the horrible, cold, falling sensation, he felt softness underneath and warmth over his legs. He sucked his tongue back in and groped through the covers with trembling fingers. With heavy gasps he spat out words of relief. "I'm in bed! It was just a dream!"

He rubbed his palms against his sweat-dampened cheeks. *No scales!* He craned his neck to get a glimpse of his back, and he tried to reach with his hands, but his tossing and turning must have twisted his pajama top enough to restrict his motion. He jumped to his feet and tiptoed toward the light switch, dodging his half-finished pencil sketches, small wrinkled ghosts in the dawn's obscure glow. With an upward swipe he slapped at the wall. *Missed!* He slapped again. *Ah! Light!*

Billy squeezed his eyes shut and then blinked at the two bulbs in the ceiling fixture. With a series of one-footed hops and careful steps, he maneuvered through his art-strewn room and headed for his mirror, almost afraid to look when he turned his back toward his reflection. He breathed a huge sigh of relief. *No wings!* A sweaty pajama top clung to his shoulders, wrinkled and wet, but it lay flat against his otherwise bare skin. He remembered his fiery breath in the dream and smacked his hot, dry lips. *I feel like I fried that knight and ate him for breakfast!*

With his school clothes tucked under his arm, he shuffled down the hall toward the bathroom, thinking about the dream. It was already fading fast, like fog chased away by a bright morning sun. *Was it a knight? I don't remember. Was I really a dragon?*

Still smacking his lips, he flicked on the light and looked around the bathroom countertop. *Ah, there's the mouthwash.* He grabbed the plastic bottle and read the writing on the side. "Makes your breath sparkling, clean, and cool!" *Well, it works for the guys on television.* Billy swished and gargled several times, but his mouth still felt like used charcoal. *What was the song they sang on the commercial? Oh, yeah. "Tired of that old doggie breath? Make it clean with Super Fresh!"* At this point, doggie breath would have been an improvement.

Billy frowned at his reflection and slammed the plastic bottle on the countertop. *Nothing helps.*

With one palm on the sink, he leaned toward the mirror, rubbing his chin to feel for any telltale signs of emerging whiskers. Not today. But the zits were under control—that was good. As he straightened his body, he examined the hair on his arms. It seemed thicker and more reddish than ever, even though there wasn't a hint of red in the company of brown follicles on his head, a flattened, ragtag mat of unruly strands that needed a dose of discipline. He brushed his hair with a quick sweep of his fingers, and his thick, short nap perked straight up and then wilted to one side.

Looking closely at his reflection, he leaned forward until he could see the individual pores in his skin. With his mouth open wide, he breathed on his image, straining his eyes to catch any results. The mirror didn't fog up. *Third day in a row!*

He drew back and blew softly on his knuckles. "Ouch!" He shook his hand and doused it with cool water. *Scalded by my own breath!* A red blister appeared under the water's spray. *Wow! My breath's never been this bad before!*

Was it finally time to tell his mom and dad about the problem? Would they make him wear a surgical mask to keep everyone safe? Some of the kids at school already called him "Dragon Breath." He didn't want a new name, like "Lizard Lips" or something.

Maybe it was a fungus, some alien life form that took up residence in his cheeks to create a new civilization. When he ran his tongue along the roof of his mouth, it felt like he was licking glazed pottery, a series of slick ridges that didn't register his tongue's caress. *Aliens that live off saliva? I guess stranger things have happened. I just can't remember when.*

"William!" Billy heard his mother calling from downstairs. "Hurry up! You still have to eat breakfast before the bus gets here!"

Billy sighed and pulled on his clothes, starting with his favorite pants—the off-white ones with deep pockets on the sides of the lower legs. The right-hand pocket still held two pens and a mechanical pencil, all tightly clipped to the opening. After throwing on a shirt and hurriedly tying his shoes, he headed toward the stairs, pausing for a minute to pet Gandalf. The long-haired cat yawned and arched his back to fully take in Billy's deep strokes. "I guess you'd never call me Dragon Breath, would you?" Billy rubbed the purring cat one more time and then bounded down the stairs, jackhammering every second stair on the way down. With a long-legged leap, he skipped the last four steps, bringing his tennis shoes in for a slap landing against the wood floor.

He stopped and listened for a second. *Mom's humming. That means something good's cooking.*

He followed the sweet sound, and his nose picked up the delicious smells of morning. He inhaled deeply, relishing the delightful aromas of fried bacon and fresh coffee, and his mood perked up, prompting him to whistle along with his mother's song, a tune he had heard recently in a movie. *What's that song called? Something about remembering the past, I think.*

As soon as he walked into the kitchen, she turned toward him and held up a foil pouch and a tall glass of orange juice. "Your father's having bacon and eggs," she said, "but I didn't know if you'd be up on time, so I didn't make you any. I don't think there's time for me to make more."

Billy grimaced at the silver pouch. "Pop-Tarts again?"

"The early bird gets the hot breakfast. You're the one who just had to stay up late, you know."

Billy took the pouch and glass, leaned against the counter, and sipped the juice while absentmindedly watching his mom bustle around the kitchen. Since his recent growth spurt, he no longer had to reach upward to take something from her hand. Her slender, five-foot-seven frame matched his own, except for the obvious differences, of course. She was definitely female, with shoulder-length hair, lighter than his own, but not quite blonde. Her skin also displayed a lighter tone, with a hint of German or Swedish facial features.

Billy glanced at the breakfast table. His father leaned back in his chair munching a piece of toast while gripping the newspaper with his strong, hairy hands. Billy carried a true blend of his mother and father, his own skin tinted with his dad's tawnier coloring. He had always thought Dad had British ancestors, though when he asked one day, his father had said, "My complexion's too dark, and I'd never be able to get the hang of drinking hot tea."

Billy shook himself out of his trance. "Mom, can I help you with the dishes or something?"

She had just put a frying pan in the sink. "No, thanks. Your dad's going to do them after he eats." She squirted a stream of soap into the pan and turned on the faucet. "Were you working on the poster for the festival last night?"

"No, I wanted to finish that portrait for Dad's friend."

"The one of the basset hound? Dr. Franklin's dog?"

"Yeah, I left it on Dad's—"

"Present and accounted for," a deep voice interrupted. "I have it right here."

Billy swiveled to see his father holding up a large sheet of paper.

"You did a great job," he continued. "It looks just like Maggie."

With two long strides, Billy stepped over to the table and sat down, placing his glass of juice next to his elbow. "Thanks," he said, reaching for his dad's cup of coffee. With his fingers wrapped around the warm mug, he waited, displaying a big smile and a "may I please have a sip?" look. His father glared at him, but Billy knew it was just an act. Although his father's thick eyebrows had curled downward, and every line on his forty-something face had taken a hairpin turn toward his chin, the gleam in his brown eyes gave away his playacting.

Billy took a long slurp and watched over the edge of the cup while his father hid a big smirk and pretended to be interested again in the drawing. Billy set the cup down, let out a satisfied "Ahhh!" and wiped his mouth with his father's napkin. "The photo of Maggie that Dr. Franklin gave you was small," Billy explained, pointing at the paper, "so I blew her up real big on my easel."

"Old Doc will love it. How do you want to be paid this time?"

Billy took a long drink of his orange juice before answering. "Just tell him to send a check to the Humane Society and put my name on the memo line. They'll know what to do with it."

"Now you're including your name? What are they doing, constructing the Billy Bannister wing for stray cats?"

"Well, they *are* expanding. Gandalf's buddies need a better place to live, you know."

"Yes, I remember when you chose Gandalf. Those cat cages were stacked higher than my head."

"So they need all the help they can get."

"True, but don't you want to keep some of the money for yourself?"

"Not really. I should get plenty at the festival tomorrow night." Billy smiled and stared at the coffee cup. "Maybe I'll get enough to get my own coffeemaker."

His father peeked around the drawing and casually tipped the cup forward to get a look at the penny-sized splotch of coffee remaining at the bottom. "So how much should I tell him to send?"

"I don't know," Billy replied, shrugging his shoulders. "Twenty dollars?"

Billy's dad held up the portrait and gazed at it again. "This may be the best you've done yet." After wiping the table with a clean napkin, he placed the drawing on the surface and began rolling it into a tube. "I'll ask for fifty. That shouldn't be a problem for Doc." He lodged the cylinder between the salt and pepper shakers and picked up his folded newspaper.

"Fifty would be great," Billy agreed.

"Right. Gandalf's friends might want to buy you a coffeemaker for Christmas." His dad let out a broad smile and whacked Billy playfully on the head with his newspaper. Billy tried to grab it, but his father snatched it out of the way just in time. Billy lunged forward, wrapped his arms around his father's neck, and pulled him to the floor. A world wrestling championship match had commenced right there in the Bannisters' kitchen, but it wasn't very convincing with both competitors laughing so hard.

"Boys," Billy's mom called from the foyer, "I heard a motor. I think the bus might be here. Kind of early, though."

Billy jumped up and gave his father a helping hand off the floor. He loved the feel of the larger hand and the manly grasp, and he swelled with pride at his own ability to pull him up, even though his dad was at least five inches taller and maybe forty pounds heavier. Not much fat in Dad's pounds, though. Billy made sure of that with their frequent tussles.

"Better keep working out, Dad! One of these days, I'll pin you!"

His father pushed his fingers through his thick, reddish brown hair and laughed. "Not a chance."

Billy didn't bother with his own mussed hair and guzzled the rest of his juice. Just before he reached the hallway, he spun around, walking slowly backwards as he spoke. "Will you still be able to change tomorrow's schedule so you can help me at the festival booth?"

"You bet. Remember what I said when you asked me before?"

Billy smiled and pointed his finger at his father, who pointed right back at him.

"Count on it," they said at the same time while winking one eye.

They both laughed, and Billy turned again to try to catch the bus. He handed his mother the orange juice glass, gave her a quick peck on the cheek, and grabbed a backpack before dashing out the front door. She winced and rubbed her face, then quickly recovered and waved.

Even in his rush, Billy noticed her pain. He waved back and continued in a fast trot, but he couldn't help thinking that he might have revealed his secret—the secret of his scorching breath. He had been careful to keep his mouth safely away while wrestling with his father; any slip-up could make it obvious.

Billy glanced down Cordelle Road, the two-lane street in front of his house, but the bus wasn't in sight, only a dark blue Cadillac idling at the corner a couple of hundred feet away.

Strange. Had he already missed the bus? He sprinted across the street to the stop and searched the other end of Cordelle. No bus that way either.

The Cadillac began rolling slowly his way, and Billy stiffened. Did this guy mean trouble? Maybe he was just lost. He squinted and tried to catch a glimpse of the driver, but the rising sun painted a glare on the windshield. A heavy uneasiness churned in his stomach, not nausea or indigestion; it was more a deep-seated worry, a nest of shivers growing in his belly, like a hundred hovering hummingbirds.

Billy was about to cross back to his home side of the road, nonchalantly, of course. He snapped his fingers and shook his head, pretending he had forgotten something, and he took a step onto the asphalt. The Cadillac gunned its engine, and Billy jumped back. The car lurched forward with a tire-biting screech, but at that moment the bus came around a distant bend in the road.

The Cadillac screeched again, this time stopping within ten feet of Billy. The driver's door popped open, and a short, stocky figure stepped out. Billy turned and quickly stepped in the direction of the school, hoping the bus would pick him up a bit farther down the road. *Probably faster than trying to go home. Besides, I can't miss the bus.*

"Bannister!" the driver shouted. "Stop!"

He knows my name. But I don't know him. Just keep walking.

Billy heard the bus engine, and he turned to see the yellow boxy truck pass the Cadillac. It pulled up to his side and stopped.

"Bannister!"

Billy turned. The Cadillac driver was now jogging in his direction. The bus doors swung open, and Billy hopped up the steps, feeling the hair on his neck sending a shot of tingles down his back. He waved at the bus driver. “Mr. Horner, close the doors quick.”

Mr. Horner pulled a lever, and the door’s two panels swung together. Billy looked out the vertical windows. The Cadillac driver stood on the sidewalk with his hands on his hips, staring at the bus. Billy couldn’t read his expression. Was he angry? Disappointed? As the bus pulled away, he leaned over and looked again. Would he run back to his car and try to follow?

Billy turned to the bus driver and gave him a questioning look, wondering if he noticed the man. Mr. Horner had never been much for words, but he communicated his thoughts with a masterful collection of at least a thousand prune-faced frowns, one for every negative human emotion imaginable. Today’s frown said, “Hurry up, Bannister. I spilled hot coffee on my pants, and I’m in no mood to watch you dawdle.”

Billy sighed and looked down the bus’s long center aisle. Out the back window he could see the shrinking figure of the Cadillac driver as he walked back to his car. The quaking he had felt in his stomach spread out into his limbs, and he shook all over. *Who was that guy? What did he want with me?*

As he stepped toward the seats, images from the weird dream once again haunted his thoughts. He remembered his hot breath and his mom’s pained expression, and he winced at the boiling cauldron still simmering in his stomach. He felt pursued by phantoms, a swarming host of invisible fears. And now a physical stalker lurked close to home, bold and real.

Billy shivered and pulled his backpack up higher. *I feel like a hunted animal, but who’s the hunter?*

CHAPTER 2

The Bathroom Incident

Billy searched across the sea of faces for his best friend. After a few seconds he spotted the back of his familiar head and his unmistakable, food-stained baseball cap. Billy stepped over a kid's outstretched leg and called, "Hey, Walter."

Walter jerked around toward the front, his brow wrinkled and his chin taut. "Hi, Billy."

Still standing, Billy leaned over to get a glimpse through the back window. "What'cha lookin' at?" He saw only empty pavement. The Cadillac was out of sight.

Walter spoke up to be heard over the din of the other students. "The car that was back there. I saw it cruising around our neighborhood earlier this morning. Do you know that guy?"

Billy sat in the aisle seat that Walter had saved for him. "The driver? I don't think so. Do you?"

"Never seen him before this morning." Walter's probing blue eyes stared at Billy from under the brim of his cap, his bushy eyebrows turning down toward his slightly crooked nose. "He came by my house and told my dad he was a reporter doing a story on people in the neighborhood and unusual things they do. He started asking personal questions about your family, so my dad told him to get lost."

"About my family? Like what?"

"Like where your dad came from before he lived in Castlewood."

Billy dropped his backpack on the floor in front of the seat. "Dad won't even tell me that one. He's pretty quiet about the past, and none of the pictures in the photo album go back before I was born, so I just stopped asking."

"Well, my dad said he'd call your dad, so I guess they'll figure out what's going on."

Billy tore open his Pop-Tart and blew slowly on the corner before he bit into it. As he repeated his blowing and biting routine, he felt Walter's curious eyes searching for an answer.

Walter finally blurted out his question. "What're you doing?!"

"Blowing on it to heat it up."

"What? One-and-a-half degrees?"

Billy tried to hide a smile as he took another bite. "You'd be surprised."

"Whatever," Walter said coolly, "but if you hate being called Dragon Breath, you'd better stop doing stuff like that." He looked out the window at the passing scenery and then back at Billy. "You want to go up to Hardin's Pass again this weekend? Last time the fish bit better than the mosquitoes for a change."

Billy took another bite and finished chewing before he replied, making sure to look straight ahead. "Sure. Why not?"

Walter shoved Billy's shoulder. "What's with you today? Can't you talk? You're acting like I'm a leper. Do I have bad breath or something?"

Billy had to laugh, but he kept his face forward. "Not you, buddy. Do you want to smell mine?"

Walter put his two index fingers together to form a cross and pushed them toward Billy's nose. "Back, foul vampire. It's a wooden stake for you if you get any closer."

Billy pushed Walter's fingers down. "Halloween's over and Thanksgiving's coming, so don't be a turkey!"

"Well, you know how I like to gobble."

"Yeah, I know. I remember what you did at the Boy Scout picnic."

"You mean the hamburger incident?" Walter asked.

"That's what you call it, but I call it the hot dog, hamburger, baked beans, coleslaw, potato chip incident."

"Well, yeah. I guess that describes it. I still don't see what the big deal was."

Billy noticed at least three other bus riders listening in, so he pulled down the bill of Walter's cap and pumped up his vocal volume. "All that stuff on one hamburger bun? And then you left it on Mrs. Roberts's seat. Don't you remember? She jumped up and screamed so loud, six different people called 9-1-1 on their cell phones. One was even three blocks away. Then Dr. Franklin's bassett started licking it off her dress, and she screamed even louder. To this day Mrs. Roberts will hardly sit anywhere but in her own chair, and she always looks down before she sits."

A hail of derisive laughter pelted their ears, but Walter just shrugged it off. "I didn't leave it there on purpose." After a few quiet seconds, he looked at Billy's hands and then at his backpack. "So, you got another Pop-Tart on you?"

Billy shook his head. "With your appetite, I don't see how you keep from getting a lard belly. But don't worry, you'll get plenty to eat at the festival tomorrow night."

"Yeah, but I'm running the Boy Scouts' dunking booth, so I have to count on good friends to bring me stuff." Walter nudged Billy in the side. "So, are you going to the festival, 'good friend'?"

"Yeah. I'm doing the caricature booth."

"Caricature? Is that like one of your animal drawings?"

"No. It's a sketch of a person's face, except that I exaggerate. If a guy has a big nose, I draw it the size of a baseball, and I make big ears look like Dumbo ears."

"And people like stuff that makes them look weird?"

"You'd be surprised. But I also draw their pets. I usually get big tips for those."

Walter held out a hand and rubbed his thumb over the tips of his fingers. "So, you make a lot of money?"

"Quite a bit, actually, but I send it to the Humane Society. I keep just enough to buy my pens and pencils and stuff."

"I'll bet the dunking booth's more fun. Did you hear that our very own history teacher volunteered to take the plunge?"

Billy laughed so hard he almost choked. "Mr. Hamilton getting dunked? Are you kidding?"

"No kidding! Can you believe it? I heard him say that it's 'for a good cause.' " Walter mimicked Mr. Hamilton's voice, a resonant tone with a dignified British accent. "He said, 'Scouting is a fine way to make gentlemen out of the young males in our town.' "

Billy wanted to stop laughing, but Walter's impersonation was too good, filled with hysterical exaggeration, and he kept it up. He even mussed his hair and widened his eyes, just like their teacher's.

"You have to go to the water closet?" Walter continued. "Did you forget to go before you left home? Did you have a bit too much tea this morning?"

"Stop!" Billy cried, holding his sides. "I like Mr. Hamilton! Stop!"

Walter finished with another British-soaked quip. "Whatever you say, Mr. Bannister."

Billy finally caught his breath, and he wiped a tear from his eye. Walter's act made him forget his problems, at least temporarily, but when his hand passed his mouth, he once again felt his breath's intense heat. He turned again toward the front and stared at the road ahead.

The droning of the bus engine and the all-too-familiar buzzing of student chitchat and chaos made the boys drift away in their own thoughts, and the two sat in silence for the rest of the trip. Walter gazed at the mountains, and Billy found himself dwelling once again on how to hide his atomic-powered breath. He could still see his mom's wincing face, and he didn't want to keep talking to Walter and risk his finding out how bad it was getting.

When they arrived at school, the boys shuffled down the bus exit with the rest of the troop. Their bus dropped them off precisely twenty minutes before first period, giving them plenty of time to get inside. Walter and Billy followed their Thursday routine, each buying a root beer from the outdoor vending machine. Next, they would go to the cafeteria and exchange belches and impossible stories with the other guys. Billy paused on the sidewalk, his can of root beer dangling at the end of his drooping arm and fingers. He stared mournfully at the school.

"Aren't you coming?" Walter asked.

"Go on ahead. I have to do something."

"You sure? You need any help with anything?"

Billy nodded. "I'm sure."

"I really have to go," Walter said, beginning to walk backwards toward the school. "Frank said he was going to tell about the time he went on a safari and wrestled a lion."

"And you have one to top it, right?"

Walter grinned. "Yeah. I have a lion story, too."

"Oh, no," Billy said, covering his face with his hand. "Not the one about you getting killed and eaten at the zoo!"

Walter had already turned his back. "I've got the teeth marks to prove it!" he called as he hurried away.

Billy shook his head. Walter was such a hoot! A morning of trading tall tales would have been great, and Billy had the perfect opening line about swallowing a blowtorch that still worked down in his stomach. But it would've been too real. The boys didn't usually bring props, and his breath would've raised too many questions.

Billy crossed the street and climbed a grassy hill on the other side, leaning forward to plant each foot while struggling against the steep incline. After reaching the top, he sat on a conveniently placed stone and pulled a small, spiral-bound notebook from his pant leg pocket along with a mechanical pencil.

Knowing about his artistic talents, the school had asked him to make a poster of the campus, something funny to attract people to the school's fund-raising booth at the festival. He had already made two drawings that were hanging in the school hallways, but this new one had to be his best work yet, something that would grab people's attention when they entered the festival gates. Billy decided now was a good time to make a quick sketch; he would transfer it to poster board tonight.

From the hilltop, the entire school campus lay before him in a mosaic of bricks, pavement, and teeming students. Imposing as it was at ground level, the complex now seemed small for the number of students it handled, filling only one neighborhood block. And in that area they squeezed in a parking lot, a ball field, and a basketball court. Most of the kids called it a dump, but it didn't look so bad, especially from Billy's vantage point. From this distance he could see how the mountains behind the school framed the campus perfectly. The colorful background of dazzling autumn leaves had faded in the last few weeks, but the scene still resembled one of those landscape photographs in a travel magazine. West Virginia had its drawbacks, but the mountains weren't one of them.

Billy took a long guzzle from his root beer can and watched his peers mill around the schoolyard. Most of them were covered by dim shadows cast by the buildings that blocked the brightening sky. With a firm grip on his favorite pencil, he let his imagination take control, working long strokes and studious doodles together to create his new masterpiece. He sketched the students as tiny escapees, running from the graphite shadows being created by the school building's caricature, an upside-down monster, a burrowing beast that had drilled its head and upper body into the ground.

The school's narrow bell towers on each side served as the monster's legs, and three sets of double doors in the middle of the first floor became a gaping hole in the giant's huge stomach. Billy drew the underground eyes of its hideous face, sinister and beady.

A bell sounded, and the monster smiled greedily as its doors closed to imprison the hundreds of children it had sucked into its hungry belly.

Billy held the sketch at arm's length and admired his work, but only for a moment. The echoes of distant laughter had quieted, allowing him to hear the autumn breeze whistle past his ears. *How long have I been up here? Is it class time yet?* He downed the last swallow of his soda and dropped the notebook and pencil back into his leg pocket.

Standing at the crest of the ridge, he looked down at the sidewalk and street, thinking about making a two-footed slide down the slope, but just as he was about to throw himself into his plunge, he stopped. A car crept slowly down the road, the same dark blue Cadillac that had stalked him earlier.

Billy waited a minute to see what it would do. It wasn't a good idea to slide right into that guy's path and get smashed into a messy pile of Bannister roadkill. And he didn't feel like having a chat with a stalking stranger. Although time was probably running short, he decided to wait and let his inquisitor move along. *I guess Dad's probably talked to Walter's dad about it by now. I can ask him when I get home.*

When the Cadillac passed the schoolyard and turned at the next corner, Billy jumped down the grassy slope, his shoes sliding as he surfed the hillside. After crossing the street, he hustled up the concrete entrance staircase, jumping as many steps as he could, but a familiar voice made him stop at the halfway point.

"Hey, Dragon Breath!"

It was Adam Lark and his clinging cohorts. Adam, the ringleader, continued his verbal assault. "How many girls' lips are you gonna shrivel today?"

While Adam and his pals laughed, Billy fumed. Walter was right; Billy hated his new nickname. He regretted Tuesday's science lab when someone had seen him try to secretly blow on a test tube to heat it up when his Bunsen burner wouldn't work. His fears were coming true; the news was spreading. He came up with a witty retort, but he thought better of using it. Maybe if he kept quiet, people would just drop the subject.

Adam and company moved on, still throwing verbal jabs as they walked away. Billy continued up the steps, ran through the doorway, and then jogged down the hall, stopping for a drink at the water fountain before continuing on his way to Room 107. *Maybe the root beer and water will keep my breath under control for a while.*

When he swung the door open, he gulped at the sight of thirty other young teenagers; they were already seated, books open and pens in hand. As if guided by remote control, every head swiveled to catch a glimpse of the offender, and a rather loud voice called out.

"Students! Unless you think the exam will ask about Mr. Bannister's clothing choices, I suggest you focus your attention on your lecturer."

The unmistakable British accent held sway over the studious automatons, and their heads swiveled toward the front again.

The teacher took a step toward the door, tapping his chalkboard pointer on his palm. "Mr. Bannister, I never thought I would see you join the ranks of the tardy."

Billy felt Mr. Hamilton's perfectly enunciated rebuke drilling through his ear like a broken pencil grinding in a sharpener. It wasn't finished yet.

"Would you care to explain to us why you are late?"

A surge of warmth radiated through Billy's cheeks. At first he thought he was in for detention, but he noticed a gleam in the teacher's eye and maybe even a hint of a grin in his pursed lips. His confidence buoyed. "I'd rather not, if you don't mind."

Mr. Hamilton pointed down the aisle. "Very well. Take your seat." He then turned to the rest of the class. "Now, as I was saying, open your book to page 119. We will begin our study of the legend of Arthur." Mr. Hamilton waited for the sound of turning pages to diminish before continuing.

With his tall, lanky form holding open the large textbook, he reminded Billy of the stereotypical country preacher, his deeply set, wide eyes and broad forehead staring with complete awe and reverence at the words before him. His thick mane of gray hair shifted, and it fell over his ears as he read. "Around the year 510, Arthur, a prince of the tribe of Britons called Silures, in South Wales, was raised to the title of Pendragon, a title given to an elective sovereign, paramount over the many kings of Britain. Supposedly, he was the only one who was able to pull a sword out of a stone, signaling that he was the rightful king.

"One legend identifies the sword as the famed Excalibur, though most authorities claim that it was the Sword of Britain that Merlin set in the stone. Excalibur, according to myth, was a gift from The Lady of the Lake, a goddess-like nymph who appeared in mysterious pools. Such is the character of legends. Who can know what is really true? The most popular legends give accounts of Arthur's victories in battle over the Saxons and of his inner circle of knights who sat in council at his famous Round Table at Camelot."

Mr. Hamilton continued his lecture, reading pieces of the text and giving his own views. He explained why he found this pseudo-history important; some of it was undeniably true, although other parts remained highly doubtful. "One of the keys to wisdom," he said, "lies in separating truth from myth, and your ability to discern reality from fantasy will make you kings in this world of knaves, the foolish believers of myth."

Billy looked over at Walter. He was spellbound. Mr. Hamilton's words had apparently transported him to another land and another time, but Walter's eyes were focused on something other than his teacher. Billy followed Walter's stare to the chalkboard where he saw a glass-covered frame resting on the chalk ledge and leaning against the board. Under the glass was a painting of a shield with a beautiful coat of arms emblazoned on the front. Had Mr. Hamilton shown this to the class earlier? The design held a knight's full helmet, silver-coated with gold trim and an ornate crown on top. Under that was a red breastplate decorated with three white clovers. Coming out from behind the armor were long red and white leaves with three-pointed ends that seemed to be trying to wrap themselves around the breastplate like snakes strangling a victim.

Billy tore his gaze away from the shield and turned to listen to Mr. Hamilton. As the teacher spoke, his passion for the subject rang with sermon-like ardor. His face rose and fell with each mystical legend, his wild, gray hair shaking with every movement of his aged head. Billy could almost see images of Lancelot and Gawain in his teacher's eyes, not only the excitement of sword-to-sword tourney, but also the nobility and valor of a knight.

Yet not even Mr. Hamilton's enthusiasm could captivate Billy when a matter of great urgency demanded his attention. From the time he was a small boy, his mother had warned him about drinking so much so early in the morning. The coffee, orange juice, root beer, and water had definitely done their job. He raised his hand in the air and waved it. "Mr. Hamilton?"

The teacher had just reached a crescendo in his story, and he stopped in mid-sentence, his arms raised to demonstrate a sword-play technique. "Yes, Mr. Bannister? What is your question?"

"I, uh . . . I have to go to the bathroom."

Mr. Hamilton lowered his arms with a brief sigh and stepped toward Billy. "You have to go to the water closet?" That friendly gleam reappeared in the teacher's eye. "It's only first period. Did you forget to go before you left home, or did you have a bit too much tea this morning?"

A wave of snickers passed through the room, and Billy glanced at Walter who was turning absolutely purple. Billy had to swallow a laugh himself. "Er, no. I didn't forget. I did drink a lot, though."

The stately teacher took another step closer to Billy and studied his face. "Are you sick? Your face is turning red."

He swallowed again. "I don't think so."

Mr. Hamilton marched back to his desk, and after scratching down a signature, he tore a piece of paper from a pad and extended it to Billy. "Here's your pass. Hurry back."

Billy hustled through the classroom door and finally let out the laugh he had worked so hard to stifle. When he neared the restrooms, he paused a minute to get more water, careful to swallow as little as possible to avoid further embarrassment later on. After every swish he tested his breath on his hand. *Not too bad.*

He banged open the restroom door and then secluded himself in a stall, preferring the privacy there to the adjacent urinals. After a few seconds his sigh of relief was accompanied by a scratching sound, something dragging on the restroom floor right outside his stall. Billy hurried to finish and then peered through the crack at the doorjamb. *It's Adam. What's he doing dragging a stool into the boys' room?*

Adam pulled the stool to a spot about two feet in front of one of the sinks and climbed to the top. It was a short stepladder, the kind that librarians use to reach a book, yet tall enough to allow Adam to stretch his lanky arms to the ceiling. At this point he must have spied Billy's head over the stall barriers. He let out a gasp, then blew a relieved sigh. "Oh, it's just you, Dragon Breath."

Billy left the stall and looked up at Adam. Standing on tiptoes, Adam flicked on a cigarette lighter and moved the flame close to the fire alarm sprinkler on the ceiling. Billy put his foot on the bottom step. "Adam! What do you think you're doing?!"

"Shut up, Dragon Breath! You'll keep quiet about it if you know what's good for you."

"You'll set off the alarm!" Billy tried to clamber up the stool to stop him. The thin metal legs squeaked and jerked under the shifting weight.

"Hey!" Adam cried. He kept the lighter poised at the sprinkler, trying to hold it steady while he fought back Billy with his other hand, pushing down on his forehead. "Stop it!" he growled. "Get off!"

Billy finally managed to dodge Adam's hand, and with a tug on the bigger boy's shirt, he hoisted himself to the top. Unable to battle any farther past Adam's flailing arm, Billy craned his neck to try to blow out the lighter.

WHOOSH!!!

The sprinkler spewed on their faces and shoulders with several jet streams of putrid smelling water. Alarms blared throughout the building, sounding like a swarm of screaming bats flying through the halls. Adam jumped off the stool just as Mr. Hamilton stepped into the bathroom.

Billy scrambled down, but not before Mr. Hamilton had seen him, and not before Adam had expertly slipped the lighter into his hand. Billy could only stare at his open palm, the stream still showering his head. Drops of water fell from his drenched hair into his hand creating a shallow puddle under the crime scene evidence, a silver lighter with a bronze, coiled snake emblem on the front.

"Well, well. Mr. Lark, Mr. Bannister," the teacher said, standing at the door, just out of reach of the smelly spray. "I thought Mr. Bannister might be ill, so I came to check on his condition, and now I see you two have filled the water closet with . . . er, with water."

Adam pointed at Billy. "It wasn't me, Mr. Hamilton! I came in here, and Billy was standing on the stool with a lighter! I tried to stop him, but it was too late."

Mr. Hamilton shook his head slowly. "Come now, Adam. If I know you, you were cheering him on." He opened the restroom door and gestured toward the hall. "We'll let the principal sort this out. Now march!"

Just as the two boys were about to exit the restroom, Mr. Hamilton barred the door with his arm. The corridors had filled with a disorganized mass of students, excited preteens haphazardly lined up by a frazzled teacher, and teenagers sauntering by with sleepy, bored expressions. They all seemed to be slowly migrating toward the exit door.

Mr. Hamilton shouted instructions to the teachers and hall monitors. "No need to panic. It's a false alarm. We must, however, continue to guide the students to the proper exits." He waved at a monitor. "Mr. Johnson, please check on Room 107. My students are likely following routine drill protocol, but propriety demands a responsible guide. I must stay here until all is clear. Please also advise Mr. Tompkins that I may arrive late for study hall should our delay extend into next period. He can supervise the students without me."

He turned to Billy and Adam. "I'm sure Dr. Whittier will deal with you severely, so I'll not subject you to further embarrassment. You may stand here until the halls have emptied." It took a while for the fire department to arrive, finish their obligatory check, and give the "all clear" signal. The sticky, smelly water clung to Billy's shoulders and back, making the wait seem interminable. He heard a bell signal the end of class, and the minutes dragged well into second period.

After the students returned and scattered to their classrooms, Mr. Hamilton allowed Billy and Adam to start their march down the hall. Everything was quiet now, and the corridor seemed much larger than usual. Billy followed his teacher toward the principal's office, walking as slowly as possible while still keeping reasonably close behind. His shoes squeaked, and he left a trail of pancake-sized puddles in his wake. He thought he had seen this in a movie somewhere. He was the condemned prisoner tramping down the final corridor. *What's at the end, Warden? The chair? The gas chamber? I'm innocent, I tell you!*

Billy threw sidelong glances at Adam from time to time, trying to gauge his reaction. Though covered with streaming water, Adam's face seemed to be made of stone. He stared straight ahead and kept his mouth in a tight line. *He's probably used to it. I've seen him follow other teachers down the hall. It's a wonder he hasn't been expelled by now.*

Billy marched on, staring at a large door at the far end, the door to the principal's office. Billy had heard rumors about the new principal. "Eccentric old guy," one friend had told him. "He's really weird," another friend had said. Billy mulled over the opinions. He thought a lot of people he knew were eccentric, especially his history teacher, but most kids said that the principal made Mr. Hamilton seem normal. Billy felt apprehensive and curious at the same time. Although he had wanted to see what the other kids were talking about, this wasn't exactly the best way to make a good first impression.

Mr. Hamilton shooed Billy and Adam through the door and then into an interior office, walking right past a girl who was waiting to see the principal. Billy caught her glance. Her eyes gleamed, and a hint of a smile crossed her face. He felt the heat of embarrassment surge into his cheeks, and he spun his head forward.

"Two miscreants for your judgment, Dr. Whittier. They were the ones who set off the fire alarm. The water clo- . . . Ahem! The restroom next to the North entrance is flooded. When I walked in, Mr. Bannister was on a stool under the sprinkler, but I suspect both of them were involved."

"It wasn't my fault!" Billy and Adam shouted at the same time.

Adam continued, thrusting a finger toward Billy's face. "He did it! I tried to stop him!"

Billy felt his tongue stiffen and his throat clench shut. What could he say? He probably *was* the one who set off the sprinklers. He felt condemned, his wet hair and shoulders shouting out his guilt.

Adam went on. "Ask Mr. Hamilton. Billy had the—"

"Quiet!" the teacher scolded. He then turned back to the principal, regaining his attitude of formality. "I will be leaving you with these two, Dr. Whittier."

"Thank you, Mr. Hamilton. I was wondering who caused all the commotion. I was helping Mr. Andrews guide his students to the exits, so I couldn't find out who triggered the false alarm. He doesn't get around any better than I do, you know."

Mr. Hamilton nodded graciously and closed the door behind him, leaving Billy and Adam alone in the strange office. As Billy gazed around at the walls, he understood what the other kids had said about the principal. But it was worse than anything he had heard. This man wasn't eccentric; he was dangerous!

CHAPTER 3

The Mysterious Principal

Billy stared in awe at the decor of the room. Broadswords, shields, and coats-of-arms hung from the walls in glass cases. *They can't be real. How could they let weapons like these into school? They must be plastic replicas, but they sure look authentic.* The collection resembled museum pieces from the Dark Ages. One display held an assortment of thumbscrews, and Billy imagined the squashed thumbs of misbehaving boys who had the misfortune of running into this hard-hearted principal.

Dr. Whittier glared at the boys, his yellow-green eyes shining like a cat's and his voice matching a feline's guttural growl. "Well, now, suppose you two tell me what's going on."

Adam coolly rattled off his story. "Ms. Albertson gave me a hall pass to use the restroom. As soon as I went in the door, I saw Billy on a stool, holding a lighter up to the sprinkler. I tried to stop him, but as soon as I got close, the sprinkler came on. That's how I got wet." Adam pointed an accusing finger at Billy. "Look! He's still holding the lighter he used to set it off!"

The principal's graying eyebrows slowly advanced toward the middle of his forehead. "Is this true, Mr. Bannister? Is that your lighter?"

Billy held the lighter out with an open palm. "I do have the lighter, but that's because he shoved it into my hand when the sprinkler went off. It's really his, not mine."

Adam kept his eyes on the principal and maintained his composure. "Dr. Whittier," he said, his finger still pointing, "I've never seen that lighter before in my life. Remember, you took my lighter last week, and I haven't smoked a cigarette since, just like I promised."

Billy scowled at Adam, amazed at his ability to lie without any hint of guilt.

The principal shook his head and ran his fingers from front to back through his gray hair. It reminded Billy of a closely cropped horse's mane, thick and bristly. "I have heard about your promises, Mr. Lark," Dr. Whittier replied. "They're not exactly from the lips of God." He then reached his hand toward Billy. "Let me see that lighter, young man."

Billy handed it to him, and while Dr. Whittier examined it, someone knocked at the door.

"Come in," the principal answered.

The door opened slowly, and a pair of bright blue eyes peered in. "Dr. Whittier?"

The principal's expression softened. Even the shimmering in his eyes seemed to dim. "Oh, Bonnie. I'm sorry I kept you waiting. That fire alarm made me forget." He extended his hand. "Here, I'll sign your note."

A young girl wearing an oversized backpack stepped up to the desk and stared quizzically at Billy while Dr. Whittier pulled out a pen. Billy was careful not to stare back, but he did cast a glance or two in her direction. *That must be the new girl from Montana I heard about. Bonnie Silver, I think. She was looking at me when I came in. Why does she keep staring at me?*

"These two rascals came in just after you did," Dr. Whittier explained. "I'm sorry they interrupted us." He studied the absence excuse and slid the lighter to the side. "Quite an elaborate story you have here." He held the paper even closer to his face. "Whose signature is this?"

Bonnie glanced at each of the boys and then drooped her head before answering quietly. "My foster mother's."

"Did she write this story?"

"Uh, no. I wrote it. But she read it and signed it."

Dr. Whittier leaned forward and lowered his voice, too. "The part about the brave drugstore clerk who walked six whole blocks to bring you Pepto-Bismol was very interesting. And I'm sure the neighbor's dog made quite a mess when he pulled the dead raccoon through the kitchen. I'm sorry you had to clean it all up yourself, even though you only had a box of tissue and a bar of deodorant soap." The principal let out a sigh and tapped his finger on Bonnie's note. "But your story doesn't mention whether or not you saw a doctor for your illness."

Her head sank an inch or two lower. "I didn't see a doctor. It was just a bug. It only lasted a couple of days."

Dr. Whittier scrawled his signature across the note and handed it back to her. "I know you're new here, Bonnie, so I signed it this time. Our policy is that a student must bring a doctor's note for absences of more than one day due to illness."

Bonnie picked up the slip and slid it into her pocket. "I understand, Dr. Whittier." Before leaving, she pointed at the lighter on the desk. "I see you have Adam's new lighter."

Dr. Whittier's eyes became narrow slits again, and he glared at Adam while raising the lighter up to Bonnie's eye level. "You recognize this lighter, Miss Silver?"

"Sure," she explained with a casual shrug of her shoulders. "Adam likes to show it off to the girls. He thinks the snake emblem on it is really cool."

Dr. Whittier motioned for Bonnie to leave. As she did, she looked back and smiled at Billy, and he offered a weak but thankful smile in return.

The principal shook his head slowly. "Adam, Adam, Adam. Why did you even try to pull this one?" He opened a drawer and drew out a file. "I should have known the lighter was yours. Look, you've been caught smoking in the boys' room four times, and Billy has no record at all."

"But I quit. Honest I did. I gave the lighter to Billy when I kicked the habit."

"But you said you'd never seen the lighter before."

"I . . . uh . . ."

Billy's smile grew to a wide grin. Dr. Whittier had Adam on the hook. Time to reel him in.

While Dr. Whittier lectured on the evils of smoking, lying, and "bearing false witness against thy neighbor," Billy tried to catch a glimpse of what was in the contraband drawer. He noticed several items: a large pocketknife, several packs of cigarettes, and a can of beer. *Are all of those Adam's?*

When the lecture finally ended, Dr. Whittier pulled two forms from his lower right-hand drawer. The sheets had dozens of blank lines and empty check boxes, and he used a sharp pencil to neatly fill in several spaces, printing names and violations in perfect block letters.

Billy spoke up hesitantly. "Does this mean I can go? Now that you know it wasn't my lighter, I can just—"

"No!" The principal frowned menacingly and pointed his pencil toward Billy. "You were caught on the stool whether it was your lighter or not. I'm suspending you both for three days."

Dr. Whittier called for a hall monitor who escorted both students to their respective classes to get their books. When they returned, the principal ushered them into a detention area adjacent to the office, giving them each a towel to finish drying off. "If we're unable to contact your parents, we'll keep you right here until school gets out."

After Dr. Whittier shut the door, Billy wiped his face and then glared at Adam who had chosen a desk on the opposite side of the room. Billy sat heavily in a nearby desk and rested his chin on his hands. He rubbed the towel through his hair and then across his arms. *I wonder how long I have to sit in here with Adam? There's no telling what he's going to say to me.*

But Adam never spoke. After about a half hour, a middle-aged, rough-looking man entered the room with Dr. Whittier. His slender frame reached about five-foot-six, and his three-day beard and dirty jeans made him look like a homeless tramp. Billy caught a glimpse of a cigarette pack in his shirt pocket, and his blackened hands told of grimy labor in the nearby coal mines.

Adam rose from his seat, a look of tired resignation on his face. As they walked out, Billy watched the man place his hand on Adam's back and grasp a handful of Adam's damp shirt, maybe even his skin, squeezing it tightly as they left the room.

Billy jumped up and hurried to look out the door's window, a square viewing port at eye level in the thick, wooden frame. He tried to catch the pair as they left the office, but by the time he pressed his nose to the glass, they were gone. When he turned back around, he wrinkled his nose. What was that awful smell? It reminded him of the brewery just outside of town.

Dr. Whittier reentered the detention room. "Curious, Billy?"

"Well, I—"

"I saw you looking out the window."

"I, uh . . . I've never met Adam's father before. I didn't mean to be nosy."

Dr. Whittier held out his hand for Billy's towel. "I'll get you another one if you need it." He folded it neatly and laid it over his arm. "We haven't been able to contact your parents yet, so I'm afraid you're stuck here for a while." He pointed at Billy's backpack. "You did get your books, didn't you?"

Billy nodded. "Uh-huh."

"Then make yourself comfortable. I left a message on your answering machine. I'll let you know when your parents call back." He exited abruptly and closed the door. Billy peeked through the window again, watching the principal limp back to his desk and sit down.

I didn't notice that before. He must have a bad leg.

Billy plopped back down in the desk and haphazardly pulled a textbook out of his backpack. *I guess Mom's on the office line, maybe rescheduling flights for Dad so he can go to the festival. She's probably just letting the machine catch all our calls.*

He finished his history reading assignment and then went on to the chapter questions. History had always been his favorite subject, so he was glad to pass the time by engrossing himself in the lesson. Unfortunately, the assignment wasn't long enough.

After counting the ceiling tiles several times, he started flipping his pen in the air, first a double flip, then a triple. A few minutes later he had successfully performed a twelve-rotation spin as well as an eleven and two tens. Finally, after a few more spins, he flopped back in his seat.

"Still waiting, Mr. Bannister?"

Billy jerked his head up when he recognized the voice. "Oh! Hi, Mr. Hamilton. I was just reading ahead. I'll be missing three days of school, in case you haven't heard."

"I heard. I'm going to see what I can do to shorten that for you." He stroked his chin and looked down at Billy with a piercing stare. "Are you a friend of Adam Lark?"

Billy's eyes opened wide. "No way! I don't ever hang out with his crowd."

The teacher nodded. "I'm glad to hear that. Well, I suspect Mr. Lark wouldn't care about his grades and keeping up with the rest of the class, but I thought you might. Would you like the lecture notes? I have them on my computer, and I can send them to you in an e-mail post."

"Sure!" Billy felt a surge of relief, but he was still worried about the prospect of staying in "The Chamber of Boredom" for the remaining hours of the school day. "I can't go home yet, though."

"Haven't they been able to reach your parents?"

Billy noted a definite hint of concern in Mr. Hamilton's tone. He had never seen a teacher with this kind of expression before. Was he worried about something? "No," he replied. "It's probably because Mom's trying to reschedule the charter flights for my dad's business, so she's too busy to answer the main phone line. He wants to come to the festival tomorrow night."

"I see." Mr. Hamilton looked at his pocket watch and then opened a booklet he had pulled from his jacket pocket. "I have my planning period free and all of lunch. Would you like a ride home?"

"Well . . ." Billy hesitated, contemplating which would be worse—to accept a ride home from his very strange history teacher, or to spend the rest of the afternoon flipping his pen and counting ceiling tiles. "Okay," he finally decided. "That would be great. Thanks."

Mr. Hamilton paused and stared at Billy as if wishing to ask a question, but he just sighed and turned around. "I'll see if Dr. Whittier will give his permission." He then strolled out of the room, and Billy stuffed his books into his backpack while he waited. Mr. Hamilton returned after a few minutes and poked his head in the door, holding out a fresh towel. "I pulled your address from your file, Mr. Bannister, and I printed out directions to your home. Let's depart."

Mr. Hamilton unlocked the passenger door of his station wagon and opened it, but Billy couldn't sit down right away because his seat was filled with books of various sizes and ages.

"I'm so sorry," Mr. Hamilton said, pointing at the pile. "Just throw them in the back."

Billy lifted the top book and read the title out loud. "West Virginia Natural Resources?" He glanced at his teacher, who was rounding the back of the car. With a flick of his wrist, he tossed it toward the rear seat and then read each title as he went through the stack. "A History of Coal Mining . . . Appalachian

Wildlife . . . Early West Virginia Settlers." After he tossed the last book, he spread out his towel on the seat and sat down.

Mr. Hamilton glanced back at the pile of books, buckled his seat belt, and cleared his throat. "One must learn about one's new home, mustn't one?" He started the engine and revved it up, and the car jerked forward before stopping again abruptly. Billy fastened his own seat belt, trying to muffle the sound of the metal click. His teacher smiled apologetically for the lurch, and Billy responded with a queasy half-grin. He turned toward the road, his right hand clutching the armrest.

"So what did you think about Arthur and his knights?"

"Huh?" Billy turned to see the teacher looking straight at him. He wasn't watching the road.

"You read the chapter, did you not?"

Billy couldn't answer. He held his breath and pleaded silently. *Please, please look at the road.*

"Well?" Mr. Hamilton said, turning to face the road.

Whew. Billy could finally breathe again. "I, uh . . . I didn't see what I expected."

"Why is that? It has the traditional legends and much of the current data speculating on the actual history involved."

"I was hoping to read about Merlin. I like stories about wizards."

Mr. Hamilton jerked the wheel, and the two right tires slid off onto the pebbly shoulder, grinding and popping the gravel beneath. Billy clutched the door handle, but it only took a second for his teacher to bring the car back onto the pavement. "How you Americans ever became accustomed to driving on the wrong side of the road, I'll never know!"

He stopped the car a moment later at a railroad crossing. A freight train made its way slowly across the road, its wheels squealing displeasure at their burden of coal. The delay seemed to please Mr. Hamilton. "Now, where was I? . . . Ah, yes! Merlin! Now there's quite a bit of controversy surrounding that chap, and, you're right; the book doesn't cover him at all."

Billy watched dozens of hopper cars grinding their way across his field of view, each piled higher than the brim with a mound of ebony grit. He loved to watch trains, but Mr. Hamilton's story kept pulling him away from the long line of rolling fuel. "What controversy?" he asked.

"Oh, opinions from every side. Some historians say he didn't exist. Some say he was a dark sorcerer, called to do Lucifer's bidding. To others he was simply a wise counselor to the king, and to a few he was a fiery prophet of the Christian faith, working miracles from the Lord. You put all these together and you get the legend—a mysterious and magical wizard. You would be amazed at how serious some people still are about these legends."

"So how can you know what's true and what's not?"

"Research. Lately, a particular interest of mine has been in the sword, Excalibur. One obscure but reliable source says that if its bearer has faith and a pure heart, Excalibur will make him invincible. You see, according to my source, God bestowed a special power on the sword such that it responds to the bearer on its own, as though it has a will. Since a sword cannot really have intelligence, it must have a material property that reacts with the holder, a sort of link with someone who emanates holiness. Therefore, the sword's power can be stolen if an evil man somehow counterfeits purity."

The train's wheels screeched, and the rumbling cars slowed to an agonizing pace. Mr. Hamilton took a deep breath and continued, raising his voice to compete with the noise. "Of course, I don't believe there was a Lady of the Lake to give and take back the sword, so there must be another source of its origin and disappearance."

"Disappearance?"

"Yes. According to my research, the sword really existed. I assume it was stolen, but the perpetrator probably could never use it to its full potential. Thieves don't have pure hearts, as you might imagine. It has been a dream of mine to find that sword and restore it to Arthur's rightful heir."

At that point, Mr. Hamilton chattered on about Arthur's knights, the "real" story of the Round Table, and several tales about his hero, Sir Gawain. Billy became so enthralled as the teacher's excitement grew that he forgot all about the train. He was fascinated by Mr. Hamilton's breadth of knowledge and inspired by how he talked about God. *Are teachers allowed to do that?*

After the last train car finally made its way across the road, the two drove on, and Mr. Hamilton launched into a storytelling mode, sounding like one of the radio narrators Billy had heard about from his father, filling the air with oral sound effects and shifting voices, from knight to damsel to king.

Mr. Hamilton became more like a bard than a teacher. His story song held Billy in a trance, the words transforming into an oracle, even telling of the future, that Arthur would reappear to help his countrymen during their greatest need. Whether that appearance would be in body or in spirit, Mr. Hamilton didn't know, but he suspected that the spirit of Arthur would reside in one of his descendants who would assume a throne, perhaps a symbolic or a spiritual one, and reinstate Arthurian rule with all of its power and moral authority.

Just as Mr. Hamilton built the story to a new crescendo, he pulled the station wagon into Billy's driveway and stopped his tale abruptly, reverting to his normal voice. "If I'm not able to do anything about your suspension, I will let you know about any new developments in class. Shall I assume that your e-mail address is in your file?"

"It oughta be. I put it on my form."

"Very good. You will hear from me soon."

Billy wasn't really ready to leave, but when he thought about his mother possibly noticing the strange car in the driveway, he jumped out quickly. "Thanks, Mr. Hamilton." He waved as he hurried away. "So long!"

Hearing the sound of his teacher's car rattling away, Billy remembered the morning's strange events. He glanced back to see if that mysterious Cadillac might still be in the neighborhood.

No sign of it.

He turned again and ran around the house, deciding to enter the back door and go through the kitchen. *If Mom's still on the phone, she'll be in Dad's office. Why disturb her work?* Besides, he needed time to decide how to explain why he was home so early. He planned to tell the truth, but he wasn't sure what to say about the fire sprinklers. Could his breath really have set them off? Was it time to let them know his secret?

He grabbed an apple, then headed toward the stairs, ready to hole up in his room to work on the English assignment from the day before. Mrs. Roberts gave them till next week, but he decided he might as well get it done. No use wasting time. He paused at the bottom step when he heard voices coming from the living room. Considering the circumstances, he decided to listen to gauge the mood of his parents. He didn't normally hide anything from them, but the day was especially strange so far. He slowed his breathing and tuned into the sounds.

"I waited to tell you, because I wanted to be sure it wasn't just my imagination."

That's Mom. She's getting dramatic. She must be upset.

"When I saw the welt, I knew our lives would never be the same. Is there any word from the others?"

"No," another voice replied. "Irene knew we moved to Castlewood, but there's still no message, not even a peep. Maybe the worst has happened, like we feared."

That's Dad. His voice always seemed to carry better than Mom's. It echoed through the house with masculine resonance.

"This is why I didn't marry for the past fifteen hundred years," his dad went on. "I didn't want to put anyone through the same kind of danger."

What?! Fifteen hundred years? What in the world is he talking about?

"But when I met you, I knew that, whether I was a dragon or not, you were the person I'd marry."

Dragon? What dragon? Billy knew he must have missed something, so he bent over to try to hear a little better.

"Is Billy in any danger?"

That's better. Mom's coming in loud and clear now.

"Yes, I'm afraid so. If his breath develops a flame, he could kill himself. He can't possibly know how to control it yet, and he doesn't know how to protect himself."

"Jared, Billy has to know. When are you going to tell him?"

The sound of his mom's choked sob lingered in the air, and sadness cut into Billy's thoughts, bringing tears to his eyes. *They're talking about me!*

After a long pause, his dad finally replied. "I don't think we can wait any longer. We should tell him as soon as possible. I think he can handle it. He's always acted more grown-up and mature than most kids, but that's to be expected since he has dragon blood. I don't think he's likely to have scales in his mouth, so if he could burn you, he must be feeling something. I also don't see how he'll be able to use normal dragon safeguards, being a—a half-breed, I guess you'd call it. He may be able to find a way to protect himself, but I can't be sure. And there are the other students to think about. It's definitely too dangerous to let him stay in school much longer. We may have to home-school him. And remember that nosy guy driving around in the Cadillac that Carl told us about. If someone's spying on us, they're bound to find out about Billy's breath sooner or later. We may even have to leave town."

"So when he gets home, what do we say to him?"

"Nothing yet. I have to consult the books. But I know I'll have to figure out what to say real soon."

After a short pause, Billy heard the sounds of someone walking. *The books? Does that mean Dad's heading for the stairs?*

Billy sneaked up to his room, absolute dread filling his mind. He hurried to his dresser mirror and stared at his reflection. "A dragon?!" he asked out loud. "A half-breed dragon?!" He looked at his hands and felt the smoothness of his skin. No hint of scales. He opened his mouth and surveyed the inside. No scales there, either, but the roof of his mouth felt weird again, hardened and insensitive to touch. *Okay, Billy. Get a grip! You're not a dragon. That dream about the knight really was just a dream.*

He stood in the middle of his room, petrified, afraid even to walk for fear of being heard. A large, purring cat stretched out from under the bed, and Billy knelt to pet Gandalf, looking deeply into his attentive eyes. "Do you have any idea what's going on? I had a dream about a dragon, but I don't remember much about it. Maybe I'm dreaming now." Talking to the cat and stroking his long silky fur calmed Billy down. "It can't be a dream, Gandalf. I know I'm awake. It just sounds like my parents have gone crazy or something. Is this some kind of bizarre joke?"

Billy glanced out his door, having left it open a narrow crack. He could see nothing but an empty hall and the top of the stairs. "It can't be a joke on me; they don't even know I'm here." He lifted his hand and blew on it softly, drawing it closer and closer until he couldn't stand the heat. *Ouch!* The sting ran through his body like an electric shock.

He wiped sweat from his brow and picked up Gandalf, hugging him close. With one arm under the cat's soft body, he continued to stroke his furry head, talking to his feline friend as though he understood every word. "It's like seeing your parents pull off masks, and finding out they're aliens underneath!"

CHAPTER 4

Bonnie Silver

Bonnie felt a sudden, painful jerk on her thick braided hair. "Ow!" She whirled around in her desk to see Adam glaring menacingly at her.

"That's for snitching on me, Bonnie Backpack. You're lucky Old Lady Roberts is coming down the hall or I'd really let you have it."

Bonnie's anger surged into her cheeks, and her voice matched her growing fury. "And you would've let Billy take all the blame for what you did, you coward!" She rose from her seat and stood toe-to-toe with Adam, staring with flashing, narrowed eyes into his, tilting her head slightly upward to compensate for the difference in height. "I'm not scared of bullies like you. You're the one who's lucky the teacher's coming."

A round of "ooohs" filtered across the school desks, and every eye in the classroom locked on the two combatants. Bonnie knew Adam would never back down in front of an audience. She had to hold her ground, too. Without a flinch she kept her fiery glare. "I heard you got suspended. What are you doing here, anyway?"

Adam pulled back a bit. "I told Whittier I forgot my English book, so he let me come back. But I really came to settle a score with you, you little snitch." With a quick reach, he grabbed a corner of Bonnie's backpack and used it to spin her around. "I've always wanted to see what you keep in that precious backpack of yours," he said loudly enough for everyone to hear. "I'll bet you're hiding some weird deformity, probably a big lump with gross, oozing sores."

Adam searched for a zipper, and Bonnie twisted and pulled to get away. "Let me go, you creep!"

"Ah ha! Here it is." Adam released the backpack to use both hands on the zipper, and Bonnie felt the sudden slack. She spun around like a spring-loaded catapult and landed a crushing right fist against Adam's left cheek, sending him flying backward over the desk behind him. Adam rolled sideways off the desk and flopped facedown on the floor, sprawled out and whining.

The class erupted in whoops of laughter and cheers, but they turned into silent statues when a nails-on-chalkboard voice screeched, "Bonnie Silver! What's the meaning of this?"

Bonnie turned slowly to see her teacher's shocked expression, her full jowls pushing downward in a bulldog frown. Bonnie felt her own face changing again, probably to a sharp crimson by now, and her anger melted into tears that soon found their way down her hot cheeks. "Mrs. Roberts, I . . ."

The teacher rushed forward and knelt down next to Adam. The boy held his cheek and moaned, "Dr. Whittier said I could get my English book, Mrs. Roberts, but Bonnie slugged me for ratting on her boyfriend." He looked up at her with sad eyes. "I guess I deserved it, didn't I?"

She stroked him tenderly on the shoulder. "Of course you didn't deserve it!" She glared back at Bonnie. "I can't believe you punched him! How could you?" Without waiting for an answer, Mrs. Roberts crooned softly to the fallen bully. "Adam, dear, do you want me to call the nurse?"

Bonnie caught a glimpse of Adam's evil smirk, and she couldn't stand the injustice for another second. She stomped her foot and left the classroom in a huff.

"Report to the principal's office, young lady!" Mrs. Roberts called after her. "I'll be there in a few minutes."

Bonnie slammed the classroom door behind her and stood in the hall with her arms straight down, her fists balled into tight weapons of rage. "Ohhh! That Adam Lark! He's always getting people into trouble!"

Bonnie stalked down the hall, her clenched teeth displaying the anger she didn't bother to resist. Why should she? After all, it was Adam who started the fight.

"Ohhh!" she cried out again. *First he gets Billy in trouble, and then he almost found out what's in my backpack. If that secret ever got out, I would just die!*

Lost in her thoughts, she nearly passed right by the principal's door, but she halted just in time to take a sharp turn into the office. Once inside the anteroom, her rage melted into dread. The last time she was here, only a few hours ago, the office seemed bright and cheery. Now it took on a different air, dark and quiet, the dismal threshold that led to the torture chamber. The devices on the wall attested to a sadistic maniac within. And what about the pictures? She had noticed them before, but now they seemed to come alive, paintings from the Dark Ages, gothic and fearsome, shadowy knights and reddish brown, fire-breathing dragons in mortal combat.

The knights, most clad in chain mail, wielded shining broadswords, and some bore horrible wounds, open and dripping red. Some of the dragons had only two legs, some four, but all had magnificent broad wings that seemed to beat furiously in battle.

The wings, in particular, caught Bonnie's eye, and she drew closer to one painting to study the dragon's beauty. *Oh, those wings!* Supported by one large sinew that resembled a wiry arm, each taut canopy also boasted a network of rib-like struts. No wonder they held such fierce power. This dragon had a tawny beige hue and deep penetrating eyes. Bonnie was so entranced, she even raised a hand to touch the image.

"Miss Silver?"

Bonnie spun around to see Dr. Whittier standing at his office door. He stared at her with one eye half-closed and his hand rubbing his chin. "Why are you back? Did you forget something?"

Her throat tightened, and her legs felt like trembling toothpicks. "N—No. I was just . . ." She stopped short of explaining. Something about Dr. Whittier's face brought a sudden fear that paralyzed her for a moment, something oddly familiar, like a phantom in a fleeting nightmare.

Dr. Whittier stepped forward, looking past Bonnie at the wall. "So you were admiring the painting?"

"Um, yes," she stammered. "The dragon is awesome."

Dr. Whittier frowned. "You like the dragon?"

"Yes, he's a magnificent creature."

Dr. Whittier glanced at Bonnie and then turned to the painting again. "She was a formidable one to be sure," he murmured.

"She?"

"Never mind. Now, what can I do for you?"

At that moment, Mrs. Roberts marched into the office shaking her finger at Bonnie while glaring at the principal. "That girl!" she spat out angrily. "That girl knocked down another student with her fist!" She gave a roundhouse swing with her own fist, wrapping her arm around her ample waist in her follow-through. "Just like that!" she finished, letting out a short gasp for breath before stopping and staring at Dr. Whittier.

Dr. Whittier merely raised his eyebrows and turned his attention to Bonnie, a hint of mirth breaking through. "Is that so?" After a brief examination of Bonnie's petite stature, he turned back to Mrs. Roberts. "Whom did she hit?"

"Adam Lark. She knocked him flat!"

Dr. Whittier's eyebrows shot up again. "Adam? I told him he could come back for a book, but I thought he'd have done that long ago."

"He's a good boy. I'm sure he was waiting for me to give him his homework assignment."

Dr. Whittier rolled his eyes. "I'm sure." He then cast a doubtful stare at the rotund teacher and gestured toward a chair.

"Why don't you have a seat, Mrs. Roberts?"

She glanced at the chair but then resumed her fiery demeanor, her nose slightly lifted. "I prefer to stand."

Dr. Whittier nodded and placed his hand on his chin. "Adam's a head taller than Bonnie, isn't he?"

"At least," Mrs. Roberts agreed. "She was a vicious one. She went just like this . . ." Mrs. Roberts twisted around, drawing back her fist for another punch, but Dr. Whittier stepped forward to catch her wrist before she could demonstrate again.

"I have the idea, Mrs. Roberts," he assured, releasing her arm. "Don't worry. I'll take care of this matter. Please send Adam to me." He scowled at Bonnie, making sure Mrs. Roberts noticed, then added a quick wink that only Bonnie could see.

As Mrs. Roberts passed by on her way to the door, she leaned over and whispered into Bonnie's ear. "Trailer-trash ruffian. It's no wonder you don't have any friends."

The teacher's insults burned like acid in Bonnie's mind. Her ears grew warm, and her heart felt like it would melt away. Trailer trash? She didn't live in a trailer, but she knew what the teacher meant. She was an orphan girl from the wrong side of town. Bonnie tried to hide a sniffle, and she tightened her chin before looking up at the principal. Would he notice her tears?

Dr. Whittier motioned for Bonnie to follow him out of the anteroom and into his office. When the door closed, he reached for a tissue from a box on the corner of his desk and handed it to her. She took it gratefully and wiped her eyes.

A big smile grew on the principal's face. "You decked Adam Lark?" He laughed out loud, bracing himself against his desk. "He probably stayed to harass you for identifying the lighter, but then you—" He interrupted himself again with another laugh.

Bonnie shrugged her shoulders, but she couldn't smile. She was glad the principal was trying to make her feel better, but Mrs. Roberts' echoing words drowned any joy that tried to surface.

Dr. Whittier walked around his desk and sat in his chair, giving it a playful spin and laughing all the way around. When he faced her again, he leaned forward and folded his hands on the blotter. "That boy has needed a good, hard licking for a long time. I'll bet he deserved it, didn't he?"

A smile finally broke through. Bonnie nodded her head, her face flushed with embarrassment.

"Tell me, what did he do this time?"

"Well . . ." Bonnie began. She hesitated, wondering how much she could tell.

"It's okay. I've heard it all. Go ahead and tell me."

"He tried to open my backpack," she blurted out.

Dr. Whittier eyed the backpack curiously. "Why did he do that?"

"He just wanted to see what was in it, I guess. Maybe he's overly inquisitive."

The principal's brow wrinkled, and he clenched his right hand into a fist. "So you decked him for trying to look at your books?"

Bonnie bit her lip, not knowing what to say next.

Dr. Whittier's expression tightened, almost as if he had suspicious X-ray eyes that penetrated the denim pack. "Do you have contraband in there?"

"Oh, no, Dr. Whittier. It's just that . . ." She paused and lowered her eyes.

"I think you should tell me, Bonnie. If you have a good reason to keep a secret, I can make sure nobody bothers you again."

Bonnie sighed deeply. After only a couple of weeks at this school, dozens of kids had asked her about her backpack. "Why is it so big? Why do you never take it off? Why do you wear it so high on your back? What are you trying to hide?" She had always been able to laugh it off before, but now she was in a tight spot. She had to tell the principal the truth.

"I . . . I have a deformity on my back, and if I don't wear the backpack, it's really obvious."

"And that embarrasses you," Dr. Whittier concluded.

Bonnie lowered her head and barely breathed out her answer. "Yes, it does."

For a moment both were silent, Bonnie keeping her head down and wondering what terrible things Dr. Whittier must be thinking about her. She looked up through tear-filled eyes, raising her tissue to wipe them again. "I know I shouldn't be so vain, but I—"

"Oh, no," Dr. Whittier interrupted. "Don't worry yourself about that. I understand completely. When I was your age, I always wore long-sleeved shirts to cover up an ugly birthmark on my arm." He rolled up his sleeve to reveal a dark, reddish blotch on the underside of his forearm.

The mark resembled a misshapen club, the playing card variety, but it had an angry look, more like an old burn than other birthmarks she had seen. "That's not so terribly gruesome," she said while trying to maintain a tone of sympathy. "It's really superficial."

"Yes, you're right, but to a shy adolescent, it was a disaster."

Bonnie turned to the side, drooping her head again and whispering in response. "Mine's much worse."

"Don't worry, Bonnie. I'm not going to ask to see it. I'll discreetly pass the word around to the teachers. They'll be more likely to support you if they know what's going on."

Bonnie just nodded her head. She knew that spreading the news couldn't possibly be a good idea. The thought of revealing her troubles for everyone to gossip about was terrifying.

Dr. Whittier gestured toward the detention room. "Why don't you sit in there until this period is over and then go to your next class?"

Bonnie nodded again and shuffled over to the side office, her head still tilted slightly downward and her long braid hanging over her chest. The plaited blonde and light brown bands were not quite as neat as they had been when she tied them that morning, and she felt the same way, drooping, haggard, and dismal.

Bonnie felt Dr. Whittier's eyes following her as she walked. What was he thinking? She knew her clothes weren't exactly the latest style, but they were clean and modest, so that wasn't why he was staring. She glanced back, and the principal quickly turned his head. *He was watching!*

When she reached the detention room, she peeked out the window. Dr. Whittier walked around his desk and into the file room adjacent to the main office. Several seconds later he returned with a folder and took it back to his desk. Just after he sat down again, Adam Lark sauntered into the room. With his hands in his pockets and his body tilted back slightly, the troublemaker exuded cockiness. Bonnie used her foot to keep the door from closing so she could watch and listen at the same time.

"Mrs. Roberts said you wanted to see me," Adam said.

Dr. Whittier put the file down and folded his hands on top of it. The principal's eyes narrowed, and he leaned forward to watch Adam's expression. A purple bruise had grown on the boy's face, and it swelled like a rodent's cheek pouch. "Did you see what was in Bonnie's backpack?"

Adam shook his head nonchalantly. "Nah. I just got the zipper open a little before she punched me. All I saw was a leather strap of some kind."

"Hmmm. Leather, you say?"

Adam blew a large gum bubble and snapped it down between his teeth. "Yeah. Can I go now? You got the goods on Bonnie, and I should be getting home to do my assignments."

Dr. Whittier breathed a deep sigh. "Yes, I know. I've seen your grades." He paused for a moment and then shooed Adam away with a wave of his hand. "Don't come back until your suspension's over."

"Sure thing, Doc." With another big bubble and snap of his gum, Adam turned and strutted out of the office.

Dr. Whittier shook his head and flipped open the file on his desk. He picked up a card that looked about the size of a photo and studied it before putting it down again and thumbing through the stack of papers in the folder.

Could that be my file? Bonnie thought. *I wonder what he's looking for. He already knows I'm living in a foster home, but what else could be in that folder?*

The principal underlined something on the page and picked up the phone, alternately punching buttons and looking back at the sheet. After a few taps of his pencil on the desk, he began speaking. "Yes, this is Dr. Whittier, principal of Castlewood Middle School. I'm looking for information on a girl who is in your foster system. . . . Bonnie Silver. . . . Right. . . . When? . . . And where did she come from? . . . Yes, I understand. . . . I'll come by and show you my credentials. Please have the information ready. . . . Thank you. Good-bye."

It is my folder! And he's checking up on me!

Dr. Whittier hung up the phone and shuffled the pages of the file back together. When he rose from his seat, Bonnie let the door close gently, and she hustled over to a desk and sat down. She leaned forward to make room for her backpack and gazed straight ahead. Out of the corner of her eye she saw Dr. Whittier peek in the window.

Brrinnggg!

The class bell made Bonnie jump, and she glanced at the window. Dr. Whittier was no longer watching. She left the detention room and saw him sitting at his desk. She let the door close softly behind her and raised her eyebrows hopefully. "So, can I go now?"

Dr. Whittier folded his hands over the file. "Yes, yes. Of course."

Bonnie left the office and walked down the hall, but the sound of the office door made her turn around. Dr. Whittier was leaving. He had a file tucked securely under his arm, and he hobbled down the hallway in the opposite direction.

Bonnie felt a blistering chill, worse than ten snowballs down her back. She could barely think. The thought of her deformity finally being revealed nearly paralyzed her. Yet, she felt torn. She had hidden the truth for so long, she wouldn't mind if a white knight rode up on his steed, shining the light of truth on her secret, ready to protect her at all costs. But what if the wrong person found out, a dark knight who would expose her to everyone?

There were too many mysteries, too many clues, and Dr. Whittier seemed like a man on a mission. But was he on the side of light or the side of darkness?

Apparently Gandalf decided he'd given enough comfort for one afternoon, and he pulled away from his master's embrace. Billy watched him prance into the hallway and down the stairs, his fluffy tail waving back in self-satisfaction. He envied the cat's freedom—no worries, no problems. His food bowl was always well supplied with tasty morsels of some kind or another, and a place to sleep was as close as any bed, sofa, or lap. He never had to worry about who he was or what his parents were.

For Billy everything he had ever known had suddenly been swept away like worthless kitty litter, and now even the floor seemed to crumble under the weight of his burdens. Every thought swirled in a Kansas-sized tornado. Stumbling about in the corridors of his own mind, he felt lost in a carnival maze of mirrors. He turned toward the door to go downstairs, ready to demand an explanation from his parents, but he stopped, afraid of what a confrontation might bring.

He glanced around the room, desperately clinging to images he held dear. There on the wall by the window hung a pencil sketch he had made with the help of his father when he was first learning art. It was a portrait of Merlin, drawn from the fantasies of his imagination. Although he had no idea what Merlin actually looked like, the more he stared at the glass-encased sketch, the more familiar the aged face looked, as though an old friend stared back to offer him help and comfort.

Over on his desk he noticed his pint jar of shark teeth. The summer before last he and his dad collected them during their vacation in Venice, Florida. He still remembered the feeling of swimming in water that had once teemed with monster sharks and pretending they were still lurking just below his dangling toes.

A relatively new treasure also sat on Billy's desk, the computer he had received for his birthday. It hadn't taken him long to learn how to get on the Internet and surf for information, both for fun and for school projects. Now its very presence gave him something to hope for. Out of the millions of web sites out in cyberspace, there had to be stuff about dragons.

After hurriedly changing his stinky shirt, he plopped down on his desk chair and began navigating the mouse cursor through dozens of web sites devoted to dragon lore, knights and damsels, and other ancient legends. The effort of wading through the mass of information dizzied his mind, and with the swirling confusion already fogging his thoughts, he just couldn't take any more. *Probably 90 percent of this stuff is just stories people make up. I need facts!*

Billy shook his head and closed the browser. With a sigh and a click of his mouse, he switched to his e-mail program. Several new messages popped into his in-box. Some were advertisements, but one looked like a personal note. His spirits lifted when he saw Mr. Hamilton's name. He opened the message and read.

> Mr. Bannister, I thoroughly enjoyed conversing with you during our ride today. When I returned to school, I spoke with Dr. Whittier. He agreed to allow you to attend classes tomorrow and clear your record if you will scrub the newly inscribed graffiti on the school's front wall. He planned to have you clean the restroom, but the janitor had already mopped the whole floor to get the water up. In my opinion, we have arrived at a good settlement. If you are sincere about wanting to keep up with schoolwork, come an hour early tomorrow; I will meet you if you need help to get started. I want to be sure you attend the next class. I will be talking about Merlin. Today's lecture notes are in an attached file.
>
> Sincerely, Charles Hamilton (1 Peter 2:18, 19)

He read the message over again and recognized the ending reference as a Bible verse. He spun his head toward a bookshelf on the opposite wall and scanned the book spines. He didn't use his Bible very much, but once in a while, when his father was out for an overnight trip, his mother would give him a lesson from it. He especially liked the stories about angels—Michael, Gabriel, and . . . and whatever the other ones were named. *There it is!* He softly stepped over to the shelf and slid out the small, leather-bound book.

After flipping through the pages for a while he found the passage. "Slaves, submit yourselves to your masters with all respect, not only to those who are good and considerate, but also to those who are harsh. For it is commendable if a man bears up under the pain of unjust suffering because he is conscious of God."

Billy pondered the words, and his mind settled into a happier mood. The fact that Mr. Hamilton had been kind enough to send such an uplifting message cheered him. The old teacher had a heart to go along with his information-packed brain.

Now there's a thought! I'll ask Mr. Hamilton my questions.

After all, he seemed to know what was real and what wasn't when it came to the legends. Maybe he knew something about dragons, too.

With his hands on the home keys, Billy started typing, but after a couple of sentences he stopped. *Boy, does this sound stupid. "Mr. Hamilton, please tell me everything you know about dragons. It's really important."* Billy held down the backspace key until his entire message disappeared, and he began again, this time typing slowly and thoughtfully.

Dear Mr. Hamilton, I appreciate the ride home today, and I enjoyed our talk about the Arthur legend. There's one part of the legend that you didn't mention—dragons. Did they really exist?

If so, what happened to them? Where can I find more information on dragons? I will be at school one hour early, like you said. I'll see you there. Thanks for getting me off suspension.

Billy Bannister

Billy clicked the send button and breathed a sigh, relieved that he had at least done something to start solving this nightmare of a mystery. A familiar noise made him turn his head. Yes, it was the engine of the school bus. *I'd better get out there fast. If Mom and Dad find I'm home already, they'll want to know what happened. I'll have to tell them eventually, but I'd rather do it in my own time. I just hope Mom doesn't notice that I changed shirts.*

He snatched up his backpack and headed toward the stairs, but the soft padding of footsteps below made him stop cold. That way was blocked. His mother was near the bottom of the steps. He ducked away from the stairwell before she noticed him.

I know! I'll go out the window! He tiptoed back into his room and sneaked toward the wall that faced the street out front. He had tried this trick before, scaling the drainpipe when playing hide and seek with Walter. After casting furtive glances all around, he opened the window slowly, looked outside at the shingles, and gauged the distance to the roof's edge.

Piece of cake, Billy said to himself as he climbed out. With his shoes grinding the gritty roof surface, he walked with bent knees to the end of the gutter, his arms slightly extended and his palms down to keep his balance. The shingles radiated the day's unusual late autumn warmth, and a fresh breeze cooled his dampening skin.

When he reached the corner of the roof, he dropped to his knees and wrapped his arms and legs around the drainpipe.

This trick was a lot easier when Walter was chasing him and they shared unrestrained bravado. Now, with all the dragon stuff going on, he felt like a wet noodle had replaced his spine.

Billy took a deep breath, gripped the metal with his shoe soles, and began sliding earthward. On the way down, his finger caught on a jagged pipe joint, and he jerked away in pain. Just before his upper body toppled, he snatched the pipe again with his bloodied hand. He rushed his descent, allowing the rough metal to scrape his bare forearms, and he shinnied the rest of the way down, landing firmly on his feet. *Whew! Made it!*

Sucking the wounded finger, he hurried around to the front of the house and hustled up the sidewalk to his front door. It looked like the bleeding had stopped, so at least the cut wouldn't give anything away.

A sense of guilt weighed him down, like the wounded finger reflected something bigger, a deeper truth of some kind. He couldn't remember ever sneaking around like this, but, then again, he had never heard his dad say he had dragon blood before. The trust he had always felt had buried itself, like a scared mole hiding from a lurking cat.

Billy entered the front door with his head held high, pretending everything was normal. "Mom, I'm home!"

He heard his mother's voice calling. "We're in the living room, Billy."

He hustled down the hall and turned into the room, finding his mother sitting on the sofa immediately to the right of his dad. A huge book lay open on his dad's lap, something like an ancient Bible, complete with a worn leather binding and yellowed parchment pages.

Billy wanted to ask about the book right away, but when his father closed it, he decided to wait. He was glad his pants were now dry, and his mother didn't seem to notice the shirt. So far, so good. He scooted to an unoccupied chair adjacent to the sofa and sat back, trying to hide his turmoil, at least for now. "What's up, Dad? You're home early."

He gazed at Billy, almost as if he were seeing him for the first time. Billy felt like his dad's eyes were fingers, poking and probing his mind and body for information and giving him shivers all over. "Your mother called me," he replied. "She wanted me to help her take care of a problem."

"What problem?"

"She noticed this morning when you kissed her that your breath was extremely hot." His mother pointed to the welt on her cheek while he continued. "We're guessing you've already noticed it, maybe for quite some time."

Billy shifted uneasily in his chair. "Well, I—" He paused. He wanted to blurt out everything, but he felt like something clamped his mouth shut.

"Go ahead, son," his mother prodded. "You can tell us."

Billy sighed and looked down at his shoes. "Yeah, I've noticed it, especially today. I had a problem in school. I tried to stop Adam Lark from setting off the fire sprinklers in the restroom, but I accidentally set them off myself."

His father shifted forward. "Set them off yourself? How did that happen?"

Billy leaned over and began retying his shoes. "Well, Adam was putting his lighter up by the sensor, and I tried to blow it out. For some reason, my breath's gotten so hot, it must have set the alarm off." He looked up, and he felt his throat tightening and tears welling in his eyes. He firmed his chin and tried to blink away the tears. "Mom, what's going on?" He turned to his father. "Dad?"

His father patted the sofa cushion on his left and reopened his book. "Come sit here, Billy. I have something to show you."

Billy stepped over and sat down, nestling into the cushion but keeping his distance. He swallowed hard, and he gripped his knees as he turned his head to see what was in the book.

His father turned a large, tawny page, revealing dozens of lines of flowing script on the ragged parchment. "What do you know about dragons, Billy?"

"Um . . . Only what I've read in books, like *The Hobbit.* They're fierce, scaly, flying lizards that can breathe fire."

"Anything else?"

"Well, they gather treasure, and they're evil. They kill people when things don't go their way."

He turned another page, this time more slowly. "In your mind, do they look something like this?"

Billy stared at the newly revealed parchment. It displayed a drawing of a knight fighting a dragon, a beautiful depiction of heated battle, the knight with drawn sword and uplifted shield, and the dragon with torrents of fire blasting the shield with outraged ferocity. Behind the knight stood a young lady in a white, flowing gown, obviously the object of the battle. Although he had never seen this picture before, something about it seemed familiar. It reminded him of a picture in the principal's office, but there was something more, something personal. Billy nodded, keeping his eyes on the page. "Yeah. Something like that."

His father turned another page, revealing several lines of centered text. The handwritten script flowed in nearly flawless curves, not quite calligraphy, but possessing the swirls of an ancient and devoted pen. The letters created odd spellings and indecipherable words.

"This is a poem," his dad explained, "written by the same man who drew the picture. He was a squire for one of King Arthur's knights."

"Arthur's knights? Like the ones of the Round Table?"

"Well, not quite. This knight was Arthur's fiercest, to be sure, but his bloodlust kept him from securing a seat of nobility. He was forever in pursuit of dragons, to the point of madness."

Billy couldn't believe what he was hearing. It sounded like a fairy tale, like his father was telling a bedtime story. "So dragons were real? They really did breathe fire and try to kill people like in the picture?"

His father's brow turned downward and his jaw tensed, but his voice stayed calm. "Some dragons killed many people, giving all dragons a bad reputation. Arthur commissioned this particular knight to eliminate the species. At the time, Arthur was unaware of the existence of good dragons."

"Good dragons?" Billy looked up from the page. He felt a tight knot growing in his stomach, and he squeezed his kneecaps like he was trying to wring out a sponge. "So why are you telling me all this?"

His father placed his hand on the page and ran his fingers across the lines of text. "To explain it, I'm going to recite this poem for you. It's written in an old version of English, but I translated it and tried to make it rhyme in modern English. The rhymes aren't perfect, but they're pretty close, and I memorized my version of it."

With dragons slain my master craves
Another beast, another prey
For dragons now wear human skin
And roam the earth to spread their sin
My master hunts and never rests
We purge the land and spoil their nests
'Tis strange to spill the human blood
But dragons hide beneath that hood.

He turned the page back to the picture of the knight and dragon, and Billy stared at it again, this time passionately searching for its mystery. The image took over all his senses, and it seemed to come alive in his mind. The eyes of the dragon glowed, pouring out evil as it unleashed its maniacal fury. Billy locked on the eyes. That was it! The eyes! This artist drew eyes the same way Billy did when his subject was furious, with tiny white dots in the center of the pupil. As he scanned the portrait, he noticed other similarities, human hands, tree leaves, boulders, all reflecting his own style, not exactly, but close enough to keep him entranced, and wondering about this even deeper mystery.

Billy finally tore away from the picture's hypnotic effect. He took a deep breath and looked up at his father. "Dad, what are you trying to say? What does this have to do with my . . . uh . . . my problem?"

His father took his own deep breath and put a hand on Billy's thigh. "I'm saying that I'm one of those dragons who now wears human skin."

Billy felt the urge to pull away from his father's touch, but he sat motionless, staring at the hand on his leg, thinking about its thick hair and imagining it morphing into a hideous claw with scales and razor-sharp talons. His body trembled with shivers. He couldn't help it. The tremors spread to his arms and legs, and his father jerked his hand back.

Billy tried to speak, but his tongue felt thick and tingly. He finally spit out his only thought. "I—I already knew that."

His mother and father turned to look at each other before his mother leaned over to speak. "You did? How?"

Billy's tongue felt more normal again, and he explained, cringing inside and half closing his eyes as he spilled his story. "I got suspended because of what happened in the bathroom, so I came home early. I heard you and Dad talking about Dad being a dragon. I climbed down the drainpipe and came in like nothing was wrong. I didn't want you to know about what happened today, at least not right away."

"I understand," his father replied without hesitation.

Billy opened his eyes again. "You do?"

"If I had heard something like that, I think I'd have run to the nearest insane asylum and checked myself in."

"Something like that did cross my mind."

His father gave him a smile. "Well, you showed a lot of courage coming in to talk to us."

Billy lowered his head. For some reason he had a hard time looking into his father's eyes. "I don't feel very courageous."

"Why not? How many other kids hear what you just heard? I think you're taking it very well."

Billy let out a short laugh but kept his eyes focused on his hands. They were still wringing out his kneecaps. As he pondered his own fear, a strange thought suddenly entered his mind, and he blurted it out, forcing himself to look at his dad's face again. "Were you a good dragon?"

His father's mouth dropped open for a second, and he cleared his throat before answering. "Yes! Yes, of course!"

Another question popped into Billy's mind and he couldn't seem to keep it from spilling out through his lips. "So, you never killed anyone?"

His father slowly closed the book and placed both palms on its dark brown cover. "I think we'd better not go any further today. You've got too much to think about as it is."

Billy could hardly believe what he was hearing. *Is Dad dodging the question? Did he kill someone and now he doesn't want to tell me?* He wanted an answer, but when his father stood up and began to walk out, he knew the conversation was over.

His father turned before leaving the living room, the mysterious book tucked loosely under his arm. "There are literally centuries of stories I could tell you, Billy, and the truth goes far deeper than even I can understand, but what you've heard is probably already a ten-ton weight on your mind. I just wanted you to know why your breath is so hot, so you'll understand what's going on."

He breathed deeply and went on, sadness seeming to envelop his mood. "You're the son of a dragon. I'm not sure how else this truth will be manifested, but you need to take care with your breath. It may bring greater problems than setting off sprinklers in the boys' room." He turned to leave, but he paused again. "I have a lot more studying to do before I can give you any more advice. There's a certain prophecy that makes me wonder." With that, he left, and Billy could hear him stepping heavily up the stairs.

Billy stared at his mother. "Prophecy?" he repeated, standing now and pointing toward the room's exit. "What prophecy?" His face reddened, and he huffed loudly. "Dad just told me I'm the son of a dragon! And then he leaves?!"

Her mouth opened and her lips started to form an answer, but nothing came out. She lifted her palms and shrugged her shoulders, then rose, extending her arms to give Billy a hug. He stepped back at first, putting his hand over his mouth, and he just stared at her. He could feel the shivers coming on again, and he tried to steel himself.

His mother shook her head slowly and smiled, reaching out even farther. Tears glistened in her eyes as she took two bold steps to pull Billy into her arms. She hugged him close and rubbed his back tenderly. Billy put his head on her shoulder, lightly embracing her in return. Her arms seemed to try to squeeze the tremors out of his body. He didn't know if he was trembling from fear or anger, but that insane asylum was starting to sound like a good idea.

"I think you'll have to wait for your father," she whispered. "Like he said, you already have a lot to deal with. I'm sure if he could explain everything now, he would." She pulled him even closer, and Billy felt warm tears falling on his shirt. "Just remember," she continued, "I will always love you, no matter what."

CHAPTER 5

Darkness and Light

Light of the dawning day illumined the office, allowing sunbeams to paint harsh stripes of yellowish white on the principal's desk. Countless dust particles danced on the multilevel stage, riding tiny air currents on an irresistible track toward a glowing computer monitor that grabbed the miniature imps like sticky flypaper. Dr. Whittier squinted at the image, trying to decipher the Internet page through the reflected glare. He finally gave up and rose to shut the blinds. Just as the slats surrendered with a loud clack to the principal's pull of the string, the phone on the desk rang. Whittier rushed to answer. "Whittier. . . . Yes, Sam. . . . You got it? . . . What's the address?"

He tapped the keyboard to record what he was hearing. "Montana? Then where? . . . Yes. That's exactly what I need. Fax me the whole report, pronto. I especially want the birth certificate and recent history. Send those first."

After a few more keystrokes and a click of his mouse, Whittier limped over to his fax machine and waited for the call. Within seconds the fax began churning out pages. When the first one dropped into the bin, Whittier snatched it up and walked slowly back to his desk, reading it as he went. He stood in front of his chair to finish and then sat down. Still staring at the sheet before him, he picked up Bonnie's photograph from her file and held it next to the faxed copy of her birth certificate and foster care records. *So you're not Bonnie Silver. Your real name is Bonnie Conner.*

Whittier typed some of the information into his computer as he kept reading. *Your name was changed to Silver when you were placed in the Montana foster care system. Let's see, what was the date? March 19?*

Whittier pulled a drawer and withdrew a personal planner booklet from the bottom of a stack. He opened it to somewhere near the middle and scanned his calendar. *That was only a few days after we did the Conner job.* He looked up from the booklet and tossed it back into the drawer, shutting it slowly as he thought. *Could it be? Is Bonnie a true mongrel or was she just an adopted human? Should we switch our focus from Bannister? Or maybe there are two of them.*

Whittier picked up the fax sheet once more and studied every entry, trying to decipher the sparse data. *But if she were adopted, how could she have Conner on her birth certificate? And why did Hartanna have her put into foster care? Did she know I was getting close and arranged to put Bonnie away? If so, why didn't she cover her tracks? And if Bonnie really was born to Dr. and Mrs. Conner, why did the good doctor keep her hidden from me?*

Whittier drummed his fingers on the desk and then moved them to the top of the telephone, tapping the hard plastic with his fingertips. *Why was she transferred to West Virginia, to Castlewood of all places, right where we tracked Bannister down after all these years?*

He rested his chin in his other hand, his eyes half-closed. *We have to find out! If she's a mongrel, we have no choice. If I'm right, then it's no wonder she could entrance me, the little sorceress.*

He grabbed the phone and punched a memorized number.

"Olga, it's Whittier. We may have to mobilize, but for now meet me in the schoolyard out in front. . . . No, don't bring the blade, at least not yet, but we may need a rope. I need you to help me catch and search a girl. . . . Why you? Because you're female. It wouldn't be right for me to search a girl. Besides, if she bolts, you can chase her down better than I can. . . . Yes, she's only a teenager. . . . Don't worry. You can go back to your surveillance of the Bannister house later. . . . Okay, one hour. It'll be right before classes, so I hope to find her in the yard. I don't want to take her from a classroom. Too many questions. We'll do it where no one can see us. . . . Don't worry. Who would believe her word over ours? I'm a respected principal now, remember?"

Whittier hung up the phone and returned to the window, opening the blinds again to look outside. He raised his hand to his brow to see below the rising sun and noticed a solitary student coming up the sidewalk toward the school entrance. Under one arm the boy carried a tube of some kind, maybe a rolled-up poster. From the other hand he swung a mop bucket back and forth in time with his gait.

The coolness of the November morning was evident in the boy's choice of dress—a thick pullover sweater and gloves. A dark bank of clouds had moved in from the west, and it threatened to blot out the dawn's attempts to warm the day. West Virginia's Indian Summer reprieve was coming to an end.

Whittier smiled at the visage. *Well, Mr. Bannister has come. That means Hamilton's probably already here, too. Maybe Hamilton was right; maybe he's a responsible kid after all. The teachers here generally have a better handle on that than I do, except for Mrs. Roberts, of course. She doesn't seem to know anything.*

When Billy disappeared around the corner, Whittier turned away from the window and looked back at the files on his desk. There wasn't enough information about Bonnie to satisfy him, at least not enough to warrant the ultimate penalty. Of course if it all proved true, sweet, innocent girl or not, he wouldn't hesitate to perform his sacred duty. Still, there were too many unanswered questions. He closed the files and stuffed them into his briefcase, grabbed his cane, and shuffled out the door. It was time to pay Hamilton a visit. *Let's see what he knows about little Miss Silver. Maybe he would become a valuable ally if he understood our noble quest; then I wouldn't have to resort to other methods of persuasion.*

Charles Hamilton sat alone in the teachers' study room. All was quiet. Not many teachers showed up at the crack of dawn carrying huge dusty books, especially crusty volumes like these that no one had opened in decades. And he could see why. Much of the material contained boring journal entries, either tittering hearsay from gossiping merchants or doubtful accounts from knights whose word choices seemed influenced by abundant wine. It was a tedious job to tackle so early in the morning, but a white china cup at his elbow sent silver vapors from the fresh, hot tea toward his nose, perking his senses.

Through half-dollar-sized lenses on his reading glasses, Charles peered at the odd script and turned the ancient pages, thick and noisy, more like cardboard than paper. Every once in a while he picked up a pen on a yellow pad, which he kept to the right of the book, and scratched a few notes, meditations that would be intelligible only to him. At one point in his study, he opened his Bible to Job, chapter forty-one, and suspended his pen over the pad as he read.

> Who can strip off his outer armor? Who can come within his double mail? Who can open the doors of his face? Around his teeth there is terror. His strong scales are his pride, shut up as with a tight seal. One is so near to another that no air can come between them. They are joined one to another; they clasp each other and cannot be separated. His sneezes flash forth light, and his eyes are like the eyelids of the morning. Out of his mouth go burning torches; sparks of fire leap forth. Out of his nostrils smoke goes forth, as from a boiling pot and burning rushes. His breath kindles coals, and a flame goes forth from his mouth.

Charles jotted down a few notes and closed the Bible, smiling as he wrote. *If that's not a dragon, I don't know what is.*

As the clock on the wall silently approached seven-thirty, another teacher walked in and greeted him. Soon several teachers had arrived and were chatting nearby, sipping coffee and munching on various doughnuts and pastries. Charles knew his study time was winding down. He turned another page, scanned it quickly, and not finding anything more to record, closed the book and began to stack his collection.

"That's quite a load you have there, Hamilton."

He turned to see Dr. Whittier standing nearby. "Yes," he replied, returning to the books. "I'm preparing for today's lecture."

Dr. Whittier picked up the top volume and examined the cover. "What's this? The Knights of Camelot?" He slid another book off the stack. "The Age of Dragons?"

"Yes, we're doing a section on the King Arthur legend."

Dr. Whittier returned the books to the stack. "Why are you studying that in a history class? Do you believe the legends?"

"What I believe matters little. I am able to mix in the indisputable with the marginal and explain the difference. What matters is that my students are interested. In fact, I acquired these books because a student asked me for information."

Dr. Whittier put his palm on the top book and rubbed his fingers on the binding. "You got these from the library? I didn't know Castlewood had volumes like these."

"They're not from a library. I drove to Cumberland last night to visit a friend who loaned them to me from his private collection. I doubt any library in our region would carry books of such antiquity."

"No doubt you're right." Dr. Whittier rubbed the cover one more time, then examined the dust on his hand. "By the way, what did the student ask you about?"

"He asked about dragons."

Dr. Whittier's eyebrows shot upward, but he remained calm otherwise. "Dragons? Who asked about dragons?"

Charles waved a finger toward the wall where Billy's school building caricature leaned. "The very same Mr. Bannister who created this beautiful poster for our school. I met him this morning to give him his assignments and collect his artwork. The same hands that sketched this marvelous portrait are now scrubbing the walls outside. As I told you, he is not the troublemaker he appeared to be yesterday. He is a bright and talented young man."

Dr. Whittier paused for several seconds, staring at the floor, obviously deep in thought. He finally murmured, "So Bannister asked, did he?" He then looked back at Charles. "And you drove all the way to Cumberland just to answer his question?"

Charles pushed his glasses down on his nose and peered over them at the principal. "Dr. Whittier, do you know how rare it is these days for a student to go out of his way to specifically ask for more information? I intend to do my part and give the very best answer I can."

The principal pushed one hand in his pocket and nodded. "As you should, of course. I'm glad to hear it. But what about dragons did Bannister want to know?"

"He wanted to know if they really ever existed."

"And what have you found?"

Charles looked back at the books and pointed to the third one from the top. "I have my own opinions, of course, but I think it's important to provide my students with good reference material. This one has several amazing dragon stories with evidence that's quite good, but I have found no truly firsthand accounts."

Dr. Whittier nodded again. "As I would expect in books like these."

Charles turned back to the principal, staring at him with his head cocked to one side. "Do you know of other sources?"

"Yes. In fact I have a number of journals in my private collection in my office, including my own journal, in which I have recorded an interesting history of the knights. I'll show them to you if you would like."

"I should like that very much."

Dr. Whittier gestured with a curled finger. "Come along, then." Charles left his books and cup of tea behind, and the two men exited the teachers' lounge. They walked side by side down the hall, using friendly nods to greet a few of the teachers and students who had arrived early. Dr. Whittier took the opportunity to continue his explanation. "They're copies, of course, but they were originally penned at the time of the dragons by actual knights." He stopped and faced Charles. "I've heard you're a religious man, Hamilton. Surely you know that the Bible speaks of dragons."

"Dr. Whittier, I am indeed a religious man, a Christian of the old school."

The principal started walking again. "Then you know that dragons are the minions of the devil. Satan himself is called a dragon."

With two quick steps, Charles caught up with his limping boss, and he replied while taking short strides to maintain the principal's pace. "He is called that, I'm sure, because of his fierceness and his determination to conquer. That doesn't mean that all dragons, if there ever were such beasts, possessed the devil's evil nature. Surely using a dragon to personify evil is symbolic, for if they existed, God created them just as he did all other creatures."

Dr. Whittier shook his head as he opened his office door. "When you read my sources, you will be persuaded otherwise."

The two men entered, and Dr. Whittier ushered Charles into a walk-in closet, probably a supply room at one time. Built-in shelves lined the walls, simple planks at eye level and above, braced with metal brackets and tightly packed with books. Freestanding book cabinets stood side by side on the flat carpet, each one stuffed to overflowing. Dr. Whittier sighed in delight as he surveyed his treasure. "I will allow you to browse my collection, Charles, trusting that you are a man of high intellect and spiritual discernment. I also trust that you will come to the same conclusions about dragons that I have." He pushed a protruding book back in place and leaned toward the door. "I have to go in a moment. I have some business this morning with Bonnie Silver. Do you know her?"

Charles smiled, and he felt a warm glow within when he pictured Bonnie's face. "Yes. She is a delightful lass."

"Have you ever noticed anything unusual about her?"

Charles surveyed the principal's face. *Why these questions about Miss Silver?* he wondered. *I suppose I should tell him what I know. After all, there isn't much to tell.* "She has quite an attachment to her backpack," Charles replied, clearing his throat nervously. "Is that what you mean?"

"No. Besides that."

Charles tried to avoid the probing eyes by looking up at the ceiling in thought. Something about the principal's manner gnawed at his conscience. He decided to give in, but only with superficial information. "I've noticed that her written work is profound and entertaining, and her vocabulary is college level. She's also more polite and charming than most girls her age."

Dr. Whittier seemed to mask a scowl, and he mumbled derisively. "Yes . . . charming." He then leaned over and spoke in a hushed tone. "I was wondering; do you know why she moved to Castlewood? She lives in a foster home on the south side."

Charles responded in kind, keeping his voice down, noting that a secretary had come into the office. "No. In fact, we did a section on heritage and hometowns, and I remember that she remained very quiet. I knew she was an orphan, so I refrained from asking about her parents, but I did ask her where she lived before coming to Castlewood and why she moved here."

"And what did she say?"

"I will never forget it. She said, 'I prefer to maintain my privacy regarding this matter.' What could I say? Of course I permitted her silence."

Dr. Whittier nodded, and his voice dropped even lower. "As you should." And he remained quiet for several seconds. With an odd stare, he looked up again and studied the teacher's face. "Hamilton, you look strangely familiar to me. You remind me of an old acquaintance of mine from a long time ago."

"Oh, really? I've lived in England all my life. Have you ever been there?"

"Oh, yes, many times, but my acquaintance is long dead. I'm sure it's just my imagination."

Charles ran his finger across a set of old bindings and then pulled several books from the shelf and collected them in his arms. "Dr. Whittier, I shall look through these books, and I shall supply you with a list of the volumes I've borrowed later today. I regret that I am unable to assist you any further concerning Miss Silver."

Dr. Whittier patted Charles on the back as they walked out together. "Believe it or not, you have."

CHAPTER 6

Bonnie's Secret

From all directions, dozens of students streamed toward the school building. A few arrived on foot from nearby neighborhoods, and many more stepped out of the various minivans and sport utility vehicles that had lined up inside the school gate. In the circular driveway, a yellow school bus fed the sidewalk with one tromping backpacker after another, some jumping over the last step for emphasis. The first truly cold day of the season had brought smiling faces and even some playful rowdiness among the young males who pushed and punched each other as they passed groups of young females.

The cliques gathered here and there to consult on the latest gossip and give their "oohs" and "aahs" over the bright new sweaters and hats sported by both friends and enemies alike, while the less popular strolled alone, looking for an acquaintance or two, someone to share the joy of the fresh new morning.

One of these loners was Bonnie Silver, walking toward the school entrance at a skipping pace, her heart feeling light and alive in the crisp, sweet-smelling air. Her walk was a long one, more than two miles from her foster home to the school. Sure, the bus would have been easier, but after the first couple of rides, the teasing became too much to take. Anyway, on a day like this, the long walk seemed nothing more than a refreshing stroll. Today she forsook her braid, choosing to let her hair flow in the fresh breeze. What a pleasure it was to close her eyes and mentally gather the sounds of other kids chatting and laughing all around her.

"Hey, Bonnie."

Bonnie turned with a smile when she heard her name. It was Jennifer Houston. She had called from a group of girls who huddled on the sidewalk near the bus loop. Jennifer carried her books in front of her with both arms wrapped around them, and they rested comfortably against her waist. Although her head was turned toward Bonnie, her body still faced her friends.

Bonnie focused on the brightly colored sleeve of Jennifer's sweater. With forest reds and yellows running through it in a mottled pattern, her arm resembled an autumn branch showing off its yearly splendor. Apparently Jennifer wasn't going to leave her klatch, so Bonnie crossed a sidewalk to enter her territory. As she approached, she admired the other girls' outfits. How soft and beautiful their sweaters and hats looked! Bonnie glanced down at her faded blue sweatshirt, but only for a moment. She refused the temptation to feel sorry for herself and instead enjoyed the warmth of its inner fleece, feeling it softly caress her neck as she walked.

"I heard that Billy's back at school today," Jennifer said, her smile revealing a row of bright white teeth under her rosy lipgloss.

Bonnie walked up to within a few feet of the group, somewhat intimidated by all the eyes staring at her. She stuck her thumbs behind the front straps of her backpack and used them to rest her arms. "Really? I heard he got suspended for three days."

Jennifer gestured with a swing of her head toward the school building. "Look over there by the corner of the wall."

Bonnie spun around to see Billy on his knees scrubbing a light gray stucco area on the school's foundation. Even from this far away she could see sweat dripping from his hair and face in spite of the cool air. Most of the section had been scoured clean, but a few faded black marks remained, and Billy pushed heavily on the scrub brush to wipe them away. She sighed and felt her heart sink in pity. "It wasn't his fault, you know," she said, turning back to the girls. "Adam Lark lied about him."

Jennifer looked back with a smirk at her grinning friends and then spoke in singsong voice with her nose tilted slightly upward. "Well, I heard that a certain Bonnie Silver stood up for her boyfriend in front of the principal and then later decked Adam for trying to get him in trouble." Jennifer walked around to Bonnie's other side, and Bonnie turned to face her again, now recognizing the girl's syrupy poison. "You sure are a forceful gal," Jennifer continued. "When you Christian girls decide to get some action, you don't mess around. I mean, I don't think I'd be picking a fight over a guy, especially not with Adam Lark."

Bonnie felt her heart race and a lump form in her throat. She tried to keep her voice calm, but it cracked ever so slightly. "Some action? What do you mean?"

"Oh, you and Billy Bannister, of course." Jennifer smiled coyly and took Bonnie's hand and patted it. "It's all right, Bonnie. Nobody really believed that Little Miss Purity act anyway. And besides, he's kind of cute, and he's a nice guy, too. Walking hand in hand with Billy would look a lot better than trudging around here alone all the time. Everyone knows you're an orphan, but you don't have to act like one."

Bonnie drew her hand back, but not so quickly that it would give away her disgust with Jennifer's game. She was determined to keep her temper, so she spread her hands and stayed cool. "You're way off base, Jennifer. I just didn't want Billy to get in trouble, so I told the principal the truth. There's no 'action' going on."

"Oh, maybe you could persuade *me* Bonnie," Jennifer said. She then gestured toward her friends, and both girls turned to look at Jennifer's seven twittering companions. "But there's a lot of other girls you'll have to convince before the rumor stops. I mean, decking Adam makes a pretty strong case that you and Billy are . . . well . . . an item. What other explanation is there?"

Bonnie shrugged her shoulders. "Adam tried to open my backpack."

Jennifer nodded slowly. "Oh . . . I see." She then spoke louder while turning toward her friends. "He tried to open your backpack. Now that's a good reason for decking a guy. I understand now."

Bonnie frowned and took a deep breath to quell her hurt feelings. She didn't know how to answer Jennifer's poisoned sarcasm. She thought she might cry if she said anything, so she just remained quiet and watched the clique drift away.

After a few seconds Jennifer called back, waving, "See you later, lover girl," and all eight girls broke out in loud laughter.

Embarrassment stung Bonnie's heart, and she tried to hold down her erupting anger, but it still bubbled like covered porridge on a hot stove. *That Jennifer Houston! What a two-face! Just yesterday she was as nice as she could be. Now, when she's with her gossipy friends, she pulls a stunt like that!*

Bonnie turned back toward the school building to find Billy again. He was sitting down, resting and wiping his brow with his sleeve. *I should go and talk to him, but if Jennifer and her cronies see me, they'll start their tongues wagging all over again.* Bonnie glanced quickly over her shoulder. Yes, they were watching. *Well, I don't care what they think. I'm going over there.*

Bonnie marched resolutely to the corner of the building while trying to think of a way to talk to Billy, some way to be natural. She knew she had no desire to have a boyfriend, at least not yet, but how could she be nice to him without making him think she was interested? Bonnie arrived at the corner, and greeted him with a big smile. "Good morning, Billy."

Billy looked up and wiped his forehead again. "Oh. Hi. . . . Bonnie . . . right?"

"Yes. Bonnie Silver." She took note of Billy's smile, friendly but tired. Jennifer was right about one thing—with his small, button nose, strong chin, and sparkling hazel eyes, Billy was definitely cute. But there was something more there, something profound that attracted Bonnie at a deeper level. She noticed a glimmer of it when she saw him in the principal's office, but it seemed stronger now. After a few seconds of uncomfortable silence, she finally spoke up again. "That looks like a hard job. Why are you doing it?"

"Dr. Whittier said he'd wipe the suspension from my record if I cleaned the wall. I'm almost done, but I have to rest for a minute."

Bonnie thought about mentioning the injustice of the situation, but what good would that do? *Billy's here. He has to do the job.* She spied the bucket and reached in to grab the scrub brush.

"Well, it looks like you've done a great job. Let me get that last spot for you." Bonnie got down on her knees and began scrubbing the wall, pushing hard to wipe out the stubborn marks. She looked back again to see the girls watching and talking excitedly, but for some reason she no longer cared. She kept on scrubbing, and within a couple of minutes the marks disappeared. "There," she said, rising to her feet. "It's done."

"Thanks, Bonnie. That was a tough stain."

Bonnie let the brush plop back into the bucket of sudsy water, and she wiped her soapy hands on her sweatshirt. "You must've been tired. My arms were fresh." She reached her hand down toward Billy. "Need help?"

Billy gladly took her hand, and Bonnie hoisted him to his feet. He marveled at the strength in her grip and took note of how well she balanced herself, bracing her legs expertly, like a swordsman or a gymnast. This was definitely no ordinary girl.

He dismissed his curiosity and reached down to get his sweater off the ground. After pulling it over his head he fluffed up his matted hair. A chilly breeze swept through his clothes, evaporating the sweat and making him shiver, but it was a good shiver now that he had thick sleeves wrapping him in comfort.

"Thanks again," he said. "That's twice you've helped me out." Billy didn't know what else to say at this point. He suddenly had a strange feeling, the same sense of worry he felt when he saw that Cadillac in his neighborhood. He clumsily extended his hand again to shake Bonnie's. "Let me know if there's anything I can ever do for you."

A deeper voice broke into the conversation. "Well, Mr. Bannister, I see you have a friend here to help you."

Billy turned to see Dr. Whittier standing a few feet away. Over the principal's shoulder, he noticed a hefty, broad-shouldered woman. At first he thought the principal's companion was a man. Her upper lip displayed more than a shadow of hair, but a closer look at her body proved her female gender. Her face looked familiar, but he couldn't place it.

"I scrubbed most of it," Billy explained, "but she did help me right at the end."

"Don't worry. I saw you working, and I've already taken care of your record. Actually, I've been waiting for Miss Silver."

Bonnie's eyes widened. "For me?"

"Yes, we have something important to discuss. Someone has reported that you keep contraband substances in your backpack. I understand the sensitive nature of your privacy concerns, so I asked Olga to assist me in searching your person, starting with your pack."

Billy noticed Bonnie's glance toward him, a look that begged him to help her out. He cleared his throat and stepped forward. "I'm sure Bonnie would never keep anything like that in her backpack," he offered. "Right, Bonnie?"

"Of course I wouldn't!"

The woman approached Bonnie with her hand extended. "Then you should have nothing to hide, dear."

Billy thought the "dear" stuff was a little too much to believe. There was something devious about her.

Olga took Bonnie firmly by the arm, and the two adults began escorting her around to the rear of the building. Bonnie looked back at Billy, terror and a pleading cry shouting from her eyes.

The school bell rang, making Billy flinch. He glanced around at the students beginning to head toward the building. *What do I do? Can they just take her like that?*

When they disappeared around the corner, Billy followed and hid behind a bushy tree to watch. Bonnie struggled to free herself, but she couldn't pull away from the woman's clutches. Bonnie's thrashing finally forced Olga to wrap her in both arms, squeezing her, chest to chest, making her give up the fight. Although they had moved nearly to the backyard, Dr. Whittier and Olga were still close enough for Billy to see what was going on, though he wasn't able to hear their conversation.

Something was said that made Bonnie start kicking wildly, and Olga lifted her off the ground, making her legs flail in the air. Her screams drowned in the woman's coat in muffled gulps.

When Dr. Whittier reached for the backpack, Billy couldn't take any more. He ran out yelling, "Stop that! Leave her alone!"

Dr. Whittier jerked his head around. "Billy, you stay out of this."

Billy rushed up and put his mouth on Olga's arm, blowing on it as hard as he could.

"Yeeow!" She threw the wounded arm upward, and Billy wrenched Bonnie away from her other arm. With a lightning fast reach, Olga snatched Billy's wrist before he could get away.

Billy pulled and twisted his arm, trying to break free. "Run, Bonnie!" he yelled. "Run!"

Bonnie scrambled a few yards away and then glanced back at Billy, her mouth open in silent terror.

"Just go!" Billy shouted, giving up his efforts to free himself from the woman's iron grip.

"Go after her!" Dr. Whittier ordered. "You know I can't run. Give me the boy."

Olga thrust Billy into Dr. Whittier's arms, and Bonnie took off again. Olga chased her, sprinting like an Olympic athlete, much faster than Billy thought she'd be able to run. When

Bonnie rounded the corner, it looked as though Olga was gaining on her, and Billy feared that the chase wouldn't last long. They had gone around to the back of the cafeteria where an alley opened into an outdoor basketball court. If Bonnie tried to escape through the alley, hoping to go through the cafeteria, she would be trapped. They never unlocked those doors this early, and there was no other way out. Bonnie probably didn't know that, being a new student.

They waited in silence for a moment, and Dr. Whittier loosened his grip, leaving his hands on Billy's shoulders with just enough firmness to keep him in place. After another moment, Dr. Whittier began to speak. "I wonder what—," but he was interrupted by Olga, who dashed from around the corner, holding her hands up in futility.

"She disappeared!"

Dr. Whittier limped toward her, pulling Billy along by his right arm. They followed Olga to the alley, where all they could see was a dumpster and bits of cafeteria trash lying around—old aluminum cans, an empty milk crate, and a few banana peels.

"Did you check the dumpster?" Dr. Whittier demanded.

Olga nodded. "It's empty."

Dr. Whittier gruffly pushed Billy toward Olga. "Hold him." Billy thought about giving the woman another blast of his breath, but he wanted to wait around long enough to see what happened to Bonnie.

Dr. Whittier rose up on his tiptoes and peered through the opening of the dumpster. "Empty," he grumbled.

"Didn't you believe me?"

Dr. Whittier searched the blacktop surface in the alley, limping around like a wounded dog. "I wasn't expecting to find her;

I'm looking for . . . Ah! Here it is." He bent over and picked up a large piece of blue and black denim. "Her backpack." He unfolded the material and displayed a large hole in the fabric, a gap that had rested on Bonnie's back.

Billy looked on with interest but wasn't able to figure out Dr. Whittier's point.

"So what do I do with this one?" the woman asked. "The little rascal bit me."

Dr. Whittier extended his hand. "Let me see the wound."

Olga let Billy go for a moment, but the two adults blocked the only way out of the alley. There was no escape.

The principal examined Olga's arm for a few seconds and then glared at Billy with a maniacal stare. "That's not a bite," he snarled. "That's a burn! No wonder you're in cahoots with the little Demon Witch!"

Dr. Whittier reached toward Billy with raging fury in his eyes. Billy was about to try to run for it when he felt a sudden jolt of pain under his arms and a shove from behind as if he were being pushed to the ground. But instead of falling, he rose, surging higher and higher into the air, leaving his breath behind in a terrified shout. "Aaaahhhh!"

Billy tried to breathe again, huffing and puffing against tight pressure on his chest. He saw Dr. Whittier and Olga shrinking beneath him, the principal shaking his fist and Olga standing beside him with her jaw dropped open, but he couldn't understand Dr. Whittier's raging shouts. He felt like he'd been thrown into a dream as bits and pieces of his recent nightmare picked their way back into his memory.

Within seconds, the scene below disappeared in a cloud, and Billy noticed for the first time that two arms embraced him, each hand holding firmly to the wrist of the other, making an interlocking grip. The sleeves were pushed up to the elbows, exposing smooth, creamy white skin. The arms weren't big and muscular, certainly not as impressive as the strength of their embrace.

The sudden shift in scenery gave Billy no time to feel any fear, but now a new queasy sensation brewed in his stomach. *Maybe this isn't a dream after all.*

"Are you all right?" a familiar voice asked.

"Bonnie?" Billy tried to turn his head to see behind him, but with his body dangling in the air, the effort was hopeless.

"Stop wiggling! You'll make me drop you!"

"Drop me?" Suddenly the realization of where he was flooded Billy's senses. He looked down and saw nothing but the top of the cloud bank that had rolled in that morning. "Bonnie!" he screamed. "What's going on?" He gasped for breath and thrashed his arms and legs in useless attempts to steady his mind and body.

"Be still! I can't hold you if you do that. You're too heavy."

Billy felt her arms grasp him even more tightly, and their strength settled him down, but only a little bit. He couldn't calm his voice. "B—Bonnie, what's going on?"

Before Bonnie could answer, Billy felt the ground press the soles of his feet, and Bonnie's arms loosened around his chest. He spun his head, looking below from side to side. "I'm on the ground, but the clouds are still below us!"

"We're on Mount Hardin. The peak is sticking up through the clouds."

Billy turned to see Bonnie sitting on a large boulder. She held a palm on her chest and took several slow, deep breaths before smiling and letting out a quiet laugh. "You're pretty heavy, you know that?"

Billy stepped toward her but then halted. "How did you . . . What did you . . ." Finally he raised his hands to the sides of his head. "What's going on here?"

Bonnie stared intently at Billy, and for a moment she sat still and silent. Then, as if growing out of nothingness, two enormous wings spread out behind her. Decorated with a light brown hue that resembled rustic gold, the wings flapped slowly, waving toward Billy in friendship. Each wing was at least as large as the girl herself, rippled with sinews throughout, with a mainstay extending from her back all the way to the farthest tip.

Now that Billy and Bonnie were above the low clouds, sunlight filtered through the higher cirrus and shone through the thin membranes of Bonnie's wings, making them brighten into a honey-glazed shimmer. With her blonde-streaked hair flowing in the breeze and her flawless innocence shining through, Bonnie's appearance was like that of a seated angel, her winged silhouette the striking portrait of Michael himself. She was stunningly beautiful.

A thousand thoughts scrambled Billy's wits. What was this creature before him? Just yesterday he had learned that he, himself, was somehow of dragon blood. That realization had come riding on the winds of an overheard conversation. It was scary, but it didn't seem real. This time, however, he rode the winds himself with only the arms of a dragon princess saving him from Dr. Whittier's fury. The revelation literally jarred his bones, pumped through his heart, and made his hair stand on end. He could only stare in bewildered silence.

Bonnie rose to her feet and her wings folded behind her, making her appear normal once again. She walked closer to Billy and stood in front of him, face-to-face. Since she was only about an inch shorter, she was able to rise up on her toes and look straight into his eyes. With her hands folded behind her back, her face flushed with sincere gratitude, she kissed him on the cheek. "Thank you for saving my life," she whispered.

Billy shook his head, waking himself from his trance, and he put his fingers tenderly on his anointed cheek. "Uh, you're welcome. But I didn't save your life. I just kept Dr. Whittier from snooping in your backpack."

Bonnie nodded her head in a fast rhythm and let out a short laugh that carried a hint of embarrassment. "And now you know what I was hiding. But I was in such a hurry I didn't have time to pick it up. I had to fly to the roof before Olga came around the corner." Her wings flapped briefly again, this time coming around her and within inches of Billy's ears.

Billy had to smile. "Your wings are awesome." He couldn't believe how calm he felt in her presence, even though she seemed almost alien. Her manner was so disarming, she could have had three eyes and four antennae and it probably wouldn't have mattered. "But I guess I can understand why you don't want anyone to see them."

Bonnie turned and peered down the mountainside as if trying to look through the clouds. "Not just anyone. Now that I know who Dr. Whittier is, he's the worst one to find out."

Billy looked toward the valley, too, but only for a moment. He couldn't see anything but the steep, grassy knoll that lay ahead, strewn with rocks and disappearing into the mist. "Who Dr. Whittier is? What do you mean?"

Bonnie turned back to face Billy, who quickly averted his gaze from Bonnie's wings and back to her very excited eyes. "I was listening from the roof," she explained. "I couldn't believe it when I heard about how you burned that woman. My mother told me about your father, but I never thought I'd find someone else like me, another dragon kid I mean. When I first saw you that day in the principal's office, I knew there was something different about you, and then when you were scrubbing that wall and we were so close together, I could feel it. Anyway, when Dr. Whittier called me Demon Witch, he gave himself away. He has to be a slayer. 'Demon Witch' is what a slayer calls the females."

"A slayer? What's that?"

"A dragon slayer. Your parents have told you about the dragon slayers, haven't they?"

"Well . . . no."

Bonnie's face contorted. "But . . . but you *are* a dragon, aren't you?"

Billy shoved his hands into his pockets and glanced toward the knoll again. "Yes . . . I mean, I guess so. I just found out yesterday."

Bonnie came up to his side and tried to look him in the eye. "You mean you've only known for one day?"

"I overheard my parents talking about it." Billy shrugged his shoulders and shifted his body to the side, away from Bonnie. "Then they told me, but they didn't tell me much."

"So your father's the dragon, right?"

"Uh . . . right. At least that's what he said. But how did you know?"

"I'll tell you later." Bonnie took his arm and pulled him around so she could talk face-to-face. She smiled and spoke excitedly again. "Do you have any other dragon powers besides breathing fire?"

"Well, it isn't really fire breathing," Billy said, his hands still in his pockets. "My breath's just real hot."

Bonnie pondered that for a moment, her head tilted upward and her eyes wide open in thought. "Then it's probably just now developing," she said slowly. "That must be why your parents waited so long to tell you." She looked back at Billy and brought the tip of her right wing into her right hand. "My wings started growing when I was five years old, so my mother had to tell me what was going on."

"So you've been flying ever since you were five?"

"No. They didn't get big enough until about three years ago. I started practicing my flying on cloudy and moonless nights when no one could see me, but after my mother was killed, I—" The color suddenly drained from Bonnie's face, and her wings slowly collapsed into a shivering huddled mass.

"What's wrong?"

Bonnie grabbed Billy, squeezing his upper arms in terror. "Dr. Whittier! He's a dragon slayer!"

"Right. You just told me that."

"But he knows where you live!" she cried, pushing and pulling him back and forth. "He's probably on his way there already!"

Billy's eyes opened wide. "You mean, he'll—"

"Yes, he'll stop at nothing to kill your father!"

CHAPTER 7

THE BAT CREATURE

Billy's face paled to an ashen, almost corpselike color, and he paced back and forth frantically. "I—I have to call home. I have to get home."

Bonnie's wings spread out fully once again, and she grabbed Billy's shirt to stop his pacing. "I'll fly there right now. Where's your house?"

"On Cordelle Road. Fifteen forty-five."

Bonnie spread her arms. "Cordelle Road? I don't know where that is. I'm new around here, you know."

Billy stooped and drew a quick map in a dirt patch. "It's one mile northwest of the main highway from the exit where the Shell station is." He stood again and turned around slowly, searching for a landmark through the mist. "Over there," he said, pointing. "The highway has to be right about there, just down the slope from where that clump of trees sticks out. Follow it northeast for about a mile. That's where the exit is."

Bonnie shook her head slowly as she surveyed the murky landscape. "If I fly below the clouds to find the highway, I'll scare the whole town. And I still might not be able to find your house."

"But the clouds are too thick," Billy countered. "If you stay above them you won't be able to tell which way is which."

Billy and Bonnie stared at each other for a moment. Billy felt the stalemate in his brain, like two solitary kings on a chessboard.

Bonnie leaned over and peered into the valley again. "Where did you say your house is?"

Billy turned and pointed again while Bonnie circled behind him to follow his line of sight. "See where that cloud puffs up and turns white? I think—Hey!" With a sudden thrust that squashed his breath away Billy felt himself being swept up into the air again, his feet nearly leaving his shoes behind.

"I'm heading that way, Billy!" Bonnie called out. "Just tell me where to go!"

"Not again!"

This time Bonnie's arms wrapped around his body near his waist, so tightly he could feel his heart pounding against her arm as it pressed under his rib cage. The uplifting pressure pushed out every breath he tried to draw in, but Billy managed to talk in gasping, short bursts. "Bear . . . right!"

"How much?"

"Two . . . o'clock!"

"Two o'clock?"

Billy extended his right arm in the proper direction, but the move made him slip an inch or so through Bonnie's grasp. He quickly pulled his hand back and clutched Bonnie's arms.

"Keep your arms still," she ordered. "I get it now. Two o'clock." Bonnie veered to the right. "Should I fly lower? Higher?"

"You're . . . fine!"

Now that he had his wits about him, Billy noticed that they weren't flying horizontally, the way Superman always did in the movies. They were almost vertical, their slight forward angle reflecting the position of Bonnie's wings versus the location of their combined center of gravity.

The realization of complete airborne helplessness unnerved Billy, but Bonnie's calm tone and her uncommonly strong arms kept him from panicking. With the fate of his parents in the forefront of his mind, he was able to concentrate on his task—finding his house, and fast. His eyes darted back and forth, straining to see through the clouds, but he could only guess, hoping his sense of direction would get them somewhere close. After a few more commands to correct their direction Billy shouted, "I think . . . we're right . . . over it!"

"Okay, I'm going to make a fast drop so no one will see us. Get ready."

Billy wasn't quite sure how to get ready, but holding his breath seemed like a good idea. Every ounce of his dangling weight abruptly reversed direction, and his heart and lungs threatened to take up residence in his throat. He and Bonnie plummeted through the clouds, white mist dampening their faces as they struggled to keep their eyes open to look for a clearing. As soon as they fell under the clouds Billy was able to yell, the pressure of Bonnie's grasp lessened by their hurtling plunge. "Pull up!" Billy yelled. "We're clear!"

Bonnie's wings stretched out once again, grabbing the air like a muscular parachute, and Billy felt the painful catch under his rib cage again. Bonnie's arms, though soft and smooth on the surface, felt like steel clamps squeezing his gut up into his esophagus.

Through his grimace he could see the housetops, and he recognized where they were. They had descended very close to his house and right above a neighbor's backyard. "Land here!" he grunted.

Bonnie glided down to the leaf-covered yard and deposited Billy carefully. His feet hit first, but he couldn't keep his balance. He rolled over three times before sitting upright. Scrambling to his feet, he hurriedly pulled off his sweater and ran to Bonnie. She was just slowing down from her running stop. "Here," he said. "Put this on."

Bonnie took the sweater, and Billy helped her pull it over her head. As he did so, he guided the bottom hem over her wings, using one hand to hold the sweater and the other to fold her wings down as flat as possible. For a brief moment he wondered about touching her like this. He couldn't help but admire the feel of her wings, smooth and leathery, not the same as the velvety texture he had already felt on her arms. No, the wings were more primitive and wild, with tactile friction that seemed to grip his skin as he rubbed across their surface. They even smelled of an outdoors freedom, of horses and saddles, or of work belts and new boots, or even of a well-worn baseball glove. Apparently she felt no shyness about his caress.

"Is this your yard?" Bonnie asked, turning around to Billy.

"No. We're three yards down," he replied, pointing to his right, "but I don't think anyone's ever home here during the day. Let's stay behind the houses and sneak up to mine from the back in case Dr. Whittier's already there."

The two ran, crouching as much as possible while still maintaining a good clip. Billy led the way and signaled for Bonnie to slow down as they approached his house. The small two-story dwelling stood in the middle of a half-acre, fenced yard. Its clean white siding and neatly landscaped surroundings created a perfect model for the quiet, middle-class neighborhood. But the peaceful scene gave Billy a creepy feeling. Had Dr. Whittier already come? Maybe he held his parents captive inside. Or worse.

With a running start Billy jumped the chain-link fence by leaping with an extended left foot, stepping on the top of the fence, and vaulting over. Billy turned to help Bonnie climb, but she was already scaling the links. He arrived in time to brace her elbow on the way down as she jumped from the top bar. The two now approached more stealthily, heads low and feet careful to pad as softly as possible. Billy was glad he had raked the yard recently. A deep pile of oak leaves would surely have sounded a crackling alarm if they tried to sneak through them.

Billy stole up the porch steps with Bonnie close behind. He crouched low and raised his head to peek in through the back door window. "Whew!" he whispered to Bonnie. "Mom's in the kitchen, and I think she's alone."

They stood up as one, and Billy opened the door, walking in nonchalantly to keep from startling his mother, who sat quietly at the kitchen table. Billy guessed she was doing payroll for Dad's business. "Hi, Mom!"

His mother looked up and cocked her head to one side. "Billy! What are you doing home? You're supposed to be at school! And why did you come in the back door?" Just then Bonnie walked out from behind Billy. His mother's eyes opened wide, and a pleasant smile of greeting crossed her face. "And who is this young lady?"

Billy spewed out an introduction. "Mom, this is Bonnie Silver." Bonnie nodded and returned the smile while Billy continued.

"There's no time to talk. We have to get out of here." He turned his head in every possible direction. "Is Dad home?"

"No. He had to run out to the airport and then the hardware store. He'll be a while." Her face wrinkled and her smile disappeared. "Billy, what's wrong?"

Billy's words poured out breathlessly. "A dragon slayer is coming. At least we think he is, and he could be here any minute."

Billy's mother jumped to her feet, her eyes ablaze. "Dragon slayer?! Who?"

Billy took his mother's hand and tried to lead her toward the front door. "Never mind. We have to hurry."

She pulled back on his hand and then pushed him toward a chair. "Sit down and start explaining right now!"

Billy plopped down while Bonnie slid into the chair next to his. He took a deep breath and tried to speak calmly. "My principal is a dragon slayer," he explained, "and since we're both dragons, he's coming after us. We have to get out of here." Billy gulped when he realized how crazy it all sounded.

"*We're* both dragons?" she repeated. "What do you mean? I'm not a dragon."

Before Billy could answer, Bonnie stood and pulled off the borrowed sweater, carefully guiding it over her head. Her wings spread out, and in the enclosed space they seemed even more magnificent than ever. They shielded the overhead light and cast a shadow over Billy and his mother. "I am," she said softly.

Billy's mother raised a trembling hand to her mouth. "Dear God in heaven! You're one, too!"

Bonnie touched her tenderly on her shoulder. "Now, please. We really have to go."

Billy's mom circled the table. "I have to get the box." She left the room and thumped up the stairs.

"Box?" Bonnie asked.

Billy spread out his hands. "I don't know, but I'd better see if I can help." He leaped up the stairs and heard Bonnie calling after him.

"I'll keep watch down here."

Billy caught up with his mother just as she came out of her bedroom. In her arms she carried a large cardboard box. A layer or two of duct tape wrapped the box in a gray mask, presumably to make it stronger, and maybe to hide any labels or markings.

Billy slid his arms under the load. "Let me get that."

She gave it up gladly. "I have to get one more thing, and we'll put it all in the Volks." She turned and ran to another room, returning within seconds with a large book under her arm. "Okay. Let's get going."

The two rushed down the stairs where they saw Bonnie holding back the edge of the curtain to peek out the front window. She had put the sweater back on, but her folded wings made obvious lumps on her back. "Looks safe so far," she announced.

Billy's mom opened the door, and all three hustled into the driveway where a yellow Volkswagen Beetle sat. "We have to pack the box and book in the back seat. Let's put them behind the passenger seat. It'll be a little tight, but Bonnie should still be able to fit behind the driver."

"No problem. I'm used to my wings getting cramped."

"I hope it decides to start okay this time," Billy said.

"It had better," his mother agreed. She opened the car door and placed the book on the back seat. "I'll run and write a note for your father in case I can't get him on his cell phone. We'll go to the airport and try to catch him before he leaves." She hurried to the house and disappeared through the door.

Bonnie climbed into the back seat. She reached for the box, and Billy helped her place it securely on top of the book. He withdrew quickly when he heard a strange rattling noise. A boy on a bike pedaled furiously toward them. With sweat plastering his shirt to his chest, he looked exhausted and terrified.

"Walter!" Billy called. "What's wrong?"

Walter pulled up and plopped his hands and elbows on the handlebars while he tried to catch his breath. "I borrowed Frank's bike . . . rode all the way . . . here." After a few seconds he was able to speak more easily, and he squinted at Billy. "How'd you get back so fast?"

"I left quite a while ago. What happened?"

"Haven't you heard? A bunch of kids at school saw a huge bat creature carry a kid away. It flew up into the clouds with him kicking underneath. I saw it, too, right before it disappeared. Everyone was pointing, so I just looked up, and there it was."

Billy sneaked a look at Bonnie out of the corner of his eye. She was hunkered down and peeking out the corner of the open window, listening to the conversation.

Walter went on. "All the girls screamed, and even some of the guys, and everyone ran for their lives. Dr. Whittier was out there limping toward the parking lot, but two moms dragged on his arms, screaming like banshees about their missing kids, and they wouldn't let him go. Some parents were still dropping off kids, and they were going nuts, yelling at them to get back in the car. Frank got a ride home with the Jacksons; that's why I took his bike."

Billy turned to look down the street. "So that's why he's not here yet."

Walter followed Billy's glance. "Who's not here? Frank?"

"Never mind." Billy put his hand on Walter's shoulder and looked him right in the eye. "Listen, Walter. Do me a huge favor. Stick around here, but stay out of sight. If my dad comes home, tell him we went to the airport and he has to come meet us right away. But if Dr. Whittier shows up, make sure he doesn't see you."

"Dr. Whittier? Why would he come here? You didn't swamp the bathroom again, did you?"

"No!" Billy rolled his eyes and tried to stay calm. He took a deep breath and looked him in the eye again. "Just do it, okay? If my dad doesn't get here in, say, thirty minutes, you can go on home. All right?"

"Sure, Billy, but aren't you wondering about the bat creature?"

"Don't worry about the bat creature. She won't hurt you."

Walter's face lit up. "She? You know the bat creature? Cool! Can you show her to me?"

Billy shook his head and groaned. "Not now," he pleaded. "Just watch for my dad, okay? It's a matter of life and death!"

Walter raised his hands in surrender. "Okay, okay! You know a female bat creature that flies away with school kids for no good reason, and you don't want to let me in on it. I understand. Makes perfect sense to me." He looked down the road again and then back at Billy. "So what's so important? What if your dad asks why you need him?"

Billy paused to think, but he drew a blank. What should Walter say?

"Walter!" Billy and Walter both spun around. It was Bonnie. She had leaned forward to speak through the front window. "Walter, tell him this: A dark knight is coming quickly."

Walter cocked his head and stared at her, his eyes narrowing. "Why is Bonnie here?"

"You know Bonnie?" Billy asked.

"Everyone knows about Bonnie Backpack." He leaned forward to get a better look at her. "She's not wearing it!"

"Never mind! Now what are you going to tell my father?"

"That it's going to get dark early tonight."

Billy groaned again and grabbed Walter's shoulders. "No! Listen! A dark knight is coming quickly. Exactly like that. Got it?"

Walter's eyes grew large, and he stared at Billy's gripping arms. "A dark night is coming quickly. Got it!"

Billy nodded and started walking to the car, but he had a feeling Walter wasn't quite on board, so he watched him over his shoulder. Walter stared at the ground with his chin in his hand, and he looked up at Billy. "But I thought it was going to be a full moon tonight. You said the other day that the fish bite better when—"

"Walter!" Billy shouted, his hand extended to stop his friend's question. "Just say the words."

Walter shrugged his shoulders. "Whatever you say, boss. A dark night is coming quickly. Who am I to argue with the keeper of the mysterious bat creature?"

Billy was about to yell at Walter again, but his mother burst out of the house and ran toward the car. "Why is it I can never find a pen when I need one?" She jumped into the driver's seat, and Billy got in beside her. He stared back at Walter and pointed his index finger at him. "Say it again," he ordered.

Walter rolled his eyes, but he managed a smile. "A dark night is coming quickly."

After one unsuccessful grind of the ignition, the Beetle roared to life. The sound brought welcome relief and made Billy's frown melt away. He felt bad about getting upset at his friend, and he softened his tone. "Great, Walter. Now remember, stay out of sight unless my dad comes."

As the car screeched backwards down the driveway, Walter pushed the bike to a clump of bushes at the corner of the house and disappeared among them. He crouched in the mulch and watched the antique yellow bug putter away, wondering what was going on.

How can a bat creature be nothing to worry about? What does Billy know about it, anyway? Was he the one the creature carried into the clouds? I guess that would explain how he showed up at home so quick. But how did Bonnie get here? He held his hands on the sides of his head. *It's all just way too weird to believe!*

A roaring engine speared his thoughts. A dark blue Cadillac thundered from the direction Billy's car had just gone and squealed to a stop in front of Billy's house. The right rear door flew open, and two men, one tall and one short, jumped out. Walter gulped when he caught a glimpse of the driver. *Dr. Whittier!* Walter scrunched down low and peeked through the leaves. Dr. Whittier shouted orders as he slung his door open.

"Break the door down if you have to! If they're not home, Sam, check with Olga. She knows what to look for."

She? Walter thought. *Okay, so the shorter one's a woman. I can see that now.*

The pair ran toward the door. Dr. Whittier limped behind them, his cane digging into the grass as he struggled to catch up.

Olga jiggled the doorknob and then thrust the end of a crowbar into the jamb. She braced her foot against the side panel and ripped the door open, allowing them to rush inside.

Walter spread the outer branches a bit wider to watch Dr. Whittier. The principal scanned the yard and then the roof, and Walter hunched down even farther to avoid detection. Within seconds Sam returned carrying the crowbar and a piece of paper.

"Here's a note," he said. "What do you make of it?"

Dr. Whittier took the scrap of paper and read it out loud, slowly and deliberately. Walter strained to listen, barely able to make out the words.

"Jared. The little bird is here and the black hawk pursues. Hurry and fly away with us."

Dr. Whittier crumpled the note and stuffed it in his pocket. "Lousy code. Couldn't fool anyone. Bannister's a pilot, so they must be going to meet him. Was that a yellow Volkswagen we passed?"

Sam nodded. "Female driver. I didn't notice anyone else. If they were in there, they were hiding."

Dr. Whittier took the crowbar and slapped his open palm with it. "I'm going to the airport. Finish the search and then burn the house to the ground. I don't want one stick of this house to curse this land. We'll meet . . ."

Try as he might, Walter couldn't hear the rest of the conversation. But he had heard enough. Big trouble was brewing, and Walter could only watch and wait.

Sam popped open the trunk of the Cadillac, pulled out a plastic gas can, and hurried back to the house, one shoulder sagging with the weight of his load. Dr. Whittier took another quick look around and limped back to his car. Seconds later, the tires spun a high-pitched squeal, leaving a puff of gray smoke behind, and the car roared down the street.

Walter stayed low, guessing that the two goons might come out of the house at any minute. He wondered what he was getting into. Burn the house down? And here he sat right next to it! His heart pounded, and he tried to slow his breathing to compensate. If not for the cool breeze, he would have broken into a sweat.

He waited, catching whiffs of smoke, stronger and stronger as the minutes passed. A swirl of smoke crawled out of the window over his head, seeping under its bottom edge. He heard a slam, and Sam and Olga sprinted out. Walter craned his neck to listen.

"Don't worry. The flames will climb the stairs . . ."

That was all he could hear. When Olga closed the door, she and Sam turned and stared at the street. Walter looked, too. A beige pickup truck had just turned onto the road about a hundred feet away.

Walter was delighted when he recognized the truck. *It's Mr. Bannister!*

Sam and Olga hurried across the grass and onto the sidewalk, pretending they were just walking by, but Billy's father apparently wasn't fooled. He skidded to a stop on the street and jumped out. "What were you doing in my house?"

Walter couldn't hear Sam's answer. He seemed to be making an excuse, but Mr. Bannister wasn't buying it.

Before Billy's dad could reply, Olga pulled a small handgun from under her jacket. With a hyper-quick thrust, Mr. Bannister kicked her wrist, sending the pistol skidding on the sidewalk. When Olga lunged for it, Billy's dad bolted toward the house. After scooping up her pistol, Olga charged after him with Sam following close behind.

The house belched smoke from under the front door, but Mr. Bannister swung it open anyway and vanished into the cloud. He left the door open, and his pursuers dashed in only a few seconds behind him, Sam first and then Olga, both waving their arms to clear the way.

Smoke poured through another window near Walter and it blew into his hiding place. He couldn't help it; he just had to cough. The choking fumes were flushing him out. *No time to grab the bike. Gotta run!*

He staggered from the bushes to find another place to hide, maybe a bush farther away from the house. He headed for the street, but the sound of someone else coughing made him turn back. Billy's father had run outside again. He was leaning over and hacking with dry, retching spasms, sucking in precious air after every coughing spell. In his arms he carried a terrified cat, and as soon as he let the struggling mass of flailing legs down, it took off like a furry-tailed fireball into the next yard.

Since neither Sam nor Olga was anywhere in sight, Walter ran to help. "Mr. Bannister! Are you all right?"

Billy's father raised his hand, signaling "wait just a minute," and coughed several more times. He nodded and tried to choke out a reply. "Yes—" He bent over and let out yet another series of dreadful, sandpaper coughs before wiping his mouth and clearing his throat. "Whoever those burglars were, they weren't very bright. I clubbed the first one with a baseball bat I keep in the coat closet. It was so smoky, the second one couldn't see what happened. So I just bashed her, too."

"Didn't you get them out?"

Mr. Bannister shook his head. "The second one grabbed me on her way down. I guess I aimed too low and got her on the shoulder. I lost the bat, and we rolled into the fire. Her clothes caught, and my shirtsleeve did, too." He held up his arm to show Walter his scorched sleeve. "When she screamed, I finally figured out she was a woman. She let go, and I got away. Her buddy was already burned up. The flames were everywhere. It was all I could do to get out."

Before Walter could say anything else, he jerked his head around. "I hear sirens." He turned back to watch tongues of flame shooting through the roof.

Billy's father sighed. "Yep. I guess somebody called 9-1-1." He turned to join Walter in watching the tragic sight. "I see the VW's gone, so Marilyn couldn't have been home. Have you seen her?"

Walter couldn't believe Mr. Bannister's calm voice. His house burned like a doomsday inferno, and a creepy lady with a gun had just tried to kill him! And now he was acting like he just had a bad day at the office! "I saw them," Walter replied, pointing down the road. "She and Billy both left a little while ago."

Mr. Bannister glanced upward. "Thank the Maker!" he said before turning his gaze back to Walter. "Billy was home? Is school out?"

"Sort of, but Billy asked me to tell you something, so I'd better tell you now."

"Okay. What is it?"

Walter quoted his part slowly and carefully. "A dark night is coming quickly."

Mr. Bannister's forehead wrinkled. "A dark night? That doesn't make sense; there's a full moon tonight."

Walter gave a shrug. "I know. That's what I told Billy. But he seemed to think you'd know what it means."

Mr. Bannister rolled his eyes upward and tapped his shoe on the ground. Suddenly, his eyebrows lifted, and he leaned over to look at Walter face-to-face. "Did he mean a dark N-I-G-H-T or a dark K-N-I-G-H-T?"

Walter shook his head. "I dunno. He didn't spell it for me."

Mr. Bannister paused, rubbing his chin. "What else did he say?"

"Just that they went to the airport. You're supposed to meet them there."

Two fire engines blared their sirens as they careened onto the neighborhood block. The pumper stopped right behind Mr. Bannister's truck, and four uniformed men spilled out, grabbing equipment and unraveling hoses.

One firefighter ran up to Walter and Mr. Bannister. "Is everyone out?"

"No," Mr. Bannister replied. "The two who set the fire are trapped inside. I think they're dead."

The firefighter rushed back to the truck. "We've got two on the skewer!" He grabbed a gas mask, and two others with masks followed as he raced to the door.

Mr. Bannister put both hands on Walter's shoulders. "Thank you for the message, but you'd better get home. Those two were looking for trouble, and I don't want you here if any others show up."

"Sure, but there's one more thing you should know."

"What's that?"

"Our principal, Dr. Whittier, was with them. I think he was going to the airport to catch up with Mrs. Bannister and Billy and Bonnie, and he's the one who ordered the house burned down."

"Bonnie? Who's Bonnie?"

Walter was about to answer, but Mr. Bannister didn't give him time.

"Never mind. I have to go." He ran to his pickup, shouting behind him. "Get home, Walter! And if you can come back with your dad and find Gandalf, I'd appreciate it. I'm pretty sure I left my cell phone at the airport, so you can't call me until I get back there." He threw open the door, started the engine, and roared away.

Walter stared at the scene around him, his mind filled with awe. A house he knew so well crackled in flames, and firefighters scrambled all around, two now anchoring a gushing hose that rained onto the roof. Three women approached from other houses to watch, and several young teenagers congregated in the street, apparently arriving at home after their early release from school. The crowd gathered around Walter and pelted him with a dozen questions at a time.

He felt a strange sense of importance and tried to answer as many as he could, but he knew he had to keep some things secret. He hoped Billy would make everything clear later. After a few minutes, the crowd grew tired of asking the same questions over and over, giving Walter a chance to muse about the excitement. A bat creature at school, burglars with guns, a house on fire. What a day!

CHAPTER 8

The Slayer's Wrath

Billy stared at the road through the car's rear window. The tailpipe coughed in fitful spasms, blowing a train of miniature gray clouds into the long line of cars slowly crawling behind. He felt like their little yellow Beetle was the head of a snaking, segmented worm, and each trailing car contributed a set of four spinning legs. One of the segments, a large, dark sedan, shot out from the line, roared ahead of a big SUV, and pushed back just before an oncoming truck could slam it head-on. It was the Cadillac! But a new driver gripped the wheel, sitting higher in the seat than did the shorter guy who had been spying on him. Billy strained to get a better look, but the car still trailed too far behind. Could it be Dr. Whittier?

The Cadillac lurched out again, zoomed past three cars, careening around the serpentine slopes, and jerked back into line just in time. Billy shivered. This guy was nuts! He turned to see if his mother noticed. She had the gas pedal smashed to the floor, and her eyes darted between the windshield and her rear view mirror. Billy slapped his hand against the dashboard. "C'mon you old bucket of bolts! Can't you go any faster?"

When the Beetle neared the top of the last hill before town, it chugged, backfired, and finally crested the top. Once on the downhill slope their car seemed to sigh as it coasted into the valley.

Billy's mom wiped her hand across her moist forehead, breathing easier but keeping an eye on the erratic driver still a few cars back. "Okay. Now we just have to get through town. It'll be crowded today, you know."

"Yeah," Billy replied, turning again to the rear. "The festival's tonight." He glanced at Bonnie. She sat low, scrunched down to keep her head below the rear window level. Her eyes told him that she knew someone was following them.

Now that they had driven onto a long straightaway, several cars passed them by, leaving only bare road between the little yellow Volkswagen and the crazy blue Cadillac. The maniacal car pulled right up to their bumper, and Billy recognized the driver's scowling face. "It's Dr. Whittier, all right!" It was too late to hide. The principal's evil glare attached to Billy like cobra fangs.

His mother mumbled her thoughts out loud. "Where's a police car when you need one?" She took a deep breath and exhaled heavily. "Maybe I can lose him when we get into town."

Billy felt the hatred in Dr. Whittier's stare, as though his principal's eyes were cutting open his head and reading his thoughts. He couldn't stand it. He turned to look at Bonnie again. Her wide, fearful eyes stared into space, but when they focused on Billy's, she smiled sheepishly. He guessed that she was embarrassed about her fear, so he gave her a smile in return and whispered, "I'm scared, too."

Bonnie reached her hand forward, and Billy hesitated, staring at it for a second. Finally, he put his hand in hers, folding his fingers into a handshake, but this was like no handshake he had ever felt before. Her cool, smooth fingers wrapped under the heel of his hand, and her thumb hugged the knuckle of his index finger. Every pressure point brought a strange warmth that overwhelmed the chill of fear in his hands, and with every ounce of energy he had, Billy tried to transmit that warmth back to Bonnie, hoping to bring her some comfort.

After a few seconds, Billy pulled his hand back, letting go slowly, allowing his fingers to caress hers as they moved apart. He had never held a girl's hand before. He didn't know what the sensation meant. Was it a romantic feeling, or was it the loving touch of a friend, a faithful sister who really understood all his troubles?

Billy's mother picked up the cell phone and handed it to him. "We should be back in range now. Let's try your father again."

Billy punched in the numbers and waited, tapping his foot and breathing heavily. After a few seconds he responded to his father's recorded greeting. Billy's fear came through in his trembling voice. "Dad, it's Billy again. The slayer's following us. We'll try to lose him, but I don't think we can do it in this rickety old car."

"Billy, if he's not there, just hang up and call 9-1-1."

"Dad, I have to hang up and call the police." Billy glanced back again at their pursuer. "There's no use hiding now. He knows who we are." Bonnie raised her head and turned around to get a look at the slayer.

Billy punched the emergency number and waited. His eyes darted around at the familiar sights as the road narrowed again, signaling their entry into Castlewood's downtown section. The small town normally had light traffic, but today a river of cars jammed the two-lane stretch through the main drag. Trucks and vans carrying the setup crew for the fall festival hugged the curb and flooded the parking areas near the recreation entrance a few blocks farther up the road. Various craft stands, harvest exhibits, and charity booths packed the sidewalks, and dozens of people milled around, putting the final touches on their displays.

A mechanical female voice finally answered, "Nine-one-one. What is your emergency?"

Billy was about to speak, but he saw something that made him shout into the phone. "Never mind!" He hung up, grabbed his mother's shoulder, and pointed down the road. "Look! There's a policeman!"

At the next traffic light, about two blocks ahead, a police officer directed cars, waving his gloved hand with robotic precision. Billy put the cell phone down and pointed again. "Mom! Pull up beside him and tell him what's going on!"

"I can't yet. I have to stop. He's stopping everyone, and there are at least a dozen cars between us."

"Then go in the other lane!"

She waved her hand at the oncoming traffic. "I can't. Cars are turning this way from the side street."

Billy looked back. Whittier's Cadillac had stopped, too, and when their eyes met, Billy felt a cold shiver again. The principal's evil glower carried a mix of unearthly hatred and sadistic delight. Would he get out now and come up to the car? Billy looked ahead. *Oh, good. Mom left some escape room in front of us.* He noticed her eyes moving back and forth again between the rearview mirror and the windshield. She was definitely on the alert.

"Why won't he let us through?" she complained.

"All those cars have their headlights on," Bonnie noted. "Is it a funeral procession?"

Billy kept his eyes riveted on the slayer. "Probably. I'll bet they're all coming from Smather's Funeral Home."

Billy's mom gripped the steering wheel and wrung it like a dishcloth. "I couldn't turn into the other lane even if I wanted to, and there's no way I could get up on the sidewalk with all those produce stands everywhere."

Billy could only watch and wait. "Whoever died must've been a popular guy." He looked back at the short distance between the VW and the Cadillac. "He's so close. He could just get out and—" Billy dropped his mouth open. Dr. Whittier's car door had swung open, and he was stepping out onto the street.

Bonnie grabbed the front seat and screamed. "He's getting out! And he's carrying a crowbar!"

Billy's mother spun the steering wheel to the right and muttered. "So I smash a few pumpkins!" She stepped on the gas, lurching the car forward, but the engine backfired with a loud "Pow!" and choked before expiring in a dying gasp. All three gulped and held their breath while she frantically turned the ignition key. The starter sounded like rocks spinning in a tin can. The motor coughed and sputtered but died away again.

The dragon slayer limped up to the left rear window and drew back his crowbar, ready to strike. Bonnie threw herself forward and covered her face with her hands. The crowbar crashed through the window, sending glass shards and pellets flying over her back and shoulders.

The slayer didn't bother opening the door. He threw the crowbar down and lunged his torso through the window's gaping hole, reaching with his maniacal fingers until he grabbed a fistful of Bonnie's hair. He jerked her upright and dragged her, faceup, toward the window. Bonnie screamed and stretched out her arms and hands, hysterically trying to grasp anything within reach.

Billy lunged toward her, grabbed one of her floundering hands, and pulled, but it slipped, and he flew back and banged his head on the dashboard. Billy's mother spun, leaned around her seat, and caught one of Bonnie's arms. She held on with one hand while wrapping her other arm around Bonnie's waist.

The enraged slayer, with both fists now full of Bonnie's hair, pulled ferociously. Pop! Pop! Bonnie's neck vertebrae sounded an alarm; they couldn't hold out much longer.

Billy reached over his struggling mom to help. It was no use. Their bodies flailed, arms and legs flying in every direction. But he had to do something! Bonnie's neck was about to snap, and the jagged glass in the window stabbed her shoulders. She could be dead in seconds! He leaped out his door. His only hope was to dash around and attack the slayer.

As he ran, he noticed the policeman finally turning their way. *Can he see what's going on? Can he possibly help in time?* The people on the sidewalks just stood and stared, apparently in a state of shock. He couldn't wait for anyone. He had to go for it.

As he rounded the front of the car, a strange light struck his eyes, blinding him for a second. It seemed to come from the slayer himself.

Billy stopped and shielded his face. He felt confused and weak, as though something was draining his energy, even his thoughts.

Bonnie's throat lay bare and stretched out just past the window base. The window frame's jagged, broken glass sliced into her shoulders just below her neck. Her terrified eyes turned to Billy, and her gaping mouth formed a silent scream.

"If I can't get you out," the slayer growled, his bright eyes now glowing yellow, "I'll just finish you off right here, Demon Witch!" He raised his hand, and a long switchblade snapped open.

Billy took a deep breath and held it. His feet wouldn't move. They felt anchored to the street. He lunged forward, releasing a guttural, explosive, "Nooooo!" An orange tongue of fire shot out and wrapped around the slayer's arm, engulfing his sleeve in flames before he could complete the fatal plunge. Still clutching the knife, the slayer stumbled backward, almost falling into the next lane of traffic. He ripped out dozens of strands of Bonnie's hair as he jerked away, and her head flew up and then whipped back downward again, springing like a clown's head in a jack-in-the-box.

Billy thrust himself toward her and stretched out his arms to catch her on the downswing. He cradled her head with his right hand, and he slid his left arm behind her back to support the rest of her body. Now gasping for breath, he made his own body a shield for Bonnie, lifting her off the glass on the window frame while standing between her and the slayer. All he could do now was wait for help.

After the sudden release of pressure, Billy's mom slipped and lost her grip on Bonnie. Her foot caught on the brake pedal as her body spun toward the passenger's side. Her elbow slammed against the Volkswagen's horn, and it stuck, sending a high-pitched distress signal throughout the district.

The slayer ran for his car, beating the air with his right arm while tearing at his sleeve with his left hand. By the time he reached the door, the flame had died, and a torn, charred sleeve fell to the street. Before he could pull the door's handle, a wiry, gray-haired man leaped on his back. Like a squirrel on a thin sapling, he wrapped his legs around the slayer's waist while grasping his face and neck with his hands. A huge, burly man jumped from his pickup truck and charged the slayer from the front, reaching forward with ape-like arms.

With a deft spin, the slayer turned, putting the man on his back between himself and his new attacker. The trucker planted one oversized boot flat on the pavement to avoid smashing the older man, and he stumbled, falling forward to the road like a toppling redwood. His forehead smacked against the asphalt, and he slowly lifted his body, bracing himself on hands and knees and shaking his head.

The slayer extended his right arm, his knife still in hand. With driving fury, he plunged the blade into his older attacker's calf. The man cried out and fell to the ground next to the truck driver, grasping his leg and writhing in pain.

Dr. Whittier flung his car door open and jumped in. Since the policeman had stopped the flow of traffic just seconds before, the slayer was able to turn his car into the opposite lane. He roared away in the other direction, and, in a heavy puff of exhaust smoke, he was gone.

Less than two seconds later the policeman finally arrived, halting his frantic sprint in a burst of heavy stomps next to Billy. He helped Billy keep Bonnie's shoulders clear of the window's sharp remains.

Billy made sure his hands were the only ones under her back as he leaned through the window to support her hidden wing structure, while the officer, an athletic, leather-jacketed man with a thick mane of gray hair, carried her head and shoulders. "That's it, son. Lift her a little higher. Everything's going to be just fine."

Bonnie had stopped screaming. Her eyes stayed tightly shut, but her stifled sobs broke through her composure. As gently as they could, her two helpers guided her back into the car where she pushed herself to a sitting position.

When they opened the door, Bonnie stepped out with the help of the four supporting hands and tried to stand. Her wobbly legs fought to steady themselves, and just before she lost her balance, she threw her arms around Billy and wept pitifully on his shoulder. Billy supported her weight and gently draped his arms around her, careful to keep his touch light on the blood-dampened sweater. He tried to pull the material away from her skin to somehow disguise the lump from her hidden wings. Would anyone notice?

Billy's mother had struggled to a sitting position herself. She gave the steering wheel a firm rap with her fist, and the horn stopped blaring. The officer helped her out of the car with one hand while reaching for his shoulder-strapped radio with the other. "I need ambulance support at the corner of Main and Millstone. Four individuals, two females, one adult, one teenager, and two adult males. Injuries may be serious. I need an APB on a Cadillac, dark blue. License plate looks like a vanity tag that starts with IHD, state unknown. Middle-aged male suspected of attempted murder. May be armed with a knife. Last seen heading southbound on Main."

The policeman paused for a second, his eyes squinting toward the horizon. He cleared his throat and began speaking into the radio again. "It's hard to believe, but the suspect looked just like the middle school principal. I think his name's Whittier."

"It is Whittier," Billy offered. "And he may be heading for the airport." When he spoke, he felt a terrible stinging pain. His tongue had cleaved to the roof of his mouth, and he spat out the words. The inside of his mouth felt like he had been gargling acid, and pain radiated back into his throat, making his whole insides burn like he had swallowed a swarm of angry bees. *What happened? Did that fire come from inside me?* He needed water to cool the burning sting, but nothing was available. He tried to create some saliva to swallow. That helped, at least a little bit.

"Suspect believed to be going to the airport," the officer continued. "Cannot pursue at this time. He'll probably take residential roads to Airport Boulevard, so seal the corner of Airport and Vine." When he finished, the officer turned to the victims and addressed Bonnie first. "Miss? Are you all right?"

Bonnie kept her face buried in Billy's shoulder. She just nodded.

With an awkward limp, Billy's mother walked behind Bonnie and pulled the sweater collar down to have a look at her wounds. She shook her head and grimaced. "Quite a few cuts. One looks pretty nasty, but the bleeding's not too bad. It's just oozing."

The officer lowered his bushy gray eyebrows, making him look like a worried grandfather. "And are you all right, ma'am?"

"Just a little ankle sprain. I'll be fine."

"Sorry I took so long. I stopped and drew my gun, but I couldn't shoot while he had the girl. Then the boy got in the line of fire, and the man got on the creep's back. I should've kept running."

"Don't worry, officer," Billy's mom said, "it wasn't your fault, and I think our injuries are minor."

The policeman looked at Billy, his eyes surveying him from top to bottom. "Where did that fire come from, son? Did you throw something at him?"

Billy glanced over at his mother and Bonnie and then back at the officer. He really didn't know how to respond, so he just shrugged his shoulders. "You got me."

The policeman pinched his chin between his thumb and index finger, apparently mulling the whole thing over, but after a few seconds he just waved his hand toward the outskirts of town. "The ambulances should be coming from the county station, but the traffic's pretty bad, so it might be a few more minutes. Just take it easy right here while I check on the men." He gave a reassuring smile and hustled over to the two would-be heroes.

While his mother continued to examine Bonnie's neck and head, Billy watched the officer tend to the fallen men. The policeman knelt and pulled up the smaller man's pant leg while the trucker rose slowly to his feet, still shaking his head to clear the fog. The officer then left the scene, jogging past Billy toward his squad car back at the intersection.

"I'm going for a first-aid kit for the girl and the men," he called back. "The ambulances might take too long."

A few seconds after he left, the faint sound of a wailing siren rode the cool breeze into town. Bonnie lifted her face from Billy's shirt and tried to speak through her crying spasms. "We . . . can't let them . . . examine me."

Billy's mother stepped back and ran her hand through her tangled hair. "She's right, and we have to get to the airport. We have a first-aid kit in the plane. I think she'll be okay until then."

Without another word, Billy helped Bonnie and his mother back into the car. As he walked around the rear, he saw the two injured men once again. Billy decided he couldn't possibly leave without thanking them.

"Back in a sec!" he called, his tongue stinging a bit less.

As he hustled toward them, he noticed an unusual sparkle on the road near where the two men rested. Clouds covered the sun like a cold gray blanket, so he wondered where the light could be coming from. He leaned over and snatched it up. It was a small stone, about the size of a quarter, shaped like a slightly flattened golf ball. Instead of tiny dimples, it was covered with hexagonal facets about the width of a pencil eraser, and a hole had been drilled through one edge, as though it had been the pendant for a necklace. A crystalline shell surrounded a black core, and it seemed to emit light from one side, dim but noticeable. The faint beam flickered, painting shadows on Billy's palm, as though it were casting the image of ghostly dancers from its glass-covered stage.

Although the pain in his mouth came roaring back, he had to ask about the gem. He showed it to the truck driver. "Is this yours?"

"Never seen it before," he replied while rubbing the back of his neck.

The police officer had just arrived and was kneeling next to the older man, who was still sitting on the street holding his pant leg up. Billy held the stone between his thumb and finger. "Does this belong to either one of you?"

"Nope," the injured man replied. "Don't wear jewelry."

The officer pulled a roll of gauze from the first-aid kit and glanced up at Billy. He just shook his head.

Several other people had ventured onto the street, talking to and comforting the men, so Billy held up the stone for all to see. "Does this belong to anyone here?"

Various shakes of the head and calls of "Not mine" gave him his answer. He dropped the stone into his pocket and spoke to the two men. "I appreciate what you tried to do. He's really dangerous."

"No need for thanks," the trucker replied. "I just wish we could have caught him."

Billy didn't know how to end the conversation, so he just waved clumsily and hurried back to the Volkswagen, which now had three or four people by the driver's side, talking to his mother and to Bonnie. As he jogged back, he noticed the pain in his mouth lessening again. *Good thing! I don't know how long I could've stood that heat without a drink! I wonder why the pain keeps changing?*

Billy jumped into the front passenger seat and slammed the door. "The police guy's got his back turned. We don't have time to file a report, so let's roll. The sirens are getting close. With all the commotion, maybe he won't notice."

His mother rolled up her window after saying a quick goodbye to her well-wishers. By this time, the cars in front had already pulled away. "Oh, please start this time," Billy's mom pleaded as she turned the key. A weak, grinding sound whined from the rear and then fell silent. Another grind, even weaker, cried like a sick puppy and died away.

Billy turned around and looked out the back window. "Try again! The cop's still not watching, but the truck driver's coming this way!" He grabbed his mother's wrist before she could turn the key. "No. Wait a second!"

She glanced at the rearview mirror. "Why is the back hatch open?"

Slam! A loud thud of metal on metal startled the riders. "Try it now," came a shout from the back. They turned to see the truck driver waving. Apparently he had done something to the engine and slammed the rear access closed.

She turned the key again, and this time the engine chugged twice and finally rumbled to life. She waved to the trucker as she pulled forward, careful to give the motor enough gas this time.

"Billy," his mother said, "do you remember the airport's main number?"

"Sure."

"Call and alert Security there. Describe the car, and ask them to put a guard on your dad's airplane."

Billy took in a deep breath and then let it out slowly. He looked back at Bonnie. She had curled to one side, resting her shoulder against the back of the seat with her eyes tightly shut. Seeing her in so much pain drove daggers through his heart.

After a quick look around, he found the cell phone on the floorboard. He snatched it up and punched in the number. "I'll have them in a second, Mom. Let's hope we get through in time."

CHAPTER 9

Hartanna's Daughter

When they arrived at the county airport, Billy scanned the access road and the parking lot for Whittier's Cadillac. There was no sign of it. Besides the two police cars at the gate, the field of blacktop held only a few widely spaced vehicles. They parked the car near the terminal, and the trio made its way toward the door. Billy wanted to run—to dash ahead and look for his dad, to check on their airplane, and to make sure the coast was clear. But having to carry the box and book in his arms forced him to step with care. He couldn't even see his own feet, much less the parking lot curb. And his mother and Bonnie hobbled along slowly. He couldn't leave them behind; that wouldn't be a manly thing to do. He contented himself with keeping their pace and watching for the slayer.

As soon as they entered the terminal building, Billy's mom headed straight to the security desk. Her limp was less noticeable, more like she had a pebble in her shoe than a sprained ankle. At the desk sat Manny, head of the security department for as long as Billy could remember, a nice old guy, but Billy wondered if the challenges of airport security in this day and age had passed him by.

Manny rose to his feet as Billy's mom approached. "Hello, Mrs. Bannister."

"Manny, is Jared here?"

"No, Mrs. Bannister," Manny replied, pulling his holster up as he walked around the desk to join her. "He logged out a while ago. As soon as your son called I sent a man to the hangar, and no one's seen the car he talked about."

"May we go to our plane now?"

"Sure. I'll escort you myself. Let me call my man to see if everything's clear."

Manny picked up a phone and punched a couple of numbers. "Jerry? Any sign of trouble? . . . Good. Did you search the plane? . . . Perfect. I'm bringing Mrs. Bannister down." He hung up the phone and pulled a cart from behind his desk. "Let's go."

Billy plopped his box and book on the cart and peered at the book's title. The old leather carried tiny cracks throughout its worn gray skin, and the darker inscription barely stood out against its background. He could still make out the words, "Fama Regis." *Hmmm. I didn't see the title when Dad showed the book to me. I'll have to remember to ask him what it means.*

Manny grabbed the cart handle and led the party across the terminal waiting area and through an exit on the opposite side. Billy paused at the water fountain near the door to cool his breath once again before hurrying to catch up.

Once out in the breeze, the cool air flapped his thin short sleeves, and he crossed his arms, rubbing them briskly with his hands. Through all the excitement, his lack of a sweater hadn't bothered him, but now he wished he had picked one up at home. It didn't matter; his sweater was being put to good use.

Billy looked over at Bonnie. With her head down and her eyelids half-closed, he couldn't read her expression, but her tense jaw and deep forehead lines revealed her agony. Billy clutched the front of his shirt and shivered again. Why did Bonnie's pain keep sending those cold daggers through his heart? After all, he barely knew her. Their only connection was a vague, mysterious dragon ancestry, and yet he felt as though he had known her for centuries, like their encounter in the schoolyard had launched an adventure planted in ancient soil along with the roots of time itself.

Bonnie glanced in Billy's direction. She gave him a brief, tortured smile, and in her wet, weary eyes he read an uninvited darkness. Was it mourning? Loneliness? He felt she was finally willing to expose her deep, crushing burden, but not just to anyone; it had to be someone she could trust, someone who would understand. Before today she had no one to tell—no mother, no father, and, it seemed, no friends at school.

Billy wanted to put his arm around her just to say, "I'm with you. Don't worry," but he had no idea how she would take it. He knew it would be innocent, like it was when they held hands in the car, but would she know that? She had also hugged him a little while ago to keep her balance, but did her warm embrace signal anything else? What was really in the mind of this dragon girl? Could he trust her? Who was she, anyway?

Billy's own dragon revelations gnawed away at his sanity. He couldn't even trust his own feelings; how could he possibly know hers? But if she felt the same suffocating gloom he was feeling, she probably could use a comforting hug. Then again, with all the cuts on her shoulders, she might not like to be hugged or even touched there. *Yes, that's it, too many cuts. Of course she wouldn't like it, right?* He saw a pebble in his path and kicked it hard across the pavement.

After walking about a hundred yards on a series of wide concrete pads and grassy medians, they reached a large hangar, a very familiar structure to Billy. Although it was nothing more than a big, elongated garage, the plain, gray metal barn was a welcome sight, his dad's workplace, a haven of safety and comfort. He had spent many summer hours there, flown with his dad dozens of times, and even helped work on the Cessna. Normally, he and his mother would have just walked right to it, but because of the danger, an escort seemed necessary.

The airport security team had definitely taken the warnings seriously. The first hangar door was the only one open, and a uniformed guard, Jerry, Manny had called him, stood watch right outside. Although Billy didn't know Jerry personally, he thought he had seen him at least once or twice.

Just as they were about to enter the hangar, they heard a loud yell coming from behind them. The whole group spun around to see a tall, athletic man sprinting in their direction.

"Marilyn! Billy!"

"Dad!" Billy ran to meet him, relief flooding his mind. For the moment, he forgot all the mysteries; the dragon inside hid itself once again, and the little boy emerged to drink in his daddy's warm embrace. The chill of autumn fled as his father's strong arms wrapped him up, generating the holy heat of pure love.

But when the warmth radiated into Billy's face, the blood-swelled sting returned to his mouth, and with it the sting of betrayal. This was the same man, with these same arms, who had hugged him good night a thousand times and chased away all the monsters from under the bed. With every bedtime story he had opportunities to explain the truth, to prepare his son for what he would surely learn some day on his own. But he wasted them.

And was this man really a monster himself? Was he really one of the good dragons? As far-fetched as it might have seemed just a few days ago, every word this dragon spoke, every emotion he portrayed, was now suspect, perhaps a hidden lie. And worse, the dragon specter that lurked within Billy's own frame came out to haunt him once again.

Billy pulled away and turned his head, trying to find something else to look at, anything but his father's eyes. He knew he still loved his father, but he felt detached, like this man just wasn't quite Dad anymore. He felt awful even thinking this way, but he just couldn't help it. It seemed that claws of anguish threatened to rip his heart in two. He had enjoyed the manly embrace, but somehow it brought the cruel, stinging fire of a dragon.

Manny spoke up from the hangar door. "I guess you won't be needing me." He turned and walked slowly back to the terminal building, leaving the cart just inside the door. He nodded toward Jerry, and the guard began walking toward another hangar.

Billy's mother and father locked both hands into one another's and kissed tenderly, a hint of passion hovering in their touch. His mother sighed. "You won't believe what we just went through."

"I'll give you the chance to tell me all about it in just a minute," Billy's father replied. He turned to greet the unfamiliar face. "You must be Bonnie."

Bonnie managed a weak smile and looked up at him curiously. "How did you know?" Her hair flew around in disarray, and dried tears painted faint trails on her flushed cheeks, making her look less presentable than she probably would have liked.

"I saw Walter back at home. He told me."

Billy jumped toward his dad, but he kept his voice low. "Then did he tell you about Dr. Whittier, that he's a dragon slayer?"

His father answered the question absentmindedly. "I figured that out." His thoughts were obviously elsewhere. For some reason his gaze lingered on Bonnie's face. He looked into her eyes, staring at her as if trying to read her mind.

"What's wrong?" Bonnie asked. Her face turned a brighter red, and she put a hand through her messy hair, pulling a few stray wisps out of her face.

"Hartanna!" he whispered. "You must be Hartanna's daughter!"

Bonnie's eyes lit up, and the joy of hearing that name broke through in a wide smile. "You could tell by looking at me?"

Billy's father glanced at the hangar security guard, who was standing by another door, and he leaned over to speak to Bonnie, smiling. "Anyone who's been around dragons as much as I have can tell a dragon child when he sees one. I'll explain later." He then looked back at Billy. His smile dissolved, and his eyes darkened.

Billy had an idea of what his father was thinking. The secrets he had kept for so many years were coming back to haunt him; he had exposed his family to danger. These dragon slayers still hunted, still lurked in the shadows, ready to pounce on the unprepared. And Billy was unprepared, unaware of his peril. Both he and his father knew whose fault it was.

Billy didn't know why, but he felt sorry for his dad. Yet, if only his father had shared the burden, they could have borne it together, man to man. He walked closer and forced himself to look imploringly into his father's eyes. "Why didn't you tell me sooner?"

His father's frown melted, and he put his arm around Billy, looking deeply into his eyes. "I have no excuses. I know that now." He then guided him toward the hangar door while the others followed. "I'll explain more soon, but first let's get in the Cessna and get out of here. If the slayer gathers his forces, we don't want to be around. My guess is he knows about our plane, so he's sure to try to get to it." With a loving pull, Billy's father drew him closer, and his charred sleeve smeared soot on Billy's shirt.

Billy's mom reached over and caressed her husband's arm. "Your sleeve's burned! What happened?"

He pulled his arm back and picked at the torn, dangling shreds that covered his reddened skin. "It's not too bad, just superficial burns. The slayer's goons torched our house."

She pulled her hand up to her mouth and cried out. "Torched our house!" Billy put his arm around her shoulder, and he stared at his father with his jaw hanging slack.

His father grabbed the cart on his way through the hangar door and gestured for the others to follow. "Don't worry. We've got insurance, but most importantly, we're all safe." He picked up the book from the cart. "You brought *Fama Regis* and our emergency box, so all our photo albums and papers are here, and we still have our livelihood." He took his wife's hand and gently pulled her along. "But we have to get to a safe place."

"But what about our other keepsakes? What about our memories?"

He put the end of his finger on her lips and then removed it to kiss her again tenderly. "Everything else is just stuff. It can all be replaced, even memories. We'll make new ones. We'll rebuild."

With tears flowing, Billy's mom sniffed and squeezed her husband's hand. "That's not as easy as it sounds."

He closed his eyes and nodded. "No . . . You're right. It's not easy. But we still have our business. We still have Merlin."

Bonnie walked slowly into the darker interior of the hangar. "Merlin? Who's Merlin?"

He released his wife's hand and walked the few paces to the first airplane in the cavernous room, reaching up to slap it on the side of the cockpit. "Bonnie, meet Merlin."

Bonnie folded her arms across her chest, her pain still apparent in her wrinkled forehead. A sweet smile graced her lips as she strolled around the nose of the plane, but her voice remained weak. "He's a handsome one, all right."

Billy's father climbed the stairs to board the plane, holding the book under his arm. "Even though we don't have to worry much about Dr. Whittier, or whatever he's calling himself, we should get going. He won't be able to battle me alone, and it'll take him some time to prepare."

The other three followed, with Billy trailing. He stepped carefully up the stairs, once again lugging the family box. With every step, a strange feeling grew, like someone was watching from a hidden corner, or the fear of being alone in the dark. The hairs on his neck stood on end, and his stomach burned. When he reached the top, he looked back at his surroundings. There was still no sign of Dr. Whittier, and the guard was nowhere in sight. He took a deep breath and tried to ignore the feeling. Everything seemed in order.

His father slipped into the pilot's seat, keeping the book at his side, and after depositing his load in the cargo area, Billy took the copilot's place. Bonnie sat behind Billy in one of the two-seat benches that lined the right side of the plane. Billy's mom slid into a single seat across the aisle, a first-aid kit already in her lap. She popped it open and began rummaging through it.

The plane's motor chugged and then purred, sounding like a pride of satisfied lions digesting a recent kill. Seconds later they taxied out of the hangar, and Billy's dad angled his head toward the passengers. "Bonnie, are you afraid of flying?"

"No, not at all," she replied softly.

Billy and his mother laughed out loud, but his father just shrugged his shoulders. "What's so funny?"

"You'll see!" Billy's mother replied. She turned to Bonnie. "I'll help you pull the sweater off, honey." She reached across the aisle and lifted the bottom hem. It wasn't easy. The combination of dried sweat and blood made the process sticky and painful, and when the sweater finally came off, Billy grimaced at the dark purple splotches showing through her otherwise blue sweatshirt. Bonnie sighed in great relief, and Billy's mom folded the sweater before turning to the cockpit. "Take a look at Bonnie now!"

Billy's father turned. Bonnie's wings seemed to fill the whole cabin. She had spread them out to flap a couple of times and then folded them back in to let Billy's mom nurse her wounds.

"Whew!" Bonnie said, arching her back. "That feels better!"

Billy glanced over at his father to see his reaction, but he didn't appear to be surprised. He smirked, chuckled a bit, and turned toward the front. "So that's why you're not afraid of flying. I knew Hartanna had a daughter, but I didn't know about the wings!" He stared out over the dashboard for several seconds. "Marilyn, could she be the one?"

"I was wondering the same thing," she replied.

"The one for what?" Bonnie asked.

Billy's father looked at Bonnie from under his dark, reddish eyebrows. "I'll try to explain when we're airborne, but I'm not sure

I can give you a very good answer." He turned Merlin toward the runway and waited for clearance from the tower while another plane settled in for a landing. "Well, I hope this machine isn't too much of a letdown for you, Bonnie. It's a Cessna Caravan. It's not as agile as a dragon, but it's a lot better equipped for what I have to do. I carry corporate execs around, maybe an occasional troop of sky divers, or cargo that absolutely, positively has to be there today."

"You men keep your faces forward," Billy's mother called out. "I'm going to have to pull her sweatshirt up in the back."

The men obeyed and listened to the conversation coming from behind them. Billy heard his mother's voice, tender and loving.

"The stitching on these holes where your wings come out is very well done. Did you do it yourself?"

"Yes. My mother taught me."

"I'll push your wings back through. They're sort of like big buttonholes, aren't they? And you sewed in hidden zippers at the bottom."

"Yes. I had to make them big enough to get my shirts on and off by myself."

"That's amazing! How did you keep your secret from your foster parents?"

"They don't pay much attention to me. I think they're in the foster system to find a younger child they can adopt, so I'm just there until the state can find someone else to take me."

"Why are you in Castlewood? We heard Hartanna was living in the Northwest and that she had a daughter, but there hasn't been any other word for years."

"Well . . . that's a long story."

"Okay. I'm going to start wiping the dried blood off."

After a few seconds of silence, Bonnie moaned softly. "Ooooh!"

"Sorry, I guess the peroxide burns; it's not supposed to. You have one long cut just above where your left wing goes into your back, but it's hard to tell how deep it is. It looks like there's also a wound of some kind on that wing, too, but I don't think it's broken."

"I think you're right. It feels more like a bruise." Both ladies were quiet for a few seconds until Bonnie spoke up again, her tone more upbeat. "Mr. Bannister, what's all that cargo you're carrying?"

Billy wanted to look back to remind himself of the payload contents, but he remembered to keep his focus ahead. He assumed Bonnie was trying to get her mind off the pain, and he hoped his dad would comply. He hadn't been very talkative, his secrets apparently keeping him in deep thought, and even now he seemed hesitant to answer.

Billy pictured the cargo area in his mind. Merlin's back half had its seats removed, leaving plenty of room for almost anything, while still providing seats for six passengers and two crew members up front. He visualized the paneled boxes in the rear, unmarked and stacked neatly in rows.

"They're crates of Bibles," his father finally replied. "I've been collecting them for months. I was going to fly them to Atlanta tomorrow, and from there a missionary society will pick them up and smuggle them into a closed country."

"Oh, then you do follow the Bible," Bonnie said. "My mother told me you didn't."

Billy waited for an answer, but none came. He noticed his father's face turning red, but his only reply was a warning to get ready. "Is everyone buckled? We're going to take off!"

"All set back here!" Billy's mother replied. "Bonnie's covered again. I'll put her wings back through the holes when we're cruising."

The Cessna picked up speed, rolling down the runway as smoothly as any luxury car on an interstate, and then lifted effortlessly into the air. Billy had flown dozens of times, but the exhilaration of takeoff never failed to suck his breath away. The force of the seat on his body and the unsteady feeling of increasing space between himself and the ground made him grip the armrests a little more tightly and made his heart pound just a bit faster. Although there was inherent danger in every flight, it was certainly more comfortable sitting here, even with the bumpy climb through the cross breeze, than dangling precariously from Bonnie's arms.

After a few moments of silent ascent, Billy's father spoke up, raising his voice to compete with the buzzing propellers. "Okay, we're on our way to Huntington."

"Huntington?" Billy asked. "Why Huntington?"

"Because I don't have any pilots there, so it's not a likely place for me to go. And I'm not comfortable with taking Bonnie out of West Virginia. I'm not sure what the laws say about transporting someone else's foster children, but we don't want to end up with kidnapping charges. Anyway, it'll be far enough to give us some time together. We have a lot to talk about."

"I'll say!" Billy agreed. He grimaced at his own words. He didn't mean to sound like he was provoking an argument, but it did sort of come out that way.

"Okay, then," his father said. "You go first."

Billy proceeded to tell their story, with his mother's occasional interruptions to fill in the gaps, and he downplayed his own role. He especially didn't want to mention the fire, but, of course, his mother brought it up.

"So, it's progressed to fire breathing, has it?" his father asked.

"Yes, and it really hurt, too."

Billy's father grabbed a penlight from a tray on the console. "We're cruising now, so I can take a look. Open your mouth and lean over here."

"Okay." Billy opened his mouth as wide as he could and even stuck out his tongue and said, "Ahhhh."

His dad flicked on the light and pointed the beam into his mouth, murmuring as he moved the light around. All Billy could see was his father's wandering eyes and the shiny silver pen waving back and forth. After several "hmmm's" his father pulled away and tapped Billy's chin to signal that he could close his mouth again. "It looks like you've started forming scales, but they aren't fully glazed over yet."

Billy licked the sore insides of his mouth. "Is it supposed to hurt so much?"

His father tossed the light toward the console and glanced back at his wife. She was busy helping Bonnie's wings back through their holes. "That's hard to say," he replied. "I don't have any experience rearing human dragon children, but back in the old days, when the young dragons started breathing fire for the first time, they jumped up and down, yelping like a Chihuahua with a hot foot." He leaned back in his seat and sighed. "It was a long time ago, but I think it was the same for me."

Billy placed his hands on his stomach and rubbed it softly. "How can I know when the fire's coming? I mean . . . I didn't plan it. It just came out."

"It's because you were so upset. When I was a dragon, I couldn't help spitting fire if I ever got really mad or scared."

Billy trembled and then laughed to hide his uneasiness. "When you were a dragon? That sounds so weird hearing you say that, especially after all these years."

His father took in a deep breath and let it out slowly. "All these years?" he repeated with a sad sort of smile. He then nodded and gazed at Billy. "You're right. Your few years are everything to you, but they seemed like only a few short days to me. I should have known better than to keep the truth from you for so long. I didn't realize you'd be exposed to danger." Everyone stayed quiet for a minute or two, and the loud buzz of the propeller droned in the ears of the passengers while they waited for Billy's dad to speak again.

"You told your story," he finally continued. "It's time for me to tell mine." He picked a microphone up from its cradle on the control panel. "The engine's kind of noisy, so this will be a good time to test out the new PA system. Are you ready?"

Billy was accustomed to hearing his father's dramatic stories, so he leaned back and closed his eyes, ready to imagine the details. "Fire away."

CHAPTER 10

Merlin's Prophecy

Billy's father settled into his pilot's seat, pulled out *Fama Regis,* and laid it open on his lap. "I wasn't there for some parts of my story, so I'm getting a few details from this book. Those parts were written by a squire you'll hear about very soon."

After clearing his throat, he spoke with a deep, storyteller's voice, his characteristic resonance playing through the speakers and carrying throughout the cabin. "Once upon a time, over a thousand years ago, during the days of King Arthur and his noble knights, an aging prophet named Merlin ascended the crags of a steep hillside."

The old man climbed the rocky bed, lithely passing over the rough, steep incline. He moved like one much younger than he appeared, more like a yearling mountain ram than an ancient, gray-headed sage. His long robe, a blunted scarlet in the dimness of the night, scarcely troubled him in his ascent as it flowed passively around his legs. After steadying his feet on two stable rocks, he set down a large leather saddlebag and cupped his hands around his mouth. "Hail! Clefspeare!"

Motionless and barely visible, the man on the rocks stood and waited for an answer. His long, spindly shadow rested on the face of the cliff, a ghost in the full moon's glow. Above him and to one side, another dark shape yawned as if stretching to swallow the old man's silhouette; it was the entrance to a cave that held the caller's attention.

"Hail! Clefspeare!"

The old man waited again, but there was no response. He turned his head and looked down the rugged slope. Another man stood on a smoother path below, a somewhat younger, sturdier gentleman dressed in the finest of riding array. Although there were no horses nearby, he seemed ready to mount and dash away at the slightest provocation.

"Come, Your Majesty," the older man said, holding out his hand to aid his fellow traveler. "We must enter the cave."

The king, using both hands and feet to find his way, slowly but steadily climbed the rocky embankment. His broad shoulders expanded and his rippling forearms strained to lift his body. As soon as he approached the old man's level, he grasped the outstretched hand and pulled himself the rest of the way up. "Master Merlin," the king said, "your strength amazes me."

"I have climbed many hills in my time," Merlin replied.

The king wiped his hands and bowed in reverence, his gray-streaked golden hair falling forward to cover his ears. "I have always respected your courage, Master Merlin, and I vowed to trust you tonight no matter what befalls us; but I did not expect to walk into the mouth of death, for I can hear the monster's breathing even from here."

"You must continue to trust me. Come. The path is easier just ahead." Merlin hoisted his bag and continued the climb for a few more yards before stopping to wait again. Within seconds the king joined him, and the two proceeded on level ground, Merlin again leading the way. After passing a few bare, stunted trees, the travelers faced the entrance of the cave. They felt a breeze coming from within, and then, seconds later, the breeze reversed, and the cave drew the air past their bodies, swallowing it deep into the darkness.

"The cave breathes," the king remarked, his yellow mustache twitching, "but I smell no rotting flesh."

"Nor will you," Merlin replied. He cupped his hands once again to address the cave's occupant. "Hail! Clefspeare! It is I, Merlin, Prophet of the Most High. With me is His Majesty, King Arthur."

Again they waited but received no response. Merlin turned his gray head to the king. "He must be in regeneracy."

"Regeneracy?" the king repeated. He peered into the shadows, his gold circlet gleaming in the moonlight.

Merlin walked forward without looking back again. "You will see," he said before disappearing into the darkness.

Arthur hesitated. The full moon's light cast the cave's interior in shadows, but the prophet's courage washed over the king, beckoning him to follow. After a few steps into the cave's arching influence, his eyes adjusted and he could see Merlin, waiting again, well inside.

"We must hurry," the prophet warned. "The others will be assembling very soon."

"The others?" The king quickened his pace. He was able to see quite well now. A strange light from deeper in the cave illumined the path, dimly at first, but ever more brightly as he proceeded.

When Arthur caught up with Merlin, the two passed together through a large archway and into a brightly lit interior chamber. In the very center, the source of the light took shape, a huge cone of swirling luminescence that pointed toward the cave's ceiling, its circular base resting a few inches from the rocky floor. It was a shimmering, inverted funnel of pure light. Yet, it was more than light; it seemed to have substance, as if you could scoop it up with your hands and carry it home in a saddlebag. And within the cone, a dazzling array of flashing glitters flew like buzzing bees from one side to the other, bouncing and dancing until they happened to strike the focus of the cone, a huge, heaving body that rested in the very center.

"Master Merlin," the king cried out, "tell me what it is that I look upon! If it is accursed I shall turn my head and pluck out my eyes rather than look upon it again; but if it is holy, I shall bare my head as well as my feet and fall now to my knees."

Merlin placed a strong hand on the king's shoulder. "My king, your colorful oaths are out of place. This light is neither accursed nor holy; it is a natural process I have called regeneracy. It is how a dragon prefers to sleep. Have you ever seen a creature like this in full flight?"

"Yes. Just several days afore this, I saw a dragon in battle with Sir Devin."

"And did you notice how his scales shimmered in the sunlight and how his eyes flashed while in flight?"

The king nodded ardently, his gaze fixed on the form before him. "Indeed I did take note. A frightful sight, to be sure."

"Yes, frightful if you are not aware of the reason. His scales and eyes breathe the light as you and I breathe the air. He absorbs energy and expels the light he does not use. If a dragon were subjected to darkness for a long period of time, he would be overcome by weakness. Without at least a candle to feed his body, he would eventually die."

Merlin set down his bag, approached the glowing dragon, and stretched out his hands over the cone as if to warm them. "At night he rests on a bed of silver and gold, and the power of the day flows into his bed. The energy grows into a shroud of luminescence around his body, and he reabsorbs the light as it passes over his scales." Merlin pointed to the base of the dragon's bed and then moved his finger around as if stirring. "Intermixed in the precious metal pieces are polished gems. They reflect the light, making it rebound within the shroud, so that more of the light strikes his body."

The king listened with complete attention and took a step or two closer, emboldened by the prophet's familiarity. "You say that he is asleep?" The creature's heavy, rumbling breaths made the king stop once again, and he instinctively placed his hand on the hilt of his sword.

Merlin walked back to join the king. "Yes, he is asleep." The prophet grasped Arthur's forearm just above his sword hand. "You have nothing to fear, good king."

Arthur returned the grasp but kept watching the dragon. "You say he is sleeping, but it appears that his eyes are open."

Merlin turned to look. "They are open. His eyes are the gateway to his mind. Through his scales he gains physical power. Through his eyes he gains both physical and mental prowess. They, too, must absorb the light."

"When will he awaken?"

"This I cannot predict. I do not yet understand the process completely, but the light eventually fades and then the dragon awakes."

"Is he vulnerable to attack while he sleeps?"

"I do not know. I believe we are the only humans ever to see a dragon in this state. Many have come upon dragons in their lairs, but a dragon can sense danger and always awakes. Since I am his friend and you have come as his new ally, Clefspeare senses none. But I must awaken him now."

Merlin unfastened a string from around his neck and used it to pull a strangely shaped object from beneath his vest, a pendant stone dangling at the end of the string, small enough for his fingers to fully envelop.

"This is a candlestone, a kind of anti-prism," he explained. "You see, a normal prism bends light and splits the colors. This stone does the opposite. It arrests fractured light and straightens it out. The light passes into it as excited energy and passes out as a simple light beam. If I place it at the base of Clefspeare's shroud, it will interrupt the circuit and disperse his shield."

Arthur gazed at the stone in awe. "It is no wonder you are called a wizard, Master Merlin. I have understood none of your words, yet I am enchanted by your explanation. A magic stone like that could make you very powerful."

"I am not a wizard, Your Majesty, and there is nothing magical about the stone. It simply uses a reverse refraction to interrupt a dragon's photorespiration, and therefore his energy flow. It can actually absorb light, and with it the life force of his body."

"Energy and life force I understand. Then could it be used as a weapon against dragons?"

"Most definitely. I wear it around my neck for defense against the evil, fallen dragons. I believe I am the only one who knows how to use it, but after today it will matter no more."

Merlin placed the stone on the ground and slid it into the base of the shroud. Instantly the dancing light radiated toward the candlestone, and a brilliant, steady beam poured forth from its opposite side. The shroud vanished, but the candlestone kept glowing, giving light to the chamber.

After a few seconds, the sleeping dragon stirred. With a great stretch and a mighty yawn, Clefspeare rose to sit on his haunches, his enormous tail acting as a balance behind him. With his yawn came a belch of smoke mixed with flying sparks, and the king drew back, once again placing his hand on his sword.

Clefspeare spied his two visitors. His deep gravelly voice erupted and echoed in the cave. "Master Merlin!" He yawned and stretched again. "I have been expecting you, but I did not expect to see the Sovereign." Clefspeare did his best to attempt a formal bow. Although dragons are graceful in the air, they are sometimes clumsy on their feet. He nearly fell on his face, but with a flap of his wings, he righted himself quickly. "Master Merlin, would you be so kind as to remove that accursed stone from my sight before I become violently ill?"

Merlin bent over and picked up the candlestone, covering it with both hands. "Are you sure the stone made you lose your balance, or are you still overcome by sleep?"

"I assure you that my eyes are clear. I recognized the king, did I not? Now please put that wicked jewel under a pile of rocks by the far wall. Covering it with your hands merely blunts its evil effects."

Merlin walked carefully to the cave's edge, guided by a dim, flickering light on the wall. He found a flat rock and placed the candlestone underneath.

With a great snuff from Clefspeare's nostrils, a stream of flame erupted and flew toward an iron stand on the wall, reigniting a rag-topped torch. "Aaah! Now we have better light." He looked back at Arthur and this time merely bowed his head. "Your Majesty. Welcome to my humble abode."

King Arthur bowed in return, much more gracefully than did the dragon, but his voice betrayed a slight tremble. "I am honored to meet you, Great Dragon."

Clefspeare nodded his appreciation and then turned to the prophet. "Master Merlin, am I to understand that your presence signals the coming transformation?"

"Yes, Clefspeare."

"How many are assembling?"

"I'm not sure. The slayers have been busy, so very few, I'm afraid. Hartanna is gathering the dragons who still honor the code."

Clefspeare let out a long, spark-filled sigh. "The corrupted ones have been our downfall, Merlin, as you prophesied. A fallen dragon is the most detestable beast on Earth, and the Book chooses them well to symbolize the father of lies."

"And who can know," Merlin added, "whether corruption hides in the hearts of the remnant? Hartanna is wise, but she cannot always detect the seeds of darkness that spread evil shadows within."

"Indeed," Clefspeare replied, closing his eyes briefly. He opened them again and nodded toward Arthur. "And the king? What is his role?"

"We will need his help after the deed is done. I can trust no other."

Clefspeare stared at the king long and hard. "I know of his deeds, but I do not know his heart."

King Arthur strode boldly forward and stood directly in front of the dragon. "How else can a man's heart be known, or even a dragon's, if not by his deeds? To me, you look very much like the dragon that murdered my brother and sister right outside the very walls of Camelot, the beast that Sir Devin slew only last week. Against my earlier judgments, I was persuaded by the wise prophet to come to your lair, in order to help the race that left me bereft of my beloved siblings. He has recounted your many great deeds, deeds that have been explained away by your enemies as mere selfish desire for treasure. I now know why you accept the gifts of the wealthy after you do your mighty works. How well I also know of the appearance of these treasures in the homes of the poor, benefiting widows and orphans who now have good food on their tables and warm clothes on their backs. Your deeds have set you apart from the others, Clefspeare, and I have come to grant Merlin's request and aid you in your time of need."

Clefspeare bowed once again, this time with more agility. "Well spoken, wise king. I suspect then that Merlin has explained why I must keep some of the treasure for myself. My bed is but a humble collection. Not like Goliath's, I'm afraid; his treasure is what makes him so strong."

Merlin picked up his bag, threw it over his shoulder, and walked up to the dragon, placing a hand on his right flank. "Do not envy that which is gained by evil means, Clefspeare. True strength lies in wisdom. Goliath has chosen his path, and his end will be destruction. I hear grumblings that the slayers have already darkened his door. Your shroud has been sufficient for your needs and is the result of your honest labors, not the greedy lust of a fallen spirit." The prophet gestured for the king to join him.

"I have summoned all the noble dragons that remain to Bald Top. Come, now. We must fly to the meeting place."

Clefspeare's voice changed to a growling rumble. "Master Merlin! You and the king must climb on my back. Make haste. I smell danger."

Merlin reached for the torch and stamped out its light. With lightning quick moves he helped Arthur climb across the dragon's scaly back. The spiny middle ridge made it easy for the men to hold on, and the scales' luminescent glow guided their way. Merlin, accustomed to such a ride, held with only one hand, keeping his other hand firmly gripped on his saddlebag. "Do slayers approach?"

"Most likely, and they are already within my walls."

"They must have followed us," Merlin said.

The dragon roared. "Your Sir Devin is quite the zealous one, Your Highness."

"It couldn't be!" the king protested. "He was sound asleep when we left. Merlin saw to that."

"No time to argue. Heads down and hold on!"

"Wait!" Merlin shouted. "The candlestone!"

"No time! And I will not fly with that cursed dragon's bane!"

With a great flap of his wings, the dragon rose from the ground and hovered in the midst of the cave. After taking in a deep breath, he blew a raging river of fire through both his mouth and nostrils. Then, slowly at first and still breathing fire, he moved forward into the stream, floating easily on the cushion of flaming air like a dragonfly in the wind. As they passed through the tunnel, accelerating as they traveled, Merlin and Arthur peered through the passing fire, flames that bounced in all directions with the beating of the dragon's wings. They could only see shadows, scurrying ghosts diving for cover in the rocks. Within seconds, Clefspeare burst out into the open and then almost straight up into the clear night sky.

"May God be praised!" Arthur cried out, both hands gripping the dragon's spines. "What a magnificent beast!"

"Indeed!" Merlin called. "We have to get higher than their arrows can reach. With us on his back, he cannot turn to defend himself, so his underbelly is vulnerable."

Arthur did not answer. He just held on tightly while the angle of ascent slowly leveled off. Finally, when they reached a safe altitude, Clefspeare spoke up. "I apologize, Your Highness, for the rough ride."

The king took a deep breath in the rarified air. "No need, my good dragon. I was exhilarated. That was a masterful escape."

"Could you tell if Sir Devin was among the attackers?" Merlin asked.

"No," the king replied. "I saw only shadows."

"I think I saw him," Clefspeare said. "But his identity matters little to me. He is a slayer and cannot be trusted."

Merlin looked out over the scene far below, a shifting gray canvas with firelight speckling the shadows cast by the ghostly moon. "I slipped a drug into Devin's food to make him sleep, so I thought our journey would be secret. But there is no time to speculate. We are only moments away from the mountain."

The light of two flashing torches filled the cave, and a pair of undulating shadows crawled along the walls. With every step of the dark images, an echoing clop replied, yet there was more silence than echo. The wary travelers sniffed the air and made their way ever so slowly toward the center of the main chamber.

"There is no hint of fresh kill to guide us," the taller one said.

"No, my liege. In fact, the air is very clean, but I am sure his bed must be right in front of us. I see flashes of light."

The two walked more boldly and then stopped again. The shorter man's cheery voice gave away his darkened smile. "Sir Devin, all is not lost. We have the treasure."

"Yes, Palin. It is much smaller than Goliath's, but we will all be paid handsomely once again. Split it up in my presence and reserve the proper portions for God and for the king."

"Of course, my liege," Palin replied, stooping to collect the treasure. He carried a set of saddlebags and deposited the valuables piece by piece, cycling through the bags to make an even disbursement. "You are most gracious to give equal shares to us all, even though the others wait outside in fear."

Devin surveyed the cave floor, taking care to hold his torch close to the ground. "What does the census say now?"

The squire pulled a scrap of parchment from his tunic and studied it for a moment before looking up again to address his master. "After your valiant conquest of Maven last week, and your extraordinary slaying of Goliath this morning, I know of only ten remaining. The Demon Witch, Hartanna, is next. She will pay for wounding you last summer, and I have already begun making a sketch of your eventual triumph."

"All in good time, my friend. She did rip my leg, but it is merely part of our holy crusade. Wars are not won without loss of blood." He continued gazing at the floor, kicking the pebbles in front of him as if searching for every last gem. "By our count, only ten of the demon spirits are left on the earth, and now that the king knows of Merlin's conspiracy with them, I shall have the old wizard's head by noon tomorrow." He looked up from the ground and flashed the torch toward his squire. "Could you tell if the king was safe on the demon's back?"

"Yes, from what I could see, my liege."

Devin shook his head. "We nearly missed our part of the plan, but you, my good Palin, will be greatly rewarded. You awakened me from Merlin's spell. Without you, we never would have found the dragon's lair, and you were the only one brave enough to stay in the cave. Count out for yourself a double portion, and be sure to commend yourself when you write all of this in the king's chronicles." Devin returned to his search, combing the floor with the light of his torch.

"Thank you, my liege. I will record every word."

After sweeping more rocks to the side, Devin stopped suddenly and stooped close to the ground. He put his hand forward and then drew it back suddenly. "Palin, what is this?"

"Where, my liege?"

"This glowing ember on the floor, a stone that spills a faint beam of light."

"Shall I touch it for you, my lord?"

"I am not a coward, Palin." Devin picked up the stone between his right thumb and forefinger. With great interest, the two men huddled to study its peculiar shape, but they had to draw it closer to their faces when the light around them began growing dim.

"Our torches are going out," Palin said.

"No. The flame lives; only the light dies. It is drawn to the stone."

Devin closed his hand over the candlestone. Instantly, the light from the flames scattered throughout the cave again.

"I have heard legends about such a stone," Devin said. "But why would it be here, in a dragon's lair?"

A strange silhouette crossed the night's skyscape: a dragon, not so unusual in this time period, and two riders, not completely unheard of, but with the lead rider sporting a wizard's robe and the trailing jockey wearing a king's circlet, it was a most unusual sight indeed. As is true with many of nature's most curious events, no human had the pleasure of beholding this one; only a pod of dragons at Bald Top's summit were in the area, and they seemed to pay no attention. To them, if you've seen one flying dragon, you've seen them all.

"Your Majesty," Merlin called out. "Prepare to dismount."

"Shall I just slide off the tail?"

"Yes. It is the safest and fastest way. Remember, find the clearing and watch the proceedings from the woods. The dragons will not sense you because you pose no danger. I know most of them, but until all is complete, it is best if you stay in hiding."

"Agreed."

"Ready yourself! He's hovering over a clear spot. Go!"

The king slid across Clefspeare's scaly hind portions, taking care to avoid the dragon's spiny middle ridge. After three huffing pushes, he dropped down, safely planting his feet in soft turf. Clefspeare's beating wings created a gusting breeze, and Arthur, leaning forward to keep his balance, slapped the dragon's flank to signal his safety. The great dragon rose once again over the tree-filled mountain and toward a nearby clearing.

The grassy field at Bald Top was a perfect circle and made an ideal secret meeting place. As the highest hill in the region, no other land vantage point offered a view over the treetops surrounding it. As it was, Arthur became only the second human ever to see the Council of the Dragons. He watched from behind a tree that stood a few yards inside the edge of the woods. He wanted to make sure he was out of sight. There was no use taking unnecessary chances. Since he had heard that dragon voices carry well, he thought he would be able to listen even from this far away. And since the full moon shone brightly upon the open field and illuminated the shimmering dragons, Arthur was able to see the whole council.

He pointed at each dragon, one by one. "Let's see, that's eight, nine, ten, eleven, and Clefspeare makes twelve. Hmmm. Goliath isn't here, so that's two more than the count Sir Devin has given me."

Although the dragons bore similar features, three of them differed from the other nine in color and size. Arthur guessed that these were gender differences, so, knowing Clefspeare, he was able to distinguish the sexes. The smaller females displayed a lighter tone, more of an orange and beige mixture in contrast to the reddish brown of the males. Since one of the females stepped forward to address their visitor, he assumed that the males were not dominant, at least not in the council meeting.

"Master Merlin, all are present, as you requested."

"Thank you, Hartanna. You have been a great help. And all are in agreement?"

"Yes, Master Merlin. We have discussed the final preparations, and we are ready for the transformation."

Merlin dismounted and threw his bag to the ground while Clefspeare joined the others. Hartanna's head turned to follow the male dragon as he crossed her path of sight. "Clefspeare, I have not interviewed you personally," she said. "I assume Master Merlin has prepared you?"

Clefspeare bowed his head graciously. "Yes, Hartanna. Diving into the human condition is an adventure that none of us covets, but we dragons do what we must do."

"Well said, Clefspeare." Hartanna turned back to the prophet and watched him expectantly, her wings gently folding and unfolding as she waited. Merlin reached into the pocket of his scarlet robe, and, even in the dark, his concern was obvious. "What troubles you, Master Merlin?" Hartanna asked.

"I just remembered that I had to leave the candlestone behind." He smiled at the she-dragon. "It is of no consequence. It should not affect you after the transformation. Let us begin." From his deep left pocket, he pulled out a skin flask and placed it in the middle of the semicircle of dragons. Then, standing in front of the solemn assembly, he addressed the council.

"The flask contains only wine, but those who drink it in faith will receive what God has promised. All who have their hearts prepared will be transformed, and when the fullness of the time has come, you will be restored to your original state. The slayers will eventually die out. Once they believe the dragons to be extinct, they will no longer train to battle your kind, and the poisoned hunger for dragon killing will cease to exist. When you return, there will be no fallen dragons to make the people fear you again."

Hartanna stepped forward. "Then let us proceed. I volunteer to go first."

"No one will change until all have tasted," Merlin warned. "Otherwise, faith would be made sight before its time."

The prophet then picked up the wineskin and lifted it toward the sky. "Heavenly Father," he prayed, "King of the Universe, bless this wine. Fill it now with the seed of Adam so that these will bear his likeness, both in his glory and in his shame. They understand that the benefit of your presence will depart from them as they share in the human curse. They also understand that should they fall after the likeness of Adam's sin, they must find their salvation through the Light of the World."

Merlin turned toward the line of dragons, extending the flask as he walked their way. Hartanna lowered her head and opened her great mouth. Merlin, not quite sure how to administer the drink, raised the opening of the skin over her teeth and tipped it forward. At first it came out too quickly, spilling a bit over her jaws, but Merlin pulled back before he lost too much. Hartanna lifted her head, dramatically swallowing as she turned toward the others. "Be brave, my friends. The drink goes down without harm."

One by one, Merlin gave the wine to the council. A few seemed tentative, but they all took it without much hesitation.

Clefspeare was the last dragon in line. "I look forward to shaking your hand," he said to Merlin.

The old man bowed his head. "And I, yours."

Clefspeare followed the ritual, and after he swallowed, the council of twelve waited in silence. For the first tortuous minute, nothing happened. Merlin decided to take a seat on the ground, but the dragons just stood and looked at each other expectantly.

Another minute passed, and then another. A few sets of dragons' eyes took on worried looks, but Hartanna remained unmoved, and Clefspeare joined her at her side. "We have not been promised the hour," he said, "only a result. We must have faith."

"In the Maker," Hartanna added, "not in Master Merlin."

Several more minutes passed. Merlin continued to sit in silence, his legs crossed and his head bowed in prayer. Some of the dragons rested, too, lying on their bellies in the cool grass, while others were too nervous to do anything but stand and watch Merlin for any sign of what to do next. One tested his wings a few times to see if they still worked.

After what seemed to be an hour, but was in reality only about fifteen minutes, one of the males broke the silence. "He's a fraud!"

Hartanna and Clefspeare turned as one to see a cowering dragon backing away from the rest of the council. "What did you say?" Hartanna asked.

"He's a fraud! Merlin has made fools of us all. There was a second man riding on Clefspeare's back. I saw him. He must be a slayer, and he will bring the others while we wait for this traitor's potion to fail."

Hartanna roared. "Silence, Gartrand! Will you destroy the faith of the others with your own infidelity?"

Gartrand flapped his wings in anger. "This is not faith. I, too, want to survive. Who ever wants to die? But we have stepped into the humans' trap. Let us kill this evil sorcerer and fly away to safety."

Merlin sat still, watching the verbal battle intently. Even when Gartrand moved forward to attack him, he sat unmoved. In a flash of wings and reddish glistening scales, Clefspeare flew to Merlin's defense. He glided into Gartrand's path and opposed the rebel, but when Clefspeare opened his mouth to attack, only hot air spewed forth. Then he turned to slash his foe with his tail, but when he swung, no tail appeared.

Gartrand backed away in fear while Clefspeare physically shrank. The dragon's scales melted into smooth skin, his claws reshaped into fingers and nails, and his giant maw shriveled into the square-jawed face of a human male. Gartrand let out a piercing scream and took to the skies, still completely in dragon form.

Clefspeare turned to watch the rest of the council. Hartanna was farther along than the others, but all were going through the same metamorphosis. Her spiny top transformed into long, silky blonde tresses and her scales into the milky white skin of the northern Europeans of the time. All had the appearance of fully mature adults, perhaps in their late twenties to early thirties, and when the process was complete they gathered together in excited laughter.

Merlin calmly rose to his feet and carried his leather bag to the huddle. He opened it and started pulling out mounds of clothing, tossing various articles onto the ground. "Get dressed," he said, in a matter-of-fact tone. "You are naked, and the king is watching."

Hartanna turned to Merlin in surprise. "Naked? Oh, yes, of course. Come everyone! Here is another new experience. Clothes!"

With some of the council laughing like excited children, the former dragons picked through the clothes, offering pieces to one another and helping each other figure out how the fasteners worked. Merlin had to help here and there, and at one point he was unable to decipher how one of the women's dresses should be worn. He had extra, though, so they discarded it and tried another. Soon, all were dressed in the garb of peasants, not the rags of the poorest members of society, but they would never be mistaken for wealthy merchants or for royalty.

During the gaiety of the moment, Hartanna and Clefspeare whispered to one another, and when everyone was settled and waiting for their instructions, Hartanna spoke up. "Master Merlin, what of Gartrand? Surely this was unexpected."

Merlin answered without even looking up. "Unexpected, indeed, and unfortunate."

"How so?"

Merlin raised his wizened head, appearing tired and worried. "He may be the only dragon left in the world. He will feel abandoned, frightened. He will not take the usual care, so Sir Devin is sure to find him. He is vulnerable, and since he knows what has happened, all of you are vulnerable as well."

"What shall we do?" Hartanna asked.

"While I was in prayer, the Lord spoke to me. His purpose remains unchanged, but with the departure of the traitor, God will accomplish it in another way."

"Traitor?" Clefspeare repeated. "Gartrand will betray us?"

"Yes, but not willingly."

"Then the slayers will pursue us always," Hartanna concluded.

"Yes, I fear you are correct. They will continue to sharpen their swords and brand their forearms. The scent of your blood will never leave their nostrils."

Arthur decided it was time to present himself. He walked out of the woods and approached the gathering, greeting everyone with a low bow when he arrived.

"Hail, great council. I salute you who were once clothed in the majesty of your race. I commend you for humbling yourselves to our estate, for taking on our bondage in order to ensure the future of your children. As long as I live, I will protect you. I cannot take the slayer's thirst for your blood out of his soul, but I can deprive him of the means to pursue his quest. And though the slayers will live on through their descendants, I shall be your guardian for as long as I live."

Hartanna bowed her head, then, discovering her new agility, she curtsied, clumsily at first, but with her second effort, as gracefully as any princess. "I trust that you will prove your promises, my king." She turned to Merlin once again. "Master Merlin, if the slayers seek our lives now, their bloodlust will surely live on in their descendants. How, then, will we ever become dragons again?"

Merlin shook his head and placed his hand on her shoulder. "Hartanna, I fear that some of you will never be dragons again. Who knows what the slayers will do or how the Lord will battle for you?"

A rumble of murmurs interrupted the conversation, and Hartanna waited for the noise to subside. She took Merlin's hand from her shoulder and held it firmly in both of hers, gazing into his eyes for an answer. "Then how will our race survive? How long shall we live? Shall we procreate? And if we do, what kind of creature shall we beget?"

Merlin slipped his hand from her grasp and reached forward to hug her. She accepted his arms willingly. He then reached one arm for Clefspeare and the three huddled in a warm embrace. Merlin signaled with his hands for the others to come close, and when they were within a whisper's distance, he looked around at the circle of concerned eyes. "You will not be able to procreate with each other," he said softly, "but you will live long on the earth. I know of no dragon who has ever died of natural causes, but death is part of Adam's curse. I cannot say how you will be affected."

The former dragons looked at each other and then to Hartanna. She knew their thoughts. "No progeny? Then all is lost?"

Merlin shook his head again. A strange passion filled his eyes, and he lifted his hands toward the sky. "No, Hartanna. All is not lost. Listen to a new word I have just received from the Lord."

When hybrid meets the fallen seed
The virgin seedling flies
An orphaned waif shall call to me
When blossom meets the skies

The child of doubt will find his rest
And meet his virgin bride
A dragon shorn will live again
Rejecting Eden's pride

A slayer comes and with his host
He fights the last of thee
But faith alone shall win the war
The test of those set free

A king shall rise of Arthur's mold
The prophet's book in hand
He takes the sword from mountain stone
To rescue captive bands

After he finished, Merlin bowed his head. During the utterance, the former dragons had moved away from the prophet, his words having a fearful effect on them, and now they waited in silence, drinking in the prophecy that reverberated through their minds. After a minute or two Hartanna decided to give voice to what all the others were wondering. "What does it mean, Master Merlin?"

Merlin sighed and picked up his nearly empty bag. "I cannot say, dear lady." He slung the bag over his back but decided to drop it before walking toward the woods. "Come. It is a long way to Camelot, and now we must go on foot. No need to carry more than we must."

Speak, Gartrand, you foul lizard, and I will let you live. Describe the humans for me."

The fully armored knight stood holding his shield with one hand and his sword with the other, the point pressing against the dragon's underbelly. Draped over the shield in the dragon's full view lay a chain with the glowing candlestone as its pendant.

The dragon cowered in the corner of the cave. "S—Sir Devin. They were still changing as I fled. I do not know. Please believe me."

Devin pushed the sword ever so slightly, and a trickle of thick liquid emerged around the point. "Think, lizard. You must have seen more."

"Have mercy, great knight. I cannot remember. I am so weak. Merlin's spell must have enchanted me."

"It is my stone that weakens you now, demon," the knight replied, holding his shield higher. "But I will not underestimate Merlin's power. I have never seen a dragon fly so stupidly as you, coming directly over the city in full view, spilling fire as you blubbered across the land. You were easy to track, and now Merlin's magic will be the death of you if you do not answer."

"Ask again," the dragon moaned. "I will try."

"You said there was another hiding in the woods. Was it the king?"

"I could not tell. It was a man, I think, but that is all— "

Devin took a step forward and thrust the sword into the dragon's belly. With another agile step and a twist of his blade, he backed away to avoid the gushing fluids of his victim's entrails.

The dragon fell forward, tumbling over like an uprooted tree, and the cracking thud shook the ground at Devin's feet. Devin calmly handed his sword to his squire and took the torch from his hand. Palin pulled a cloth from his vest and began cleaning the soiled blade.

Devin draped the candlestone's chain around his neck and let the sparkling gem dangle over his breastplate. "If the dragon spoke truly, Palin, then our mission is complete. There are no more dragons."

Palin finished wiping his master's sword and handed it back to him. "Yes, my lord, but what of the humans?"

Devin handed the torch back to Palin and put the sword into its scabbard. "A new mission, Palin, a very different one. Now we hunt our own kind; we must put twelve humans on our list."

"Twelve, my lord? Are you including Merlin?" The two walked toward the cave entrance and squinted at the growing light. "Killing humans will not seem a noble venture. The king will not approve."

"If I am right," Devin countered, "the king will help us, even with Merlin."

When they reached the open air, they stopped and took in the view. From the high cliffside, they could see Camelot in the distance, torches and lanterns illuminating the outer walls and windows. "Come," Devin continued, mounting his horse. "Let us seek an audience with the king. Have our chronicles prepared and include today's activities."

Palin drew a book from his saddlebag, just far enough for Devin to see it, and then pushed it back down. "I will, my liege. Every word, as always."

CHAPTER 11

A Dragon's Faith

And so," Billy's father continued, "we all chose common human names for the time and place, and as you may have guessed by now, I was Clefspeare. I have lived for about fifteen hundred years as a human, sometimes as Jared Bannister, sometimes using other names when I had to."

Billy sat and stared. What a story! A zillion questions raced through his mind, too many to even know where to begin! He just had to sit and think about it for a couple of minutes. With spellbound eyes still wide open, he leaned forward in his copilot's seat and gazed out the windshield. There wasn't much to look at; no dragons meeting in secret councils on grassy hilltops, no shadows of the great creatures flying in search of good deeds to do; just a thick layer of clouds covering the woods of the West Virginia mountains below. Billy meditated on one part of Merlin's prophecy that stuck in his mind, *A dragon shorn will live again, rejecting Eden's pride. I think getting shorn is like getting a haircut, so I guess it means the dragons had their dragon bodies removed. Would they ever really get them back?*

As he thought about the prophecy, he imagined being a dragon and flying over the gray puffy blanket below. He knew the landscape in this part of the state, rough and wild. Of course his trance-like attention to the story made his guess of where they were somewhat suspect, but he had a pretty good idea.

In the plane's cabin all was quiet, save for the buzzing prop engine and the whirring blade outside. In fact, the sudden smell of peanut butter was the only input that could shake Billy out of his daydream. He turned back to see his mother and Bonnie munching on peanut butter crackers. They were now sitting together in the dual seat behind Billy.

"Are you holding out on Dad and me?" he asked playfully.

His mother laughed. "I just got them out. Here are some for both of you."

Billy reached to grab the plastic-wrapped crackers and tried to catch Bonnie's eye at the same time. She had once again donned the sweater he had loaned her, and she sat awkwardly, head down and body shifted forward slightly to make room for her hidden wings. She glanced up at him, but only briefly, giving him a tired smile before staring downward again.

The story clearly had a profound effect on her; it seemed to have hypnotized them all, revealing a dark secret that shrouded life itself, a revelation almost too fantastic to believe. Surely his mother had heard the story before, perhaps many times, but had Bonnie? Had her mother disclosed everything? Maybe Bonnie knew, and the old story gave her a different perspective, even gave her new light to chase the shadows away. Maybe. But could it have cast new shadows and raised more dark questions than ever before?

Billy turned to his father, who was also staring quietly, and he tossed the cracker package onto his lap. "Wake up, Dad!"

His father grinned and deftly unwrapped the plastic with his right hand while holding his other on the control yoke. Although the flight had started out smoothly, the weather front brought unpredictable winds, forcing his father to keep a firm pilot's hand on the helm. Billy watched his dad pick a cracker from the wrapper, and he noticed an old ring on his hand. A red stone was mounted in the center, a rubellite he had once been told, a dark red tourmaline that reminded him of a very important question. He reached into his pocket.

"Um . . . Dad," he said, pulling out the stone he had recovered from the street. "Did the candlestone look anything like this?" He held it out in his open palm, but something felt strange when he did, as though he were getting airsick.

His father's eyes opened wide, and he reached out, hesitating briefly. With one finger, he touched the stone, rocking it back and forth. Then, with thumb and forefinger, he picked it up and held it close to his eyes.

"There was a time when holding this stone so close would have sent me into convulsions. I remember when—" He turned suddenly to Billy, his face aflame with passion, and he held the stone right in front of Billy's eyes. "Where did you get this?"

Billy drew back for a brief second, surprised at his father's sudden change, and he again felt nausea boiling deep in his stomach. "F—From the street. I—I guess Dr. Whittier must have dropped it."

His father stared at him for a moment. He looked confused at first, but then sympathetic. "Are you all right, son?" He pulled the stone back and clenched it in his fist.

Billy breathed a sigh and held his stomach with his hand, pausing a few seconds to take inventory. "Yeah, it's a little better, but now I have this really weird feeling."

"What's it like?"

Billy looked over the instrument panel, reading all the gauges and looking for a warning light. "Like there's something wrong. I felt it when I got in the plane, and I feel it again now."

His father uncovered the stone but this time kept it well away from Billy. He passed it slowly in front of his eyes and caressed it with his fingers, rubbing them over the smooth edges of each facet. "There's no doubt about it," he said with a low trembling voice. "This was Merlin's very own candlestone, passed down from Sir Devin, himself, I would guess." He slipped the stone into his pocket and turned to Billy again, this time with his usual fatherly countenance, his teaching mode, upraised brow and thinned out lips. "That means your Dr. Whittier is likely a direct descendant of the worst of all the dragon slayers, Sir Devin the Dragon's Bane."

A rough voice spoke up from the back. "You could say that, Clefspeare, but I would say the best of all the slayers."

Four heads spun around to see a human form stepping out of the cargo area and into the aisle. He stooped because of the low ceiling in the cabin, but his face was unmistakable.

Billy gulped. "Dr. Whittier!"

The slayer stopped and pointed a pistol directly at Billy's father, extending his arm fully. "I didn't have time to get my prophetic host together, Dragon, but I would wager a hefty sum that a well-placed bullet would kill you now."

Billy's mother screamed. "Jared! Get down!" She pulled Bonnie to the floor and then reached over to try to push Billy's head lower. He budged, just a little, keeping enough of his head above the seat to watch what was going on.

Dr. Whittier fired the gun, and the bullet whizzed by Billy's head and clanked into the instrument panel. His father stretched out his hand and yelled. "Stop! What do you want?"

"That was just a warning shot," the slayer growled, now pointing the gun directly at Billy. "Give me the candlestone, and I won't shoot your kid. I'll just jump and be on my way." He motioned with his hand toward something on his back, a parachute, Billy guessed, but it was concealed in the shadows behind him. "I was a paratrooper in the war. I'm sure I can do it again."

Billy's father got up and gave a hand signal. Billy took the cue and grabbed the copilot's steering yoke. His father took a step toward the slayer, leaning forward to avoid bumping his head. "It's me you want. Leave them alone."

The slayer turned the gun toward Billy's father. "Indeed, you are one of the fallen spirits, but your son is equally condemned. Haven't you explained that to him, or did you tell him your sweet fairy tale about good dragons and bad dragons? Did that bedtime story make him feel better about being a mongrel?"

Billy saw his father's eyes glance his way. The slayer went on. "Now give me the stone, and you'll be the only one I shoot."

"Why do you want the stone so badly? It doesn't affect me anymore."

The slayer's face grew red, and a throbbing blood vessel rose near his temple, drawing a crooked blue line across the side of his forehead. His voice shook with passion as he spoke slowly through his teeth. "You're testing my patience, Clefspeare. I could have killed you right after we took off." He took a deep breath, cooling his anger, and went on. "I decided to bide my time and try to listen in on your conversation. Now I know one of you holds the candlestone, and I know for sure that you're the last true dragon. I had long suspected there was only one left; now it's all the mongrel puppies your kind has whelped that I have to worry about." He extended his open palm even further. "You may not like my methods, but you know I'm no liar. Give me the stone, and you'll be the only one I shoot. What do you say, Clefspeare? If you really believe the prophecy, you should take my offer."

Billy saw the determined look in his father's eyes. *Is Dad going to take that deal? Is he really going to let that creep shoot him?*

His father pulled the stone from his pocket. With cautious steps, he walked down the aisle, reaching the stone toward the slayer, but Dr. Whittier backed away, extending the gun with a trembling hand.

"Wait." He motioned toward Bonnie with his gun. "Give it to the witch."

Bonnie sat huddled in the gap behind the copilot's chair and in front of the dual passenger's seat, but after the slayer referred to her so casually by that derogatory name, she rose with a defiant glare and held her hand out for the stone. Billy's father handed it to her, and she glanced at it briefly before closing her fist around it. As she stood to face the slayer, her eyes lost their gleam of bravery, and a painful frown spread wrinkles across her forehead. She took a deep breath and walked through the narrow aisle toward the slayer, extending the stone in the palm of her hand.

Dr. Whittier snatched the stone and dropped it into his pocket, but when Bonnie turned to go back to her seat, he stepped forward and grabbed her from behind with his left arm, gripping her tightly while holding the gun to her head. Both the girl and the slayer scrunched over, with Bonnie's hidden wings squeezed between their bodies. She let out a single painful grunt, but she didn't struggle.

"Now, open the cargo door," the slayer demanded.

Billy's dad took a heavy step forward and stopped, keeping his eye on Dr. Whittier's gun hand. "You said you wouldn't shoot anyone else. That gun could go off!"

"It won't if you cooperate."

He turned toward the front. "Think you can hold Merlin while I open the door? It'll get real bumpy."

"I think so." Billy tried to act confident, but he wasn't really sure he could hold the plane. He considered jerking Merlin with a sudden tilt, hoping his father could take advantage of the surprise, but he was afraid it might make the slayer angry enough to shoot everyone.

Billy's father stepped around the slayer and threw open the door. A stiff, frigid breeze buffeted the three in the rear of the plane while Merlin bounced angrily. Billy held the copilot's yoke and kept glancing toward the rear. His mother had risen from her crouch, and with the extra light pouring in, he could see the silent fear in her eyes as she stared at him as if crying for help. He could also see the parachute on Dr. Whittier's back. It looked familiar, like one of the stock parachutes from the hangar.

With a maniacal grin, the slayer pointed the gun toward the cockpit and fired toward the front of the plane. Billy threw his body to the right, away from the line of fire. Each crack of the gun popped in his ears like a firecracker.

Pow! One bullet hit the windshield, drilling a precise hole through the glass and sending crooked streaks in every direction.

Clank! Clank! More bullets plowed into the instrument panel, bending and breaking the metal and plastic gauges. Thump! A fourth bullet ripped through the carpet and lodged somewhere under the floor.

As soon as the gun went silent, Billy jerked back up in his seat and tried to hold the bucking plane in check. After a slight adjustment to the left, however, Merlin yawed and kept leaning more and more to the left while slowly losing altitude. "Dad," Billy yelled, "I can't correct." A cloud of gray smoke erupted from the left side of the panel while he struggled to maintain control. "We're gonna crash!" His father took a step toward the front of the plane to help.

"Halt, foul dragon!" the slayer commanded, causing his enemy to turn toward him once again. The slayer pointed the gun directly at his chest. "This bullet's for you, Clefspeare. The twelfth of the council finally meets his end."

The gun sounded again, and the bullet smashed into the former dragon's body, slamming him against the cabin wall.

"Dad!"

"Jared!"

Neither Billy nor his mom dared to move.

"I must be going now," the slayer said while bracing against the plane's slow spiraling turn. "Of course I'll have to take the witch with me. She could just jump and fly away. We can't have that happen." The slayer dragged Bonnie to the open door. After first leaning over to look below, he hoisted Bonnie up off her feet and jumped. Without a sound, they disappeared into the open sky.

Billy's mother leaped from her seat and scrambled to her husband's side. She put her hand on his heaving chest. Her voice trembled, each word barely escaping in tightened squeaks. "How—How b—bad is it?"

He opened his eyes halfway, and his wincing face breathed out a tortured reply. "Very."

She ripped open his shirt and grimaced at the wound.

Billy grabbed the radio handset, squeezed the talk button, and shouted into it. "Emergency! If anyone can hear me; plane in trouble, pilot shot and can't operate. We're losing altitude, big time. I can't do anything with the controls." Billy let go of the button and leaned over to listen, but all he could hear was static. He slapped the handset back in place and moaned, "The bullets must've killed it." He waited a couple of anxious seconds, staring at the radio, his heart pounding, his chest heaving through rapid, shallow breaths. *C'mon radio! Work!*

"What's your position?" came a faint, scratchy reply.

Billy snatched the radio again and squeezed the button. He coughed. His words squeaked through his swollen throat. "I'm—I'm not sure. We were flying—I mean, we were heading for Huntington, coming from Ca—Castlewood. We had over a hun—hundred miles to go." Billy's throat pressure eased, and he kept on talking in case he didn't get another chance. "We're in a Cessna Caravan, two adults and one teenager. The shooter is Dr. Whittier, the principal from Castlewood. He jumped with a parachute and carried another teenager with him. Her name is Bonnie Silver."

Billy waited for a reply but could only hear static once again. He looked back at his father. His mother crouched over his dad's quivering frame, and she pressed a towel on the wound. Blood oozed through the towel and over his mother's fingers. *Dad's blood!*

Billy's throat tightened again. He squeezed his eyes half-closed, fighting the tears. His father . . . his dad . . . lay mortally wounded. The tears flowed. There was no way to stop them.

His mother rocked her body and nodded her head in rhythm with her sobs and the bounces of the plane. "Jared," she cried. "I don't know what to do. Help me."

He breathed out a faint whisper, his voice gurgling as he spoke. "Para . . . chute . . . behind . . . seat. You . . . and . . . Billy."

She jerked her head around and yelled. "Billy, check behind Dad's seat! Is there a parachute?"

Billy jumped up and lunged toward the rear of the pilot's seat. He could barely choke out a reply. "Yes!" he said, desperately trying to hold back his sobs.

His mother's expression softened and her tone calmed. "Bring it here . . . please."

Billy had found the chute in a space behind and under the seat. It was stuffed in tightly, but a quick tug dislodged it. There was no use trying to steer the plane, so he left the cockpit and brought the bundle to his mother. With one hand on her husband's wound, she used her free hand to fumble with the parachute straps.

"Do you know how it goes on?" she asked.

Billy took the chute again and separated the straps. With his heart racing, he stumbled through his words. "I've seen—seen Dad's jumpers put them on. . . . H—Here." His mother had to release the pressure on her husband's chest while Billy hoisted the pack over her shoulders and tightened the straps. "It's just an emergency chute," Billy explained, "there's—there's no backup."

"It'll have to do. Do you know what to pull?"

Her calm demeanor helped him speak more easily. "Yes. We'll have to hold each other, but I'll be able to reach the cord."

Billy's mom leaned over and caressed her husband's face with a tender, open palm.

He whispered into her ear. "No . . . time for . . . good-byes. I can't . . . die yet. The prophecy . . . must be fulfilled."

Two large tears splashed onto his chest, mingling with the spreading blood that had painted his shirt crimson. She kissed him, her trembling lips only managing a weak peck on his deathly pallid cheek. Billy helped her to her feet, and the two crossed the few steps to the open door. The wind buffeted their faces and dried their streaming tears.

Billy and his mom grasped each other. He felt her arms squeezing tightly around his back, and he held the ripcord with his right hand while wrapping his left arm around her shoulders.

He tried to stop trembling, but even his mother's tight embrace did little to calm him now. Was his fear for his father's safety or for his impending jump? He honestly couldn't tell; everything he had ever known was falling apart before his eyes, and so quickly that he couldn't take it all in.

His mother's soothing voice whispered in his ear. "Don't be afraid, Billy. We can do this."

His only answer was a tighter squeeze with his arm, and he laid his head down on her shoulder. With his mouth so near her neck, he didn't want to risk burning her skin. He really had no idea what to say, anyway.

Billy looked back at his father's writhing body. He could barely spit out the words, but his emotions forced his shaking voice to push forth his tearful lament. "Good—good-bye, Dad. I—I love you!"

There was no answer. His father's tall frame lay deathly still.

After briefly looking down at the slowly spinning cloud bank, they jumped.

Let me go!" Bonnie screamed. Although the rushing wind drowned out her cry, her struggling arms and kicking feet relayed the message.

The slayer shouted into her ear. "I should have known you'd be strong." He held her tightly from behind, both his arms wrapped around hers. The parachute had already opened, and they had penetrated and passed the gray wall of clouds that acted as a blanket to hide the ground below. Now they could see a mass of dense treetops drawing closer, and the shifting wind made their eventual landing point impossible to predict. With each heavy gust, the wind jerked the chute, dragging Bonnie and the slayer at random angles, and the slayer had to reposition his arms to keep his prisoner in check.

Bonnie decided to rest for a few seconds. She had to gather her strength to be ready to kick and struggle with all her might at the next gust of wind. *Maybe, just maybe . . .*

She didn't have to wait long. A gust hit the chute and threw it to the side, and just as she sensed the pull, Bonnie thrust her elbows into the slayer's ribs and bit his right hand. With a mighty two-legged kick and another thrust with her elbows, she felt his grasp slip over her head. She was free . . . and falling.

She tried to flap her wings. She was almost in flying position, facedown and body in a horizontal spread, but something was wrong. Somehow her wings were stuck. The sweater! She was still wearing the sweater! She reached down and yanked at the hem, trying to rip it over her wings in the back. The trees raced toward her from below. The stinging air brought tears streaming back toward her temples. In a few seconds her body would be dashed against the branches.

She pulled at the front of the sweater and snatched it over her head, then after two quick tugs, each arm was free. She wasn't able to reach to her back, so she flapped her wings ferociously, hoping they would throw off the sweater. The trees were so close, she could distinguish individual twigs, and she could almost feel sharp branches thrusting into her body, impaling her, leaving her dangling as a morbid decoration in the lonely forest.

She flapped again with all her might, knowing the next second would bring the first stabbing knife. A splash of color rushed at her face. Branches scraped her legs, snagging and pulling her jeans as her failing wings thrust her body horizontally across the deadly spikes. A stream of twigs and leaves flashed by her eyes, threatening to slice her face. "Ohhhh! Help!" With a pain-filled gasp she pulled through a desperation flap. She caught a gust of wind and vaulted just above the treetops.

Pain stabbed the top of her left wing near her back. The outside half collapsed, spinning her to one side. Spying a narrow gap in the trees, Bonnie lunged for it. After brushing against an outstretched hickory branch with her injured wing, she swerved to avoid the other wooden spears and fly into the treeless gap, a rainwater trench in the mountain slope.

Bonnie spread her wings to slow her descent and hoped for the best. Barely missing a few more protruding limbs, she resembled a huge falling leaf, zigzagging downward on the ever-shifting cushion of air. Finally, she crash-landed into the trench, tumbling forward along the downslope, face-first into the dense floor of decaying leaves.

CHAPTER 12

The Chase

It's okay, Mom. The parachute opened. We're going to be all right." Billy's voice trembled as he whispered into his mother's ear while trying to avoid breathing on her. He was locked tightly in her arms, and he had his own arms wrapped around her, careful to avoid the parachute lines.

She didn't answer. Billy followed her line of sight and spied their falling plane, still making a spiraling descent. Since they were now floating more slowly downward, the plane passed them by, missing them by several hundred feet. As the wind blew them in the opposite direction, Merlin grew smaller, and the tiny airplane disappeared into the trees, hundreds of yards away. Billy's mother stifled a sob, and he could feel her arms grow ever stronger around him. "He said he wouldn't die, Mom," Billy said tenderly. "I believe him."

"I do, too, honey. If I didn't, I don't know what I'd do."

They stayed quiet for a few moments, but their reverie was cut short. The treetops below rushed toward them, their spiny fingers reaching to catch their prey. "Mom," Billy called out. "It looks like we could get scratched up."

"Close your eyes and pray!" They both squeezed their eyes shut and hoped for a narrow, vertical entry into the forest. The idea seemed to work. Billy felt twigs lightly scratching his arms, and he heard the pops and groans of bending branches, but he felt no pain. A strong tug from above and a swinging sensation finally signaled the end of their fall.

Billy opened his eyes and looked around. They were suspended in midair! Their parachute had entangled itself in the arms of a tall oak tree, actually two trees that grew side by side, and the two jumpers, still clutching one another, bobbed slowly up and down like a dying yo-yo.

His mom spoke up first. "Now how are we going to get down from here?"

Billy looked below. There was nothing between him and the ground except for a few skinny limbs that were much too far away to reach safely. "I'd guess we're about fifty feet up. Too high to jump." He looked around again. Since he couldn't point, he had to gesture with a nod of his head. "But if we can swing to my right, toward the big tree over there, I might be able to catch that branch and drop to the limb just below it. Then maybe I could pull you toward it."

She clenched her teeth. "I see it. It looks too dangerous."

"Do we have any choice?"

"I guess not."

At first they moved in opposite directions, but within a few seconds they were rocking in sync, waving back and forth, suspended in space. Their motions sent a cascade of leaves raining down on their heads, the stubborn ones that had not yet succumbed to the cold weather. Billy heard a slight cracking sound from above, but the branches held firm.

Billy and his mom pulled and pushed through a fourth swing, then a fifth, drawing closer and closer to the protruding branch. They spun around like a twirling pendulum, first clockwise until the parachute lines wound up, and then counter-clockwise. Billy wondered if he would be closer to the branch than his mother would when the time came to make a lunge for it. Would he have to reach in front of himself and around her or would his back be toward it?

The cracking sound grew louder. On their next swing the branch came within reach, directly behind him. He released his mother with his hands but kept a firm grip on her with his legs as he twisted to stretch toward his target. There was no room for error. The slightest miscalculation would send him downward, dangling with his legs around his mother's hips, at best, and at worst, diving headfirst into who knows what below. He reached high, knowing he would start falling as soon as he let go of his mother, and he thrust his whole body outward.

He did it! His hands struck the branch! His left hand slipped away, but he hung on with his right, stubbornly refusing to lose this chance. A loud pop sounded from above and a dozen small crackles. "I got it, Mom!" he grunted.

"You'll never make it unless you let me go!" she called back.

"Okay. I'll drop down to the limb and you can swing back to me." He pulled with his right arm and threw his left hand up again to get a double grasp on the branch, then, after releasing the scissors grip he held on his mom with his legs, he yanked his body upward to get a better hold. His fingers screamed in pain as the extra weight dug the bark deeper into his hands.

He spun his head to see his mother swinging wildly away in the other direction. The branches snapped her up higher, and when she came back down, they finally gave way, sending her plummeting toward the ground. Billy could only watch in terror as she alternately fell and stopped with each snag of the parachute. Her legs swiped against small branches twice, but her head cleared all the deadly obstacles. She finally reached bottom with a sickening thud, and Billy leaned forward to try to see through the tangled mesh of woods.

Still dangling, he screamed toward the ground. "Mom! Can you hear me? Are you all right?"

There was no answer.

He had no time to lose. He had to get down, now! But how? That limb underneath was close, but not close enough. Dropping straight down to it was possible, but if he missed, the next step was about another fifty feet away, ground zero . . . and zero chance of surviving.

Ouch! My fingers! They're slipping. Gotta go for it.

He let go with his left hand and watched his shoes stretch for the limb, maybe five feet down. *Here goes!* He released the branch, and when his shoes slapped against the limb, he bent his knees to absorb the shock. With a quick turn toward the tree, he dropped down to straddle the limb and then slid his body across the bark until he could grab the trunk.

He took a deep breath and rested, but just for a second. There was no time for a break. He looked down. The trunk stretched to the forest floor without more than a gall and a few knots in its rough skin, hardly anything to grab with his hands or to use for foot support.

With a surge of adrenaline, he hugged the supporting limb, swung down, and clutched the trunk with his legs, giving him the grip he needed to release the limb and wrap both arms around the tree's middle section. From there, he shinnied down the trunk like a monkey racing down a palm tree. A sharp knot dug through the skin of his hand, sending a trickle of blood into his palm, but he couldn't worry about minor wounds—not now.

The downward slide seemed an eternity, but when his feet finally landed in the crunchy matted leaves, he broke into a cold sweat and his legs turned wobbly, two strands of cooked spaghetti struggling to hold up a desperate boy. He didn't have time to wait for them to recover. He lumbered through the leaves toward where his mother had landed. Grabbing armfuls of the torn parachute, he called feverishly. "Mom! Mom! Where are you?"

He finally found her lying faceup, partially covered with leaves. Her eyes were closed. Billy fell to his knees next to her body. "Mom! Can you hear me?"

He put his hands on her cheeks. They radiated soft warmth against his cold fingers, and her face winced. Billy started crying. "You're alive! Thank God! You're alive!" He could feel tears streaming down his cheeks, but he didn't bother to wipe them. He placed one cold hand on her forehead and one on her throat to try to revive her.

She finally opened her eyes. What a welcome sight that was! Two eyes had never been more beautiful.

"Your face is dirty, Billy."

Billy smiled through his tears. "Mom, do you know where you are?"

She nodded. "Somewhere in the West Virginia mountains. But that's about the best I can do."

"Can you get up?"

She braced herself against the ground with both hands and pushed while Billy cradled the back of her head to help. She sat and stretched her neck to each side as if trying to get a crick out. "Ohhh! I feel awful."

"Did your head hit the ground? Do you think you might have a concussion?"

"I don't remember. I know my feet hit first, but I don't remember after that." She reached her hands forward to signal for her son's help. "Let's see if I can walk. We have to find the plane right away."

"Right! The plane! How could I forget?"

He hoisted her to her feet, and she tried to walk. On her first step she lost her balance, but she caught herself on Billy's hands and stood on one foot. "Owww!"

Billy helped her sit down again, and she rolled up her pant leg to reveal a swollen ankle. "That's the same one you hurt in the car. Do you think it's broken?"

"I can't tell. I'd better not try to walk on it, just in case."

Billy stood up fully and raised his arms in the air. "Then how're we gonna find Dad?"

His mother pulled on his pant leg and brought him down to his knees. She spoke softly and slowly. "You'll have to hunt for him by yourself; I'd just slow you down." She turned her head and pointed to a place higher on the hill. "Help me up to that clearing, and I'll try to signal for help if anyone comes looking for us from the air. When you find your dad, then both of you can come back and find me."

"You mean if he's still alive."

She put her hand on his shoulder and squeezed it tenderly. "He's alive. He has to be."

He watched his mother rub her ankle deeply with her free hand. She really believed! So shouldn't he believe, too? And what about the slayer's words? Was Dad really a good dragon? Just a few days ago he would have sided with his father no matter what. Now, with his father snatching away his foundation like it was just a thin, ratty carpet, he didn't know what to believe. And besides, why should he trust in a fifteen-hundred-year-old prophecy, especially when it lived only in the memory of the one who relied on it?

Billy placed his hand over his mother's and stroked it. His fingers trembled over her cold skin. "Mom, do you really think it's true? He looked real bad, you know."

"I know, but I'm not ready to consider the alternatives."

"Okay, then. What about Bonnie? If we know Dad's going to live, shouldn't I look for her first?"

"You've got a point." She shrugged her shoulders. "But I guess it doesn't really matter. We don't know which way to go in either case."

"Then what do we do?"

She looked around and then stared, and Billy followed her line of sight. Downslope he saw hundreds of various sized trees, both standing and fallen. They were sparse enough to get a view of much of the mountainside. Everything looked the same, no matter which way he turned, tall, white and gray trunks, bare and skinny, with their shed leaves covering the ground as far as the eye could see. Although some of the leaves still held their autumn shape and yellow hue, most were flat and brown, creating a matted carpet that shifted with each gust of wind. He listened to their faint whisper and took in the mountain's scent, a sweet, woodsy aroma, clean and cold, biting gently into his nostrils. He turned back to his mother and waited for her to answer.

"I suppose you should search for the road," she finally said. "Getting help may be our best option."

"Yeah, I don't know if anyone on the radio understood my call. Maybe no one's even looking for us. I saw the road while we were floating down. I think I can figure out which way to go."

"Then you'd better get going. Your dad usually flies pretty close to a highway if he can, so it shouldn't be too far. And you'd better hurry. It'll be getting dark soon."

Walter Foley loved the city's fall festival. For him, next to Christmas, it was the most fun day of the year. As was his custom, he arrived at the park early to help with setting up the Boy Scouts' dunking booth. Being a high-ranking scout in the local troop, it was his duty to help manage the festivities, but it was also his pleasure. Where else could he play carnival barker and poke fun at the various teachers who had bravely volunteered to become the objects of ridicule and the victims of an icy dip in a big washtub? But they knew the risks, and Walter had assured them that there were enough volunteers to make each chilly turn on the dunking platform a short one.

Walter grabbed one of the softballs out of a wicker basket and repeatedly tossed it a foot or two in the air, catching it in the same bare hand. Each smack of leather on flesh stung a bit in the chilling late afternoon, but it was a good sting, one that promised lots of fun.

As usual, the city council had timed the festival to coincide with the approach of Thanksgiving. Long ago, the founders of the city designated a community feast two Fridays before Thanksgiving; nobody alive today knew why for sure, but local legend tells the story of an early settler who fell off his horse on this very weekend over a hundred years earlier. He slid into a deep pit, and for six days he sat at the bottom eating nuts and berries that sympathetic chipmunks dropped in. Finally, a passing hunter noticed a gathering of chipmunks around the hole and investigated, finding the settler at the bottom, covered with berry stains, but very much alive.

The town celebrated the weekend of his rescue every year, hauling out a three-foot-high bronze chipmunk and placing it at the park entrance for six days. Everyone patted it on the head as they passed by or placed acorns at its feet in memory of the friendly chipmunks that kept the poor settler from starving so long ago.

This year, cold air dominated the weather, but not unusually cold for West Virginia in November, just chilly enough to give the festival its late autumn flavor. Somehow the sight of everyone bundled up made the evening more like a family get-together. Ladies in double-thick sweaters and men in lined jackets strolled from booth to booth, sometimes attached glove-in-glove and trailed by prancing children in knit ski caps carrying corndogs or half-eaten plumes of cotton candy. White puffs streamed out of red noses, laughter became contagious, and people ate, talked, and played together late into the evening.

Walter's enthusiasm this year, however, was tempered by the worries of the day. With the strange bat creature at school that morning, and with Billy's house burning down, people seemed on edge. Gossip buzzed around town. The police had interviewed Walter right after the firefighters finished saving what was left of the house, and they talked to everyone at school who knew Billy. The police wanted to interview Dr. Whittier, but nobody knew where he was. Walter told them that Dr. Whittier had gone to the airport while his goons burned down the house, but the rumor mill said there was no sign of him at the airport. Not only that, the Bannisters' plane had taken off without leaving a flight plan.

Theories bounced around town, sounding like plots from bad detective novels. One had Dr. Whittier as a foreign spy who had used a flying robot to snoop on kids, and when Billy stole it to take a joy ride, Whittier burned down his house to scare him into giving it back. Another had Billy as a genius kid who had built a new kind of flying machine, and Dr. Whittier as a government agent who was trying to steal the secrets for the military.

But nobody mentioned Bonnie. And it seemed that nobody cared about her part in the story. Walter knew she had gone with the Bannisters, but he didn't mention that to the police. They didn't ask. Besides, with Billy acting so secretive, Walter decided not to volunteer any more information than he had to. Billy was his friend, and they trusted each other. Anyway, Bonnie's foster parents would report her as missing if they didn't know where she was, wouldn't they?

"Walter? Is that you?"

Walter spun around to find the owner of the familiar British accent. "Hi, Mr. Hamilton." He smiled and pointed at his booth. "Are you ready to take the plunge?"

Mr. Hamilton shook his head, and his creased brow made Walter drop his tease.

"Walter, I regret that I shall not be able to participate tonight."

"What's the matter, Mr. Hamilton? Are you sick?"

"No, Walter." Mr. Hamilton looked at Walter's booth and sighed. "I know how much this activity means to you and your fellow scouts, but I feel I must ask you to come with me on an urgent matter."

Walter tossed the softball back to its basket and paid close attention to his teacher. "Is it something about Billy? Do you have news?"

Mr. Hamilton put his arm around Walter and began walking him toward the entrance of the park. He kept his tone low. "Yes, I have news, a great deal of news, in fact." He waited to speak again until they found a secluded area, away from the booths and still a hundred feet or so from the entrance. He stopped Walter and looked at him gravely, his deeply set eyes shaded in the dimming light. "Can you come with me to the school?"

Walter hesitated, sobered by Mr. Hamilton's frown. "Uh, I guess so. What for?"

"I think the police are on the wrong trail, and word has it that you know the Bannister family better than anyone else. I need you to help me investigate."

"And it can't wait until tomorrow?"

"No. There's more. I heard on the news that a plane was reported in trouble over the mountains, the same kind that Billy's father owns. The police believe it went down perhaps ten or twenty kilometers east of Elkins. A sheep farmer in a place called Sully heard the laboring motor and saw a smoke trail."

Walter suddenly felt sick to his stomach and light-headed. Mr. Hamilton grabbed him by the shoulders and held him up for a few seconds, just enough to keep him from falling. Hot blood surged back into Walter's face, and he pulled away, waving his arms excitedly. "What can we do? Can we go and help them search the mountains?"

"Yes, but not yet." Mr. Hamilton pointed to the cell phone on his belt. "I'm waiting for a call from someone who will give us a more precise location. We can drive there and join the volunteer search team." He glanced around the park. "Are your parents here? Can you ask their permission to go?"

"They're coming later. They're probably still at home."

Mr. Hamilton extended his hand, gesturing toward the park exit. "Then please come with me and phone them from the school. I must leave the cell line open for the call I'm expecting. I never bothered to purchase that call-waiting feature."

Walter hesitated, but only for a moment. He had already set up the booth, and the other volunteers could work it without him. Billy needed his help.

Bonnie opened her eyes and tried to see past a dark, wrinkled ocean, a wet brown pile of stale-smelling leaves. She felt dizzy, confused.

While she lay prostrate, she mentally took inventory, asking each part of her body what was going on. Her lips held a damp leaf and she spat it out, leaving an earthy taste on her tongue. Her arms spread out across the soft, wet mat. Apparently she had tried to stop her fall but failed. Any pain? Yes. Her left wing ached, her right knee complained of a stabbing throb, and both of her hands reported a burning sensation. Not too bad.

Bonnie raised her head, lifting it out of the pile of leaves. She squinted and turned in every direction, gazing in a dreamlike trance. Now she could see the forest and the mountain downslope that served as her bed. The skies had darkened. Thick clouds obscured the setting sun.

Something in her brain prodded her. *Get up! Get going!* But why? She turned her eyes upward, trying to roll back the events of the day, but she was interrupted by the voice in her head. *Run! Fly!* Suddenly the sound of rustling leaves shook her out of her trance. The slayer!

Billy tramped hurriedly through the leaves, making his way down a relatively easy slope. His mother was probably right; the highway shouldn't be too far away, but it had seemed like a skinny gray ribbon when he saw it from the sky. Just before he left his mother, using the notepad and pencil he kept in his pant leg pocket, he had drawn a quick map of what he had seen while drifting down. All he could do now was try to head in the right direction and hope to hear the sound of cars or see the flicker of distant headlights when darkness fell.

Everything looked so different at ground level, but he knew most highways passed through the mountains at the lowest points, so a steady downward trek had to be the logical way to go. Although he found a hiker's trail, he knew it wasn't wise to follow a path that probably wound through the mountains to reach vistas for sightseers. Down was the smart direction. He had to ascend a hump from time to time, but he was always able to find a declining slope again.

He had to concentrate. The torture in his mind was almost too much to bear. Did he have a father anymore? Would he be able to find his mother again? What about Bonnie? What would the slayer do to her? Did they even land safely? Like a hundred hammers his doubts pounded his emotions, and through welling tears, he ran on and on.

Bonnie burst out of the leaves and flew, crying in pain as she lifted herself a few feet off the ground. It was no use. After flying only a dozen or so feet horizontally, she fell again.

The crackling sounds of footsteps drew closer. Bonnie searched every direction for a hiding place. There was only one chance. Up! With every ounce of heart she had left she flung herself into the air. She grabbed a low branch, flapped again to sling herself to the next branch, and then rested, breathlessly waiting in the crook of the tree. The skinny trunk barely shielded her body, and she tried to hold back her panting gasps. She feared her pounding heart might give her away as she listened to the sounds below. A voice! She heard a voice!

"That's right," the rough voice said. "In my office. The doctor sent the sword last week. It's in the panel I told you about."

Bonnie listened for a few seconds before noticing a limping man hurrying across the slope as fast as his gimpy leg would allow. It *was* the slayer! He was talking on a cell phone and pushing through the leaves while looking around in every direction.

"Wait! Hold on! There's something here."

The slayer stopped, and Bonnie tried to squeeze her body behind the trunk and peer out as secretly as she could, painfully folding in her wings as tightly as possible. He was standing right where she had first fallen to the ground.

"I think I found where she landed. It looks like she flew again . . ." At this point he looked down at the palm of his hand.

What is he looking at? A compass? Yes, it must be a compass.

"She's heading southeast, or at least she was." He limped over to another area a few yards away. "She landed again right over here." The slayer stopped and searched the area while keeping the cell phone at his ear. "I don't see any other disturbed leaves, so she must have flown away." He looked up and scanned the intricate matrix of branches. Bonnie tried to follow his gaze, alternately watching him and the trees. A few were still decorated with rusty leaves, making a confusing patchwork in the dimming light, and the evergreen firs stood out as the living sentinels of the winter, but all the others stood naked and still in the stiff, cold wind.

"I think she's around here somewhere. She was flying hurt; I could tell." He kicked through the leaves and did a complete three-sixty scan before speaking again. "Get the sword and the book, and bring Randall and Jerry. . . . Yes, Jerry will be at the airport. . . . I don't care how long it takes; just cruise highway thirty-three in the area I told you until you see me at the side of the road. I'll get there eventually. My instincts tell me there's an injured dragon around here somewhere, and I'm going to find her."

Walter handed the office phone to Mr. Hamilton, who had stooped to read something on the desk. "My dad wants to talk to you."

Mr. Hamilton took the phone and stood erect. "Charles Hamilton, here. . . . Yes, I am the same. . . . Carl Foley? You mean Crazy Carl Foley? . . . Of course I remember you. My days at Oxford weren't that many years ago. You looked after my dear, sick wife while I gave Elizabeth away in marriage. I'll never forget that. . . . Ah, I remember now; Walter was absent when we had our unit on heritage, but I should have guessed that this fine young man was your son."

Mr. Hamilton listened for several seconds, rapidly nodding his head. "Yes, we're doing some detective work. He is secure in my care. . . . Yes, we will be in touch."

The teacher hung up the phone with a satisfied smile. "Your father has approved."

"Good thing," Walter said, "since I'm already here."

"Yes. Quite." Mr. Hamilton gestured with his hand. "Come over here. Since you're Carl Foley's son, I'm sure you will be very interested in seeing a fascinating book."

Walter stepped cautiously through the principal's office. He wanted to ask his teacher a bunch of questions, about how he knew his dad and about the "Crazy Carl Foley" nickname, but creeping through the dark, eerie room brought a tight lump to his throat. He decided to wait.

Since he had never been in much trouble himself, Walter rarely visited the principal's office. The last time he was here, he was delivering papers for a teacher, but he had just zipped right in and out, not wanting to stick around and meet the man behind the strange rumors, the eccentric Dr. Whittier. Now, with the office dark, save for Mr. Hamilton's flashlight, the eerie paintings and gothic displays seemed to stare down at him, looming much larger than reality.

Walter tiptoed forward. Mr. Hamilton had explained on the way to the school about all the books he had looked through in Dr. Whittier's office. He also asked a lot of questions about Billy. But why? Why was his teacher so curious about Billy's family, his grandparents and aunts and uncles, and what did all of this have to do with the plane crash? And why did the principal keep a personal library in a supply closet?

When Walter entered the closet he saw that Mr. Hamilton had already laid open a huge volume on a low table. The teacher's finger ran down the page, and the light focused on the strange type. His voice trembled with excitement. "See this? It's a genealogy. I mentored your father for his research project on family histories, so perhaps you've seen them before."

"I've seen them," Walter admitted, "but I don't really understand them."

"Look here." Mr. Hamilton tapped the page. "Bannister is the family name of Reginald, a man whom Arthur adopted."

"So? I'm sure there are lots of Bannisters."

"Right you are, Walter. But I was searching to find any reason for Whittier's actions. You see, I discovered that our principal is not Whittier. His name is Devin. His Whittier character is just a disguise for him."

"A disguise? How did you find that out?"

"From his own books." Mr. Hamilton turned around and pulled out another volume and laid it on top of the cabinet, throwing it open to a marked page.

"You would have to understand how genealogies work, but he has placed the name 'Devin' where his own name should go. Notice the handwriting and compare it to that of the original Sir Devin."

"They're the same!"

"Yes, it's as if Whittier copied the script. I think he fancies himself a true knight, and he is very proud of his name. I knew beforehand that Sir Devin's first son was also named Devin. So it's no surprise that any descendant would have the same name, even after so long."

"What's so special about Devin?"

Mr. Hamilton looked away from the book and stared toward the dark ceiling. "Sir Devin was a knight, very close to King Arthur, but the two had a bit of a falling out." He looked back at Walter. "Nobody knows why they argued. I think it's because Devin was never allowed into the king's inner circle; he never had a seat at the Round Table. But the legends say the strife was over Devin's rabid interest in killing dragons. Supposedly, Arthur thought him mad and sent him away, but in either case, ever since that time Devin's family has had a cruel interest in making life miserable for any of Arthur's descendants. They made the Christian name into a surname as a threat to Arthur's family."

"So Billy's descended from King Arthur, and Dr. Whittier—I mean, Devin, has it in for him and his father."

"Precisely! And not only that, legend tells us that Arthur will return some day to rule once again. My own theory is that his return will be in spirit, in the form of one of his descendants, and not necessarily to rule. But rule or no, it is a return that Devin and his ilk would surely oppose. Perhaps William—"

A doorknob rattled, making both boy and teacher jump. Mr. Hamilton slapped the book closed, flicked off his flashlight, and pulled Walter deeper into the closet, sliding to the side of a bookshelf near the back. The office light flashed on and then the closet's fluorescent bulbs flickered to life. A relatively short man entered, stocky but not obese. Walter decided to label him, "Rocky," because his build reminded him of a boxer.

Walter watched while Rocky pulled books out one by one with small, nimble hands, reading each title, then pushing each book back in place. Finally, he pulled out an old metal box that had been placed vertically on the shelf as though it were another book. He then fished in his pocket and drew out a key. With quick, surgically precise hands, Rocky unlocked the box and opened its creaky lid. Then, moving his hands much more slowly, he withdrew a book from the box and smiled. It wasn't an evil smile, but somehow it seemed less than happy, more relieved, maybe, than joyful.

The book was old and worn, smaller than the huge journals that weighed down the bookshelves. With its ornate cover it gave the impression of royal significance, and Rocky's reverent handling proved its worth. He put it carefully back in the box before placing the whole package in his trench coat pocket. Then Rocky did something that struck Walter as really weird. He pulled out a pocketknife and used the blade to pry at the side of the bookshelf. The panel came off rather easily, exposing a narrow chamber inside, maybe four inches deep. Walter couldn't see what was in the chamber until Rocky turned to the side and held a long metal object out in the open to admire.

It's a sword, or at least a sword holder. What's it called? Oh, yeah, a scabbard.

Walter thought he heard a stifled gasp from Mr. Hamilton, but Rocky apparently didn't hear it. He delicately grasped the end of the scabbard and slowly pulled out a shiny, silver blade. This time his smile revealed true joy. How could he help but admire this beautiful shimmering weapon, etched with all those strange markings? After a few seconds, he returned the sword to its scabbard and put it under his coat, hurriedly fastening the buttons in front to secure his load. He reached into his pocket and pulled out a cell phone. He punched two numbers—a speed dial, Walter guessed.

Rocky waited and then patted his coat with his hand, looking very pleased with himself. "I have the sword. The host will soon triumph."

The slayer moved on, and the sound of his feet scattering the leaves disappeared in the distance. Bonnie was pretty sure he hadn't seen her. His departure didn't appear to be a ruse to bring her out of hiding. She decided that going in the same direction the slayer went might be dangerous, but since he was heading for the road, she had to follow anyway. What other hope did she have?

Now all she had to do was get down. In theory, going down should be easier than getting up, but she knew it wouldn't be. Fear had spurred her upward leap, and besides that, she had probably used her last ounce of energy. Climbing down would be impossible. One limb hung directly beneath the one she was on, but nothing else between her and the rest of the twenty-foot drop gave her any hope of descending in steps. Maybe she could just spread her wings and try to float down and hope for the best.

She tried, but the results proved painful. She hit the ground, chest first, with a hard thump, and if not for the leaves, she might have broken a rib. As it was, she lost her breath, banged her knee again, and took another mouthful of leaves. She coughed and gasped, fighting to catch her breath, pushing the ground with her arms to make room to breathe. She tried to gulp precious air, but her muscles clenched again before enough came in. She coughed the shallow breath out and tried again, another gasp accompanied by the grinding sound of her throat locking closed. She felt light-headed and woozy. Would she faint? Finally, after her third try, the air flowed more freely, and a rush of blood charged into her head.

She pushed back to a sitting position and breathed gratefully. But instead of sighing in relief she simply cried, and cried hard. She sniffed and tried to hold it back, but it was no use. She erupted into a pitiful sob. A powerful slayer was chasing her, she was seriously wounded, her friends were surely dead, and worst of all, she was alone, alone and far from a home that didn't even care.

CHAPTER 13

Shelter

Bonnie tried to stifle her sobs. Any sound might bring the slayer back. She sat motionless in a relatively open spot under the tree canopy. With the sun setting, only a few beams of light penetrated the woody skeleton above. Bonnie sniffed one last time and scanned the darkening trees around her. With various sized trunks sprouting at different elevations on the slope, they looked like huge soldiers struggling to scale the mountain. All she could see were their hardened legs, skinny hairy ones, smooth muscular ones, all stretching skyward toward the invisible bodies they carried. Were they soldiers announcing freedom to the land, or were they cruel conquerors threatening an invasion? They were dropping multicolored leaflets, floating, misshapen papers that spun and weaved their way to the ground, wasted and tromped upon by the advancing army. The leaflets whispered their message as they blew into one another and against the marching legs, making a musical rustle in the breeze.

With the slayer nowhere in sight, Bonnie closed her eyes and listened to the theme, caught in a moment of bliss. For an instant she didn't care where she was, oblivious to the pain, awash in a daydream about flying above it all, above every care in the world. The blowing leaves sang a hypnotic hymn with mournful arias and tinkling bells. But did she hear something else? Yes! A loud snap out in the brush! She shook herself out of her trance, struggled to her feet, and limped toward a dense group of trees. Her knee buckled, but she stayed up. Her weak wings flapped just enough to hold her weight, but her stumbling, sliding feet managed only a few paces in the slippery leaves. Between her own gasping breaths she heard rustling footsteps, louder and louder. She could never get away. Even if she made it to the trees, the slayer would still catch her.

A hand clamped around her mouth, and she tumbled forward. She threw her arms out, but stronger arms held her fast. Lying on her stomach, she kicked backward, but her foot struck only air. Then she heard his voice.

"Bonnie! Settle down or the slayer will find us!"

She spun her head as far back as she could. "Billy! It's you! Thank God!" She pulled free and sat up, throwing her arms around his neck.

Billy pushed her away and whispered, his voice hoarse in the cold wind. "No time. We have to hide. The slayer's coming this way." He lifted Bonnie to her feet and pulled her arm around his back. With his hand gripping her shoulder they trudged across the dim mountainside, wading and kicking through ankle-deep leaves. He helped her over a rise, then downslope, crossing flat rocks to hide their path, and they hid behind a huge stump that stood in the midst of a hedge of short evergreen trees. The lush, dark foliage promised a much better hideout than anywhere else she had seen, but would it be dense enough to hide them from the slayer's evil eyes?

"I saw the slayer down the slope," Billy said, pointing over the rise, "so I followed him. Then I heard you crying. He heard you, too, and started this way, but I got here before he did. He's got that limp, you know."

"What—" Bonnie started, but Billy shushed her.

"Let's watch and listen," he said in his softest whisper.

Bonnie quieted herself, though she kept trembling, and every few seconds her whole body heaved; her sobs were trying to come back. But what could she do? She was scared. A madman lurked only seconds away. Would he find them? And if he did find them, what would he do? *Oh God, please, please, don't let him find us! Please keep me calm!*

Bonnie felt Billy's arm fall gently around her shoulders and then his tight, encouraging squeeze. The pain it brought to her wounds pierced like a hundred tiny knives, but the warm reassurance was worth it. Her spasms stopped, and the two waited quietly for the inevitable appearance of the slayer. They knew he was close; the sound of a ringing cell phone announced his arrival. They both leaned forward to concentrate, trying to listen in on his side of the conversation. At first they could only see him nodding with the phone to his ear, but as he drew closer, they could hear his gruff tones.

"Good. You found the sword . . . Yes, I'm on the trail of the witch. I'm sure I heard her. She's wounded and crying somewhere around here. . . . Yes, keep to the schedule, but make sure you bring the papers and the badges. And bring a syringe and a vial. I'm sure I'll be able to get some blood yet. Did you get all that?"

The slayer stopped suddenly and looked down at the leaves. He turned his head to the right and then to the left, obviously trying to follow a trail. He finally made up his mind, and with his head still down he walked slowly, raising his feet high to keep from making noise. But his efforts didn't matter. Bonnie could see which way he was heading, straight toward their hiding place!

Walter and Mr. Hamilton listened, still hiding in the closet. Since they had huddled in a kneeling position between a bookshelf and the back corner of the closet, the tight squeeze was making them uncomfortable. Walter's left knee cried out for a stretch, and his thigh cramped. Why wouldn't the man in the trench coat just leave so they could get out of there?

The man Walter had dubbed "Rocky" spoke loudly into the cell phone, as though he had a weak connection. "Think you can find the girl? . . . If anyone can find her, it's you, Sir Devin. What dragon has ever escaped your grasp? Shall I still pick up the others before I come to look for you on thirty-three? . . . Yes, I got it. Every word, sir, every word."

Rocky slid the phone back into his coat pocket, turned off the closet light, and then doused the office light before closing the door softly behind him. After waiting a few seconds to make sure the mysterious man was gone, Mr. Hamilton jumped up and grabbed Walter's arm. "Come, Walter. We must hurry."

The two skulked out of the office, guided by Mr. Hamilton's flashlight. Walter knew better than to ask questions now. Besides, his throat felt so tight he would probably squeak. And what made his back tingle like that? Was it excitement or fear? Danger brought a buzzing thrill, but it could also bring a painful end, sort of like jumping from the top of a building. The feeling of flying through the air was awesome, but the splat on the ground kept a guy from taking the leap.

When they reached the exit, Mr. Hamilton switched off the flashlight and cracked the door open just enough to peek out.

Walter whispered. "Do you see anyone?"

The teacher kept his focus on the scene outside. "A car is just now leaving the parking lot. I wonder if the driver noticed mine parked in the teachers' lot."

Mr. Hamilton pushed the door fully open. "Come. The man is gone." After emerging into the cold evening air, he turned to Walter, his eyes gleaming. "At least we know to drive on highway thirty-three. When my call comes in, we'll have a better idea of where to go. We have to find them before Whittier and this man do. Are you with me?"

Walter spread out his hands. "I don't get it. What was that about dragons, and why do we have to get there before they do?"

Mr. Hamilton bent over to speak to Walter face-to-face. "It's clear that Dr. Whittier is mad. He fancies himself to be the real Sir Devin, and he still thinks he's chasing dragons. Remember, he mentioned 'the girl.' Do you know about whom he may have been speaking?"

Walter felt that lump in his throat again. "Bonnie?"

Mr. Hamilton slapped himself on the forehead and leaned back. "Of course! Why didn't I think of it? Whittier asked me about Miss Silver. He somehow thinks of her as the fair maiden whom he must rescue from the Bannister family. Because of Arthur's refusal to allow Devin to go out on his insane dragon missions, the king's descendants, the Bannisters, symbolize the dragons for him! I know it sounds totally mad, but don't you see?"

Walter watched the teacher blankly. "Uh, if you say so, Mr. Hamilton." He read the earnestness in the aged man's face and shrugged his shoulders. "Okay. I'll go with you. But can I stop by my house first?"

Mr. Hamilton stepped quickly toward the parking lot, and Walter followed, nearly running to keep pace with the spry gentleman. "Of course, of course," he said, waving his hand while he walked. "We shall be in a great hurry, but I should like to see your father again. We shall both explain the situation to your parents. I'm confident they'll still allow you to accompany me."

Walter caught up to the teacher's side and looked up at him hopefully. "But leave out the dragon part, okay?"

Mr. Hamilton stopped suddenly and stared at Walter, fumbling nervously with his keys. "Oh . . . very well . . . As you wish, Mr. Foley."

The slayer stood atop the small rise on the slope and scanned the mountainside. Bonnie tried to follow his gaze, looking back at him every couple of seconds to see where he might go next. The dense patch of trees they hid in stretched out in a tapered hedge for at least a few hundred feet, following a narrow footpath along the mountain's face as though the hedge were trying to wrap the whole mountain in a leafy garland. How could the slayer possibly search through all of those trees?

The slayer turned to stare directly into their hiding place, his unearthly eyes seemingly piercing the dense growth. He bent his head forward and squinted, keeping his gaze pinned on their refuge. *He's staring right at me! He's going to find us! Dear God, please help us!*

The slayer raised his head again, and a long stream of white vapor gave away his sigh of frustration. He looked at the leafy floor and kicked up a few leaves before turning to march downslope. When he finally disappeared over a ridge, Billy turned to Bonnie and whispered, "He's out of sight. I saw which way he went, but if we don't keep up, we'll never find our way to the road. I have a map I drew, but it won't be any good when it gets dark, so it'll be better if we can just follow him from a distance."

Still throbbing all over, Bonnie reached for Billy's hand, and he helped her to her feet. She held onto their interlocking grip and caressed his fingers while keeping her voice low. "Your hands! They're ice cold!"

Billy pulled away and rubbed his hands together briskly. "Yeah. It hurts too much to blow on them while I'm running. I can't be careful enough."

"And I lost your sweater on the way down. I only have a sweatshirt, but it's warmer than what you've got on."

Billy extended his hand. "C'mon. Let's get going again, and we'll both stay warm."

Bonnie took his hand and leaped forward on her left foot, but she hesitated when her right knee refused to keep pace. She reached down and rubbed both hands on the aching joint.

Billy spun around. "Can you walk at all?"

She looked up while still rubbing. "Walk? Maybe. Run? I don't think so. Fly? Uh-uh." She flapped her wings, her grimace giving away her agony, and she swallowed a yelp of pain. "I—I guess you'll have to go without me."

Billy shook his head fiercely. "No way! I already left my mother behind, and she's hurt. I'm not about to leave you behind, too." He pointed down the slope and looked back at Bonnie. "I don't think we have much farther to go, so we'll just—"

Bonnie stood straight up. "Your mother!" she cried, embarrassed at her forgetfulness. "I'm so sorry. I didn't ask you what happened."

Billy sighed and nodded slowly. "Yeah, the slayer's got us both spooked. Mom and I jumped with a parachute, and she hurt her ankle. Dad stayed in the plane, and it crashed somewhere."

Bonnie threw her hands over her mouth and gasped. "Oh, Billy! I'm so sorry!"

Billy nodded again and cast his gaze downward. "I know it sounds weird, but Mom's sure he's alive. It can't be too much farther to the highway. That's probably where the slayer's going, so we need to get help to find the plane before he does."

Bonnie took Billy's hand again, but this time she pulled it around her back just under her wings. She wrapped her arm around his shoulders to prop herself up, keeping as much weight as possible off her sore knee. She looked into his eyes, determined to show courage. "I'll do the best I can."

For the next half hour or so, the two worked their way down the slippery, leaf-covered slopes, slowly, painfully, and Bonnie was careful to keep from crying out. She knew Billy would slow down even more if she were to give even a hint of the torture she was feeling. Whenever she thought she couldn't go another inch, Billy's strong arm pulled her up and forward once again, giving her the courage she needed to go just a few more steps. His only words were spoken to motivate her, to give her strength: "C'mon. We can do it," or "Probably just one more rise. It'll be downhill the rest of the way." His face was like flint, but dripping sweat gave away how hard he was working. How could he do it? Bonnie didn't want to wimp out on him, but she feared that any minute the pain would overcome her will to go on.

Walter, we just passed county road ten on the left. How much farther is it to Alpena?"

Walter pulled the road map close to his face. The spotlight from the overhead pilot lamp gave too little light to make much difference. He had given up on the flashlight a while back; its batteries died much more quickly than their advertisements promised.

A growing darkness covered the land, and out in this mountain wilderness, there were no streetlights to break the black monotony. "I think it's a couple of miles," he finally decided. "It's too dark to be sure."

Mr. Hamilton tried to glance over at the map. "They said they would have a cruiser at that intersection, so I assume there will be flashing lights to signal where it is."

Walter clutched the armrest tightly as Mr. Hamilton sped up. He had already been going fast on the curvy mountain road, but on this straightaway he had to be doing ninety!

"Lives may be at stake," the teacher mumbled nervously. "Mustn't worry about a speeding ticket now."

Within a minute or two Walter bent forward, pointing. "Lights! I see flashing lights!"

"Indeed! It won't be long now."

After leaving the main highway, Mr. Hamilton received instructions from the policeman and drove north on county road twelve for several miles. It was a dark, narrow strip with hairpin turns, plunging dips, and breathtaking rises—a trackless roller coaster through an ink-black forest. Finally, Mr. Hamilton slowed down and made a sharp left onto a forest road, marked with a sign calling it number 162. Then, just a few hundred feet up the road, he turned left into a parking area next to a foot trail that led into the wilderness. He and Walter got out, fastened their coats, and looked around for someone in charge.

Several men ran here and there, putting up and testing light standards near the trailhead, and a couple of the big lamps flooded the area with light. An assortment of sport utility vehicles and pickup trucks had lined up perpendicular to the road, and one truck bed held a big steel cage with two baying dogs scratching to get into the action. Their barking was drowned out by the roaring of a huge generator, which sat right next to where Mr. Hamilton had parked.

Walter pulled up his hood and then pressed his gloved hands against his ears. He followed Mr. Hamilton toward a uniformed man standing by a state patrol car about fifty feet away. The teacher waited for the policeman to finish his radio conversation before introducing himself.

"Good evening. My name is Charles Hamilton. My young friend, Walter Foley, and I are here to join the volunteer search team. His father, Carl Foley, will also be joining us in the morning if the search is still underway."

The patrolman pointed in the direction of the trucks behind him. "Look for a red-headed guy with a full beard. That's Scott. He's organizing the next group to go out."

Mr. Hamilton strode on, and Walter followed, bundling his coat even closer to his body. The breeze was picking up, a much colder, more biting wind than back at Castlewood.

When they found Scott, he welcomed them with hearty handshakes. A thick, red beard masked his square jaw, and a checkered flannel shirt covered his stocky arms and spilled over the zipper of his thick vest, making him look like the stereotypical lumberjack. He had a deep voice, but it didn't bellow like Walter expected. He spoke to Mr. Hamilton in the manner of a college professor, with no trace of any of the local accents.

"A low pressure area is riding northeast on the cold front," Scott explained, "so we have to get out there before the precipitation begins. Air support is at a minimum, and locals are still arriving." He pointed across the access road. "One group will go east across Glady Fork toward Panther Camp Ridge and Sully; the other group will go west on the footpath toward Shavers Mountain. We'll have one chopper on each side with searchlights. I don't know how long they'll be able to stay up with all the crosswinds at mid-levels, so we have to get moving."

The two adults discussed their options while Walter looked out over the barely visible mountaintops. Was his friend out there somewhere? He pulled his coat closer again and pressed his hands tightly against his belly. The worries of the night and the smell of the diesel generator worked together to stir his stomach into an evil, boiling swill pot. His anxiety mounted as he scanned the skyline, dark clouds announcing the end of twilight as they shrouded the tallest peaks. Would they be able to find Billy up there? He watched a helicopter guiding a beam of light through a driving wave of low clouds. What hope did that overgrown flashlight have of finding anything in such a big place? Not much, he guessed, but if anyone could find his way out of those woods, Billy could . . . he hoped.

Walter heard Scott mention the huge number of square miles in the search area he called the Otter Creek Wilderness. A wilderness? The lump in his throat swelled to the size of a goose egg.

Men and women walked around him with hurried steps and glum faces. Did they know something dangerous about this area? Did they have any hope? Walter looked up again and tried to choke back the tears. "God," he whispered, "please help Billy get home."

I'm so sorry, Billy!" Bonnie looked up from her seated position, rubbing her knee again. She did everything she could to keep from crying, but the pain was too much. Her tears flowed freely, though she kept the heaving sobs in check.

"It's all right, Bonnie. I need to rest, too, but we'd better move to a safer place." Billy helped her up, and, almost fully supporting her, headed across a leaf-filled channel to a large tree with smooth, white bark. The two sat at its base and leaned back against its massive trunk. Bonnie scrunched up her wings to sit close to Billy; she knew they had to huddle to stay warm.

Billy stroked his arms, massaging friction heat into his frigid limbs. "It's really getting cold. My sweat's drying up, and I'm getting numb." He blew on his cracking hands and rubbed them together. His frequent attempts at keeping them warm with his superheated breath had taken their toll on his skin.

"Then we can't stay in one place long or you'll freeze. I'd give you my sweatshirt if I could, but it's all I have."

Billy tightened his lips and stopped rubbing. "No, I'm okay. We'll stay. You have to rest." He got up and began sweeping leaves toward the trunk with both feet. After just a few minutes, he had pushed enough together to make a chest-high nest around Bonnie. He sat next to her again and used his hands to gather the leaves toward his own body, enough to cover up to his elbows.

Their leaf blanket helped, but Bonnie noted the goose bumps on Billy's bare lower arms, and she recognized his chivalry. He had been taught by a true dragon. "The leaves are great, Billy," she said, bending at the waist. "But we're still cold at the top. Lean forward for a second."

Billy seemed taken aback for a brief moment, but he obeyed. When they had bent forward enough to make a gap between them and the tree, Bonnie extended her wings fully. "Now, please slide closer to me," she said gently.

Again, Billy did as she asked, sliding up to her, hip to hip. "I'll bet I stink by now," he warned.

"No worse than I do." Bonnie then wrapped her wings around their upper bodies. "Pull your arms in to your sides so I can close the gaps." Billy complied, and Bonnie made a shell with her wings so that only their two heads poked out through the top. With leaves covering their lower portions, the wind had no way to enter their makeshift shelter.

"Warmer?" she asked.

"Definitely!" Billy looked around at their leather-like blanket. "It's amazing how you can bend your wings in all the right places to do that."

Bonnie laughed. "I've had a lot of practice. On some nights I fly up to the top of Mount Hardin and look at the stars. The peak is usually above the low clouds, and it can get real cold up there, so I just make a cocoon and I'm fine. My wings don't get cold, so it works out great."

"You just look at the stars? Doesn't that get boring after a while?"

Bonnie stared up into the starless sky for a moment. "Well . . . I pray quite a bit. And I think about things. You know, what I'd like to do, where I'd like to go."

Billy turned his head, and their eyes met within inches of each other. The darkness now was almost complete, and only the slightest glow from the moon-painted clouds allowed Bonnie to see Billy's face. It was tired, but warm sincerity poured forth. "What would you like to do, Bonnie?" he asked. "Where do you want to go?"

Bonnie looked ahead and sighed. "What I'd really like . . ." Her voice trailed off into a trembling whisper. "I'd really like to have my mother back." She remained quiet for several seconds. Then she sniffed, and through a tortured, cracking voice, she went on. "I know you'll try to understand, and maybe you will understand now that your father's missing, but it's real hard to talk about." She stopped again.

"Take your time," Billy said softly.

Bonnie nodded thankfully and went on, still in a choking voice.

"I watched my mother die. I didn't see how it happened, but when I got to her, she had a huge gash in her stomach. It was awful. She was barely alive, lying there on the living room floor, and she told me to run, to get to the state agency as fast as I could, just like we had planned. I knew what to do, but I didn't want to leave. I held her hand for a few seconds, and then I heard a noise, like heavy footsteps. Her eyes got real big, and she said, 'Run! Don't look back! Just run!' Then her eyes closed and she stopped breathing. I didn't dare scream or cry. I just ran out the back door and all the way into town."

"To go into foster care?"

Bonnie sniffed again and gathered herself together before continuing. "Yes. I knew who to ask for, and all the paperwork was already done. They had a new last name for me and a place to go. And Mom had already arranged for me to get transferred to Castlewood, because she knew that's where your father lived.

She even had a train ticket for me. The only problem was that she didn't tell me exactly where you live. I'm not sure if she knew that herself. And she never even told me your father's human name. I suppose she was going to contact him if things got too dangerous. Mom never finished her plans, but obviously she knew all this could happen."

"Because the slayers were after her?"

Bonnie tightened her lips and nodded.

"And you've been looking for my dad ever since?"

She nodded again, her eyes clenched shut to keep in the tears.

Both stopped talking for a minute or so, and Billy let out a sympathetic sigh. "So . . . I guess you really miss your mom, huh? I guess you want a new home? Some real parents?"

She nodded her head once more, her eyes still closed. She turned to him and felt the warmth of his breath caressing her cold nose, but when she opened her eyes, she couldn't see him at all. The darkness had enveloped them. "That's the part I hope you never have to go through," she went on. "Can you imagine going from one home to another, having a new set of brothers and sisters every couple of weeks? Nobody wants me, because I'm so weird." Her voice sputtered and cracked more and more as she spoke. "Sometimes I wake up and I'm afraid to open my eyes. I wait until I can picture where I am, and sometimes I can't remember. Then, I hear strange voices in the hall, and I don't even know who they belong to."

Her voice grew louder, and sobs punctuated her sentences. "Sometimes I'm not even alone in bed. Can you imagine trying to keep my secret when I have to sleep with a little sister? Can you imagine trying to explain to new parents why I can't go to the doctor, why I always wear a backpack, why I never even let them hug me?" For a moment Bonnie couldn't go on. Her voice was overcome by her turmoil, and she tried one more time, her words interrupted by heaving sobs. "And sometimes . . . when I think of my mother . . . and how she would hug me—" Bonnie broke down, her head bobbing pitifully as she wept.

Billy put both of his arms around her. The two leaned their heads together, and Billy sniffed away his own tears, hugging her close and rocking her gently. "Forever and ever, Bonnie," he said tenderly, "I will always be your friend."

The two stayed quiet for several minutes, and Bonnie's crying subsided. Although her face was now moist with tears, she noticed a new wet sensation on her head. "Is it raining?"

Billy shook his head to fling off the wetness. "No. It's snow. At least we'll have clean water to drink if we need it. Those mountain streams are nice and cold, but that last one was pretty muddy."

Bonnie put her head down toward her chest. "Lean your head forward as much as you can."

Billy complied, and part of Bonnie's wings moved to cover their heads. "Amazing!" was all he could say.

"Now, if you can stand the smell, try to get some rest."

"I guess there's no use trying to find the road in the dark."

Bonnie yawned. "Nope. Not a chance."

"I suppose my mom's huddled in a big pile of leaves or something."

"Yep. She's a smart one." Bonnie yawned again, and in a few seconds she was sound asleep.

As dawn broke, a group of weary searchers stepped out of a Ford Expedition and into a field of white powder. Walter, though bleary-eyed, couldn't help but enjoy the sight. "How much snow do you think we got, Mr. Hamilton?"

The teacher kicked the snow with his boot. To Walter he looked a lot different with his wild gray hair stuffed under his royal blue ski cap. Only a few wispy locks poked through alongside his ear lobes. "Oh, I would estimate about fifteen centimeters."

"Centimeters? I guess that's about . . . uh—"

"About six inches, Walter." Mr. Hamilton patted him on the back. "I'm sure you're tired. We had only three hours of sleep in that seedy motel, but we must get to work."

Walter gazed into the awakening skyline. "Yeah. Billy's still up there somewhere."

The teacher tilted his head to the side. "I hear the helicopter. Perhaps daylight brings us good news." They watched the metal bird buzz away over the ridge as they headed for the search team's morning rendezvous.

Walter and Mr. Hamilton followed the directions of their group leader and formed a sweep line, each person staying within sight distance of the next, and they walked into the mountains. When they had moved well into the trees, they kept contact with each other through various calls and shouts, slowing their progress as they scaled the mountain. Their group leader carried a walkie-talkie and kept barking out updates that had been relayed from the helicopter. Finally, after an hour or so, he let out a whoop. "They found the plane! They found the plane!"

Everyone else in the party followed the sound of the shouting, and they gathered to listen.

"It's on Shavers Mountain, south of us. Let's get back to the base, and get exact coordinates. I'm sure we'll be concentrating the search in that area."

With renewed enthusiasm the search team hurried down the mountainside and into the valley. When they arrived at base camp, Walter and Mr. Hamilton found the police officer they had met the night before. He was in heated debate with another man who apparently was the leader of a trio that waited alongside.

"Look, I don't know who you are," the patrolman snapped. "What makes you think you can come down here and take over something you know nothing about?"

The other man flashed a badge in a leather case. "I'm not taking over; I'm just telling you to report all findings to me. If you don't, I will take over."

The patrolman left in a huff, and the man with the badge looked back at his three friends and laughed. "They're just a bunch of local yokels! Come on. Let's get to the crash scene."

Walter tugged on his teacher's coat and whispered. "Mr. Hamilton. Look at that guy. Is that—"?

Mr. Hamilton pulled Walter to the side. "Don't show your face. Yes, it does look like Whittier, or whatever he's calling himself, and he's walking with a limp." He lowered his voice to a whisper. "I suggest that we call him Devin, at least for now, to prevent confusion. Let's talk to the patrolman and see what's going on."

The two high-stepped through the snow-covered grass to the patrolman's car. They found the officer sitting behind the steering wheel, talking on the radio. "Yes, Special Agent Albert Devin. He says he's FBI." The officer twisted his neck to see who had approached. "Yes?"

Mr. Hamilton cleared his throat and tried to sound confident. "We know who the agent is. He is not who he claims to be."

The patrolman squinted, a curtain of doubt crossing his face. "Who is he, then?"

Mr. Hamilton raised his eyebrows with a knowing sort of air. "Have you heard the name, 'Whittier,' in your investigation?"

"Of course. The missing principal, the guy who tried to kill the girl back in Castlewood."

Walter tugged on Mr. Hamilton's coat again.

The teacher waved him off. "Just a moment, Mr. Foley."

Mr. Hamilton went on. "Albert Devin *is* Dr. Edward Whittier."

The patrolman's eyes shot wide open. "What?"

Walter tried to speak up. "Mr. Hamilton?"

"Just a moment, Mr. Foley."

The officer got out of the car and glanced briefly over at the supposed FBI agent. "And he's the one who tried to kill the mystery girl?"

Mr. Hamilton crossed his arms and nodded. "The very same."

The squad car radio crackled back to life, and the patrolman listened to the static-filled transmission. Walter couldn't decipher the words, but when the patrolman came out again, the look on his face told him something was wrong. His shoulders had slumped, and his eyebrows bent down toward his nose. "Devin checks out. I'm supposed to do whatever he says."

Mr. Hamilton jerked his head fully upright. "What? Impossible!"

"Mr. Hamilton?"

The teacher turned sharply to Walter. "Yes, Mr. Foley! What is it?"

"The plane. Were there survivors?"

Mr. Hamilton stared at Walter for a second and then slapped himself on the forehead. "Yes, of course!" He turned back toward the patrol car. "Officer, what of the crash site? What was found?"

The patrolman slammed the car door shut and gazed up toward the hills. "Good news and bad news I suppose. The good news is that the plane didn't explode, and there were no bodies around anywhere." He then looked back at Mr. Hamilton. "The bad news is that they found a lot of blood and signs of something being dragged away. There are bears in the area, you know."

Walter gulped. "Bears?"

The patrolman continued. "But the snow's making the search for footprints very difficult. Aviation is consulting by phone, and they said the plane could have had parachutes. Maybe the passengers jumped."

"You mentioned the mystery girl," Mr. Hamilton said. "Her name is Bonnie Silver, and we have reason to believe she was on the plane."

"Bonnie Silver?" He rolled his eyes upward in thought. "I'll call that in and see what Missing Persons says." He opened the car door again and slid into the seat. "We did assume that the mystery girl was on the plane." He looked back at Mr. Hamilton. "And you're sure that Agent Devin couldn't be FBI?"

He sighed. "I'm not sure what to think anymore." He then pointed discreetly toward Agent Devin. "But that man is the Castlewood Middle School principal who calls himself Whittier. There's no doubt about that. I'm a teacher there, and I know him personally."

The patrolman nodded and grabbed the radio. "I'll try to get a photo faxed over here. If that really is Whittier, we'll find a way to keep him off that mountain."

Walter stepped forward to address the officer. "If they jumped, any idea where?"

"They're mapping the possibilities now. Get back with your search unit and you'll find out."

Walter took another step closer to the open car door and bent over to look the patrolman in the eye. "I'm sure Bonnie was on the plane. I bet it'll help if everyone's calling out her name, just in case."

The patrolman gripped Walter's shoulder. "You can count on it, son."

Walter and Mr. Hamilton reunited with their team, which had been joined by new search groups. The number of people was growing dramatically as the morning progressed. Walter guessed that the locals had already heard about the finding of the plane. A lot of people probably listened to police scanners or something, and now with the news reporters and their TV cameras showing up, the whole world would soon know about it.

The search leader spread a map out over a car hood and began explaining the color-coded highlights painted on it. "The red area is the most likely jump zone," he said, pointing at the map. "We'll start there and work our way back to the orange zone and then to the yellow."

Walter tuned out the rest of the explanation while trying to move closer to Devin. Keeping his head turned so the principal wouldn't recognize him, he tried to listen in on what he was saying to his cronies. His usual gruff voice was unmistakable.

". . . with the team closest to the crash site. If you find Clefspeare, radio me. I have a good idea where the witch is, so I'm going after her."

Walter's eavesdropping was interrupted by the sounds of shouts from far away. "They found someone on the mountain!"

Cheers went up all around, and the buzz grew so intense Walter could no longer hear the announcer's voice. Walter stood on tiptoes and saw a big man raising his hands to quiet the swelling crowd, his panting breaths blowing clouds into the breeze.

"A woman," he said, still panting. "The chopper spotted a woman near the very top of the ridge, and they were able to pick her up a few minutes later. She's fine. Very cold, but she'll be fine."

"Who is it?" about a dozen voices shouted out. Several microphones pushed through the tight throng to catch the rescuer's answer.

"The pilot's wife. And, man, what a story she told! Anyway, a boy and girl are still out there somewhere, and the pilot went down with the plane. The boy's trying to find his way back, and some maniac named Whittier has the girl. Parachuted out of the plane with her in his arms. Whittier caused the crash and wants to kill the girl."

Walter looked for the patrolman to see his reaction, but he wasn't at his car. Then he looked back toward Devin, but he was gone, too. Walter's eyes darted in every direction, trying to find the principal while listening for more news.

"The woman refused medical help," the messenger continued. "They're taking her to the crash site to join the search parties."

There was no time to lose, but could Walter convince the patrolman that Devin had gone out to try to kill Bonnie? The police already knew that Whittier tried to kill her back at Castlewood, but would they believe this FBI agent was really a maniac who was now hunting for her again?

Wait! There he is! And he's alone.

Walter spotted Devin slowly easing away in a large, black pickup truck. Walter didn't have time to plan or go back to find Mr. Hamilton. He sprinted to the truck just as it turned out of the parking area and onto the field, and he leaped into the payload bed. He hoped Devin didn't feel the bounce he made. Maybe he would think it was just one of the many rough bumps from the trail's parking area. Walter slid toward the front of the bed and into a corner, out of the rearview mirror's line of sight.

So far, so good. He's still driving.

Walter rode out the bumps, struggling to maintain a hold on the metal frame. The truck must have been a four-wheel drive. It pulled through the snow without much trouble, but Devin ran it like a tank, ignoring run-off ditches and any other obstacle. It was full speed ahead, it seemed, and Walter felt every painful bounce.

After a few minutes, the truck started climbing, and when it would go no farther, slipping in the melting snow, the driver turned off the engine. Walter curled up in the corner and listened for the sound of the door closing. He then waited a minute or so before poking his head up to try to find Devin.

Walter spotted him trudging up the side of the mountain on a narrow, snow-covered foot trail, and he scrambled out of the truck to follow. Devin had a good lead, but that was okay.

Walter knew he could follow Devin's footprints, and he didn't want to alert him with the sound of crunching leaves that each of his own footsteps would bring as he pushed through the snow.

Walter dashed from tree to tree, hiding himself and then watching for a few seconds until Devin moved out of view behind a rock or over a rise. After stopping behind a massive oak in a dense part of the forest, Walter was unable to find him again. He rushed ahead, searching the snow for the principal's trail. At least eight lines of footprints scattered in every direction, and none looked any fresher than the others. Walter kicked at the snow and hundreds of glittering specks rained all around. He couldn't wait. He had to guess.

"Wake up, Bonnie. It's morning."

"Huh? What?" Bonnie yawned and turned toward the voice. "Oh. Good morning, Billy." It was still pretty dark under Bonnie's homemade canopy, but she could see Billy's face, tired and dirty, yet more rested than the night before. She smiled sweetly. "Are you ready to face the weather?"

"Yeah. I'm itching to find Mom and Dad."

Bonnie spread her wings out, opening the shell and exposing them to the glistening morning sun. Her eyes drank in the sparkling glitters on the blanket of snow. "It's a beautiful day!"

Billy got up and stretched his legs, kicking away the nest of leaves. "Beautiful, but still cold." He reached his hand down to help Bonnie up. "C'mon. We'd better get moving."

Bonnie took his hand and pulled, but her right knee gave way again. "Ouch!" She had to balance on her left leg and hold tightly to Billy's hand to keep from falling, and Billy lowered her to a sitting position. "My knee's stiff as a board. There's no way I can get down the mountain, especially in the snow."

Billy clenched one fist and let out a frustrated sigh while cocking his head upward. "Can you fly?"

"Good thought." She held out her hand. "Help me up again."

Billy pulled Bonnie to her feet, and, standing on one leg, she began flapping her wings. She grimaced as she flapped, and she started rising, an inch or two at first, then almost a foot, but she dropped back down to her good leg and reached out for Billy's hand again. He was quick to catch her.

"My left wing's a lot better, but it's still too weak. I think I could get off the ground, but it would be impossible to steer or stay up for more than a minute or so." Bonnie eased her right foot down and let go of Billy's hand. She was able to stand, but painfully.

Billy raised his hands to his hips and frowned. "Look at you. You can barely stand. I can't leave you here by yourself."

"Why not? I've got my wings. I'll stay warm enough until you come back with help."

"I don't know. I think—" Billy turned his head suddenly. "What was that?"

Bonnie craned her neck to listen. "It's an engine of some kind."

Billy ran to a fallen tree and stood on tiptoes on its horizontal trunk, trying to see over the treetops. "I think it's a helicopter! Maybe someone's looking for us!"

Bonnie turned her head one way and then the other. Because of her lame knee, she didn't dare try to turn around. "Which way is the sound coming from?"

Billy pointed toward a dense cluster of tall oaks. "Upslope." He jumped off his perch and helped Bonnie sit back down at the tree they had used for their overnight stay. "Okay. Wait here, and I'll try to find the helicopter." He stood and scanned the entire area. "There," he said, pointing to a tall, rotting tree about thirty feet away. "I'll use that old snag as a marker to find you again. I think it's tall enough to see from anywhere around here. If I don't come back pretty soon, do you think your wings are strong enough to get you up in a tree to try to flag down a helicopter?"

Bonnie sighed. "I'll just have to do what I have to do."

Billy walked backward a couple of steps, holding his hand out as if he were telling a small child to stay. "Okay. I'll be back. I promise." He hustled away, slipping against the snowy incline. Within seconds he disappeared into the forest.

Bonnie folded her knees up to her chest and listened for a moment to the faint chopping sound of the distant helicopter. *Yes, it's definitely quite a bit higher up the mountain, but Billy's bound to find it.*

Although the snow had stopped falling, the fresh breeze from the north persisted. Bonnie remade her shell and closed herself in again, listening intently for a while but then wandering off in her thoughts. The searing pain still burned through her knee, but warm comfort flowed gently into her thoughts. She finally had a good friend she could count on, someone who really cared and could identify with what she was going through. Yes, he was a guy, but she didn't feel like he was a boyfriend. He was what she imagined a brother would be. No, not like the mean brothers that a lot of the girls talked about;

he was a real brother who cared. She knew he would do anything to help her.

With those thoughts waltzing through her mind, she dozed for a minute or two before being aroused by the sound of footsteps. *Billy's back!*

She unwrapped her shell and opened her eyes. A large, bony hand slapped tightly over her mouth, and strong arms clasped against hers, wrapping her up like a crushing straightjacket. She grunted and tried to struggle, but it only brought a tighter hold and a brutal threat.

"Quiet, Demon Witch! One scream and you're dead!"

CHAPTER 14

In the Hands of the Slayer

Devin slowly relaxed his grip on Bonnie, making shushing sounds as he let go. She stared at him with firm brow and lips, still seated with her knees drawn up. He unfastened his heavy coat and drew out a long, shining sword.

"And what do you plan to do with that sword?" Bonnie asked, trying to sound stern. She didn't want to give away any hint of fear.

"For now, just get some of your hair." He pulled several strands of Bonnie's blonde-streaked locks, stretched them out, and with a deft stroke sliced them off right at her scalp and tucked them into a pale blue envelope. "I pulled out your hair once before, but I didn't get to keep it."

Bonnie scowled at him. "What kind of weirdo are you, anyway? You've been trying to kill me; now you just want my hair?"

The slayer slipped the envelope into his coat pocket and pulled out a glass test tube and a hypodermic needle. "Your hair, and some blood."

Bonnie slid away on her backside, but when the slayer raised his sword again, she stopped. "Hair and blood?" She tried to appear confident. "I suppose you'll want my autograph next?"

His voice kept its nasty edge. "I'm not getting samples for my scrapbook, Witch. The good doctor needs your blood for his research." The slayer methodically went through the routine of drawing blood, sliding Bonnie's sleeve up her forearm and pressing the needle into the soft crook of flesh. She watched the tube slowly fill with blood, and the slayer's eyes seemed to sparkle with desire. "I see you've had blood drawn before," he said, pulling out the needle. He tucked the vial into a velvet-lined case before sliding it into an inner coat pocket. "Many times, perhaps?"

He was right. There had been many times, many blood-sucking needles. But that was a painful story she didn't want to dredge up. She just pulled her arm back and examined the mark. "What doctor are you talking about? What kind of research?"

"If Doc never told you, then I'm not going to, either. I will tell you that I need DNA markings so I can find any more dragon mongrels that might be out there. I've never had access to that kind of technology before I met Doc. Who knows how many mongrels may have slipped through my grasp over the years?"

Bonnie had no time to ponder the slayer's mysterious words since his next step would probably be to kill her, so she tried to stall, faking curiosity. "Mongrels? What do you mean by that?"

The slayer smiled, this time without his usual menacing sneer. He sat on his heels in the snow and held his sword in his lap. "A mongrel is a mix between two breeds, in your case, dragon and human."

Bonnie rubbed the wound on her arm. "I know you hate dragons, but why do you hate me? I'm not really a dragon, and neither is Mr. Bannister."

"No, you're not. Technically, you're both anthrozils, fully human and fully dragon. Clefspeare, or Bannister as you call him, was a real dragon who now happens to be in human form, but it's not so much his presence I seek to destroy; it's his potential."

"His potential?"

"Yes, to bring a fulfillment to the prophecy and thereby the restoration of the accursed dragon race. If I eliminate him and any dragon offspring, the prophecy cannot be fulfilled."

A tinny voice sounded from the slayer's coat. "Devin. Agent Devin, are you out there?"

The slayer pulled a walkie-talkie from his pocket and answered. "Devin here."

"This is Officer Caruthers. You asked for an update. They found the pilot. He's alive and he's with me at base camp. Do you want to talk to him?"

A big smile crossed Bonnie's face. *He's alive! Praise the Lord!*

The slayer glowered. "Yes. Hold him there. I'll be right down." He put the radio away and turned back to Bonnie. "Looks like I have more work to do."

Bonnie knew she had to keep stalling. Would Billy never show up? She put on an innocent expression and spoke in the most childlike voice she thought she could get away with. "But why do you hate the dragons so much, Dr. Whittier?"

He coughed and cleared his throat. "You might as well call me by my real name—Devin." His tone softened, and he didn't seem to be in any hurry. "Haven't you ever read the Bible?"

Bonnie drew in the snow with her finger, and she continued in her innocent voice. "Yes. I know it pretty well. We had lots of Bible stories in Sunday school." Her simple lines in the snow created a fire-breathing dragon.

Devin ignored Bonnie's markings; he seemed absorbed in his explanation. "Then you may remember in Genesis about the demons taking human women as wives and creating a super race called the Nephilim. God hated them because they were pure evil, and he destroyed the world with a flood."

Bonnie began drawing a boat in the snow. "Noah's flood? The one with the ark?"

"Exactly. But the spirits of these mongrel creatures survived and had to choose a body to inhabit when the flood subsided. As you know, the serpent is the manifestation of the devil on the earth, so these evil spirits chose the dragons and possessed them."

"So dragons weren't always evil?"

"No, but they became nothing but evil. They may not have taught you this in your little Sunday school class, but the Bible says that the dragon is king over all the sons of pride."

Bonnie jotted down "Job 41" next to the dragon while still gazing at the snow. "How do you know they're all evil? Maybe some dragons were possessed and some weren't."

The slayer finally noticed Bonnie's marks, and he wiped them away with a swipe of his hand, his hate-filled growl returning. "You think you're smart, don't you? Typical Demon Witch deception! You pretend to be young and innocent, but you're no better than the full-blooded dragons. They lie out of their very nature, and Clefspeare probably lied to you about everything, too."

Bonnie's ire shot into her eyes, and she shouted back. "He did not! He's not a liar like you!"

"Oh, really?" His voice changed to a mocking singsong. "He probably told you he was one of the good little dragons, didn't he?" He gripped the sword hilt tightly and reverted to his normal voice. "I'll bet he didn't tell you how he killed a merchant just because he had no gold to give him."

Bonnie felt the wind's cold chill and a shiver crawl across her arms. "Killed him for gold?"

"As if you didn't know! Dragons always lust after gold and jewels. They can't get enough of them, and they go insane when they can't satisfy their lust."

She stared at the slayer, her brow now creasing with more defiance. "I don't believe you."

"Then let me tell you a story, Witch. The merchant's name was Andrew, and Clefspeare knocked down a row of trees for him so he could build a wall. Andrew had no payment, so Clefspeare scorched him like a pile of old kindling, right in the village just outside Camelot."

Bonnie felt her breath catch, and her heart beat wildly. Could Clefspeare have done something like that? She knew her own mother, the great Hartanna, was good and noble, but she had heard stories of evil dragons, too. Didn't her mother have reservations about sending her to find Clefspeare? Could he possibly be one of the evil ones? It sounded impossible, but the slayer's presence seemed to bring into doubt everything she ever believed.

She tried to keep her boldness from melting away. "Camelot? Wasn't that way over a thousand years ago? How can you know what happened?"

"I have my ways." He stood and extended the sword with both arms. "You have no idea how high my power extends." He pointed the sword's tip toward the sky and then slowly lowered it toward the ground. "Or how deep my influence goes." As the slayer followed the sword's descent, he looked at his shirt and cursed. "The stone's underneath," he muttered as he pulled the candlestone out from beneath his shirt and let it dangle from its glittering chain. "Can't leave it hidden. If your boyfriend's still alive, he might show up."

The slayer's theatrical sword display was obviously more than a threat; it somehow generated real power. Devin looked younger now, stronger, and the sword glowed with a streaming halo. The brightening candlestone seemed to drain Bonnie's courage, absorbing strength from her muscles, even breath from her lungs. As she stared at its hypnotizing sparkle, she noticed a blemish on one facet, a dark red smear. Was it blood? Her blood?

She tightened her chin and clenched her fists, not wanting to reveal her weakness. Through half-closed eyes, she looked at the slayer with disdain. "Well, I must say you have a flair for the melodramatic, Devin, or whatever your real name is." She gestured toward the woods with a nod of her head. "But if Billy's hiding out there somewhere, he could blast you from behind a tree, and you'd be a smelly mound of soot before you could wave that flashy sword again."

Devin glanced around and listened. Bonnie thought she heard something. A shuffling sound? Was someone coming? She knew this might be her only chance. "Billy!" she screamed. "Help!"

The slayer clapped his hand over her mouth and nervously scanned the woods, whispering, "If you want your boyfriend to show up, keep screaming. You can die side by side." After a few seconds of silence, he uncovered her mouth, and Bonnie held her breath, paralyzed, yet shivering. He used the candlestone's chain to dangle the gem in front of Bonnie's eyes. "Bannister can't fight me. This stone will absorb his power, just as I'm sure you feel it draining your strength right now." Bonnie grimaced and turned her head, closing her eyes tightly. The stinging pain was too much to bear, like a million pricking needles slurping her life's blood.

The slayer stood up again. "You can't hide it, Demon Witch. You testify against yourself that you possess the spirit of evil. The virgin bride now meets her doom."

As he raised the sword, his coat sleeve slid on his arm to reveal the club-shaped mark on his skin, and his voice deepened into a growling rumble. "And since you think you know so much about the Bible, try this one, 'This sword is sharpened, and it is furbished, to give it into the hand of the slayer.' " With a maniacal grin, he pulled the sword back, ready to swing.

A loud cry of "No!" bellowed from a thicket, and a lightning stream of fire burst out of nowhere and encircled Devin's arm. The flames engulfed his coat, and he flung the sword to the ground.

Devin buried his arm in the snow and screamed. "Not again, you cursed pye-dog!"

Billy dashed out of the woods, snatched Bonnie by the hand, nearly lifting her off the ground, and half carried her down the slope. They alternately stumbled and got back up again, and between sliding and running, they scrambled away. But how long could they stay ahead?

Walter's ears perked up. That was Bonnie screaming! He sprinted across the snowy mountainside, found a trail of footprints, and followed them, running with all his might. With a burst of energy, he leaped over a boulder and landed with a sliding stop. He couldn't believe his eyes. He felt his heart skip two beats when he saw Billy's stream of fire blast Devin's arm. *Billy really does have dragon breath!* He then looked at Bonnie. *She has wings? She's the bat creature? Wow!*

Devin grabbed his sword and started after Billy and Bonnie. Walter snatched up the biggest, strongest limb he could handle and ran up behind the slayer. Devin stopped and glanced from side to side, apparently noticing the sound of footsteps coming from somewhere.

Walter pulled the limb back and smiled. "Good night, Sir Devin." He swung with all his might. Devin turned, and the limb smacked him square in the face, sending him sprawling to the ground. The wood in Walter's hand cracked with the force of the jolt, but he didn't wait to see how badly he had injured his foe. He rushed down the slope, trailing Billy and Bonnie, staying far enough behind to keep from being noticed. For now, it was better not to reveal that he had learned his friends' secrets.

Walter watched Billy and Bonnie, keeping close behind and jumping from tree to tree, as they followed the long trails of footprints and tire tracks. When they approached an open, snow-covered field, Billy and Bonnie stopped and cocked their heads as though they heard something. Bonnie grabbed the lower hem of her sweatshirt, and Walter heard Billy's voice protesting.

"Wait! Don't take it off! We'll just stuff your wings back inside."

"I don't have any choice. My wings won't stay hidden with the holes back there. I have to turn my sweatshirt all the way around. Just close your eyes for two seconds."

Walter turned his head, and after a short pause he heard Bonnie's voice.

"Okay, I'm covered. Just help me straighten it all out in the back."

Walter looked again, and Bonnie was clutching the sweatshirt in the front, keeping the holes tightly closed. When the two came in sight of the base camp, several members of the search team started a huge buzz and called out to them.

"Billy? Is that you? Bonnie?"

Billy shouted, "Yes!" and with one arm fully supporting Bonnie's weight from her left side, the two lumbered down the rest of the trail. Walter finally decided it was safe to show himself. He rushed up behind them and pushed his left shoulder under Bonnie's right arm, lifting to bear half the weight. Billy's look of surprise was followed by a broad grin. "Walter! Thanks, Buddy!"

Walter had a hard time deciding where to hold on. He could feel the base of Bonnie's wings, so he dodged them and slid his gloved left hand lower and around her waist, moving it under Billy's supporting arm. With his other hand, he draped Bonnie's right forearm over his shoulder and clutched her wrist.

At least a dozen men and women came out to meet the trio, and they offered to carry Bonnie the rest of the way.

"I've got her!" Billy assured them. He looked over at Walter hopefully. "You got her, Walter?"

"Absolutely!" he sang, smiling back at Billy.

Billy and Walter carried Bonnie down to a waiting ambulance and laid her faceup on a stretcher. An attendant covered her with several blankets and offered one to Billy. He gladly took it and wrapped himself in its warmth, and for the first time since the day before, he shivered, and shivered hard. The attendant distributed cups of hot cocoa, and Bonnie supported herself on an elbow to drink. Lying flat on her wings was obviously not the most comfortable position.

Billy smiled down at Bonnie, and after a warm, steamy sip, she smiled in return. People in the crowd shouted out dozens of questions, and a couple of microphones pushed toward Billy's face, but he didn't want to answer right away; he was shaking too hard. For right now, he just wanted to stay with Bonnie and make sure she was all right.

He looked around at the throng of people. "So, where's my dad?" His voice quivered with his body, and his mouth stung from the fire-breathing episode, so he tried to keep his talking to a minimum.

Several of the search team members stared at one another, and some shrugged their shoulders. Billy tilted his head, confused at the blank responses he was getting. "Bonnie said she heard on the radio that he was down here."

A patrolman stepped forward. "I can explain." He put a hand on Billy's shoulder. "I'm sorry, son. We received a faxed photo that proved Agent Devin is really Dr. Whittier, so we made up that story to lure him down from the mountain."

"Agent Devin? What are you talking about?" The horrible realization crashed onto Billy like an avalanche. "You mean he's not here? My dad hasn't been found yet?"

"No, son. But we're still looking for him. We found your mother. She's up there with the main search team. She's fine."

Billy drooped his head. He felt a cramp in his throat, and he swallowed hard and let out a long relieved sigh. "Thank God for that." He tried to compose himself and looked up again. "Can I go up there, too?"

The patrolman smiled. "Could we keep you down?"

Billy smiled back, feeling a surge of energy. "No way!" But he paused and turned toward Bonnie. He leaned over and whispered in her ear. "Can you keep them from examining you?"

She nodded. "I'll tell them it's just my knee. That hurts more than anything."

Walter piped up. "Go on, Billy. I'll keep an eye on Bonnie."

Billy beamed at his faithful buddy. "Thanks, Walter. I'm sure glad you came." The two embraced, patting each other with manly slaps on the back. "Watch out for Dr. Whittier. He's really out to get us."

Walter laughed. "Not any more, he's not."

"What do you mean?"

Walter posed as though he were ready to swing a baseball bat. "Remember how we used to have a contest to see how big a branch we could bust on a tree?"

"Yeah. I remember."

"I used Whittier's head for the tree." He swung his pretend bat as hard as he could. "Pow!" he yelled, dropping his "bat" and laughing again. "I think I won our contest."

"Wow! When did you do that? You didn't kill him, did you?"

Walter shrugged his shoulders. "I don't know if he's dead or not. I didn't stick around to find out. Could be, I guess. I really let him have it."

The patrolman reached for his handcuffs. "You assaulted an FBI agent?"

Walter lowered his chin beneath his coat collar and backed away. "But I saw him . . . uh . . . chasing someone with a sword. I thought he was after Billy, so I had to stop him."

The officer's grim face burst into a smile. "Just kidding, son. Can you lead us to where you dropped him?"

Walter let out a loud sigh. "I could find him, but I'm not leaving Bonnie's side."

A new voice entered the circle. "So there you are, Mr. Foley! Where have you been?"

Walter grinned and made a half swing with a new "bat." "I guess you could say that I've been out taking batting practice, Mr. Hamilton." Walter's eyes brightened when he saw another new face appear behind his teacher. "Dad! When did you get here? Have you heard all the news?"

"I got here a while ago, and the professor filled me in on everything. We were searching in the yellow zone and heard all the buzz on the radio and hurried back."

Mr. Hamilton surveyed the scene. "Mr. Bannister! Miss Silver! Welcome back!"

Billy swallowed a big gulp of cocoa and wiped his mouth. "Thanks, Mr. Hamilton." He nodded at Walter's father. "Hi, Mr. Foley!"

"Good to see you, Billy," he replied. "You and Bonnie have had quite a night! How did you stay warm?"

Billy glanced at Bonnie, smiled, and turned back to Mr. Foley. "We stayed on the move until pretty late, and then we found a sheltered spot to rest and gathered together a bunch of leaves."

Walter tugged on the teacher's coat sleeve. "Mr. Hamilton. Can you and Dad stay with Bonnie while I show the police where Devin is?"

"Yes! Of course! I overheard the part about the branch." He punched the air with his fist. "Great going, old chap!"

Billy laid his hand on Bonnie's shoulder. "You won't leave Bonnie's side while I'm gone?"

"Not even for a second!" Mr. Hamilton knelt down next to Bonnie and took her hand, clasping it tenderly. "I am yours, fair maiden, your knight in shining armor! My squire and I will protect you from every foul fiend."

Bonnie gulped hard to keep from laughing, and a radiant smile crossed her face. The patrolman laughed and raised the radio to his lips. "Sky One. This is Caruthers. Come in!"

"Sky One. Go ahead, Caruthers."

"Meet me at the base field. I have Billy Bannister. Repeat. I have Billy Bannister."

Caruthers turned back to Billy and put an arm around his shoulder. His voice cracked with emotion. "Let's go see your mom!"

Billy kicked a pile of snow, scattering it in every direction. He had kicked through a ton of snow already, and he had no idea what he was searching for any longer. The dogs hadn't been able to find any new trails, he and his mom had picked through the wreckage three or four times, and he had already stacked all the Bibles he could find and covered them with a tarp. He still held a pocket Bible in his hand. He didn't know why he was carrying it other than it just made him feel better.

He stared gloomily at the twisted metal that was once Merlin. Now he understood the reason for the airplane's name. Over a thousand years ago the real Merlin had taken away Clefspeare's ability to fly, but his passion to soar through the heavens and look down over his domain never disappeared. This trusty plane had given the skies back to him, at least in a way.

He looked over at his mother and mentally traced each worry line on her face. He missed her usual shining glow, the smile that burst forth every time her husband walked into the room. Billy caught a glimpse of the old radiance just a little while ago when he and his mom were reunited. Her smile was real, but not quite whole. She needed Dad.

Billy, of course, was exhausted, but he dared not mention it. At least he was warm. On the way to the helicopter a kindly older lady had given him a fresh set of clothes and a heavy coat. They were all a little too big, but they felt heavenly, especially the shoes, a dry pair of mid-top hiking boots that fit pretty well with thick wool socks underneath. After getting his bundle of clothes he saw the lady wheel a wagon toward Bonnie. He guessed she was in for the same treat. Since he still had a blanket draped around him at the time, he changed on the spot, anxious to get out of his freezing, wet clothes.

Up to this point, Billy had bottled up his emotions. He felt them trying to smash through; heart-breaking sadness, self-pity, and anger, especially anger. He thought if he allowed even one tear, everything would burst out at once. It would mean he had given up. It would mean he believed his dad was really gone. After all, if Dad was still alive there was no reason to cry; everyone else was safe, and Walter had probably stopped the slayer for good.

He looked once again at the streaks of blood the investigators had exposed and pictured what might have happened. He imagined where arms or legs might have smeared this line or that line on the cabin floor and out into the leaves. He saw his father's limp frame stretched out, pale and cold along the horrible path. He cringed, and his whole body shivered at the thought.

Dragged off by some slobbering old bear? He shook his head to sling the image away, but it bounced right back. He pictured a massive, drooling beast crouching in a cave and crunching on his father's bones. Suddenly a wave of nausea swept over him, and he bent over to heave out all the hot cocoa he had drunk earlier.

His mother limped to his side and patted him on the back while wiping his face with a tissue. "Let's get you back to the camp," she said softly.

Billy looked up at her caring face through his tear-filled eyes. "Mom, if Dad's really still alive, he has to be around here somewhere. I can't give up. I want to go out with the new dogs when they get here."

"He's already here," his mother replied.

"He? Only one dog?"

A gruff voice with a heavy Appalachian accent made Billy turn his head. "Iffin ol' Hambone caint find him, ain't no dog in the world that kin."

A thin-faced man slouched next to the plane. Through the man's open coat, Billy saw a flannel shirt, much of the shirt's tail sticking out of his two-sizes-too-big overalls. In his long, skinny fingers he held a wide leather strap, and on the other end sat an elderly hound. The dog, a bluetick, Billy thought, seemed sleepy but not disagreeable.

The man tipped his greasy baseball cap. "Arlo Hatfield's the name. Ol' Hambone don't like to go out in the cold, but it don't take 'im long to find a soul."

Billy stood up and wiped his eyes and nose with his gloves. He stepped cautiously over to the hound, took off a glove, and put out his hand. The dog sniffed it from thumb to pinky. The thin man laughed with a bellow. "Haw! Now iffin you was ever to git lost, ol' Hambone'd find you! That's fer shur!"

Billy pulled off his other glove and stooped, petting the dog's head lovingly with both hands. Hambone's face perked up. His tongue dangled, dripping through his puffy panting, and his tail jerked back and forth like a high-speed metronome.

Billy leaned over and whispered in the dog's ear. "Hambone, you'll find my dad, won't you?" He looked up at his mother, pouring on as much pitiable sadness as he could muster. "Can I go with him, Mom?"

"Billy, you were throwing up just a minute ago, and you were running soaking wet through the mountains most of the night!"

"I know, but maybe I can help."

The mountain man spat out a stream of brown juice. "Nope! Hambone and me, we works alone. You'd just be a distraction. We been huntin' Otter Crick fer years, so we don't need no help."

"You heard him, honey. I think we should both go back to the camp and get some rest. We're just walking in circles here. This man and his dog know the area, and they don't want us getting in the way."

A loud voice rang out in the distance. "All ashore that's going ashore!" The helicopter's pilot was calling from a clearing. He had just delivered the mountain man and his dog and was ready to go back to base.

Billy's mother took a step toward the voice, partially turning her body to leave, but she kept her eyes trained on Billy. He gave a reluctant nod and grunted as he rose to his feet, petting Hambone one more time before walking away. "We're coming!" he called back.

Billy put on his gloves and picked up the Bible again, but finding it soiled from his spell of nausea, he tossed it back into the pile of debris. The two made their way toward the makeshift chopper pad, and Billy kept moving his eyes and head in all directions, trying to get some clue, some sign that might help him find his father.

At the same time, nagging doubts thrust their way into his mind. How could he be alive? He was shot through the heart, the plane crashed, and there's all that blood. Who could survive that? He had to keep prying his mother for the truth.

"Mom, do you *really* still believe Dad's alive?"

She paused, and every second Billy had to wait for an answer buried him in more doubts. Finally she said, "I have to believe in him, Billy. He said he wouldn't die, and he's never lied to me before."

"But why should *I* believe in him?" he asked, nearly shouting now. "Up until a couple of days ago, my whole life's been a lie!"

"A lie? What do you mean?"

"Never mind." He felt childish after that outburst, especially when Bonnie suddenly came to mind. He knew his own troubles were nothing compared to hers. Still, doubts remained. Even if his father walked right down that mountainside, Billy wondered if he had it in his heart to forgive him. Yet, he knew he still loved his dad. How could he just forget all those years of good times?

A spirit of betrayal stalked his mind. No real father would keep a secret like that, would he? Billy saw a small piece of Merlin's fuselage and kicked it, making it slide across the snow. He felt like his heart was being torn in two.

As they walked, a shadow passed over them, and Billy jerked his head up to look. A huge vulture circled low, his V-shaped wingspan casting a black stripe on the treetops. Did the bird know something the rescuers didn't know, or did it just smell blood? The thought of gluttonous scavengers made Billy shudder again, and he folded in his coat and kept his eyes on the ground the rest of the way to the helicopter.

CHAPTER 15

The Ring and the Stone

As soon as Billy stepped out of the pickup truck that ferried them back from the helicopter pad, he scanned the rescue staging area to find Bonnie. He picked up his pace and strode up to her, trying to mask his inner turmoil.

"No good news, huh?" Bonnie asked, speaking softly to keep their conversation private.

"You could tell?" he whispered in return.

Bonnie just nodded, her own face telling a sad story. Although she had managed to sit erect on a lawn chair, her right leg, wrapped ankle to thigh in Ace bandages, was propped on an ice chest, a huge lump bulging over her knee.

The rest of the faces in the huddled group reflected Billy's gloom—Walter, his father, Mr. Hamilton, and Officer Caruthers all frowning in varying degrees.

Billy's mother caught up and joined the group. Her shoulders sagged, and dried tear tracks smudged both cheeks. She looked like she could use a three-day nap.

Mr. Hamilton gave them a weary saluting gesture. "Hello, William, Mrs. Bannister. From your expressions, I take it you bear ill tidings?"

William? Billy thought. *Why is it William all of a sudden?* "Well, no good news. We haven't found my dad yet." He looked around at the glum faces again. "What's everyone so upset down here for? At least everyone else is safe, and we're all together."

Walter spoke up. "Devin's gone."

"Gone? I thought you said you really decked him!"

"I did. We found the place, and there was lots of blood where I bashed him, and then a trail of blood with footprints. But all of a sudden, the trail ended."

Billy had tried to keep up a good humor, but the whole world seemed to turn gray and cold. He stuffed his hands into his pockets and took a deep breath. "Let's just hope old Hambone finds my dad."

"Old who?" Walter asked.

Billy waved him off. "I'll tell you about it later."

Officer Caruthers slapped his thigh and laughed. "Old Hambone is the best hound in the state. It took us a while to convince that hillbil—uh, his handler—to bring him up, especially since it's so cold. I'm sure they'll find your father. Old Hambone's never failed, and the colder it is, the faster he finds his man. He hates the cold."

Billy stuffed his hands deeper into his pockets and bounced lightly up and down on his toes. "Brrr! Then we oughtta hear from them real soon."

As evening fell, and more frigid air descended, the volunteers dispersed, giving way to professional search crews and their fresh teams of dogs. Billy wanted to stay and find out if Hambone had found anything and why other dogs were coming in, but the searchers persuaded him and his mother to go home and rest. They had to allow the bloodhounds to search that night, and perhaps the next day, without interference. They reluctantly obliged, their weariness overtaking their will to go on.

A rescue volunteer offered to drive them back to Castlewood in his recreational vehicle, promising a ride of comfort with beds and blankets. Billy, his mother, and Bonnie took him up on his offer. Mr. Foley told them to go straight to his house. Mrs. Foley would have hot food and steaming drinks waiting for them, along with a place to sleep for as long as they wanted.

Walter stayed with his father and Mr. Hamilton. He offered to help them clean up the rescue staging site to get his mind off the tragedy. With hopes of finding Jared Bannister fading, the number of volunteers dwindled, leaving only a few to do the dirty work.

After a couple of hours of cleanup duty, Mr. Hamilton asked Walter's father to accompany him on his walk toward his station wagon. He had parked well down the road due to the large number of cars that had packed the narrow throughway. Walter stuffed the last of the food wrappers and used coffee filters into a garbage can and then followed his father and the professor, wrapping his arms around his coat to battle the freezing temperature. The crisp, cold air made it easy to hear their conversation, even from a dozen or so paces behind.

"Professor," Walter's father began, "thank you for all your help and your interest in Walter and Billy."

The professor walked quickly, forcing Walter and his father to step up their pace. "That's quite all right, Carl. They're fine young men."

"Yes, I know." Walter's dad puffed as he pumped his long legs. "I was wondering, though, how much do they really know about you? Do they realize that you're—"

"No!" The professor slowed down as they descended the last slope, which led to a wider section of road where he had parked. Walter lagged farther behind, wondering if they knew he was listening. He leaned over and tied his shoe but kept his ears trained on the conversation.

The professor stopped and faced Walter's father. The teacher's voice lowered, but Walter could still make out the words. "When we visit that issue we tread dangerous ground. It would not help matters if they knew about the Circle, or about my role in it."

"Matters? What matters are you talking about?"

The professor's eyes gave away deep concern and more than a little love. "That's what I wish to discuss. With this mad Sir Devin still about, William and Miss Silver will not be able to attend school safely any longer."

"Yes. I was wondering about that. Go on."

"And William's mother will have neither the time to teach nor the money to hire a tutor. Surely Miss Silver's foster home is no better equipped."

"I agree. Exactly what are you trying to say, Professor?"

The professor took a deep breath and exhaled in a cloudy white stream. "Carl, do you remember me mentioning something called 'The New Table' back during your Oxford days?"

"It rings a bell. Wasn't that the weird group that thought they were Arthur's knights or something?"

The professor sighed. "More than a weird group, I'm afraid. They're a secret society, powerful and cultic, and they believe they're the rightful authority in England, the true Round Table of Arthur, or some such nonsense."

"Okay. But what do they have to do with Billy and Bonnie?"

"I can only tell you that the society seeks to kill them both. Their conspiracy has branches all over the world now, so protecting the children will require my personal attention."

"Your attention? What are you talking about?"

"I have a proposal to make to you, but if you agree, you must continue to keep what you know about me and my mission a secret. You may, of course, relate to anyone my official capacity at Oxford. There is no need, however, to arouse fears in William and Bonnie, or in Walter for that matter, by reporting my unofficial business. I will reveal what I know over time."

Walter's father nodded. "Go on. I'm listening."

The professor glanced back at Walter and lowered his voice further. Walter could see their conversation in the spurts of white leaving their mouths, but the sound died away. He knew they were leaving him out on purpose, so he walked back toward the camp to find his dad's car. With every step he wondered about "The New Table" and Arthur's knights. What could it all mean?

The night grew suddenly darker and colder, and Walter hurried his pace. When he reached his dad's car he threw open the door and jumped inside. He bundled his coat together and shivered hard.

Billy sat with Walter at the kitchen's breakfast table. Mrs. Foley had set a fabulous morning meal before them—pancakes with butter and warm syrup, a big slab of ham, steaming hot hash browns covered with a fried egg, a tall glass of fresh-squeezed orange juice, and a fat blueberry muffin, split from the top with melted butter dripping down the sides. Billy just stared at it, poking at the egg with his fork. He popped the yolk and stirred it into the potatoes.

Walter munched on a huge mouthful of potatoes and swallowed, chasing it with a gulp of juice. "Just because Hambone couldn't find your dad, it doesn't mean he's dead. It just means the old dog ain't what he used to be. At least he didn't find a body."

Billy took one bite of egg and chewed it halfheartedly. "We know something's up there. Hambone wouldn't have gone crazy barking at a cave if nothing was around it. We heard that Arlo tripped and broke his foot. Maybe they would've found something if he hadn't gotten hurt."

Billy dropped his fork on the plate and rested his cheek in his propped up hand, gazing around the large eat-in kitchen and out into the family room of Walter's house. "I'm glad you have such a big place."

Walter pointed at Billy's breakfast. "You gonna eat that?"

Billy shoved his plate toward Walter, who grinned at the sight of another whole meal coming his way. "Ever since my sister moved out," Walter said while chewing, "we've had her room open, and we have the guest room, too. We've got lots of space."

"Yeah, it's a nice house and all, and it's a great place to sleep, but I can't believe Mom's making us just sit here when we should be up at that cave searching."

Billy's mother walked gingerly up to the table. She looked refreshed and clean and smelled like she had just come out of the shower, but her limp proved that her ankle still bothered her. "You know why, young man."

"I know. I know. Bloodhounds work better when other people aren't there stinking up the place. But what if Dad's on his way home? What if he's hitchhiking back? He won't even know where to go!"

"Billy," his mother warned, "now you're getting irrational."

Billy sat up straight in his chair, wide-eyed, and he sputtered his words. "Irrational? Has anything *rational* happened the last few days? People setting our house on fire, a school principal with a sword chasing us through the mountains, bodies vanishing at the end of bloody trails, dogs that can't track anymore, and now we can't even go to school, because . . ." He wiggled his fingers creepily and imitated a deep radio announcer's voice, "Who knows where the mad Sir Devin lurks?"

Billy looked into his mother's sad eyes and felt bad about his outburst. He clasped her hand tightly. "I'm sorry, Mom. I'm really out of it today." The entire kitchen area fell silent for a moment, and an overall gloom took control.

Walter leaned back and put his hand on his stomach. "Well, if it makes you feel any better, Mom and Dad decided it was okay for me to homeschool with you."

"Yeah? That's pretty cool." Billy looked over at his mother. "So have you decided if you're going to be our teacher?"

She lowered her head and shook it slowly. "I don't see how I can. Since we don't know when your dad's coming back, I have to run the business by myself. Until the insurance company pays for the house, we're going to need the money, and the other pilots are counting on me."

"Well, if you can't stay home, then who's going to teach us?"

She looked at her watch and then at the front door. "I hope you'll find out very soon."

Billy followed his mother's eyes to the door, and he sighed. "You went out and hired a tutor?" He covered his face with his hands and moaned. "Oh, no! Some spinster lady who can't keep a regular job! What else did you do to me yesterday when I wasn't looking?"

She ignored Billy's grousing. "Well, I had a long talk with Walter's folks, and then Walter's mom and I went shopping with Bonnie while you were napping. Since all our clothes burned in the fire, I had to get at least a few things. You can wear Walter's clothes, but his mother and I aren't the same size."

Billy felt a sudden burst of energy, but he kept his voice under control. "You went with Bonnie? How is she doing?"

"Fine. She was feeling a lot better yesterday, except for the knee, of course. The store had a wheelchair for her, and my ankle wasn't bothering me much, so we got around just fine."

"What did the doctor say? If I know Bonnie, she wouldn't let anyone examine her."

"Well, she let the ER physician look at her knee. He said there might be some permanent damage, but since she doesn't want to get an MRI, we'll just wait to see if it starts healing on its own. For now, she's crutching around."

"Who's watching her? I mean, if Devin knows where she lives, won't he try to come after her? Since she's crippled, she won't be able to . . . you know . . . get away."

"Don't worry. The house is under twenty-four-hour surveillance. The police are hoping he does come by so they can grab him."

Billy looked toward the front window. The drapes had been drawn closed, so he couldn't see outside. "Why aren't they watching this house?"

"A police cruiser comes by now and then, but since the Foleys have a fancy security system, they can monitor us remotely. Mr.

Foley decided to allow the security company to keep the audio lines open during the day, and when he arms the system at night, they can only listen if the alarm goes off. I'll show you how to disarm it later so you can go out the door if you're the first one up in the morning."

"You mean the security company can listen in right now if they wanted to?"

"Right. So don't—"

BRAAAAP! Walter's belch echoed throughout the room, and he put his hand back on his satisfied stomach. "Aaaah! That'll give SOS Security something to think about!"

Billy was about to bop Walter on the head, but a loud rap at the door grabbed his attention. His mother looked at her watch again. "Yep. The old spinster's right on time."

Walter wiped his mouth and stood up. "Come in!"

The door opened and a tall, wild-haired man strode in carrying a large briefcase, his ever-familiar accent sounding out strong and lively. "Good morning, pupils! Are you ready to explore the wonderful world of learning?"

Billy laughed. "Mr. Hamilton! You're going to teach us?" He passed a plate to Walter, who was stacking dirty dishes on the table.

Mr. Hamilton stepped back and raised his head high. "And what's wrong with that, young man?"

Billy waved his hand apologetically. "Oh, nothing—nothing at all. But what about your classes at Castlewood?"

Mr. Hamilton pulled off his coat and draped it over his arm. "I resigned, effective immediately."

Billy glanced at his mom. "But what about your income? I'm sure we can't pay you what you were making."

Mr. Hamilton walked slowly into the kitchen and set his briefcase down by Billy's chair. "My wife passed away years ago, my house is paid for, and my only child is married to a prominent nuclear physicist. I require very little."

Billy's mother poked Billy playfully in the side. "Mr. Hamilton offered his services to Mr. Foley, and we're sharing the expenses. How could we say no?"

Walter's father walked in, his large frame making his shoes squeak across the vinyl floor as he entered. He placed his hand on Billy's shoulder. "And you and your mother are both welcome to stay here indefinitely. We have plenty of room." He turned to the teacher and extended his hand. "I look forward to seeing you in action again, Professor."

"Indeed!" the teacher replied. "I trust that I shall not disappoint you."

"Professor?" Billy asked. "Why did you call him Professor?"

Mr. Foley pushed his glasses up higher on his nose and slid a business card in front of Billy. "Because, I studied under him at Oxford as a Rhodes scholar. He's the most—how shall I say it?—the most 'interesting' professor I've ever had."

Billy picked up the card. It read, "Dr. Charles Hamilton, Centre for the Study of Ancient Documents, Oxford University."

Mr. Foley put his finger on the department name. "That's where he worked right before he moved here. When I studied at Oxford, he was a professor in the department of anthropology."

Billy looked up at his teacher. "Why would you ever want to come to a hick town like Castlewood?"

"William," the professor replied, shaking his head, "we must all have a few secrets we're allowed to keep to ourselves. Mustn't we?"

Billy smiled and nodded. "I can't argue with that."

Walter picked up the stack of dishes and walked toward the sink. "Sounds cool to me."

The professor looked around the house. "Have you decided on an appropriate room?"

Mr. Foley gestured for everyone to follow. "Yes, I cleaned out the back den last night and set up a table." The professor grabbed his briefcase again and followed along with the two new pupils. After passing through a short hallway, they stopped at a room at the end.

Mr. Foley stood at the doorway and pushed his hand through his thinning hair. "We can get a marker board later today, and I have chairs for the table already set up."

Walter and Billy stood by the square, Formica table and gazed around at their new schoolroom. Billy slid one of the chairs out from under the table. "I see four chairs. Is Bonnie coming, too?"

Mr. Foley laughed. "We couldn't leave her out, especially after we acquired a master intellect to be the house tutor."

"Where is Miss Silver?" the professor asked. "Will she be joining us later?"

Mr. Foley glanced out the room's solitary window. "My wife went to pick her up. Don't worry, though. A police car will escort them here." He turned to leave and gave them a comical salute, clicking his heels together and raising a ramrod straight arm to his forehead. "Learn well, men! I have to get ready for work. My clients will be waiting."

Billy walked to the window, and Professor Hamilton followed, stooping to look over Billy's shoulder. "I assume Miss Silver will be here shortly, so we'll wait for her arrival before we begin."

"I can't believe her foster parents never reported her missing," Billy grumbled. "How could anyone not care where someone like Bonnie is?"

Walter's expression brightened and he nudged his friend with an elbow. "Are you getting the hots for her, Billy?" Billy's glare made Walter put his hands up in surrender, and he backed away. "Whoa! Touchy subject!"

Billy reached for Walter's shirt and tugged him back to the table. "That's not it. I like Bonnie . . . as a friend. She's the coolest girl I've ever met, but when you say things like that, you make her sound so . . . so—"

"Common?" Professor Hamilton suggested.

"Yeah, common. Like she's one of the popular girls at school, you know, playing their stupid games like they do."

"And your willingness to discuss it," Professor Hamilton added, "proves that you have a pure and honest relationship with her, as one does with a close sister."

"I have a sister," Walter snorted. "I think she must be one of those 'common' ones."

"Oh, come on," Billy countered. "Shelley's not so bad. But when you get to know Bonnie, I think you'll find out what I mean."

All three heads turned when they heard the front door open and then the sound of Walter's mom giving directions to the schoolroom. Several seconds later, Bonnie appeared at the door to the den. At first she just peeked in, her wide eyes revealing their ivory white borders and her thick braids framing her elegant neck. She leaned on crutches, but her beaming face belied her injury. Her eyes shone with an inner joy that captivated the three males in the room, and her infectious smile spread to every face.

Under her new backpack, she wore an ankle-length dress that sported a simple flower design, mostly pale blue over bright white, and its newness made her sparkle. The crutches added an aura of helplessness, of deprivation, the image of a lost orphan. Billy knew better. He knew the heart of a lioness beat within her delicate frame, fearless and confident.

Walter's chin dropped an inch or two. He stared, and his voice shook. "I think I already know what you mean."

"What?" Bonnie asked. She crutched fully into the room and looked around at everyone. "What do you mean?"

"Never mind," Billy replied, stifling a laugh. "Is that a new dress?"

She leaned on her right crutch and spread out one side of the dress with her left hand. "Yes. Your mother picked it out, and Walter's mom bought it for me. It wasn't a perfect fit, but your mom altered it when we got home."

Billy tried to tell her with his eyes that he knew what she meant. *Mom must have cut holes for her wings.*

"I really like the dress," she went on. "It even has pockets. Speaking of which—" She reached into her left pocket and pulled out a ring. "I found this on the welcome mat outside." She held it up for Walter to see. "Your mom didn't recognize it. Do you?"

Walter shook his head, and they both turned to Billy. She held it right in front of his eyes. "How about you, Billy?"

Billy dropped to his seat and stared at the ring with his mouth wide open. With the color in his face quickly draining, he looked as though he would faint at any second.

Bonnie put the ring down on the table. "Billy! What is it?"

"It's my dad's ring! It's his rubellite!"

Professor Hamilton reached over and snatched up the ring. He looked it over closely. "William is absolutely correct. It is definitely a rubellite, a red tourmaline."

"Mom!" Billy yelled at the top of his lungs. "Mom, come quick!"

Within seconds Billy's mother and Walter's parents ran into the room, and Professor Hamilton presented the ring to Billy's mother. "Discovered on the mat outside, madam."

When she saw the ring, her face contorted, tears forming in her eyes. "It's Jared's!" She held her hands over her face and cried. "What does it mean? What does it all mean?" Mrs. Foley put an arm around her and hugged her close.

Bonnie dug her hand into her pocket again. "There was something else right next to it, but it's just a dirty old rock." She placed a large, crusted pebble on the table. Professor Hamilton reached for it first and brought it up close to his eyes. He brushed the dirt off with his fingers, letting the sand fall to the floor, and then looked apologetically at Walter's mother. "I'm so sorry, Mrs. Foley. I will be sure to clean it up." He reached for his handkerchief and wiped the stone clean. After several more seconds of eyeing it closely, he cleared his throat and gazed at everyone in a formal manner. "It is a ruby," he concluded. He waited for the surprised gasps to subside before continuing. "Not the finest quality," he went on, "but with its size, I estimate it would fetch six or seven hundred American dollars."

Billy watched the professor's hands fingering the gem. "Then what does it mean? Devin wouldn't leave a ring or a ruby here, would he?"

"Let's think about this logically," the professor replied. "What benefit would Devin gain in delivering the ring?"

"Scaring us?" Billy offered. "Letting us know he's around?"

The professor shook his head. "Scaring you? I don't think so. He wants to kill you and Miss Silver, although his desire to kill the fair maiden rather squashes my theories as to why he is persecuting you. Anyway, giving away his knowledge of where you are would only injure his strategy. It would be more expedient for him at this point if you thought he was dead."

Billy cocked his head doubtfully, but he was ready to hear more. "Okay, go on."

The professor held up his hand. "The conclusion is quite simple, really. Since Devin has no logical reason to leave a valuable gift, that leaves only one possibility."

Everyone in the room froze, waiting for the professor's explanation. Even Mr. Foley stopped still, right in the middle of pulling up a knot in his necktie. The professor kept waiting, bouncing lightly on his toes.

Billy looked up at his mother. She knew. Her eyes told him so; they were confused but delighted at the same time. Billy picked up the ring and slid it onto his right index finger. With everyone watching, he closed his fist and gazed at it, not knowing whether to jump for joy or cry out in confusion.

"Dad left it," he finally said.

CHAPTER 16

The Gift

"It's obvious, isn't it?"

Billy sat with the Foleys at the dinner table and addressed his mother who sat across from him. A marvelous meal graced the table once again. A big roast of beef rested near the center with a gravy boat to one side. A huge bowl of mashed potatoes sat next to the roast, with broccoli, carrots, and warm bread on various platters spread from one end to the other. Billy wondered if this kind of meal was normal here, or if the Foleys were showing a little extra hospitality for their guests.

Billy's voice came alive with new hope, and he chattered like an over-caffeinated parrot. "We don't have to worry that they called off the search today. You see, Dad's alive, but he's not showing his face. He's worried that Devin will find out where we are, so he's trying to protect us. He used the ring to tell us he's still alive, and he gave us the ruby to make sure we had some money."

"But how could he get it?" his mother asked. "There can't be rubies just lying around on the ground out there in the mountains. How did he get back to Castlewood? And where is he staying?"

Mr. Foley reached into his shirt pocket. "Here, Marilyn, before I forget." He pushed a folded sheet of paper across the table. "It's an appraisal from the gemologist. He says the ruby's worth six hundred bucks."

Billy's mother picked up the sheet and unfolded it slowly, her brow wrinkling as her eyes scanned the numbers. She then refolded the paper and made a fist around it. "I—I'm not selling it." Her trembling lips forced a smile. "At least not yet. We'll be all right, and besides, the ruby might hold a clue we haven't figured out yet."

Mrs. Foley placed a comforting hand on her knuckles. "Of course you don't want to sell it." She turned to her husband. "But isn't six hundred what Dr. Hamilton said it would be worth?"

Mr. Foley nodded while finishing a mouthful of potatoes. "The old professor knows a lot about everything. He's going to be great to have around!"

"Yeah," Walter agreed. "What a setup! Learning everything from the professor and staying at home to do it. It's perfect!"

Billy stirred gravy into his potatoes, turning it into thick brown soup. "Perfect except for one thing."

"What's that?" Walter and his father said at the same time.

Billy let his fork fall to his plate, making a loud clank. "Bonnie. She has to keep going back to her foster home every night."

Mrs. Foley sighed and her lips turned downward. "I'm not sure there's anything we can do about that." She glanced at her husband and intertwined her fingers with his before turning back to Billy's mother. "So what's the next step, Marilyn? How do we contact Jared?"

"We can bet that Devin knows Billy and I are here. So I don't know if it's safe to leave a note on the mat, but that's our only point of contact so far."

"Or just let Dad give us more clues," Billy offered.

Mr. Foley pulled his napkin from his lap and wiped his lips. "Billy's right. If Jared's alive, he's smart enough to tell us what we need to know. For now he just wants us to know he's alive and he's thinking about his family. At least it seems that way."

"We have to trust him," Billy's mother agreed.

Everyone at the table nodded and then continued eating quietly. Billy swirled his fork through his potatoes again and wondered about the silence. Did everyone have pet theories they were pondering? Were they trying to answer the same questions that gnawed away at his mind? How did his dad survive? How could he have disappeared? Why hadn't he called?

Those were the easy questions, the ones Billy dared ask himself over and over. But there were other questions that he hid deep within. He was scared to peer into that dark portion of his soul. He knew the questions were there, and every time they broke through to his conscious mind, it became easier and easier to dwell on them.

Could he really trust a man who had hidden his secret dragon identity for so long? What other dark secrets was he hiding? A few short days ago these questions would have been absurd, but a few short days ago he didn't know he had a former dragon for a father.

And last, but not least, what was the slayer up to?

Billy lay awake in the darkness of late evening reliving Monday's events in his mind. School was really a blast now, and the second day promised to be even better than the first. They had been distracted from their lessons, preoccupied with the rubellite ring, but now Billy felt sure his dad was still alive, so he stopped worrying about that.

Professor Hamilton had given a sneak preview of what learning would be like. The professor arrived with masks from Africa for social studies; he had them act out parts of "Julius Caesar" for reading appreciation, including the stabbing scenes; he brought an ancient abacus for math; and he even taught a Bible class from the book of Matthew. "Couldn't do that at Castlewood," the professor said. And that was all on the first day! Best of all, his only classmates were Walter and Bonnie, the two best friends he had in the world. With these thoughts in mind, he was able to drift off to sleep.

Through the night, Billy floated in and out of dreams, strange visions that reflected his jumbled thoughts. In one dream he and Bonnie were walking in a dark cave filled with flickering lights and dancing shadows. A stone floor greeted their shoes with echoing clops, and a breeze wafted through, caressing their faces with cool dampness and filling their nostrils with musty odor. Suddenly the cave became completely dark, and Billy felt a strange sense that sent chills across his back. Something was watching, something large and fierce, looming in their presence like a rising shadow.

"How will we get out of here?" Bonnie asked in an unearthly voice that only dreams can create.

Billy pulled his father's rubellite ring from his finger and held it up. With a sudden flash it emitted a blinding, radiant light, sparkling red like a crimson lantern. "My father will show us the way," Billy replied. "There's nothing to be afraid of."

Billy woke up and glanced at the clock. Five a.m. He shuddered at the dream. Were he and Bonnie walking in the cave at the mountain? What might be happening back there? Where was his dad now? Did he leave something else on the doormat?

He arose while it was still dark and ran to the front door. After punching the buttons on the burglar alarm panel to disarm the system, he flung the door open and looked all around the porch.

"Nothing!"

With cold, bare feet, he stepped out onto the painted wood deck and scanned the yard, a span of brown grass with just a few patches of dying green here and there. At least five streetlamps illuminated this section of Cordelle Road, spilling light into the adjacent properties and painting crisscrossing shadows over land and houses.

The snowfall had confined its coverage to the mountains, but the cold sweep of the northwest wind had definitely paid a visit. Billy listened to it blow newly fallen leaves and watched the little dry imps dance across the lawn and then squat like defiant settlers, never to budge until the next rake came to persuade their exit.

Billy was ready to go back inside, but a rustling sound in front of the porch made him stiffen his body. He took a deep breath and tiptoed slowly toward the stairs, whispering, "Who's there?"

He climbed down the steps and started poking through the hedge that bordered the house. Could it be? Dare he hope? He whispered into the thin branches. "Dad?"

Suddenly a human form burst out from the bushes and ran across the lawn. Billy knew immediately that the runner wasn't his father; he was too short.

He didn't have time to think. Though he was barefoot and wearing only pajamas, he dashed after the intruder. Adrenaline pumping, he ran faster than he ever had in his life. He had to solve the mystery and find his father. He did have one other thought—Old Hambone. Just like the dog, he wanted to get the chase over with, and fast. It was way too cold!

The runner, bundled up in a heavy coat, couldn't stay ahead of Billy for very long. A hundred feet down the sidewalk, the intruder tried to cross the street, but Billy reached out for his shoulders and pulled him to the asphalt. They fell hard, tumbling on the rough pavement like two grunting football players.

The intruder tried to roll away, but Billy kept him pinned, strength flowing through him like shots of liquid muscle. He pulled down the runner's hood and snatched his ski cap off.

"Adam!"

Adam struggled underneath Billy's weight. Billy jammed the bully's wrists against the pavement, and he noticed a book in Adam's right hand. Billy moved up to sit on Adam's chest and grabbed the book with one hand while trying to keep Adam in check with the other. "It's a Bible!"

"So what!" Adam growled.

Billy looked at it more carefully. "I know this Bible; it's the one I had back on the mountain." Adam struggled again, wrapping his free arm around Billy's waist and trying to wrestle him to the side. This time Billy pressed his knees on Adam's upper arms and pinned his head to the road with one hand. "Talk fast, Adam. Were you delivering it or stealing it?"

Adam smirked. "Wouldn't you like to know, Dragon Breath?"

Billy pulled on Adam's hair and then jerked it back toward the road, slamming Adam's head on the pavement and shouting. "Yes, I would like to know!"

Adam angrily kicked and pushed, forcing Billy to fall back. Both boys scrambled to their feet, and Adam pushed Billy backward as hard as he could, sending him flying toward the curb. He landed heavily, tearing his pajama sleeves and scraping his elbows on the pavement, and the Bible flipped out of his hand and slid across the sidewalk. Adam took off in the opposite direction, his footfalls clopping loudly on the pavement in the silence of the early morning. Billy scrambled to his feet, but Adam was already well down the road. There was no catching him now.

Billy retrieved the Bible and brushed it off. He jogged back to Walter's house, staring at the newfound treasure all the way. He knew he ought to be cold all over, but only his bare feet complained. He burst back into the house yelling. "Mom! Come here, quick!" He ran toward the guest room, and his bleary-eyed mother met him in the hallway.

"Billy! What do you mean shouting through the house this early in the morning?"

Placing one hand on his knee and trying to breathe without coughing, he showed her the Bible. "Look!" He took two gasping breaths before continuing. "The Bible I was carrying up on the mountain!"

She took it and turned on the hall light. "You were carrying this up there? I didn't notice." She flipped through the pages. "So, why is it here? Did you bring it back to Castlewood with you?"

"No! Don't you get it? I left it up on the mountain!"

Billy's mother rubbed her eyes and finally seemed to wake up. "You mean it was out on the front porch this morning?"

"Not exactly. Adam had it. He was hiding in the bushes, but when he ran away I tackled him and took it."

She stared at him with her head cocked to one side. "You mean he's the one delivering things to us?"

"He wouldn't say, but I don't think so. I think the Bible was already there, and he was stealing it."

The kitchen light flashed on, and Mr. and Mrs. Foley came in from the other side of the house, both in long pajamas and bedroom slippers. "Is there a problem?" Mr. Foley asked.

Billy took the Bible back from his mother and handed it to Mr. Foley. "Adam Lark was hiding in the bushes out front, and he had this. I tackled him in the street and took it from him."

Mr. Foley looked at the Bible and then back at Billy. "Adam was carrying a Bible and you mugged him for it? Doesn't seem like the Christian thing to do."

Billy grabbed the Bible back and sputtered. "No, that's not it at all, I—" He then noticed Mr. Foley's big smirk and stopped.

"I heard what you told your mother, Billy," Mr. Foley said. "The whole neighborhood did. Don't have a heart attack."

Billy felt his face turn red, but the embarrassment died quickly. He just stared at the Bible and rubbed its imitation leather cover. "What's Dad trying to tell us now?"

"But could it be Devin this time?" his mother asked. "Adam had it. Could he be doing something for Devin, trying to confuse us maybe?"

"No! He was stealing it. He had to be!"

"Let me see it again." She took it and opened it to the blank pages in the front and then to the rear. Her frown gave away her disappointment. "No message. Just this brownish stain on the cover."

"Oh, yeah. I guess that's where I threw up on it." Billy took it again and started flipping through the pages rapidly. "But I don't see any other marks. Whoever owned this Bible never wrote in it, so if Dad left a message in here somewhere, I should be able to find it."

Mr. Foley pointed at the clean pages. "Don't you think your dad would have made his message easy to find?"

"I guess so, but Devin would have, too, if he were trying to fool us."

"Good point!" Mr. Foley conceded.

Walter finally joined the gathering. He staggered with stiff legs, hands in his bathrobe and eyes barely open, mumbling something about all the noise. When he got to the hall, he raised his head and opened and closed his eyes several times while everyone watched, snorts and chuckles filling the room. He finally kept his eyes open and focused on the Bible. After a few seconds of staring he said, "Revival meeting?" He then turned around and headed back to his room, loud laughter following him down the hall.

Expecting Professor Hamilton to arrive at any minute for class, Billy and Walter sat at the table, each one staring at the pages of the Bible. Every few seconds or so, they nodded to each other and turned the page.

Billy raised his head and rubbed his eyes. "Okay, Exodus is done," he said, closing the Bible. "No clues yet."

Walter looked at his watch. "The professor's late. That's not like him."

"He's picking up Bonnie this morning," Billy explained. "She's probably still moving kind of slow."

Billy rolled his eyes around a couple of times to rev them up for the work ahead and then looked at Walter. "You ready?"

"I guess so."

Billy opened the Bible again and sighed. "Leviticus chapter one."

After a few minutes Professor Hamilton strode in, followed by Bonnie, still on crutches and wearing her usual jeans and sweatshirt. The professor sported a new look, a full-fledged safari outfit, complete with khaki shorts and an elephant gun.

Both boys stared at him until Billy finally said, "Africa again, professor?"

"Yes, of course. It's a very large continent, you know. Much ground to cover."

Walter laughed. "You never dressed like that at Castlewood."

The professor stared at Walter, his gray eyebrows twitching. "Of course not. Do you think they would let me carry a gun into school? And shorts, especially on a frigid day such as this? That would be a professional embarrassment of the highest order!"

"And how are you feeling today?" Billy asked Bonnie.

"About the same. The knee feels a little better, but it's still real sore. I don't think I'll have to get an MRI, though." She glanced over at the open Bible on the table. "Homework? I thought we were studying the New Testament first."

Professor Hamilton looked over Billy's shoulder. "Good idea. You cannot understand the new without the old, right William?"

"No, we weren't studying for the class, we were just—" Billy stopped and stared at the teacher. "What did you just say, Professor?"

"Oh, nothing, just that you cannot understand the New Testament properly without a solid understanding of the Old

Testament. We were going to discuss that today, actually. That's why I brought it up."

"Can't understand the new without the old," Billy repeated softly, his voice trailing away at the end.

Walter picked up the Bible and showed it to the professor and Bonnie. "Adam Lark had this in front of the house early this morning. It's the same Bible Billy was carrying around up at the crash site, and he's sure he left it there."

Bonnie took the Bible and looked it over, flipping through the pages. "Adam had it? Why would he have it?"

"Billy thinks it was already on the porch, and Adam was stealing it."

Bonnie put the Bible back on the table. "Do you think your dad left it there, Billy? What's he trying to tell us this time?"

Walter waited for a second for Billy to answer and then shrugged his shoulders. "We don't know. We were going over every page looking for clues, a mark, a symbol, anything." He waved his hand in front of Billy's eyes. "Earth to Billy. Come in, Billy."

Billy blinked his eyes and smiled. "Sorry, I was just thinking."

Bonnie's face lit up, and she held out her hand. "May I see it again? There's something I want to look for." She reached for the Bible and opened it to the book of Job, then slowly turned the pages to chapter forty-one. "I'm looking for my mother's favorite passage. It might be one of his, too. . . . Here it is."

Billy stood up, and he and Walter looked over Bonnie's shoulder. "What did you find?"

"No writing; no symbols; only this tiny black smudge in the margin next to verse twenty-one. 'His breath kindleth coals, and a flame goeth out of his mouth.' "

"What?" Billy said, nearly shouting. "Let me see that."

Bonnie handed the Bible to him, and Billy pulled it close to his face. "It *is* a smudge, just a dirty black smudge."

Bonnie put her hand on Billy's shoulder. "But the verse, Billy. It has to mean something."

Billy didn't answer. He just handed the Bible to the professor. "What do you make of it?"

Professor Hamilton eyed the page closely and then pushed the book out to arm's length. After another second or two, he brought it back up to his face and sniffed it. "It's coal," he finally said. "Yes, it is definitely a coal smudge."

"Coal?" Billy repeated, sitting down. He looked at Walter and Bonnie. They just raised their hands, perplexed. Professor Hamilton kept staring at the page.

All four sat silently for nearly a minute until Billy started mumbling. "New without the old. . . . A coal smudge. . . . His breath kindleth coals." He was quiet for another minute with his eyes squeezed shut. Finally he opened them wide and said, "A dragon shorn."

"What?" Bonnie asked.

"A dragon shorn," he repeated, louder this time. "The prophecy, remember? 'A dragon shorn will live again, rejecting Eden's pride.' "

Walter looked at his friend like his head had sprouted horns. "What are you talking about?"

Billy closed his fist and banged the table. "I've got it! I know what's happening!"

"What is it?" Bonnie asked, her voice rising to match Billy's. "What's happening?"

Billy gestured for Bonnie to follow. "Come on." He hurried out of the schoolroom and shouted down the hall as he ran. "Mom!"

"Yes, Billy?" she answered from somewhere in the house. "I'm in the living room."

Billy jogged to the living room and Bonnie tagged along, her crutches clopping on the floor in time with her squeaking tennis shoe. He found his mother sitting on a sofa, a tablet on her lap and a pen in hand. She was talking on the phone, taking notes as she spoke. She held up one finger of her pen hand to signal for Billy to wait a minute.

"What do you mean 'criminal arson'? All arson is criminal. . . . But Jared didn't start it; someone else did. . . . Who? I told you who. . . . Didn't the police report mention the ripped open door jamb? . . . No, of course he didn't fake it!"

Billy paced frantically while Bonnie watched, and in a few seconds Walter and Professor Hamilton walked in.

"Oh!" the professor started when he saw Billy's mother on the phone. "Pardon the intrusion, madam."

She hung up the phone with more than a delicate landing. "The insurance company won't listen! It's as if someone is pulling their puppet strings."

"Mom! I figured it all out. At least I think I did."

She sat up straight in her chair. "You mean the ring and the Bible?"

"Yes."

A new fire kindled in her eyes. "Tell me!"

He looked around the room at the others. "I—I can't. At least not right now. It's too weird to talk about. Can you just get me back to the mountain, to where they found that cave, the place where Hambone went crazy?"

"I don't know where it is," she said, tapping her pen on her knee.

"How about Officer Caruthers? Can you contact him?"

She placed her hands on her knees and let out a slow sigh. "Billy, nobody's going to help you if you keep this hunch of yours a secret. Please, just tell us!"

"I have an idea. Can you ask him to tell us where Old Hambone lives? Tell him we want to thank him and his master and give them something?"

Her face began turning red, but her voice stayed calm, yet stern. "Billy, I'm not going to lie for you."

"Well, I really do want to thank him. I like Old Hambone, and I really will bring him something. Then maybe he can lead us back to the cave."

She took a deep breath and let it out slowly. "Billy, if you have a serious idea, you need to tell me right this minute, and then we have to tell the police."

He gestured with his head toward the professor and Walter. "Mom, I can't!"

Walter grabbed Professor Hamilton's sleeve. "Professor, come and show me that gun." He led the teacher out of the room.

"The gun? Why do you want to see . . ." The professor's voice trailed off down the hall.

Billy waited a few more seconds and walked closer to his mother, signaling for Bonnie to follow. "Mom, if I'm right," he said softly, "we don't want the police to know. We can get what we need today for hiking and leave for the mountain first thing in the morning, that is, if your ankle's okay."

"My ankle's doing fine." She sighed and sat back in her chair. "Okay, let's hear your idea."

"Mr. Hatfield! Are you there?"

A chorus of barks and howls greeted Billy's call. He stopped, petrified at the thought of a hundred hound dogs crashing through the trees and jumping all over him.

"Let's keep going, Billy." His mother continued down the trail with just a hint of a limp. "The dogs are probably penned up. It doesn't sound like they're getting any closer."

They kept walking the beaten-down path in the woods and finally saw an old shack in the distance. Snow still speckled the flattened leaves, and Billy and his mother hiked through the dappled landscape, bundled in heavy coats, gloves, and ski caps to battle the piercing wind. After the snowstorm, the sun melted whatever layers it could reach through the thinned, autumn canopy, and the cold front brought a bitter sting, battling the sunshine to keep the mountain in its winter grip.

When they arrived at the shack, Billy gave a small box to his mother and knocked on the door. The howling songs rose to a crescendo.

A voice bellowed from inside. "Whoose thar?"

"It's Billy Bannister and my mother, Marilyn Bannister."

"The kid what lost his pa?"

Billy couldn't help smiling. "Yes. My fath—uh, my pa was in the airplane that crashed in the Otter Creek Wilderness."

There was silence from inside the house for a moment, and Billy and his mother waited, trying to listen through the terrible dirges being sung by the various beagles, blueticks, and mongrels they had seen fenced in at the side of the shack. The dogs had a large, covered kennel area that looked as cozy as the man's house, but they roamed out in their yard, jumping with their forepaws on the fence, their noses upturned and sniffing the air and their tongues dangling like pink welcome mats.

Then, from within the house, the sound of clumping shoes came closer and closer. The door opened, and Mr. Hatfield appeared, pulling up a strap on his overalls while leaning against a crutch on his left side. "What choo want?"

Billy felt his jaw tremble. "A couple of things." He took the box from his mother again. "I have a gift for you and Hambone to thank you for helping us look for my pa."

Mr. Hatfield reached out and took the box, opened it greedily, and looked inside, sticking his nose through the top. His eyes brightened, and he took out a foil bag.

"Chawin' toback-ee!" he chortled. "And it's my favorite kind!" He reached in the box and took out another foil bag and inspected it with his eyes half-closed, first sniffing it and then trying to decipher the label, his lips moving as he read.

"It's doggy treats," Billy explained. "Old Hambone will love 'em."

"Hambone ain't never had nuthin' like them before, but we'll try 'em out." He stuffed the two bags back in the box and rubbed his free hand on his opposite arm. "Well git on with it. What else you want? It's colder'n a metal seat in an outhouse."

Billy looked at his mother and then back at Mr. Hatfield. "We want to borrow Hambone and look for my pa again."

The leathery creases on the man's thin, wrinkled face turned downward, and he drew his head back an inch or two. "You want to borry Hambone?"

"Yes, sir. We'll just take him back to the crash site and let him lead us to the cave." Billy glanced down at Arlo's bandaged left foot. "I'm sure I can lead him. You don't have to go."

"It ain't me to worry about. It's Hambone that don't like the cold! And I already been to that there cave. There ain't nothin' in it."

"But Mr. Hatfield, my pa is out there somewhere, and Hambone is my last hope. Please let him come with us."

Mr. Hatfield's mouth opened a notch, and he stared at Billy. With each passing second his expression softened, and a glistening sparkle appeared in one eye. "I'd lead 'im out there agin, but I busted up my foot huntin' for your pa."

Billy lowered his head. "Yeah, I heard about that." He scraped his shoe on the porch floor and then looked Arlo in the eye. "I really appreciate what you did."

Arlo shivered again and started to close the door. "Iffin Hambone wants to go, take 'im. His leash is there on the pawrch." With that, the door slammed shut.

Billy didn't waste a second; he didn't want to give Mr. Hatfield a chance to change his mind. He grabbed the leash and ran toward the side of the house, his mother following close behind. When they got to the gate, Billy glanced over the entire yard, searching for the old bluetick.

"He wouldn't be in the yard, Billy," his mother reminded. "He'd be in the shelter. He hates the cold, remember?"

"Right. Close the gate behind me, okay?" Billy took a deep breath, opened the gate, and proceeded cautiously into the yard. Three dogs jumped playfully up on him, trying to lick anywhere their long tongues could reach, and at least four others sniffed wherever Billy's shoes landed. He bent over to go through the kennel's low door and peeked inside. There he was, Old Hambone, lying on a tattered blanket near a space heater that looked to Billy like a kennel fire waiting to happen.

Hambone raised his eyelids, then his head, but only to let out a big, stretching yawn before plopping his head back down again. Billy removed a glove, reached into the kennel as far as he could, and let Hambone sniff his hand. The hound immediately perked up, and his tail started wagging. “Hambone, old buddy. Please come and help me find my dad. I know it’s cold outside, but it’s real important.”

Hambone laid his head down again and whined mournfully, his tail slowing to barely a wiggle.

Billy couldn’t quite reach him to drag him out, and, besides, he didn’t want to force him; that would be against Mr. Hatfield’s wishes. Billy had another idea. “Hambone, if you go with me, when we’re done, I’ll give you a nice, warm bath and a thick, warm doggy sweater for keeps.”

Hambone whined again, and his tail stopped wagging.

Billy sighed and reached into his pocket for a pouch of doggy treats. He had hoped to save them for the hunt, but he knew they wouldn’t do any good if he couldn’t coax the dog out. He tore open the foil and held out a nugget for Hambone to sniff. With a wet, pink tongue the hound licked it out of Billy’s hand and crunched it contentedly. Billy scratched behind his long left ear. “Hambone, there’s more where that came from. If you’ll go with me, I’ll give you the whole bag. I promise.”

Hambone’s tail started up again, and he rose slowly to his feet.

“ ’Atta boy!” When Hambone got to the door, Billy hooked the leash in place and led him out into the yard.

Billy’s mother stood at the gate, her hand on the latch. “So he decided to go?”

Billy smiled as he led Hambone out of the yard. “He’s a tough negotiator, but we struck a deal.”

CHAPTER 17

A Sixth Sense

Driving up the primitive mountainside, Billy and his mother coaxed their borrowed SUV as far as it could go on the rough forest road. This was normally a restricted footpath, reserved for hikers of Shavers Mountain, but because of the plane crash, the forest ranger left the gate open to allow search vehicles to enter. Finally, when the path narrowed to only a few feet across, they set out on foot, carrying a map and compass and following the sniffing nose of a champion hound.

Billy wished for a helicopter to lift them over the dense trees and rocky slopes, but cold wind answered his feeble prayer, whistling across the mountain range and biting through his garments to bring a chill to his bones. Billy felt more sorry for the dog than for himself. He wore a heavy coat with double layers underneath. Hambone had only his natural coat and bare paws.

After a couple of hours of guessing the correct route, the scenery became more familiar. Billy pointed to a flat clearing in the distance. "That's where the helicopter landed. It's not far now." A few minutes later they arrived at the crash scene, and Billy planted both feet and nearly dropped the leash. "It's all cleaned up!"

His mother walked over to the main fuselage and kicked it with her boot. "You mean burned up!" She pointed all around the plane. "The metal's charred, all the bushes are either gone or blackened, and even the blood's been scorched away." She picked up a mangled, unreadable soda can and threw it back down. "What's Devin up to now? Why would he try to burn the evidence of his crime when we already know who did it?"

Billy ran over to where he had stacked the Bibles. "They're gone!" He picked up a scorched canvas blanket from the ground. "Only the tarp's still here."

Billy's mom put her fists on her hips and huffed. "Then Devin really did deliver that Bible? Why would he steal all of them?"

"I'm not so sure it's Devin, Mom. C'mon. Let's get Hambone started."

She tilted her head forward. "Do you know how to lead a tracking dog?"

"I was hoping he'd be smart enough just to lead me." Billy felt a jerk on the leash. "Here we go!" He raced ahead, trying to keep Hambone in check.

Billy's mother ran behind, and they jogged to keep up with the veteran tracker. The dog obviously knew where he was going, having followed this trail before, and he tugged at the leash, apparently anxious to get on with it and get out of the cold.

Hambone led them across the face of the mountain ridge and then down a slope toward a valley for about a mile before finally emerging onto the valley floor. They stepped cautiously into the open and surveyed the grassy field, a stone's throw in width and at least a couple of football fields in length. The dog, still with his nose to the ground, proceeded to the middle of the field and stopped at the edge of a creek, lifting his head to stare at the upslope on the opposite side of the valley floor.

The bubbling creek wound through the open field of tall, snow-speckled brown grass. The long, winter-worn blades looked like trampled wheat sprinkled with sugar, and a winding channel cut through the middle in a two-foot-wide highway of steaming water. On the other side of the valley, green fir trees bordered the field, making the quiet meadow a secluded sanctuary.

Billy pulled up the leash and patted the dog's head. "There's no cave here, boy. What's the matter?"

Billy's mom caught up and tried to catch her breath. "He must smell something."

They both looked around, stone silent. They listened. They sniffed the air. Billy heard the creek's gently running water and the wind whistling through the naked trees at the edges of the field. His nose detected the musty aroma of rotting leaves the wind had blown into the clutches of the thick grass. After a few seconds he sensed something else, not a sound or a smell, just a feeling. "Mom, do you feel something weird?" he asked in a whisper.

His mother stared straight ahead and kept her head still. "No."

"I do. Maybe I feel what Hambone's sensing." Billy scanned the trees while rubbing his thumb up and down the leather leash. He felt naked out in the open field, and they weren't close enough to the forest edge to make a dash for it. "Remember what Dad said about dragons?" he asked, still whispering. "He said we can sense danger."

"But you're not a—" she started, but then she paused. "Well, I guess you are . . . sort of."

A gunshot rang out. Billy and his mother jumped, and both fell to a crouch. Hambone bayed wildly and strained at his leash. Billy searched the trees for any sign of movement.

Nothing.

No, wait. He did see something, a flash of movement behind a big trunk.

"Who's there?" he called out. Billy's mother squatted by his side and looked down his line of sight. With a choked snarl, Hambone strained at the collar.

A man stepped out from behind the tree, a rifle raised to his shoulder, his eyes looking down the long barrel. Billy pushed his mother farther into the tall grass and covered her with his body. Hambone jerked away and rushed at the man, but with a heart-stopping crack from the rifle, the hound snapped backwards and fell to the ground, motionless.

"Nooo!" Billy yelled, and a stream of fire spewed forth toward the assailant. The flaming surge crossed the grass and nearly reached the forest, but it stopped well short of its target, igniting a path of grass and leaves on the valley floor. Billy didn't move. He kept himself sprawled over his mother.

"Billy," she whispered from underneath. "What is it? Who is it?"

"Some guy with a rifle," he said, his voice trembling. The burning sensation had returned, but it wasn't as bad this time. "I've never seen him before. He's already shot Hambone. Stay still. He won't dare come near us."

The man shouted from the tree. "It's not your mom I want, Dragon Boy. It's you! Now get up and take your medicine, and I'll leave her alone."

"You'll have to come and get me," Billy shouted back.

"You think I'm stupid? I'm not coming anywhere near you, not where your yap can spit fire on me." He raised his rifle back to his shoulder. "I guess I'll just have to shoot from here. I'm not that good a shot, so if I hit your mom, it'll just be too bad. I'll give you to five."

Billy breathed heavily, and his eyes darted around.

"One . . ."

What should he do? Stand up and get shot? Let his mother get shot?

"Two . . ."

He was about to ask his mother for help when he noticed the ring on his finger, his Dad's rubellite.

"Three . . ."

Seeing the ring brought a flood of images to his mind, his father's strength, his bravery. Without a doubt, he knew what he had to do.

"Four . . ."

"Wait!" Billy shouted, raising one hand high. "Wait!" He rose slowly, first to his knees and then straight up. With trembling legs, he took a deep breath, closed his eyes, and waited.

His mother tried to pull him down, screaming, "Billy! No!"

The gunman cackled and taunted loudly. "Wait till I tell Devin that I killed one of the mongrel pups!"

Billy tensed his frame, resisting his mother's frantic pull. She tried to get up, but he kept his foot on her back, pushing against her struggling body.

Just get it over with! he thought as he waited for the bullet to tear through his body. *I don't think it will kill me, but I bet it'll really hurt!*

But the shot never came.

"Aiieee!"

Billy's eyes flew open, and he saw the man running in tight circles, covered with flames. After a couple of seconds, he dropped to the ground and rolled. Billy cupped his hand over his mouth. *That fire didn't come from me, did it?*

He pulled his mom to her feet, and they rushed toward the gunman. As he neared their assailant, Billy slowed down to search the carpet of leaves for the rifle while his mother kept running. After a few seconds he spotted it and snatched it up. When he turned back to the man, he saw his mother kneeling at his side. A thin swirl of smoke rose from where the man lay, but he couldn't see his face; his mother blocked his view. He started to dash toward her, but his feet slipped, rustling the leaves, and he dropped to one knee.

Her wailing voice drilled into his ear. "Don't come any closer!" Billy stood up, and his knees locked in place.

Her voice lowered, trembling as her breathy wisps joined the gray plume of smoke. "He's—He's dead!"

"Dead?"

He watched the back of her nodding head.

"You mean . . . I killed him?"

She nodded again. "I don't want you to see this. Just turn around, and let's go on."

Billy obeyed and waited for her to join him, shivering from the cold and the terrifying thought of what he'd done. He felt her gentle arm around his neck and a reassuring squeeze.

"Mom, I didn't mean to—I mean, I was just trying to— I didn't even feel any—"

She tightened her grip. "I know. You were protecting me."

Billy swallowed hard as they stepped away from the stench of death. “Yeah, I was, but it was more than that. I felt this boiling anger, and it just erupted like a volcano. I couldn’t control it. But after the first blast that missed, I didn’t feel another.”

She patted him on the back and then pushed on his shoulder to urge him forward while kicking the smoldering leaves into the mix of snow and grass. “I know, but we’ll talk about it later. Right now we have to see about the dog.”

Billy jerked his hands up to his face. “Hambone!” They sprinted toward the spot where the dog had fallen, but a loud flapping sound made Billy jerk his head up toward the sky.

What greeted his eyes was easily the most wonderful and the most terrible sight he had ever beheld. An enormous winged creature was flying away, its long tail waving and its armor-like scales shimmering in the bright sun.

Billy jumped up and down. “Dad!” he screamed. “Dad!”

His mother looked up and stared at her son, her head cocked to the side. “Dad? What are you talking about?”

Billy pointed to the sky. “I didn’t kill that guy after all.” He jumped up and down, waving. “Dad! Come back!”

His mother stood up, and her eyes froze on the huge flying shape. She clutched her coat and gasped. “Heaven help us!” She fell to her knees, and her eyes followed the amazing sight as though hypnotized by the rhythmic beat of its wings. Billy rushed over to help her up while trying to keep his eyes on the majestic creature in the sky. It wasn’t flying away; it just sort of glided in a small circle.

“Is Hambone dead?” Billy asked, still looking up.

Billy’s mother shook herself out of her daze. “What? . . . Oh. . . . No. It looks like a pretty bad wound in his shoulder. I think he’s in shock.”

Billy threw down the gun, tore off his outer coat, and covered the injured hound. "C'mon! Let's follow Dad!"

"You mean the dragon?"

"Exactly!"

Billy scooped up Hambone with both arms, coat and all, and jogged toward the dragon while his mother carried the rifle. He had to be careful, looking up, running on mountain terrain, and carrying a heavy dog at the same time. But nothing would stop him now.

Once Billy arrived at the dragon's shadow, the dragon flapped his massive wings and glided to another spot, using his shadow to guide Billy and his mother to the next destination. Billy had a hard time seeing the shadow when the dark undulating shape fell on treetops and barely filtered to the ground. But the dragon flew in tight circles, and the shadow moved around, as if waltzing on a stage until he could spot it again. Finally, they traveled into a dense part of the forest.

"Can you see it anywhere?" Billy asked, his arms hugging Hambone close.

"No. Let's just keep going in the direction we were heading and—" She stopped.

"What? What is it?"

She pointed with the rifle toward the dark hillside, too dark for the ample amount of sunshine the bare trees allowed through. "It's the cave!"

Billy laid Hambone just inside the entrance, out of the wind, and reached for his mother's hand. She hid the rifle under a bush, and together they stepped slowly forward. The opening was high enough for both to pass through without ducking, but it was so shrouded by tree trunks, it was no wonder the searchers hadn't seen it until Hambone sniffed it out.

As they tiptoed farther in, daylight faded, but a flicker from deep within beckoned them. Although the walls and ceiling were invisible in the darkness, they felt as though the cave had opened up into a yawning chasm. A gentle breeze wafted across their faces as they stepped, and gravel crunched beneath their shoes. Each keeping an arm extended in front, they held hands and shuffled toward the light.

The cavern breathed. For a few seconds the frigid air seeped through from behind, and then, after a second or two of absolute calm, a warmer mass from within caressed their cold, chapped faces. The warmth smelled stale, the spent exhaust of the massive cave.

Billy's mother whispered. "Is that light what I think it is?"

Billy clutched her hand even more tightly. "I think we're about to find out once and for all." He tugged on her arm. "Let's run. If my father's in there then I know he's already cleared the way!"

Billy's mother lurched forward, her feet barely keeping up with her lunging body. "But what if we're wrong?"

"Then I don't care what happens to me!" Billy let go of her hand and ran even faster toward the light, and in a second or two he was there, passing into an inner room where a torch, fastened to the wall by a metal strap, illumined the cavern with dancing flickers of burnt orange. His mother caught up with him and stopped at his side. Billy's eyes darted around the cave until they rested on a huge, glowing mass in the center, a magnificent dragon.

It had to be—

"Dad?" he whispered. The weak call swirled around the inner room, echoing back to his ears several times. Hearing his own simple call of faith, Billy trembled. He slipped his arm around his mother's waist, grabbing a tight handful of her coat.

A deep, echoing reply came back. "Yes, son. It is I . . . present and accounted for."

The sound was more of a rumble than a voice, but its reverberation passed repeatedly into Billy's ears, filtering through coal-soaked rocks with each journey around the room until the last dying echo whispered the familiar voice of Jared Bannister.

The droning rumble drilled its way into Billy's soul, filling him with fear and melting away his confidence. Although he had figured out the prophecy's message, actually experiencing the fulfillment both in sight and sound brought back all his fears and with them the nagging distrust that only bitter betrayal can raise.

Billy stepped back from the armored beast. How badly he wanted to embrace the scaly neck, filling his aching, hungry arms with his father's masculine presence, but an awful feeling held him in place, like chains binding his arms and legs. How could this creature be the father he had trusted all of his life? The long-kept secret felt more and more like a stinging lie that burned more deeply with every passing second.

He reached out his hand but took no steps. His reach wasn't enough. He could only grasp a fistful of dark air.

Billy's mother stepped forward cautiously and put her hands on the massive body, feeling her way across his radiant flanks and up toward his head. She looked back. "Billy!" she cried joyfully, stretching out her hand for his. "It's your father. Come on!"

Billy took one step and reached again—still not enough.

"Billy, can't you see? It's Dad! You knew it all along; you believed in him!"

Billy tried to answer, but his quivering lips refused to form the words. Finally, he pushed out his pain-racked thoughts. "I—I said I believed, but . . ." He forced back the tears and just stood motionless.

She stepped back and took his hand, pulling him toward the center of the room. His body tipped forward until his feet had to follow. He offered no resistance, and he threw his hands in front of himself to brace for a fall. His palms slapped heavily on the scaly armor, and his arms sprawled out over the enormous body. The armor felt surprisingly smooth, and radiating warmth spread from his palms up to his shoulders, chasing every chill out of his body. But his doubts remained, his heart resisting and strangely cold.

Billy's mother turned to the dragon and rubbed her arms all over his strong back. "Jared, Jared, it's really you!"

A new sound rumbled forth from deep within the heaving form. "Yes, my love."

"Jared, please forgive me. Billy figured it all out. I guess I knew what he was thinking, but I didn't want to admit it. I just had too many doubts."

The dragon covered Marilyn's back with an outstretched wing and pulled her even closer. He spoke in a soft murmur. "And where are your doubts now?"

"They're gone," she said, crying, still rubbing his scales. "I'm here; you're here. There's nothing left to doubt."

"That is all that matters. The prophecy is fulfilled, and I am again Clefspeare. You are blessed for believing, even though you once held doubts."

She lifted her head, tears streaming down her cheeks. "Billy kept pushing me. I said I believed, but he's the one that got the dog and hunted for you, even though everyone else was ready to give up."

"Then his blessing is the greater, for he has believed without seeing." The dragon looked at Billy, who knelt trembling at his flank. "But where is his faith now?"

Billy reached to take his mother's hand, and his voice shook. "I—I believe, that is, I believe you're a dragon. I knew I had to keep looking."

The dragon moved his wing to cover Billy, too. "And I never would have stopped trying to draw you to myself."

Billy tried to find the dragon's face, but the creature's glow diminished along with the size of the scales as its neck tapered toward his head. Two red points of light floated in the darkening cave. "You mean the ring and the Bible?" Billy asked.

"Yes. That is what I used to call you here."

"To call me? But how could you get to the Foley's porch without being noticed?"

"We dragons have our ways."

Billy wanted a better explanation. He pictured a huge dragon gracefully soaring over Walter's house and gliding to a pinpoint stop in the front yard and then lumbering up the steps to drop a trinket or two, but he felt he wasn't going to get any more information about that. "How did you know the Bible you brought was the one I had?"

The dragon inhaled deeply and then let out his breath, a stream of sparks spewing into the air along with it. "I detected your scent," he said in a matter-of-fact tone.

"Oh, yeah. I got sick and threw up on the cover."

"In fact," the dragon continued, "I discovered that I can feel when you are near. It is not quite the same as what I feel when danger approaches; it is sweet instead of bitter."

"Only when I'm near? How about Mom?"

"No, not your mother. I think it is because you have dragon blood in you and she has none."

Billy thought about that for a moment. Dragon blood, the blood of this huge beast flowing through his own veins. In one flash he was both honored and disgusted, feeling nobility mixing with the coarse brutality of a strange monster.

Clefspeare shifted his weight, and Billy thought he could see the head, a dark outline in the dying flicker. "Please, tell me," the dragon rumbled. "What is the fate of the daughter of Hartanna?"

"We rescued her," Billy replied, glad to talk about someone else. "She's fine, except for an injured knee and wing, but she seems to be getting better. She should be walking, and flying, real soon."

"Very good! You also mentioned the dog. I saw what happened. Is it dead?"

Billy pulled away from the dragon and stayed in a crouch. "No. He's not dead—at least he wasn't. Mom says he's in shock."

"I remember that hound. He came by here with a mountain man. I made it out of the cave right before they arrived. Take the torch. Bring him to me."

Billy looked at the weak torch hanging on the wall, but before he could rise to get it, Clefspeare let out a snort, and a ball of fire hurtled toward the rag-topped stick. It burst to life, and the room cast off much of its darkness.

Billy jumped up to get the torch, and with the new light all around, neither he nor his mother could resist gazing at the magnificent creature before them. Clefspeare lay on his belly, his noble head raised up at the end of a sleek, long neck. The details of his face were still dim, but the beauty of his eyes was obvious, perfectly circular orbs with sparkling, fiery red pupils surrounded by a shimmering dark iris, a corona seemingly painted by the cave's bituminous coal.

Billy ran to the wall, snatched the torch from its blackened frame, a familiar looking strip of metal, and dashed toward the cave's entrance. With the torch in one hand, he tried to wrap both arms and his coat around Hambone. The hound's body, still warm but deathly still, sagged as Billy lumbered back into the cave. When he approached the inner room, Hambone began to slip away from his grip, so Billy placed him gently on the floor to try to get a better hold. Now on his knees, he heard voices echoing from within, his mother's voice, frail and sad. He stopped and listened, mesmerized by the ghostly sounds.

Clefspeare's gentle, low growl drifted into Billy's ears. "Marilyn, you have always known about my past as well as the prophecies. There is nothing I have hidden from you. My Garden of Eden test finally came, and I did not fail. Your husband is now dead, and Clefspeare lives again."

The dragon let out a deep sigh. "Although I cannot live in your home, I will never forsake you. I cannot say how often the gems I find will appear on your doorstep, but I will always provide for your needs."

A coarser growl seeped into his voice. "Protecting you from the slayer, however, will be more difficult. While I was human, I lost my ability to sense danger. Now I can feel the darkness of a growing conspiracy, a distant evil that has marched an army of shadows into this realm. It is strange, a sort of unearthly influence that I cannot fully describe—sinister, treacherous. And being a dragon in a time that has never known our species, I am stranded in my own world of shadows, unable to freely defend my loved ones. I have a feeling, though, that your protection will be provided no matter where I am."

The conversation paused, and Billy shook himself out of his trance. He struggled through the remaining steps to the inner chamber, once again carrying Hambone and the torch at the same time. His mother jumped to help, grabbing the torch and guiding Billy to the center of the room. The fire was already dying; the oily rag had lost most of its fuel.

Billy set Hambone down and smoothed out his coat over the deathly still hound.

"Remove the covering," Clefspeare ordered.

Billy pulled the coat, gently rolling Hambone to the bare cave floor, and he put it back on his own body, turning it inside out first to avoid the dog's blood. Clefspeare's head moved toward the hound, seemingly floating down as his neck stretched out. He sniffed Hambone while nudging him with his nose.

"He is alive, but just barely. I will cauterize the wound and then make him warm. Billy, go outside and bring back as much snow or ice as you can."

Billy rushed out and returned within a minute, out of breath and his arms loaded down with an unwieldy boulder of icy snow. "There was a bunch in a shady spot right outside," he explained, setting it down. "I rolled it into a ball."

"Good." Clefspeare opened his huge mouth and crunched the ball in his teeth, leaving only a scattering of sparkling crystals on the floor. He pushed his nose into Hambone's shoulder and let out a short snuff. A tiny stream of smoke arose, and the smell of burnt flesh filtered through the room. Clefspeare then pulled his head back a few feet and breathed a cascade of steam toward Hambone. The white gas spewed far enough to bring a jet of moist warmth to the dog's body, and the cloud dissipated before striking him.

Clefspeare continued the therapy for nearly a minute. The dog's shallow, chaotic breathing changed, becoming deeper and more rhythmic. His tail twitched, the end flipping up and down, and finally, he raised his head.

Clefspeare turned off the steamy jets and then breathed fire on the torch again, reigniting the dying lamp.

Billy's mother jumped back from the flame but hung on to the torch. She extended her arm to avoid the heat. "Is there anything you can't do?"

"I cannot make a torch out of nothing. If I am unable to get more oil and a new rag, I will have no torch at all."

Billy scooped up Hambone and caressed him in his lap, allowing him to lick the few ice pellets that lay on the ground. The hound whimpered weakly, but his wide-open eyes told them much more. He was going to make it.

"I salvaged the rags and oil from Merlin," Clefspeare explained, "as well as the torch frame that's on the wall. It's the nameplate from the dashboard. I recovered everything I could and then burned the wreckage. I didn't want anyone poking around to try to put the pieces of our lives together. Everything important is safe. The Bibles are in another chamber in this cave, and so is *Fama Regis* and our box of papers."

"*Fama Regis,*" Billy repeated. "What does that mean?"

"The title is Latin. It is the story of the king, King Arthur's chronicles, and the scribe I told you about back home was Sir Devin's squire. Although he wrote most of the contents in an old dialect of English, he sometimes preferred Latin for titles and prayers. The book is very valuable, so I am sure Devin would like to get it back. His host has been all around this mountain, so I have to stay here most of the time. I sense when one of them is near, and I also sensed your approach. That is how I knew to rescue you from that gunman."

"I sensed danger, too. And another time on the mountain, I saved Bonnie from Devin. I left her behind, trying to find help, but I sensed something was wrong and ran back. Sure enough, Devin was about to kill her. I got there just in time."

"Then your fire-breathing is not your only dragon trait."

"What's the other one?" Billy asked, laughing. "Arriving at the very last minute after someone's scared half to death?"

The dragon laughed, and, oh, what a laugh! The merry rumble swept through the cavern, creating tiny tremors beneath their feet that traveled up their legs, and the noisy tickling made them all laugh together until new, joyful tears rolled down their cheeks.

For a minute, Billy felt lighthearted, just like old times. But it couldn't last; a dark shadow pushed into his mind, the realization that the old times were gone forever.

He put Hambone back down on the floor and stood to face the dragon. "So what now? 'The dragon shorn lives again.' Is the prophecy fulfilled? Will the host come to fight you?"

Clefspeare moved his head to look his son in the eye. "So you have come to understand. Tell me. Where do you fit into the prophecy?"

Billy looked toward his mother, partly to see her expression and partly because the dragon seemed to be able to see right through him. It was uncomfortable, but he forced himself to make eye contact again. "I guess I'm the child of doubt," he replied softly.

"And why are you the child of doubt?"

"Because I doubted you and Mom. You never told me about being a dragon, so I wondered if I could ever trust you again. I felt like I couldn't trust anybody."

"And now your trust has returned?"

Billy shuffled his feet and he looked down at the dark, stone floor. "I—I'm not sure."

"Then why did you pursue me so faithfully?"

"It was something that Professor Hamilton said. He said I couldn't understand the New Testament without understanding the Old, and then I thought about you. I couldn't understand what you did until I really understood what you were before."

Clefspeare pored over Billy's face, the dragon's gaze penetrating Billy's every thought. "And now you understand?" His loud voice rumbled through the cave.

Billy just stared back, petrified once again.

The dragon's fiery eyes brightened even more, and the glowing stare grew ever more piercing. He let out a low growl. "Now that I am no longer in your home, you have to remain as your mother's only protector. Why did you stand to let yourself be shot?"

Billy gulped and forced himself to answer. "Ju—just like you said. To—To protect Mom, just like you did on the plane to protect us." He gulped again and took a deep breath to make himself strong. "It was the honorable thing to do; it was what a brave and trustworthy man would do."

The dragon put his nose right next to his son's, and Billy felt hot, dry gasses surround his neck. The rumbling dragon voice settled into a soft purr. "But that is not all, is it?"

Clefspeare's gentle, warm breath settled Billy's trembling body. "No. When my father—I mean, when you were on the plane, you knew the prophecy had to be fulfilled. You weren't afraid to be shot."

The dragon drew back his head, but only a little. "And you were not afraid?"

Billy took another deep breath. "I was scared stiff, but I thought, well, I was really guessing, that I still had a part in the prophecy. If I *am* part of the prophecy, I guessed it would all be okay. If I wasn't, and everything was a lie, well . . . then I guess I really didn't care what happened to me."

"And what is your part?"

Billy scraped his shoes on the cave floor again. "I think I know, but . . ." His voice trailed away.

Clefspeare pulled back and raised his head high. "I think you know, too." The dragon paused. His cherry-red eyes seemed to burst into flames, and his voice growled. "The slayer will be back, and I must do battle with him. I do not know when that will happen."

Billy cringed at the sudden growl, and the flaming eyes made his bones feel like rubber. Clefspeare's words brought a new question to his mind, but he wasn't sure how to ask it. He sat down and spoke quietly, almost hoping no one would hear. "Will you win?"

Clefspeare dropped his head back to Billy's level. "The prophecy says that faith will win the war. That is all I know."

Billy noticed that his cold hand rested on the dragon's scales. The skin on scale contact reflected his feelings, warm and cold at the same time.

He looked back at Hambone, who seemed to be resting comfortably, and wondered what to do about him. "I guess I have to take Hambone back to Mr. Hatfield. He won't be happy about his champion dog getting shot."

The dragon looked the hound over again as if appraising his value. "Offer to buy him."

"Buy him?" Billy shuffled his feet to where Hambone rested, and he scratched behind the dog's ear. "He must be worth a lot, and Mom says we'll be tight for money. Besides, I don't think he'll want to part with a champion hound."

Clefspeare moved his head toward the back wall. "Come and see what I have over here."

Billy followed the dragon's lead, but the light grew dimmer where the floor met the wall, so he tiptoed until he reached the back of the cave. He knelt and bent over to get a look at the floor. "I see two piles of stones."

"They are all gems. I will polish some to start my regeneracy dome, and others I will give to you. For now, pick out the largest stone from the smaller pile and offer to buy the dog with it. If he won't sell the dog, at least he will be able to pay the medical bills. I have seen Mr. Hatfield, and he is a lot smarter than you might think. I know his skill; I had to hide from him. He knows these mountains, and I think he will recognize a ruby when he sees one, even in the rough."

Billy picked up a large stone from near the bottom of the pile, spilling the others from the top. "Mr. Hamilton said rubies aren't easy to find in West Virginia." He looked back at the dragon. "How did you find so many?"

"I am a dragon. Finding gems is in my nature." Clefspeare swept his pile of stones closer together with his wing. "I have already flown south to mine a richer territory. Just tell Mr. Hatfield what the stone is. He will believe you."

Billy's head jerked up. His voice and legs trembled. "I feel . . . something."

Clefspeare raised his head, and his ears perked. "Yes, son. Danger. I feel it, too. It is not very close, but too close for you to stay. Take the ruby with you, redeem the dog, and go home. I will watch over you until you are off the mountain." He winked at Billy and added, "Count on it."

Billy remained silent, staring at Clefspeare's strangely familiar eyes. The winking dragon made him shudder deep within, and hearing his father's signal phrase made him feel cold and bitter once more, like an imposter had appeared and posed as his missing dad.

His mother stood and caressed her husband's neck. "Jared, when will we see you again? Can I come—"

The dragon pushed her away with his head and touched her shoulder lightly with the tip of his wing. "There is no time. Go. I will erase the tracks you make near the cave, and I will contact you later."

Billy put the ruby in his pocket. He then slid both arms under Hambone and lifted him to chest level. Clefspeare reignited the torch, allowing the two to see their way back to the cave entrance. As they stepped out into the frigid wind, Billy tried to shield Hambone by sliding him under his coat while allowing the dog's head and front legs to poke through at the top. It was very uncomfortable for Billy, but Hambone cooperated.

"Billy, do you still sense danger?"

"No, not really. Not anymore."

"Then let's go back the way we came. Your father said he'd watch over us, so I guess we'll count on that even if we can't see him."

The two retraced their steps. Sometimes that was easy, especially in the unexposed ground where the snow preserved their tracks, but in the more open areas, they had to guess.

After several minutes they came upon the shooting scene. The path of burnt leaves that Billy's breath had made was still there, but the dead body of the gunman was gone. "Not another missing body!" Billy complained, his head swiveling to search the area.

"We can't stop to look around. Whoever took it might still be nearby."

Billy shook his head. "Maybe. I don't know. I'm still not very good at this danger-sensing business."

CHAPTER 18

The Meeting

With the morning's light filtering into the schoolroom, Billy sat at the table, busily drawing a picture of Arlo Hatfield for Walter and occasionally taking a sip from his root beer. Billy knew that Walter expected a wild, Thursday morning story. Although his pencil sketch caricature was quite exaggerated, anyone who knew the mountain man would have recognized him right away. Billy slid the page across the table, and Walter laughed out loud.

"So that's the old hillbilly?" Walter asked, admiring the art. "And this isn't one of those Thursday morning tall tales?"

"I wouldn't have believed it myself if I hadn't been there. He has a real outhouse, and the dogs have a better home than he does."

Walter slid the drawing back to Billy. "That's a great picture. Maybe you ought to sign it and hang it up somewhere."

Billy drew a symbol at the bottom of the portrait with a swirling flair. It was a simple design, the letters "BB" with the first B reversed to sit back-to-back with the second one, the same symbol he used to sign all his artwork. With an impish grin, he held the drawing next to his own face.

Walter peered at the symbol and then again at the caricature. "I think it's really a self-portrait."

Billy held up a fist and playfully swung at his friend, and when Walter tried to snatch the drawing, Billy pulled it back. After a short tussle, Billy sat back with his picture and thought about Mr. Hatfield and the day's events. "So what did you do yesterday while I was up on the mountain?"

Walter had a piece of paper, too, and he looked down at it while making it into an airplane. "Professor Hamilton came over to teach."

"He did? I thought we agreed to cancel school yesterday since I had to be gone."

"We did, but I called to tell him that he left his elephant gun here. He said as long as he was coming over, seeing that I was so interested, he would teach me about a few other exotic weapons. He brought a crossbow, a dart blowgun with real darts, a boomerang, and a big rock."

Billy stared at his friend. "A big rock?"

"Yeah. He said he couldn't fit the catapult in his station wagon." Walter couldn't hold his straight face any longer, and he burst out laughing.

Billy held up his root beer can. "You're kidding, right?"

Walter shook his head and got up to act out his story. "No. For real. He really brought a rock. And we tried to build a little catapult out in the back yard. When we launched the rock—"

"Don't tell me. You broke a window."

"No. The rock went about ten inches to the side and landed on my foot." Walter lifted his knee and hopped around for a few seconds. "It really hurt, but we had a blast."

Billy laughed long and hard, his spirits feeling higher than they had in several days. When he settled down, his thoughts drifted from one delight to another. "Did you hear from Bonnie? What'd she do yesterday?"

"I don't know. She didn't call. I don't think her foster parents let her use the phone. Why don't you ask her when she gets here?"

Billy got up and looked out the window at the new kennel in the yard, a large covered cage, complete with a modern space heater. "So did you get a look at Hambone? I get to keep him until his wound heals. Arlo said, 'he ain't no good for huntin' with that thar bullet hole innim.' "

Walter laughed. "Yeah. He's a cool dog. Too bad you'll have to give him back. Dad's always wanted an excuse to take up hunting again."

Billy came back to the table and gave Walter a proud smile. "He did a great job trying to find the cave for us yesterday. He'd be a good tracking dog for your dad."

"Yeah. But if Hambone's going to be a hunter again, he has to lose that ugly doggy sweater you got for him." Walter snickered. "Did you get it off a dead basset hound or something?"

Billy raised his fist again but dropped it when he heard a noise.

The front door opened and closed, and Professor Hamilton strode hurriedly into the room. His eyes darted around, and his trembling hands fumbled to pull off his gloves. "Walter, is your father still here?"

"I think so. What's wrong?"

The professor shook his head. "Oh, it's terrible, just terrible. Please, summon your father at once."

Walter left in a hurry, and the professor paced from one side of the room to another. Billy stood and grabbed one of his teacher's upper arms. "Professor Hamilton, what is it?"

The professor stopped and stared at Billy, but his lips failed to move. Billy looked around the room. Something was missing. "Where's Bonnie? Didn't you give her a ride this morning?"

The professor mumbled something and then turned to greet Walter's father as he hustled in. Billy's mother followed, along with Walter and his mother. "Professor, what is it?" Mr. Foley asked.

"It's Miss Silver," the professor said, his face anguished and pale. "She's gone. Someone accused her foster parents of neglect, and the authorities have shipped her back to Montana."

Billy clenched his fists and shouted. "To Montana?!"

Mr. Foley's face turned sunburn red. "Who ordered this?"

"You're an attorney," the professor replied. "I assumed you would be able to find out. When I went to her house, nobody was home. A neighbor told me what happened."

"What did the police say? They were supposed to be there."

"There was a policeman there," the professor explained, "but he refused to tell me anything."

"Could Devin be behind this?" Billy's mother asked.

"If he can pull off being an FBI agent," Mr. Foley said, "then he might have been able to stick his nose into this, too."

Billy wadded up his drawing and hurled it across the room. "But he doesn't want her in Montana. He wants her dead."

The professor ran his hand through his scattered hair. "And we have no idea who's transporting her."

Mr. Foley checked his belt clip for his cell phone and kissed his wife on the cheek. "I'd better get over to Bonnie's house and see what's going on." He put his hand on Walter's shoulder. "Son, get the brown folder on my desk and meet me at the car." He grasped Professor Hamilton's elbow and led him toward the hallway. "Walk with me. I have a couple of questions to ask you."

The professor nodded, and the two hurried from the room. Within seconds the front door slammed shut. Walter raised his eyebrows and shrugged his shoulders at Billy before hustling toward the office.

Billy began pacing the floor in front of his mother. "Now what?" he said, punching his palm with his fist. "We can't just sit here and wait!"

"What else can we do?" his mother asked. "Where can we go to look?"

"Make some calls! Find out where they took her."

"If I know Carl," Mrs. Foley interjected, "he'll make calls while he's driving. If he needs our help, he'll let us know what to do." She folded her arms across her chest and tapped her foot. "I'd better go see if Walter found that folder."

When Mrs. Foley left the room, Billy pressed his hands on the windowsill and watched the professor close the car door for Mr. Foley. Walter handed a folder to his dad through the window, and Mr. Foley reached out and pulled Walter into a manly embrace, ending with a firm pat on the back. As he watched the car roll back on the driveway, Walter's smile grew into a wide grin, and when the car disappeared around the corner, he and the professor walked toward a side door that led to the home office.

Billy leaned over and whispered in his mother's ear. "Mom, let's go see the dragon. Maybe he'll know what to do."

She brushed a piece of lint from Billy's shirt, and her hand lingered on his shoulder. Her voice stayed low, just above a whisper. "He said he would contact us. I don't think we should."

Billy shook his head. "The dragon said he'd seen Devin's men around the mountain. Maybe he heard them say something. Maybe if he tells us what he's heard, we'll figure out a clue. It's not like he can pick up a phone and tell us what he knows."

She put her hand to her chin. "Do you think we can find the cave again without Hambone?"

"In a heartbeat."

A knock at the front door made them stop and turn, and Walter's tennis shoes squeaked down the hall until he reached the doorway. Billy and his mom kept quiet, trying to listen.

"Adam! What are you doing here?"

"I have a message for Dragon Breath."

Billy rushed out of the schoolroom just as Walter closed the door, turning a pale blue envelope over and over in his hand. He held it out. "It's for you."

Billy snatched it and ripped it open. A creased piece of paper fell out along with a neatly clipped lock of light brown hair. He quickly scanned the words and looked up at Walter. "Um, sorry Walter. I'd better keep this private."

Walter shrugged his shoulders. "Whatever." But when Billy turned, Walter tapped him on the back. "Can I look at the envelope?"

Billy dropped the lock of hair back into the envelope and handed it to Walter. The professor walked in from the office, his head nodding as though he were counting the people in the room. "I thought I heard Mr. Lark's voice. Is there a new mystery at hand?"

Walter showed his teacher the envelope and lock of hair, and the two buzzed about it while Billy and his mother bent over to read the note.

> I'm sure you've heard by now that your girlfriend is supposedly Montana bound. I know you killed one of my host; I saw your work. If you ever want to see Bonnie again, meet me at the scene of your crime this afternoon at two. Come alone!

Billy folded up the note, and he and his mother stared at each other with their hands on their hips. Billy spoke first, loud enough for everyone to hear. "Devin says he has Bonnie and he wants me to meet him back at the mountain by two or he'll kill her. So much for the police protection; it didn't help—"

"I don't think he has Bonnie," Walter interrupted.

Billy turned to see Walter holding the envelope and the professor still studying the lock. "Isn't that her hair?" Billy asked.

The professor held up the tawny strands. "I took careful note of Miss Silver's hair some time ago. When we had our class on origins, she was quite reticent, so I tried to make an estimate of her heritage. Her hair gave away a strong English tie with a healthy mixture of Scandinavian highlights. This lock has the same characteristics. A counterfeit is highly unlikely."

"And besides that," Walter added. "Do you remember that Bonnie told us he cut off some of her hair and put it in an envelope?"

"You're right," Billy agreed. "She did."

"Well, when I whacked him," Walter went on, holding the envelope at eye level, "I remember seeing a blue envelope sticking out of his coat pocket. That's not a new lock of hair. He already had it."

Billy gazed at the note again and spoke slowly. "Then if Devin doesn't have her, why would she be going to Montana all of a sudden, and how does Devin know about it?"

The professor reached for the envelope and tucked the hair inside. "I assume, William, that Devin learned of Miss Silver's fate the same way I did. When he could not find Miss Silver, he simply asked one of the neighbors."

"But if she really did go to Montana," Billy said, "it would be easy to find that out. It would prove he doesn't really have her."

Walter gave Billy a cynical glance. "And still get to the mountain by two? I doubt it. If she really is on the road to Montana, there's no way you could find out for quite a while. Devin's counting on you to believe his lie because you don't have time to find the truth."

The professor pulled out his pocket watch. "Mr. Foley is correct, William. Mr. Lark's visit was timed precisely. If you wish to reach the mountain by two o'clock, you will have to leave right away."

"So Devin doesn't think I'll even try to check the story because he sent the hair."

Walter pointed a finger at Billy. "Exactly."

"But what if you're wrong? What if he kidnapped her and just decided to send the hair he already had? Maybe he planted the story about Montana."

"That is possible, William," the professor said. "However, it would mean that the police allowed someone to enter and forcibly remove the child without checking on his credentials. That doesn't seem likely. And I think Devin would have attempted the kidnapping earlier, if he were able."

Billy nodded and let out a sigh. "You may be right, but Devin's pulled off some big maneuvers, so it's possible the police are on his side, too." He ran his fingers through his hair and bit his lip. "But how can I take a chance either way? And what could I do against Devin? Even if he does have her, if I go up there, he'll just kill both Bonnie and me."

Billy's mother put a hand on his shoulder. "There is a way." She looked at Walter and the professor apologetically. "Please excuse us," she said before leaning over and whispering in Billy's ear. "You wouldn't be alone. If Devin gets that close to the cave, your father will sense him. And since he'll feel your presence, too, he'd be out there in a heartbeat if there's any danger. Maybe this will be your father's chance to get rid of Devin once and for all. We can't keep on living in fear."

Billy whispered back. "But if Devin has his host there to fight, would the dragon be afraid to come out because of the prophecy?"

His mother's brow cast a shadow over her eyes, and she frowned. "Please excuse us again, Walter, Professor." She led Billy out to the kitchen, and she spoke in a low, angry tone. "He's not just 'the dragon.' He's your father. And after all you've seen, do you think your father would be afraid? Remember the prophecy said that faith will win. You showed a lot of faith before; it's about time you found it again."

Billy felt a surge of heat radiate across his face. Her rebuke stabbed his soul. He gritted his teeth to hold back his rage. "And you want me to go up there to face him alone? You talk about faith, but you won't even let me go out fishing at Hardin Pass unless Walter's with me. You tell Dad that I'm not old enough to fly Merlin even though he's with me in the cockpit. Where has your faith been?"

He felt a tear roll down his cheek, but he refused to wipe it. He just kept his angry glare, afraid he would break down and cry if he moved. When he could trust himself to continue, he said, "You've known about Dad being a dragon for years, but you never told me. And you want me to believe in you and Dad now?"

His mother gazed silently at him, her expression softening with each second. New tears formed and made a pathway to her cheeks. Suddenly she reached out and hugged him close, whispering into his ear. "Oh, Billy. I'm so sorry. You're right! You're so right!" She drew in a long breath and pulled back, letting her arms fall to her side. Her tear-streamed face shimmered in the kitchen's soft light. "It's been hard, you know, living with this secret. We struggled for years about whether to tell you or not. And you're right; I have worried about you, how you would turn out, what you would become. We thought telling you slowly, when you were older and could handle it, was the best way to protect you."

She took another deep breath and rested her hand on the nape of Billy's neck. "But now your father's become a dragon! The secret's come out in one huge blast instead of a trickle. How can I expect you to accept something so crazy? How can I expect you to trust in your father as much as I do when I've known about the secret for years?" She pulled him slowly into an embrace, and her weeping began afresh.

Her shoulders shook as she cried, but she kept her arms wrapped around him. Her tears seemed to absorb his fiery anger, but nothing could ease his loneliness or fill the void his father's absence created. He gently slipped his arms around her and pulled himself even closer. At last, his own tears flowed, and the two wept together.

After a minute or two, Billy pulled himself away. "I have to hurry. There's no way to know for sure if Devin has Bonnie, so for her sake, there's really no choice. I have to go and just hope that . . ."

"That Dad helps you," his mother finished. She put her hand on his shoulder, and the squeeze she gave reminded him of his father's strong grip. "He *will* be there," she whispered. "I *know* he'll be there."

Billy dropped his gaze to the floor and nodded. He then hooked her arm in his and pulled her toward the guest room. "Let's get going before I change my mind."

Walter heard a car honk, and he jumped up from the sofa and threw open the front door. He spun back toward his mother who was sitting in a chair adjacent to the sofa. "It's Dad!"

His father leaned his head through the driver's window and yelled, "Walter! Come with me! I need your help."

Walter snatched a jacket from a coat tree. "Mom! I'm going with Dad!" He thrust one arm into a sleeve while running out the door. He jumped into the front seat next to his dad and finished putting on his jacket. "What's up, Pop?"

His father pressed the accelerator, and the car zoomed backwards. "I called everyone I could think of. Nobody's seen her. Nobody."

Walter snapped his seat belt in place. "So what do you need me for?"

"I drove by Bonnie's house and did some checking. I wanted to go inside but a couple of policemen are watching the place. They wouldn't let me in. I have my suspicions about them."

"You think they might be working for Devin?"

His father pointed at him. "Exactly."

Walter sat up straight, pulled one knee up to his chest, and began retying his shoe. "Say no more. I'm working on a plan!"

As they drove, Walter told his father about the note with the dubious lock of hair and how it led to Billy's departure with his mother. When he finished his story he gave the dashboard a swift kick. "I don't like it. It sounds like a trap."

His dad tapped him on the knee. "I don't like it either, but don't take it out on the car." As he drove he hummed a soulful rendition of *Rock of Ages,* adding whispered lyrics from time to time. "We'll try to call Billy after we're done," he finally said. "I hope they have a cell phone with them."

They cruised past Bonnie's house, a small bungalow in a rundown neighborhood, and parked across the street. A bearded man in a police uniform leaned against an oak tree in the middle of the unraked lawn. Dark smudges here and there marred the house's off-white paint, and cobwebs draped the corners of the windows.

Walter glanced at the side of the house and noticed another uniformed man poking a baton through a hedge. His officer blues were neat enough, but his hat couldn't keep his stringy hair from hanging out around the edges.

Walter's father pointed at another house on the left. "According to those neighbors, Bonnie's foster parents reported her missing right away, but the police assumed she was just another teenaged runaway and never checked other possibilities." He moved his pointing finger to indicate a house on the right. "That family heard from some guy standing in Bonnie's yard that she'd been shipped to Montana because of her foster parents' negligence. According to him, Bonnie's parents were both drunk and never even noticed she was missing. The police hauled them away a couple of hours ago."

"I'll bet that guy was Devin or one of his men," Walter said. "He made up a lie to get at Bonnie."

"Could be, but how could he manipulate the police? And who are these uniformed clowns? They look like they just rolled out of a sleazy bar."

Walter eyed the two men again. "So what do you want to do?"

"I want to go inside and look for clues."

Walter swung open the car door and jumped out. "Leave it to me." He sprinted toward the man leaning on the tree, panting heavily as he approached. "You'll never . . . guess . . . what I saw!"

The man's eyes flew open, and he stood up straight. "What?"

Walter leaned over and whispered. "A girl . . . with wings!" He flapped his arms like a drunken albatross. "Huge bat wings!"

The man stepped toward the side of the house and yelled. "Randall! Get over here!" He then turned back to Walter. "Where did you see her, kid?"

Walter waved a shaking finger toward the road. "At the middle school! Hurry!"

"Thanks kid!" The two officers dashed to a car in the driveway, backed out, and squealed away.

Walter turned toward his dad with a smirk and he spread his arms. "Not a problem!"

His father jumped from the car and hurried toward the front door. "What did you tell them?"

"Let's just say that I told them what they wanted to hear."

They stopped at the porch and his father looked him in the eye. "You didn't lie to them, did you?"

Walter put his fingers on his chest. "Me? No way! Every word was true."

His father sighed and shook his head. "Okay. I won't ask."

They walked into the house and scanned the cozy interior. Walter opened a door at the end of a short hallway and piped up. "This must be her room, Dad."

They entered the small bedroom, a room so neat even the pencils on a little desk were lined up according to size. Since those goons were looking for Bonnie, Walter had expected a ransacked house with books, papers, and clothes scattered everywhere. Maybe her obvious absence kept them from trashing the place.

Walter glanced from wall to wall. A stand-up calendar, a framed photograph of a woman, and a hardcover Bible sat on top of the pockmarked desk. Blue cloth upholstery covered a thinly padded seat of the matching dark-wood chair, a decent chair for a little kid, but not for someone Bonnie's age.

To the right of the door sat a neatly made bed, a thick blanket tucked securely all around, but the bed had no frame or headboard, and the clown characters on the blanket were better suited for a girl in kindergarten, not a teenager in middle school. Walter kicked at a circular braided rug that covered about two-thirds of the pine floor. The opposite edge abutted a dresser in the corner that had at least one pull handle missing from every drawer.

Walter's father opened the folding doors of the medium-sized closet, revealing a shallow storage space. Bonnie's brand new dress hung by itself on the left, and two more dresses hung on the right, along with a modest collection of blouses, sweatshirts, and jeans. On the floor sat a fairly new pair of tennis shoes, a pair of black dress shoes, and an open cardboard box filled with stuffed animals.

Walter picked up a stuffed bunny that had a newly stitched ear and threw it back in the box. "Dad, are you thinking what I'm thinking?"

"That this house isn't run by a couple of negligent drunks? Yeah, that's what I'm thinking."

Walter's dad walked over to the desk and opened its file drawer. Dozens of sheets of wrinkled notebook paper stuffed each hanging folder, some with the edges pushing out the top. He sat on the chair and rifled through the files. "I'm looking for anything that might stand out, maybe a note, any clue that Bonnie might have left behind." He pulled out a thick handful of paper and placed the stack on the desk.

"Would she leave a note where the wrong person could find it?" Walter asked.

His father sighed and stared at one of the crisp, white sheets that had dropped onto his lap. "Good point." He handed the fallen page to Walter. "This one looks new. Check it out for me."

Walter began reading the neatly penciled story. An evil wizard captured a fair maiden and locked her in a windowless vault. After many brave attempts to escape, she was aided by a dragon, who, after being transformed into a noble young man, married the damsel, and the two had many children together and lived happily ever after. The story nearly moved Walter to tears, but he didn't let on to his father. He just handed him the sheet. "Read the last paragraph on the back."

His father took the page and read out loud. "Such is the beauty of unshackled love. It is the beacon that finds lost sheep, the oil that fills virgins' lamps, the seed sown on fertile soil. A heart in chains is a slave to passion; it moves and breathes by the will of another. But when it is set free, true love abounds, for the will of another can never dictate love's free choice. Jesus said, 'If the Son shall set you free, you shall be free indeed.' Glorious freedom! Oh, let my heart ever be unshackled! My body, my words, and my thoughts are all His. I freely set my heart in His hands, and I have no other true love."

He set the sheet down and sighed. "Bonnie's dreams." He looked up at Walter, tears welling in his eyes. "Remember what we discussed last night?"

Walter nodded. "Yeah. You and Mom made the right call. No doubt about it."

His father stuffed the pages back in place, closed the drawer, and returned to searching the room. Walter reached for a poster taped to the wall next to the desk. It had a drawing of an angelic girl praying by her bed. Her eyes were focused upward, and the caption said, "Trust in the Lord with all thine heart; and lean not unto thine own understanding. In all thy ways acknowledge him, and he shall direct thy paths." Over by the bed, another smaller poster hung right above the pillow. It had no drawing, just a splash of rainbow colors with another Bible verse, "Call to me, and I will answer you, and I will tell you great and mighty things, which you do not know (Jeremiah 33:3)."

"Dad," Walter said, holding the edge of the smaller poster. "Check out this verse. Think it's a clue?"

"That's probably been there for weeks. A clue would have to be something new."

Walter placed his finger on the verse. "Yeah, but look. The first part is underlined with a red marker. Maybe Bonnie did it."

His father leaned over and read it again. "Call to me. . . . Call to me, and I will answer you."

Walter shrugged his shoulders. "Why not give it a try?"

"Give what a try?"

Walter gestured with his finger. "Follow me." He jogged out of the bedroom and stood in the foyer. "Bonnie!" he shouted as his father joined him. "It's Walter! Are you in here anywhere?"

They stood still and listened. "Was that a thump?" Walter asked.

His father cupped his hands around his mouth and yelled. "Bonnie, are you in here?"

More thumps echoed over their heads and then a voice. "Walter! Wait! It's me. I'll be there in a minute!"

Walter felt goose bumps popping up all over his arms, and he bounced up and down on his toes. His father's teary eyes darted all around as they listened to scratches and bumps coming from the ceiling.

Covered with clumps of pink insulation, Bonnie limped into the family room from the kitchen. She no longer used crutches, but her grimacing walk told them her knee still ached. When she saw Walter's father, she shuffled up to him with a tired smile. He reached out for her and swung her around in a wide circle.

When he set her down, she tried to catch her breath. "I was hiding . . . in the attic. I found out . . . one of the policemen works for Devin, so I couldn't go to them." She wiped her dirty, wet forehead with her sleeve. "You wouldn't believe how close they came to finding me, but it gave me a chance to hear some of their plans."

Walter's father brushed the crumbs of insulation out of Bonnie's hair and a pile of pink fluff from the top of her backpack. "Let's get out of here. You can tell us about it in the car."

Bonnie shook more fibers from her hair. "But how will we get past the police?"

"Walter took care of that," he replied, gesturing toward Walter with his thumb. "Devin's pigeons flew the coop."

Bonnie beamed at Walter and landed a friendly punch on his arm, but her smile faded the next instant. "We have to call Billy. I heard them say Devin's going to try to lure him back to the mountain using me as bait. We have to tell Billy I'm okay so he won't go."

Walter shook his head. "Too late for that. Billy and his mom left at least half an hour ago."

Bonnie's eyes opened wide. "For the mountain?"

Walter tightened his jaw. "Yeah, whatever that creep's plan is, it's working so far."

"Can't we call Billy?" Bonnie asked, her voice growing frantic. "Do you know their number?"

Walter's father held out his arm. "Come on. I'll help you to the car." Bonnie hooked her arm in his, and he supported her weight as they walked. "We'll call while we're driving. I don't know what Walter told those fake cops, but we'd better get moving before they come back."

Walter burst through the front door. "Mom! Where are you? Professor?"

A familiar British voice greeted him from another room. "Hello, Walter."

Walter slammed the door and found the professor in the kitchen. "Prof! I saw your car outside. Are you ready to go?"

The professor lifted a large briefcase to chest level. "Yes. When your mother called I packed what we would need and rushed right over."

"Good thing. We need to get going. The cops won't let Bonnie's parents out of jail unless she shows up personally, so it's up to us to find Billy. Dad and Bonnie'll come as soon as they can."

"Your mother filled me in, Walter." He patted the briefcase with his palm. "And she has already packed dinner for us and left to give Bonnie's parents a ride home when they are released." He then gestured with his hand toward the front door. "Shall we go?"

Walter pumped both fists and flashed a big smile. "Let's go pick a fight with a knight!"

Walter's father clapped his cell phone closed. "Okay, everything's set. Since Walter's going to the mountain with the professor, we don't have to hurry."

Bonnie reached over and squeezed his shoulder, hoping her tight grip would communicate her urgency. "But we do have to hurry! They might not be enough."

He glanced down at her fingers, and his eyes revealed more concern than adults usually showed her. "But we'd just have to wait in the car. You're in no shape to be climbing mountains."

"But I know something you don't." She gazed up at him. Tears welled in her eyes and trickled down her cheeks. "Mr. Foley, I have to get to the mountain to save Billy. If I don't get there soon, all could be lost."

"But you can hardly walk. What could you possibly do?"

She retightened her grip on his shoulder. "Please, you have to trust me. Just get me as close to the crash site as you can, and I'll handle it from there."

He reached over to wipe a tear from her cheek with his thumb. "Okay. What could it hurt? We'll get your foster parents out, and we'll go straight over there." He wrapped the fingers of both hands firmly around the steering wheel and sighed. "I may be crazy, but for some reason I really do trust you."

Billy trudged up the mountainside. This time he had no faithful hound to lead him, no adult to counsel him, and no idea what in the world he was getting himself into. His mother had driven into the hills and dropped him off, leaving him with only a road map to go by. The note gave him no other option; he had to come alone. Convincing himself to go solo was a huge battle, but in the end, there was no choice. Bonnie's life might hang in the balance.

The map didn't help much; the multicolored symbols included no contour lines, no hills, no valleys, only the roads and larger creeks in the area. The path he had made on his previous venture was still visible in spots. In many places he could see obvious footprints in the snow. In other places he had to track by memory, watching for familiar tree formations, a narrow part of a creek he remembered, and certain ways the slopes undulated and bent.

He and his mother had agreed that she would drive to Alpena and call the police if he failed to return after two hours, so he used a penknife to scratch his signature symbol in prominent trees along the way. He had told her to look for his mark if worse came to worse; it would be a trail the slayer's men wouldn't recognize.

As he walked, his thoughts burned miserably over Bonnie's disappearance and on whether or not the dragon would show up to help, not to mention the fact that an evil slayer's sword loomed somewhere over the horizon. The path seemed to go on forever. He wanted to go to the cave first, alert the dragon, and then go back to the slayer's meeting place, but he wasn't sure he could find the cave without retracing the way he had gone before. Getting lost was the worst option, but he knew if he could just find the plane wreckage again, finding the meeting place wouldn't be a problem.

And there they were, the blackened remains of Merlin scattered like tossed trash, strewn in every direction. Would the FAA ever come and finish the investigation, or had Devin squelched that somehow?

Billy didn't slow down at the crash site. He was pretty sure he knew the path, so he marched on. A quick pace and a steady course helped his confidence, but as he neared the spot where the dragon had scorched Devin's crony, he paused and scanned the area nervously. *I don't feel anything. No danger. I guess I'll just go on.*

When he reached the burned path near the open field, he stopped and turned in every direction, watching, listening. There were no birds chirping, no twigs popping, only the dry song of the cold northerly breeze. The journey had helped him stay warm, but now the wind tried to bite through his coat, making him bounce on his toes to stay active.

He glanced at his watch, borrowed from Walter for this trek. *Not quite two. Is the slayer going to show up? Who'll feel the slayer's presence first, me or the dragon?*

"I hope I haven't kept you waiting, son of Clefspeare."

Billy gasped and turned his head.

Oh no! The slayer! But I'm not ready—I didn't feel him coming!

Devin stood by a tree only a few yards away with three other men behind him. He was bundled up for the cold, and in front of his coat, the shining candlestone dangled from a chain necklace. The slayer's face was black and blue on one side, but there was no doubt who he was, especially with the menacing voice and its biting sarcasm. "I knew you would come, Dragon Boy, but did I surprise you? I told you I would be here."

"Uh, no. It's just that . . . well, I thought . . ."

The slayer nodded. "You thought you would sense my presence. What a shame." He glanced back at his companions, speaking in a loud, mocking tone. "Good thing I remembered to keep my stone out in the open." He then turned to Billy, holding the candlestone up with his hand. "It has amazing properties, you know, and reducing dragon powers is one of my favorites."

Billy knew he should say something, a witty retort that would make him appear brave, but nothing came out. His throat had frozen, tightly clamped in fear. Was it the stone's power that strangled him? Or was it panic? With the candlestone around, would the dragon be able to sense the danger and fly to his rescue? He looked around for Bonnie. She was nowhere in sight. Walter and the professor were right about the note, and he had fallen into the slayer's trap.

"Walter, if the rescue map is correct, we should be nearing the crash site." Professor Hamilton studied an instrument in his hand and then looked up the mountain.

Walter carried the professor's briefcase and followed behind, lifting his feet high to get over a series of rocks. "Does that GPS whatsit tell you how cold it is?"

"Global Positioning System receiver, Walter. No, it only shows the topography of the area and our exact location within it. The plane crashed about two hundred meters to our east, so we will be there soon."

"But Billy told me he was supposed to meet Devin at some other place, someplace that wasn't real close to the plane."

"My guess is that William stopped at the wreckage first to orient himself. We should be able to track him from there."

Walter marched on, following the professor's spry lead. Both were bundled in heavy coats, boots, and gloves, but their clothes didn't slow their determination. The professor stopped to check the map, and Walter took a breather. "I don't understand why we didn't see Billy's mom. If we could have reached her on her cell phone, she could have told us how to get there. Do you think they parked somewhere else?"

The professor looked up from the GPS and then down the mountain. "It stands to reason. They were driving a Sport Utility Vehicle. My old station wagon would never be able to climb as far. And it's safe to assume their cellular phone was lost in the crash, so communicating with them is impossible."

"Too bad Hambone's still injured. He could find anything, especially since he's been up here before."

The professor raised a finger in the air. "Since we have no dog, we must use our wits in concert with our physical senses."

The two walked on, Professor Hamilton often glancing at his handheld map, and Walter lugging the briefcase. "Are you sure this is going to be enough, Professor? What if Devin has a dozen men with Uzis?"

"I'm quite sure, Walter," the professor replied without slowing down or looking back. "If I understand Devin's psyche properly, he is too proud to use weaponry so boorish as an Uzi. He fancies himself a knight. His only protection will be a sword and a shield, perhaps some chain mail armor. We also have the element of surprise."

"If you say so, Professor, but—"

"Look! That must be it!" The professor pointed to a blackened section of brush in the distance. The two hurried their pace and found several large twisted pieces of metal thrown about the mountainside.

"So, now," Professor Hamilton began, searching the ground for clues, "we need only find evidence of a dragging trail and then—" He pointed dramatically to a place near a wing section. "Aha! Here it is."

Walter joined the professor, who was already following the trail. The beginning of the path was obvious, but as they looked upslope they could see only a few footprints in the remaining snow and trampled leaves here and there.

The professor studied the ground, picked up a freshly fallen maple leaf, and tossed it to the side. "Keep your eyes and ears open, Walter. I have done some tracking in my time, but this will be difficult."

"You're not kidding. Too bad we can't sniff him out."

The professor raised his head. "Yes, of course." He tilted his head back to smell the air. "We must keep our noses alert, as well."

CHAPTER 19

The Final Conflict

Devin walked a step closer to Billy and stopped. "So, Young Bannister, my sources tell me someone has been leaving gifts for you."

Billy's anger rose, and with it a morsel of returning courage. "You mean that creep, Adam, is your source? I wouldn't trust anything he has to say, if I were you."

"I'm sure you wouldn't, but Adam has all the incentive he needs to tell the truth." Devin twirled his necklace, gazing at the stone as each facet glowed with stolen light. "His father is a miserable creature, but Adam still loves him and doesn't want anything bad to happen to him."

Billy felt the fire kindling inside, and his face turned hot. "You think you're a knight," he shouted, "but you're just a coward, fighting girls and drunk old men!" The developing flame in his belly swelled his confidence. "Why don't you take on someone with a few more weapons at his disposal?"

Devin opened the front of his large overcoat, revealing an inner suit of chain mail. He gently dropped the candlestone to let it dangle in front of his breastplate and reached over his shoulder to draw a shiny sword from his back scabbard. With a skillful swipe he flashed the metal blade out in front, slicing the air from left to right, and then raised it in both hands to eye level. He glared at Billy. "Someone like you, Bannister?" he asked in a derogatory tone. "You have no idea what you're asking for."

Billy couldn't hold it back any longer. His anger surged, and with it his fiery breath gushed. This time he actually watched the bright orange tongue of flame shoot out, but it sputtered. The stream of fire extended only a few feet in front of him before it disappeared in a cloud of vapor in the frigid air.

Devin turned to one of his men, took a shield, and held the strap with his left arm. It covered Devin's body from mid-thigh to the top of his chest, and on the front of the shield a colorful coat of arms gleamed in the sunlight. One of the panels looked like a screaming dragon with a sword protruding from its midsection.

Devin charged forward, his sword raised to attack. Billy, taken by surprise at the sudden move, slipped on the snow and fell backwards, tumbling a few feet down the slope. He squirmed around enough to right himself, but Devin was nearly on him. With all the strength he could muster, Billy gushed forth another stream of fire, but this one was weaker than the last, and it sprayed feebly on Devin's shield, vanishing in a puff of smoke.

Devin laid his shield down and slid his sword back into its scabbard. He snatched Billy up by his hair with one gloved hand, and grabbed the scruff of his coat with the other. Billy felt stiff and weak, and the slayer half-dragged him back to his companions like a wounded dog. With a final push, the slayer sent Billy sprawling at the men's feet. He lay dazed and helpless in a mixture of dirty leaves and wet snow.

"Get my shield, and move to that clearing over there," Devin ordered, pointing to the field where the creek ran, "then tie him up and gag him with the asbestos. Our timing has to be perfect. The mongrel's recovery will be slow, but his fire will return." He then took the candlestone and hid it under his chain mail. "Bring on the dragon."

The three men tied Billy to a tree trunk at the edge of the clearing while Devin removed his coat, fully revealing his chain mail armor. After stuffing Billy's mouth with a fibrous rag and fastening the gag behind his neck, the men also stripped down to armor, and each brandished a sword. Although their swords appeared to be sharp and just as deadly, theirs didn't bear the strange etchings along the blade nor the ornate designs on the hilt.

Two of the men carried their weapons clumsily. They were Neanderthals, cavemen with clubs of iron rather than paladins with blades of lightning. One of them looked familiar to Billy, but he couldn't remember where he had seen him before.

The third man seemed more comfortable with his sword. It glided with his body as he walked, shimmering alongside the gleam of his black chain mail at every move.

Devin crossed in front of Billy's glare, his limp still evident. "I'm assuming that your father's been hiding somewhere nearby, but I'm not sure what to expect from him. Has the prophecy been fulfilled? Is he a dragon again?" He smirked at Billy's scowling, gagged face and raised his hand. "Oh, don't answer. You wouldn't tell the truth anyway." He thrust the sword toward Billy, halting it expertly with the sharp point barely pricking Billy's throat. "But don't worry. We're ready in either case." He pulled out the candlestone again. "If he's a dragon, he should be on his way. I appreciate your willingness to serve as bait."

Billy struggled to speak, thrashing to get loose and wrestling against the scratchy gag with his jaws. He wanted to say that there was no way four men could ever stand against the dragon. It was huge, with a tail that would smack them down like bowling pins and with flames that would cook them like rats on a grill. But when he looked at the candlestone, his bravado melted away, and he began wondering if the slayer had good reason to be confident. How could Devin know what a dragon would do? How could he have ever faced a real dragon?

The slayer gestured to his more competent crony. "Palin, do you have the book?"

"Yes, my liege."

Billy couldn't believe what he was hearing. *Palin? My liege? These guys really think they're those old knights from Dad's story!*

Devin extended his open palm. "Then give me the witch's blood, and prepare to read. We have to make sure he comes."

The dark knight put his hand under his vest of mail, removed a glass vial from a side pocket, and handed it to Devin. The slayer pulled the stopper from the top and stood with his eyes on the cloudless sky above. The dark knight opened an old book, and Devin stood next to him, scanning the page and then reading with a singsong baritone. Billy had a hard time following the words, a melodic chant that sounded like a poem. He caught some of the language as English, but it seemed too symbolic to make any sense.

After a moment or two the dark knight pointed upward and to their right. "The dragon comes."

Devin slapped the book closed. "That worked faster than I expected. Put the book away." Devin lifted the candlestone and poured a few drops of blood on its surface, careful to ensure that no other blood spilled. Billy turned his head toward the sky, horrified at the sight of Bonnie's blood being used by the evil knight.

The dragon's body grew larger against the blue background, and his shadow passed over the humans, briefly enshrouding them in its mantle. Billy didn't know whether or not to hope for rescue. If the dragon saw them, would he attack and possibly sacrifice himself? Would the dragon even care about his own safety?

A sparkle made Billy turn back toward the slayer, and he gasped at the sight. A brilliant beam flashed from the candlestone, and an aura flowed out of it like a river of gleaming light. The flash moved first into Devin's breastplate and then throughout his body and into his upraised arms, engulfing his uplifted sword, streaming from bottom to top and finally out the point, sending a laser-like beam high into the sky.

The dragon dove away from the blast, and he turned his sparkling eyes toward the gap in the trees where the four men stood. In his descent, he appeared to be falling, his reddish-brown body diving toward the clearing, closer and closer. But just before the massive form smashed to the earth, the dragon's great wings unfurled like two huge canopies, and his mouth opened, sending a torrent of blazing fire toward the mail-clad knights.

All four raised their shields as one, and the river of fire crashed on the front of the metal wall, splashing around and over the edges. Globs of blistering heat bounced off their leg armor and bit smoldering holes into nearby trees, catching some of them on fire. Devin and the dark knight took the two middle positions, and the men set their feet to brace against the onslaught while trying to squeeze their upper bodies and heads behind their shields. One of the inexperienced knights on the end fell backward, and when he hit the ground, he rolled away and scrambled behind a spindly ash tree.

Clefspeare, now flapping his wings furiously to hover in place, spotted the weak one and torched the tree, sending flames shooting up the trunk. The knight bolted from his spot, but Clefspeare, with two mighty beats of his wings, pounced toward him, and with one great snuff, buried the man in a storm of fire.

Devin shouted over the din of beating wings and crackling fire. "That was his best volley, men! He can't have much left." With the candlestone flashing like a rabid strobe and his limp now gone, the slayer ran the few yards to the edge of the clearing and took cover behind a massive oak. "Palin! Jerry! Find shelter! He'll come back with the tail."

Billy watched in dismay as Devin's prediction came true. Clefspeare lunged back to the clearing, spun around, and swiped his tail at the other inexperienced knight, smashing the trunk of the woodpecker-riddled snag he had chosen. Once exposed, the knight cowered on his knees, too scared to remember to raise his shield, and he awaited the dragon's fiery wrath. It came in a jet of flame, but smaller in volume and with less force. It was enough, however, to transform his chain mail into an armored toaster, cooking the villain where he knelt.

Clefspeare charged back, but he seemed slower, more deliberate in his actions. Instead of hurtling himself again at the two remaining knights, he headed toward Billy. With his terrible claws bared, he scratched at both tree and ropes, easily breaking the bonds. Billy fell away from the tree, his wrists still tied in the back, his ankles still fastened together with duct tape. He wriggled and rocked to a sitting position, but he couldn't stand up.

"See to the sword!" Clefspeare shouted.

Billy swung his head around and looked for one of the fallen slayers. There he was, a swirling column of dark gray smoke rising from his blackened armor. He had dropped his blade during his flight, and it lay dirty but unharmed within twenty feet of Billy.

Devin darted out from behind the oak, his shield in front and his sword raised to attack. Clefspeare slapped his tail at the other knight's tree and sent him flying away, knocking him senseless against another tree. With Devin closing in and the candlestone shining brightly in his eyes, Clefspeare flapped to launch himself into the air, but his wings faltered, giving him only enough lift to help him scratch along the ground as he scrambled away.

Billy scooted toward the abandoned sword, pulling furiously with his legs while watching the battle. Even in the cool air, sweat poured down his face. He had to hurry. The dragon had now fallen flat; the candlestone had sapped his strength. His swiping tail slowed down, and his fire smoldered to dripping sparks and spittle. Devin danced around the futile tail swipes and nimbly hopped closer and closer to his prey, his shining sword raised to attack.

Billy pushed his back toward the sword's point and raised the blade on edge. With frantic shoves, he slid his bonds back and forth. Would the sword be sharp enough? Would it cut through in time? He still had to free his feet, too, and the slayer would be in striking distance of the dragon in just seconds.

Clefspeare let out a final desperate heave from his chest, a slow stream of gas that carried more smoke than flame, and he flopped forward, his head striking the charred ground. Devin leaped from the fire's path, and sensing the dragon's desperation, strode confidently to his enemy's face, the candlestone gleaming on his chest. "Foul lizard! At last you are mine!" He glanced at Clefspeare's position and then put the point of his sword directly in front of the dragon's eyes. "Shall I convince you to expose your belly by decorating my sword with one of your eyeballs, you cowardly snake?"

Clefspeare maintained his stare and lifted his head just enough to answer weakly. "Who is the coward, the dragon who comes willingly to save his son, or the armed band of self-proclaimed knights who bind children and use them as bait?"

Devin placed the tip of the sword just below Clefspeare's left eye. "My methods have changed, but I need not explain them to you. Your eyes will find a fitting place on my mantle, and if I have to hack you to pieces to kill you, I will." With an evil smile, he held the sword in one hand and slid it slowly forward.

The dragon jerked back, and another sword clanked against Devin's, thrusting it up and wrenching it from his hands.

Billy reared back for another swipe, this time aiming for the slayer's neck, but Devin was too quick. He ducked and leaped for his sword, sprawling to the ground and reaching through the fallen leaves. Billy swung and lunged forward, almost losing his balance as he swished through empty air. Still swinging the sword wildly, he dashed toward the slayer once again. Devin had no time to defend. He grabbed his own sword's hilt and rolled to the side, barely dodging his young attacker. With a mighty surge, he jumped to his feet, twisting his body to watch Billy as he passed by.

With fury in his eyes and the hilt of his sword in both hands, Billy again advanced slowly toward Devin. He had no idea what he would do next; he just hoped he could keep from being killed while the dragon had time to recover. He had to feign bravery and skill, at least for a little while.

The slayer lifted his necklace to make sure the candlestone still dangled in the open. The gem pulsated at the end of its chain, shooting radiant beams into Billy's eyes. Billy's legs wobbled, and the sword felt heavier by the second. He panted, sweat pouring from his chin. *He's so strong, so fast. My only hope is to lunge at him and hope for the best.*

Billy hacked with his sword, but Devin blocked it, cleanly swiping the attacking blade to the side. The slayer glared at Billy, his eyes glowing an unholy red. With a deft swing, he slashed at Billy's sword. The beastly strength of the slayer's blow yanked the sword from his hands, throwing it into the air and making it spin lengthwise and land with a ringing thud a dozen feet away.

"No more delays," Devin snarled. He threw back his arms and swung again, aiming at Billy's neck. Billy gasped, ducking and backing away, but he couldn't dodge the swing in time. He felt the sword's blade strike the side of his head, a glancing blow that stripped off his ski cap and cut into his skull. The razor edge then slid away, ripping skin and scalp as it scraped across his hair.

Billy fell to his knees and raised one hand to guard against the next strike while desperately trying to wipe dripping blood away from his eyes. The light of day faded, going gray and then almost black. He tried to hold out, gasping for breath. Death lay just seconds away. He could almost feel the blade cutting into his throat, and he wondered when the last strike would come.

A growling shout came from somewhere in the darkening mist. "Come and fight like a real knight you coward!"

It was the dragon. Billy tried to watch. He could see the slayer like a shadow in the growing dimness as he turned to face Clefspeare again. The dragon's presence shone more clearly, seeming to glow in the distance as it fled into the forest. Another human form emerged. Billy guessed that the dark knight had recovered. His garbled conversation with Devin was barely audible.

"Kill the mongrel," he heard Devin growl. "I'll take care of the serpent! He can't get far."

Billy heard wings slapping against tree branches and chain mail jangling in pursuit. With ash and smoke choking every breath, Billy gasped, fighting off his dizziness. He could sense the dark knight drawing closer, and he opened his eyes wider to see his raised sword approaching, ready to slice his throat.

✦

Mr. Foley stopped the car and turned off the engine. "Okay, Bonnie. This is as close as we can drive to the crash site. And there's Professor Hamilton's car."

Bonnie opened her door and supported herself on the frame as she stepped out. "Good. Now this may sound strange, but please help me get part of the way up the mountain and then come back to the car."

Mr. Foley walked around the car and knelt at Bonnie's feet. "Bonnie," he said softly, looking into her eyes, "this doesn't make any sense. You want me to help you part way up the mountain, but I know you can't go any farther, and you can't walk back!"

"I know it sounds weird, but you have to trust me. There are some things about me you don't know, and . . ." she paused, letting her head droop for a moment, then she looked up at him again with teary eyes. "And if you can't trust me now, then I can't—" She stopped short and stared at him, trying to regain her composure. "I'm sorry," she said stoically. "I'm not going to bargain for your trust in me."

Mr. Foley let his mouth drop open. His eyes grew wide and a hint of wetness formed at the lower lids. After a few more seconds, he lowered his head and nodded with a sigh. "I guess it won't hurt anything." He helped her stand away from the car and then shut the door. "Okay," he said, lowering his body to a squatting position, "It'll probably be faster if you ride on my back."

Bonnie shuffled up behind him. She grabbed his shoulders and pulled up, while he slipped his hands under her knees and hoisted her up on his back. Being a hulking sort of man, he had no trouble bearing the load, at least for a while. He grunted a few times on the steeper inclines, but after the first fifty yards or so, the going became easier, and his panting slacked off.

Bonnie tried to find a good place to hold on. Mr. Foley's shoulders seemed as wide as a barn door, so she hooked her arm around his neck, making sure not to squeeze his throat. She accidentally put her bare fingers on his skin, and he cried out, "Your hands are freezing! Where are your gloves?"

"I left them at my house. We were in such a hurry."

"You could've borrowed some when we stopped at my house to get the coats."

For some reason Mr. Foley's remark cut through to her heart. She knew he was just trying to watch out for her, but getting any sort of rebuke with all that was going on brought a stabbing pain. She felt her nose beginning to run and she hoped it was just the weather bringing it on and not a new round of tears. With a quiet sniffle, she tried to stop the drip.

"Are you crying?" Mr. Foley asked.

Bonnie hiked herself up higher on his back and tried to wrap her arms around his frame again. She laid her head on his shoulder and squeezed tightly. "No, I'm just cold."

Mr. Foley shook his head. "I'm sorry," he said softly. His labored breaths puffed forth like an old steam engine. "I'm really sorry."

After they rounded the bend, Bonnie whispered into his ear. "Okay, I think right here's fine."

Mr. Foley squatted again and let Bonnie slip down. He turned quickly to catch her hands and helped her steady herself. "So do you want me to come back for you in a while?"

She tested her knee but kept most of her weight on her good leg. "I'm hoping that won't be necessary, but if I don't come back in say, one hour, then, yes, please come and get me."

"One hour? You'll get awfully cold in an hour."

She hugged her coat closer to her body and laughed, blowing out a long stream of white vapor. "I don't think there's any getting around that."

Mr. Foley turned back toward the car and walked several steps, but he hesitated, looking back at Bonnie. His long arms drooped below his sagging shoulders, and he seemed ready to run back and snatch her up again. She had an idea of how he must have felt, leaving an injured, orphan girl standing out on a cold mountain alone. She gave a reassuring smile and waved, but she pulled her hand down again when she remembered the missing gloves. She wrapped her borrowed coat more tightly, thankful that Walter's sister, Shelley, hadn't taken it to college. She had protested going back to Mr. Foley's house to get it, but when she saw that it was big enough to go around her backpack, she relented.

Mr. Foley sighed, and a new stream of steam engine vapor poured out. He buried his hands in his pockets and trudged down the path. He didn't look back again.

Professor!" Walter called, rubbing his finger on a tree trunk. "Another one of Billy's marks!"

Professor Hamilton strode to the tree and then looked back to the path they had taken. "That's the fifth mark, the last one coming precisely northeast of here. I suggest that we continue to follow William's lead and—"

A load cracking sound interrupted the professor, followed by a series of strange noises. Walter spun around and looked in every direction. "What's all that racket?"

The teacher tilted his head to listen. "I hear men yelling, wood splitting, and . . ." He put his hand to his ear. "Fire?"

Walter pointed, ready to run. "Over there?"

The professor studied his GPS device for a few seconds. "I believe you're right, and it should all be downhill." With Professor Hamilton leading the way and Walter still lugging the briefcase, the two rushed toward the sound of the commotion.

From his knees Billy watched the scene before him through a veil of dripping blood. Behind the dark knight, Devin rushed into the smoky woods, hacking with his sword at anything that got in the way. Within a few seconds, Devin vanished into the cloud.

The dark knight showed no emotion as he walked toward Billy, his sword in his right hand, his shield up and covering his left side. Billy wiped away the blood and steeled himself. The dark knight marched on, never altering his pace. When he reached

Billy, he snatched a handful of his hair, pulling against the gaping wound and forcing him to stand on his feet. Billy didn't struggle; pain and helplessness paralyzed both mind and body, and a new eruption of blood flowed down his forehead.

The knight released Billy's hair and stepped back with his sword raised and his shield in place, as if daring him to attack. The fire's darkening, smoky haze encircled his sinister form. "Any last words, mongrel?"

Billy glared at the knight. He wanted to fight, but with his fire literally squelched, he had no weapons. He looked in the direction Devin had run. Was the evil host winning? They had lost two, but they were obviously Devin's sacrificial lambs, their only role being to sap Clefspeare's strength.

And had the dragon escaped? It didn't look to be faring very well with its weakened attempts to fly failing so miserably. Billy thought about the dragon's face, the nobility he saw when it severed his ropes, even at its own peril. Wasn't that love? Wasn't that the same look his father had when he stood in the plane to take a bullet for his family?

What other proof did he need? Dragon or no dragon, this was his true father. He had to get away and help. Somehow he had to keep his dad alive.

Without any other options at his disposal, Billy decided to try a bluff. The candlestone was gone. Maybe if he could stall long enough, his flames would have time to return. He turned back to the dark knight and scowled. "If you give up now," Billy said with all the confidence he could muster, "I'll let you live."

The knight let out a loud, bellowing laugh. "Let me live? Bannister, I don't think you understand your position here. I am Palin, squire of the last of the great knights. I'm going to cut your head off with one swing of my sword, and Sir Devin will have another trophy for his collection."

Billy's throat tingled at the thought of the blade slicing through, and he tried not to gulp. He had to keep his composure and buy time. Maybe, just maybe, Palin was more cowardly than he was pretending. He scowled again and took a defiant pose, resting his hands on his hips and cocking his head. "Remember the scorched body of the last person who tried to kill me? Where are you keeping that trophy?"

Palin laughed. "That stupid hillbilly couldn't beat a dragon in a video game." The knight held up his shield and braced his legs. "Go ahead, Dragon Boy. Give me your worst."

Billy tried to create fire. Surely his anger was hot enough. But he felt nothing, no boiling in his belly, only the return of dizziness as blood drained from his head, coursed around his eyes, and dripped to the ground. He cast his eyes downward and sighed deeply, dropping once again to his knees and trying not to faint.

Palin lowered his shield. "Just as I thought." He stepped closer to Billy and raised the sword in a striking pose. "Time to die, mongrel!"

Billy gulped hard. There was no way he could run. His only hope was to duck away at the last second.

With a mighty thrust and turn of his shoulders the dark knight swung the blade toward Billy's neck. Billy watched the deadly blade coming, hoping somehow to evade the swing, but blood and dizziness made everything blurry. He closed his eyes and dove under Palin's lunging body, wondering if he would be looking up at his decapitated body just before he died.

Billy threw out his arms and tried to grab anything within reach. He felt two fistfuls of chain mail, and in a flash of armor and swinging metal he heaved his attacker to the side. His blurred vision caught a glimpse of Palin rolling down the hill and colliding with a tree stump. He had bought some time, but would he be able to fend off another attack?

The wounded knight struggled to his feet and trudged up the hill, limping heavily. He hesitated, glancing at the small fires that smoldered all around. A second later, a sound like a whistling arrow zinged through the forest, and Palin grabbed his arm, crying out, "Arrrgh!"

"Got him!" came a shout from the woods.

The dark knight reached with his left hand to pull a short arrow from his right upper arm. When he gave it a tug, agony flashed across his face, and the arrow stayed put. He raised his sword again and staggered back into the clearing.

Zing! Another arrow zipped in from the forest, catching the knight on the arm in almost the same spot, and he took three lumbering steps backwards to get his balance.

"Got him again!" the voice in the forest cried out.

Billy tried to stand up. He wanted to run away while he had a chance. He braced himself with one hand on the ground while leaning over to wipe the blood from his forehead onto any dry part of his body he could reach. It was no use. He was so disoriented he could barely remember what he did from one second to the next.

Palin righted himself, shook his head, and switched the sword from his right to his left hand. Two arrows protruded from his arm, blood flowing down to his elbow and falling to the ground. He raised the sword and advanced toward Billy once again, wobbling, staggering.

Billy's head throbbed, his vision dazed. He saw two figures dash out from the trees. Was it? Yes! Professor Hamilton was running toward the knight with a crossbow raised to his shoulder. Could he possibly handle the powerful knight? Would that crossbow be enough? As the questions swirled in his mind, the curtain of blood seeped into his eyes. Seconds later, the people, the trees, and the smoky haze fled away into darkness.

"I suggest you halt!" the professor shouted to the knight.

Walter rushed to Billy's side and carefully turned him faceup. He cradled Billy's head and wiped a sheet of blood from his eyes. "Take it easy, buddy. We'll get you out of here."

"Dad," Billy moaned, his eyes tightly shut. "Have to help Dad!"

The dark knight, pain and anger in his scowl, stopped, lowered the sword, and slowly reinserted it into his scabbard. The professor dropped the crossbow to his hip and turned to Walter. "How is William?"

Walter tried to examine the gaping wound on Billy's head. "I can't tell! There's too much blood!"

"Keep him still!" He turned back to the dark knight. "I'll be—" The professor swiveled his head all around. "Where did he go?"

Walter thrust his finger toward the woods. "Check that clump of bushes over there! He couldn't have gone far."

The professor squinted at the curtain of smoke that draped the forest scene. "It would be too dangerous to search the bushes for a man with a sword, and we must help William immediately."

Walter frowned, but he nodded reluctantly and then turned back to Billy. "He's moaning something about his father, and he's breathing real fast."

The professor squatted and looked Billy over. "He's delirious, and he's likely going into shock. We have to get him down the mountain right away." The professor hurriedly stripped off all his upper garments and handed his tee shirt to Walter. "Wrap it around his head. Make it rather tight, but not too tight."

Walter followed the orders, trying hard not to cry as blood soaked through the white shirt before he could even finish tying it.

"We must find something on which to drag him," the professor said while putting his sweater and coat back on. "Carrying him down that slope will be too slow and too difficult, and we must hurry. William's life depends on our pace."

Walter pointed to the clearing. "That guy left his shield! It's right there next to that old book."

The professor spun around. "Perfect!" He ran to get the shield, and after stuffing the book into his coat pocket, he and Walter lifted Billy onto the makeshift litter. They took the ropes that had bound Billy to the tree and used one to tie their gear to the shield. With the remaining rope, they secured Billy, and they each took one end of the line and dragged the shield from the front, walking with the rope over their shoulders.

The shield bounced Billy around, and their progress was terrible. They had to stop every few seconds to help the shield over stones and tree roots. After their umpteenth stop, they decided that the professor would pull while Walter pushed, and this way they glided through the dirty mixture of leaves and snow without much of a hitch.

Walter called ahead, puffing clouds of white as he pushed the sled down the slope. “You think he’ll be all right, Professor?”

“I won’t try to deceive you, Walter,” he replied without slowing down. “I don’t like the look of that wound.”

The two continued across the silent mountain without saying another word.

CHAPTER 20

The Sword of Faith

Bonnie's left wing throbbed, but the pain wasn't nearly as bad as it had been the last time she tried to fly. She wanted to stay high enough to get a wide view, but she worried that someone might notice from the nearby camping area she had spotted, so she settled for a low glide close to the treetops.

She looked down over the leafless trees, searching for movement, anything that would tell her where Billy was.

Where is he? Oh, dear God, please help me find him.

She felt cold, very cold. Although she had boots on, she had to leave the borrowed coat and her backpack under a pile of leaves. Only an old sweatshirt over her regular shirt kept the wind from blistering her skin.

What was that?

Movement. Something big. She folded in her wings and dove toward the mountain. With a painful stretch, she pulled up and glided, skimming the tops of the trees and peering down to the snow-speckled ground. It had to be around here somewhere.

There it is!

She squinted and then rubbed her eyes. *It's a dragon!*

She watched the dramatic scene before her. A wildly flapping dragon battled a sword-bearing man. The dragon seemed much weaker than its size indicated. Its tail swiped like a limp celery stalk, and its claws pawed the ground to keep its body from falling over. Its wings still beat with passion, but they barely lifted the huge form more than a foot or so with each desperate flap.

The man charged with a swinging sword and then stepped back to avoid the claws and tail. He repeated the strategy several times, seeming to dance with expert moves. After each attack and retreat he held up something that glimmered, and the dragon reacted by staggering and letting his wings and tail droop.

The battle theater told Bonnie the whole story. She knew exactly what was going on. *That has to be Devin, the sparkle is the candlestone, and the dragon must be—Wow!*

She flew in a circle and looked for a place to dive in to help, but what could she do? *Oh, no! The dragon is down!*

Devin walked toward the thrashing dragon, the point of his sword leading the way. Clefspeare lay on his side, convulsing and trying hopelessly to slap his attacker with his tail. Devin pricked Clefspeare's belly with the sword and stepped up, ready to thrust.

Bonnie dove, folding her wings in again to force herself into a vertical free fall. Just before she reached the ground she spread her wings and pulled up, screaming in pain. Devin jerked around, and she rammed into him, shoulder to shoulder, smashing him to the leafy floor. Bonnie hit the ground in a scraping slide, rolling over and over away from the slayer. She sat up, dizzy and stunned, and she tried to stare through her foggy vision to see if she had saved the dragon.

The slayer lay on his back, groaning, and he sat up slowly, shaking his head. He stared stupidly at his sword, which was now lying on the ground, and he turned to look at the deathly still dragon. He got up on his knees and crawled toward the sword, his hands sliding through the leaves.

Bonnie knew there was no time to lose. She had to stop him, but her head throbbed and she could hardly move. Like the slayer, Bonnie had to crawl on her hands and knees, but with one knee aching she had to scramble along, using her sore wings to keep her knee off the ground. She reached the slayer just as he grabbed the hilt of his sword. She knew she could never fight a man of his size and training, so she lunged for his chest and snatched the candlestone, breaking the necklace and pulling it away. She covered the stone with one hand and tried to pull her body forward as she desperately scratched at the ground.

What's wrong? I'm not moving.

Bonnie fell to her stomach and rolled to her side to look. The slayer had a death grip on her ankle, and his nails dug into her skin like sharp, dirty knives. His evil eyes glowed. He dragged her back, his sword in his other hand, ready to strike.

Bonnie pushed herself up to her knees, crying in pain as her weight pressed on her injury and the stone burned in her palm like a heated coal. She threw the necklace as far as she could, and the sparkling stone bounced off a tree trunk and then down into a wide rainwater trench.

The slayer released her ankle and sprang to his feet, never taking his eyes from where the stone had landed. With his chain mail jangling, he stumbled like a clattering drunkard toward the trench, his sword dropping to the ground behind him. Falling to his knees, he scattered the leaves with both hands, frantically searching for his precious stone.

Bonnie, still feeling dizzy and her head pulsating, stood up and staggered toward the slayer's sword. She leaned over and grabbed the hilt with both hands. The sword was heavier than she expected, and being weakened from her fall and from holding the candlestone, she could barely lift it to an attack position. She held it with the point straight up and stood between the slayer and the dragon. She had to protect him. The slayer might still have a knife or something hidden in his armor, so she couldn't simply fly away with the sword even if she had enough strength to pull off an escape.

Rising to his feet with his left hand clenched, Devin turned toward Clefspeare, a sinister grin crossing his face. He looked at Bonnie and laughed disdainfully.

Did he find the candlestone? Is he holding it in his fist?

She took a deep breath and stood firm, her lips stiff and her eyes stoic, the sword extended with her elbows locked in place. Her knee ached horribly, but she couldn't afford to let the slayer know that.

The slayer crept toward her, a confident smirk lifting his bruised cheek, making him look like a stalking monster. As he approached, Bonnie slid one foot forward to keep her balance. She felt her own heartbeat, blood pumping through her head and knee, squeezing bullets of pain through her vessels. She took a deep breath and waited, silently praying with all her might.

Devin rushed forward, and Bonnie swung the blade. The slayer dodged underneath her arms, and with a lowered shoulder he crashed into her chest, falling headlong over her body. She slammed against the ground, thumping heavily on her rear, and slid over to her left side. The rocky ground ripped flesh from her rib cage and from her left arm, elbow, and cheek, but she kept her fierce grip on the sword.

Using her wings for lift, Bonnie hustled back to her feet and took to the air. She spotted Devin rising to his knees and flew closer to Clefspeare to reposition herself between him and the slayer. With dirty leaves smeared across her bleeding face, she once again held out the sword and planted her feet.

Now the metal blade was no longer a hopeful weapon; it was an anvil, an anchor that weighed down her failing arms. Ripping peals of agony roared through every limb. The slayer rose from the ground, his evil smile and piercing eyes mocking her as he lowered his shoulder again and took a step forward for another attack. Bonnie tried to steel herself. Her arms quaked. Her knees threatened to buckle. Through wet, trembling lips she prayed aloud in tearful entreaty.

"Oh, God . . . please help me. . . . I—I can't hold out much longer."

Devin stopped and rose to his full height. He put his hands on his hips and snorted. "A dragon girl praying?" He pointed a gloved finger at her, his yellow-green eyes seeming to penetrate to her soul. "God can't love a miserable creature like you."

A single tear tracked down Bonnie's dirty cheek to her quivering chin, but her determined gaze stayed riveted on her attacker's every move.

Devin crouched again. Bonnie drew in a deep breath and lifted the sword even higher, ready to strike. She could almost feel the slayer's blazing eyes burn through her skull. With a sudden vault, he charged forward. She closed her eyes, aimed for where she thought his head would be, and swung the blade. Instead of a thud or a scream of pain, she heard a swish as if the sword had barely managed a weak swipe through the air.

She opened her eyes expecting to see the slayer lunging at her again, but the weight of the sword had spun her backwards. She whirled around to find her enemy. There he was, crouching, cowering on the carpet of rotting leaves. Had she hit him and somehow not felt the blow? She stared at the sword. It no longer felt heavy, and she carried it easily in her outstretched arms. From its tip a dazzling beam shot high into the sky, disappearing into the blue.

Feeling a surge of energy, Bonnie pointed the sword at the slayer, ready to defend herself once more. The beam shifted, casting its light across his brow, and a shimmering, translucent curtain materialized between them.

The color in the slayer's face melted away, and his mouth dropped open. The flashing light seemed to come alive, wrapping itself around him like a sparkling swarm of hornets. He squirmed as though struggling to escape from a straightjacket while the flashing mantle grew brighter and brighter. Within seconds, the whole scene transformed into a shining white blaze. Bonnie blinked hard. She had to keep watching. How else could she know what the slayer might do next?

After a few more blinks, her vision became a sheet of pulsating spots. She could see the ground and then the trees, but where was the slayer? She swiveled her head, craning to look in every direction, but he was nowhere in sight.

When the spots finally disappeared, she turned toward the place where the slayer had stood. A few remaining sparkles of light danced above a dark pile of rubble, and they twinkled, as if trying to tell her what had happened. They spun around a single point and then disappeared, like water swirling into a drain. On the ground lay the candlestone, bright and shining, no longer attached to its necklace.

With the sword still in her left hand, Bonnie flapped her wings and lunged toward the sparkling point. She scooped it up in her right hand with one quick motion. It felt like a bauble of pure poison, draining her energy like a blood-sucking leech. As she drew her arm back, hot needles stung her palm, as though the stone had sprouted vampire teeth and plunged them into her skin. She flung it into the woods and watched the glittering rock streak like a meteor into the shadows.

Bonnie stood in place, wondering if she should try to remember where the stone landed, but she couldn't bear the pain any longer. She dropped the sword next to the rubble, a mound of crumpled chain mail and a shield that had once enveloped the slayer. The strange glow had vanished, and through a gap in the trees the sun cast a ray upon her. "Oh, God, thank you," she prayed, her voice breaking. "I—I don't know what you did, but thank you."

Her wings set her down gently, and she sat and cried, the horrible pain combining with her sense of relief to bring flowing tears. A crushing burden still remained, however; what could she do to get help for a dying dragon?

A low rumble sounded from behind her. "O brave, brave lass. Your faith has saved us both."

Her wings snatched her to her feet and spun her around, but she stayed back. "Clefspeare?" she called, her voice trembling.

The dragon lifted its head up and down. "Yes, most blessed one."

Bonnie raised her hand to touch him, but she withdrew it and backed away a step.

"Do not be frightened, child. It is I, Billy's father. I have changed in form but not in spirit."

Bonnie's wings fluttered to help her balance. "I . . . I know. It's just that—"

"Speak, child. What is your fear?"

Bonnie drooped her head. She felt like a worm for doubting, but she just had to ask. "Did you really burn up a merchant named Andrew just because he had no payment for your work?"

The dragon's eyes closed for a moment, and when they reopened, they seemed more lucid. "I did kill such a man, and it is true that he could not pay, but it was not for this that I attacked him. He sought to obtain his payment by stealing from the daughter of a nobleman. Disguised as a highwayman, he attacked her right after sunset, and I happened to be overhead. In rescuing the maiden, I disposed of the thief."

Bonnie felt her fears melt away. "Oh! Devin didn't give me the details."

"Devin told you the story? I wonder how that phony could have heard it."

"Phony? Because he thinks he's a knight?"

"Yes, lass. No true knight would threaten children and take unfair advantages, using that cursed stone as a weapon."

She smiled and then laughed, wiping away her tears. "And old Devin's not so brave when he's not wearing his candlestone, is he? Did he run away? What did you do to scare him? Did you shoot some flame toward him? I couldn't see what happened."

The dragon, still lying on his side, stretched his neck to get as close to Bonnie as he could. "I blew no flame; I was too weak. I could only watch you defend me and listen to your prayers."

"Then what scared him away? Was it that strange glow? It was too bright to see anything."

"I merely raised my head. When you threw the stone away, a sliver of strength returned. If he ran in fear, then perhaps it was because he could tell I was recovering, but that seems unlikely. I, too, was blinded, so I can only guess. I suggest that we allow the mystery to remain and just be thankful."

Bonnie bowed her head, and Clefspeare rose to a sitting position. "Have you seen my son?"

"No. I looked for him, but I didn't see him anywhere."

"He was tied to a tree, and I freed him. I was so weak, I could not fight them and protect him at the same time, so I tried to lead them away. Devin followed me, but he had one black knight remaining who did not follow. I fear that he had murder in his heart."

Bonnie's wings fluttered, lifting her a foot or two off the ground. "We'll have to find him, and fast. Can you fly?"

"Not yet. My strength is coming back, but slowly. Take the sword, find my son, and bring word back to me if you can. Even if Devin reappears, he cannot harm me without the candlestone or his weapon."

Bonnie flew the short distance to the dragon and hugged his neck. "So is the prophecy fulfilled?"

"One thing remains," he said. "But you must go. All will be explained in time."

Bonnie pulled away, grabbed the sword, and flapped her wings, sending her body zooming upward. Her strength renewed, she found the sword more manageable, though it had regained much of its former weight. She glanced back at Clefspeare and wished she could wave, but she dared not take a hand off the sword. She just smiled at him and then flew across the tops of the trees, searching the slopes for any sign of movement. She decided to head back toward the cars, hoping that Billy might be somewhere along the way.

As she flew, the sword grew heavier and heavier, weighing her down, forcing her to fly lower. She tried to shift her grip on the hilt in order to reposition the sword. *Maybe I can put it on my back somehow or*— The sword slipped away and hurtled toward the ground. *Oh, no!* Within seconds it disappeared through the treetops. *Should I chase it? No, I don't have time! I have to find Billy!*

She kept flying as fast as her aching wings would take her.

Surely the slayer will never find it, and I don't think it'll hurt anything if I just leave it way out here. I hope nobody was down there. At the speed it fell, it could've killed someone.

After a few minutes, she spotted something. *Two men? Yes! Yes! It's Walter and Professor Hamilton, and Billy's on a sled between them!*

Bonnie could tell they were nearing the bottom of the ridge and would be back at the car in a few minutes. She stayed close to the treetops and passed the rescuers. She saw Mr. Foley waiting by the car in the distance, so she dove quickly and landed back where she had started over half an hour before. Bonnie pulled her coat and backpack from under the leaves. She knew she was supposed to report to Clefspeare when she found Billy, but that would have to wait until later, at least until she knew his condition. When she pulled the backpack's zipper closed, she called out while pulling on the coat. "Walter! Professor! Can you hear me?"

"Bonnie?" a surprised Walter called back. "Is that you?"

"Yes!" She waved when Walter and the professor came in sight. They hurried toward her, arriving with gasping breaths, and slid Billy's litter in front of her.

She limped to Billy's side and tried to kneel, but the pain was too much, so she braced herself with her left hand and caressed his bloody cheek. His eyes were closed, his skin ice cold even to her frigid fingers.

"Bonnie," Walter huffed, "what are you doing here?"

She lifted her head. "Your father and I came to try to find Billy. He's waiting next to the station wagon." She looked down at Billy again and then up at the Professor. "How badly is he hurt?"

The professor held out his car keys and pointed to the landscape in front of them. "Walter, can you push the shield around that bend? It's downhill about a hundred meters after that. Please ask your father to warm up my car." He reached one hand down toward Bonnie. "I'll help Miss Silver."

Walter didn't hesitate. He snatched the keys and, digging his feet into the ground, scooted the shield down the path.

The professor lifted Bonnie to her feet, put his arm around her, and helped her stand. "Your face is bleeding! What happened to you?"

"Never mind me. What about Billy?"

"His injury is very serious. That's why we cannot stop."

"Don't worry about me; I'll be fine. Just send Mr. Foley back to get me."

The professor nodded and ran ahead. In seconds he disappeared around the bend. Bonnie tried to walk, but it was no use.

Between her aching knee and throbbing head, she couldn't go on; she would have to sit and wait. Within a minute or so, Mr. Foley came running up the path, and, without a word, he helped Bonnie onto his back again and trudged slowly toward their parking place.

When they arrived at Mr. Foley's car, the professor's station wagon was already gone. After helping Bonnie get seated, Mr. Foley started the engine and turned the heater on full blast. "I can see tire tracks," he said, getting out of the car again and pointing toward a secondary path. "My car would never make it up there, so I'll follow the tracks on foot to see if I can find Marilyn. I'll be back as soon as I can."

Bonnie just nodded and watched Mr. Foley lumber away. She put her stiff fingers in front of the vent. The warming jet thawed them enough to return blood flow and with it, throbbing pain. It was a good pain, enabling her to bend her knuckles and flex her hands.

She yawned and laid her head against the window, trying to sleep in the soothing warmth. She was too tired to worry about any dangers—the slayer, the dark knight, or the candlestone. Only one thought kept her in prayer, Billy's condition. He looked awful, like a frozen corpse being shuttled home on a failed shield, a dead hero returning from battle.

Bonnie alternated between dozing and wakeful prayer for what seemed like half an hour until a new noise roused her senses. An SUV rumbled down a mountain path in her direction, its wheels spinning and biting into leaves, dirt, and snow. When it arrived, Mr. Foley jumped out, and the truck zoomed away. Bonnie caught a glimpse of Billy's mom driving the SUV as she passed by. Her face looked worried, tired, and scared.

Mr. Foley got in the driver's seat and started the car down the unpaved forest road. He turned to Bonnie, who stared straight ahead, leaning forward to make room for her backpack. She grimaced, wondering what Mr. Foley must have thought of her. Her forehead and cheeks had tightened with drying mud, tears, and blood. She probably looked like a frozen street urchin.

"Are you cold?" he asked.

"No, not anymore." She sniffed and choked back a sob.

"The hospital's not real far. I'm sure the professor and Walter got Billy there in time."

Her throat tightened, and her voice squeaked. "I hope so," was all she could manage.

Mr. Foley slowed to ease over a very large bump and then stopped on the deserted road. He pulled out a clean handkerchief and tried to wipe a clump of dirt from beneath Bonnie's left eye. "What did you do all that time after I left you?" he asked gently.

"I'd rather not say." Bonnie couldn't hold it back any longer. She started crying and buried her face in her hands.

Mr. Foley put a hand on the shoulder of her coat and gave it a squeeze. "Take your time," he said quietly. He pressed the accelerator. The car moved ahead and turned onto a smoother road. "I have no idea what happened up there, but there's something I do know." He took a deep breath and went on. "That blood on your face was the cost of doing the right thing."

Bonnie lifted her head and busily wiped the tears away. She sniffed hard and nodded. "Thank you." She looked at him, and their eyes met. She smiled through the pain. "Thank you for believing in me."

Billy opened his eyes. At first all he could see were white walls in front and to the left, with instruments of some kind dangling from shiny silver hooks. To his right, pale yellow curtains hung from tracks in the ceiling, and directly in front of him a portable table held a water pitcher and a Styrofoam cup. He tried to turn his head to the right, but a sharp pain near his left temple made him stop. As he raised his hand to touch his head, he noticed layers of medical gauze and tape wrapped around the base of his index finger. A thin plastic tube followed his movement, stretching out and tightening when he extended his arm. He followed the line with his eyes to an IV bag hanging from a metal pole.

"A hospital?" he murmured.

He felt a warm hand touch his right arm. "Billy?"

Billy turned toward the voice, this time ignoring the pain. "Mom?"

His mother stood and clasped his hand in both of hers. "Billy. Welcome back."

"Back? Where have I been?"

Her smile was as broad as an ocean. "Unconscious, for going on two days. Do you remember what happened?"

Billy squinted and tried to sit up. "Ohhh! My head!" He slowly laid his head back on the pillow and turned to his mother. "Did the dragon—I mean, did Dad get away? Do you know?"

"Yes. Your father is fine." She stroked his arm soothingly. "But you got hurt pretty badly, so you were brought here."

"Here? Where's here?"

"Davis Memorial Hospital in Elkins."

Billy lifted his hand again. "Why's this tape on my finger?"

"I wouldn't let them take it off, so they just taped it."

"You wouldn't let them take my finger off?"

"No, silly! Not your finger."

He felt more dazed than ever. Nothing his mother said seemed to make any sense. "What happened?"

"There's someone in the waiting room who wants to tell you the whole story."

"Who? Walter? The professor? I remember seeing them, but—"

Billy's mother put a finger on his lips. "Just stay still. The doctor said you would probably wake up this morning, so everyone's waiting to see you, but they can only come in one at a time." She got up and stepped toward the door. "I'll get the first one, and I'll be back later."

Billy still felt confused. "Everyone?"

Right after his mother left, a nurse came in the door. She took his vital signs, checked the IV, and spoke a few soft words before leaving, but Billy wasn't really listening. He just stared at the door, wondering who would come in to let him know what was going on. Dazed and throbbing, he recalled only images of his father's battle against the slayer. The rest of his time on the mountain was a blur.

A few seconds later, Bonnie peeked in. When she saw Billy's eyes open, she limped to the bed as fast as she could and threw her arms around his shoulders. She grabbed his right hand, and her voice sang like a meadowlark. "Billy, I'm so glad to see you again. I was afraid we were going to lose you."

He smiled weakly. "I guess I'm like a bad habit. You just can't get rid of me."

Bonnie laughed, and her infectious joy spread. Billy tried to laugh, too, but he had to stop. He spread his palm over his bandage.

"Sorry. My head's killing me." He looked back at Bonnie and squeezed her hand. "I'm glad you're my friend, Bonnie. You're the best."

Glistening tears formed in Bonnie's eyes. "And you're the very best friend I've ever had. When you thought Devin had me, you risked your life again to save me."

"I figured out that he didn't have you, but a little too late. Did you come all the way back from Montana just to see me?"

Bonnie laughed and explained the whole story, relating the tale of Devin's defeat and Clefspeare's recovery. She told him about dropping Devin's sword, and they pledged to search for it together when he got well. Billy, his memory quickly returning, told about the evil knights and how two died and about how he tangled with the dark knight, Palin. They both concluded that they still didn't know what happened to him or to Devin.

"But," Bonnie explained, "I'm sure at least one of them is still around. When I went home to get my stuff, my room was torn apart. Someone was obviously looking for something, but I didn't notice anything missing."

"Did you find the candlestone? Maybe he thinks you have it."

Bonnie shook her head. "I didn't want to try to find it, and I hope the slayer never goes back to look for it. But I suppose he might, if he's still alive. I guess we'll have to look for it eventually."

Billy breathed a deep sigh and gazed at Bonnie's glowing face. Even with the painful abrasion under her left eye and the purple bruise on her jaw, he had never seen a more beautifully noble sight. *Those wounds are love scars*, Billy thought. *Yes, love scars.*

He glanced toward the door. "Who else is out there?"

Bonnie started counting on her fingers and stifled a giggle. "Your mom and the professor are here. Walter and my parents were here, too, but when the doctor said it might be hours before you woke up, my parents went out to get something for everyone to eat. They'll be back soon."

Billy watched Bonnie's hands and then turned to face her again. "Your parents? You mean your foster parents showed up? That's great! Were they cleared of the neglect charges?"

Bonnie nodded. "They were cleared, but . . ." She leaned over and whispered in Billy's ear. "I meant Walter's parents and mine. The Foleys are adopting me!"

Billy's eyes opened wide, and he grinned. "That's awesome, Bonnie. So you're Bonnie Foley now?"

She shook her head. "The paperwork's not all done yet, but I asked if I could keep my old name."

"Your old name? What did you say it was? Conner?"

She shook her head again. "That was my mom's married name. I'm keeping the name she gave me, Silver. Actually, that was one of the names my mom's used over the centuries."

Billy narrowed his lips and nodded approvingly. "That's okay by me. Bonnie Silver has a nice ring to it. But didn't you like your father's name?"

Bonnie turned her head to the side and frowned. "If you knew what my father did to us, you wouldn't want his name, either. And something Devin said makes me wonder . . ."

Billy decided not to ask for details. "Did you tell the Foleys about your . . . ?" He stopped and pointed at her backpack.

"No. I haven't decided about that yet. I've hidden it this long; I think I can hide it a little while longer. But I guess I'll have to say something before everything's finalized."

"So," Billy said, "at least for now, we're all in the same house, you, me, and Walter, and we're going to school at home with the professor teaching us. This is going to be great!"

Bonnie pulled on the straps of her backpack and smiled. "Couldn't be better."

Billy was about to nod, but his happiness suddenly died away. "Well it could be better," he said coldly. "My father's still living in a cave." He turned his head and stared at the fluorescent lights, and Bonnie rested her elbows on the bed rails while he went on. "No more fun times together, no trips to the beach, no ball games . . . But at least he's alive." He turned again to face Bonnie. "It's kind of weird, but I still dream about him as a human, like I'll go home someday and everything will be back to normal."

Bonnie listened quietly, letting Billy's words sink in. He noticed her lower lip tremble ever so slightly and pools of wetness form in her eyes. "I have a favorite Bible verse," she finally said. "Trust in the Lord with all thine heart; and lean not unto thine own understanding. In all thy ways acknowledge him, and he shall direct thy paths." She wiped her eyes with her knuckles and went on. "I don't know what's left in the prophecy, but I'm sure your father's involved somehow. And since you and I can both fly, we can go see him any time we want."

"Fly? I can't fly."

"In Merlin, you can! Or should I say Merlin the Second?"

"Merlin the Second?"

"The insurance is going to cover the plane, and you and your mom can fly to Elkins in less than an hour. She told me she has her pilot's license."

Billy nodded slowly. "That'd be cool," he said, but his voice was only halfhearted.

Bonnie took his hand again, and she gazed at him with probing eyes. "Billy, we have to have faith. It's all going to work out."

Billy felt the coolness of Bonnie's soft touch and also something new. He held up her hand to take a look and noticed a ring on her finger. "What's this? I haven't seen this before."

"It's a rubellite, just like yours. Your mom went back to the Foley's to get some clothes, and the gemstone was there on the porch. So she went right out and had it cut and polished and put into a ring for me. She said she's sure that's what your dad wanted."

Billy gazed at it for a moment while Bonnie went on.

"Your father said there's still more to be fulfilled in the prophecy, and it's all been true so far. That's good reason to have faith."

Billy released Bonnie's hand. "Yeah, that's true, but what about Devin and Palin?"

"We'll just have to deal with whatever comes."

Billy didn't answer. He just smiled and gazed at Bonnie's face, amazed at her ability to overcome anything.

"I've spent more than my share of time here," she said. "The professor's coming in next, and he has something for you." She limped toward the door, and when she reached it, she turned, smiled, and blew a kiss. "Get well soon, Billy. I have a feeling we have a lot more adventures ahead of us." She opened the door, stepped into the hall, and then looked back again. "Just remember," she said, holding her hand over her heart, "even though I'm going to be Walter's sister, I'll always be your sister, in here." With that, she shut the door, and Billy stared at the wall and then closed his eyes, listening to Bonnie's uneven footsteps as they faded in the distance.

Within a few seconds, the door opened again, and a familiar British accent boomed. "William! It's so good to see you again!"

Billy opened his eyes and watched the professor stride in. "Hi, Prof—"

"William," the professor interrupted. "I have something very special for you." He didn't wait for Billy to respond and turned toward the hallway. "Walter! The coast is clear!"

Walter walked in, hunched over, with his coat fully zipped. With a wiggling lump struggling under his coat, he looked like he had swallowed a live wolverine. Walter held his hand over the thrashing bulge and grunted, "Be still!"

"Shhh!" the professor warned. "If the nurses find out, we're . . . how do you say it? Dead meat?"

Walter unzipped his coat, pulled out a squirming, hairy mass, and laid it on Billy's stomach.

"Gandalf!" Billy cried out. "Where did you find him?"

Walter stripped off his coat and shook his head. "You don't want to know!"

"The solution was quite simple, actually," the professor said, "but the journey was very trying. We found Gandalf's old bed in the ruins of your house, and Hambone sniffed it and did the rest. He ran us all over the neighborhood, under cars, through several gardens, and into and out of two homes. I had to climb into three trees, onto a slippery roof, and over a barbed wire fence."

"And I had to carry a shovel all over the neighborhood," Walter added. "Wherever he stopped and sniffed, I dug a hole to see what he found."

Billy bit his lip to keep from laughing. "And what kind of stuff did you find?"

Walter began counting on his fingers. "Gandalf's squeaky rat toy, the collar he lost a year ago, and various—" He looked up at the professor. "Uh . . . various kitty leavings."

Billy laughed in spite of the pain, and he stroked Gandalf's long, lush coat. The cat arched his back and then curled up on Billy's chest. "So, where did you finally find him?"

"Oh, yes," the professor continued. "Actually, he was under your bed at the Foley's house."

"What? What was he doing—"

"And that's not all!" the professor interrupted again. He slipped his hand under his vest and pulled out a glass, baby-food-sized jar.

Billy stared at the black, angular pieces inside. "Shark teeth?"

"Yes," he said, placing the jar next to a flower vase, "quite a number of fine specimens. Walter discovered them on his doorstep yesterday morning, and he said you would probably like to have them here at your bedside."

Billy gave Walter a thumbs up sign, and Walter returned it, adding a quick, tight-lipped nod.

The professor reached under his coat again. "And last but not least . . ." He pulled out a miniature tape player and wedged a small earphone into Billy's ear. "Yesterday's lecture notes," he announced proudly, "all recorded on tape. You can play them while you relax."

Billy adjusted the earpiece to make it more comfortable. "Uh, thanks Professor, but I think I'll be too tired to—"

"Nonsense." The professor gathered the cat and put the tape player at Billy's side. "Surely you're not too tired to lie here and listen. Later I'll ask you some questions, and we'll have a nice talk.

Miss Silver told me some of her story, but she seemed quite reticent. I should like to learn more about the sword I saw in Devin's supply closet and to study the rubellite ring on your finger as well. I also wish to show you a most interesting book Walter found, but everything must wait until your wounds are healed." He paused and gazed down at Billy's head bandage. "I discovered that you have quite an interesting lineage, William, and I predict you will learn much about yourself in the very near future, physically, mentally, and spiritually."

Walter gave Billy a strong handshake, holding on as if he would rather not let go. Their eyes met, and they each nodded with firm-set jaws. They didn't have to say a word. Their friendship had been sealed forever.

Walter took Gandalf from the professor and tried to hide him under his coat again, but the cat had other ideas. He leaped from Walter's grasp and zoomed into the hall. "You crazy cat!" Walter yelled. "Come back here!" He gave Billy a quick wave and dashed from the room.

Professor Hamilton grasped the bed rails, his eyes dancing with mirth. "Well, I should be going, too. It's wonderful to see you recovering." He pointed at the tape player. "Did I mention that Miss Silver read the notes for me on the recording?" The professor winked. "Get well soon, William." And he left the room.

Suddenly, all was quiet. The old gentleman's words settled in Billy's mind, gently caressing his soul. They echoed and whispered questions over and over, reminding him that many mysteries remained unsolved. What would the professor teach him from the book? Would they ever find the sword? And, of course, how in the world did Dad get shark teeth into a jar and deliver them to Walter's house?

He slowly shook his head in wonder. *I guess we dragons have our ways!*

Billy glanced at the cassette player at his side and noticed once again the gauze tape on his finger. He picked at the tape until he was able to unwind it. Slowly, as each layer peeled away, the shape of his treasured ring became clear. When he stripped off the final bit of tape, the rubellite appeared. He used his thumb to rub away the sticky remnants and then held the stone close to admire its beautiful, dark red shine. For the first time, he noticed how it reflected everything in the room, the ceiling, the lights . . . and his face. He saw himself in his father's ring. The image was sharp, the details clear. For some reason, he no longer grimaced at the thought. He was indeed the son of a dragon.

And he wasn't alone as a dragon child. He thought of Bonnie, his partner in adventure, a friend closer than a sister, and now she, too, shared this symbol, a simple rubellite ring that reflected more than what lay on the surface; it somehow revealed their inner character and represented their faith in each other. Billy knew he could trust Bonnie with his life, yet he couldn't help but feel that something was still missing, a void within himself, a strange, deep-seated hunger that even this amazing young lady could never fill.

He took a deep breath and sighed. Bonnie was right. Their adventures together were only just beginning, and maybe the future would hold the answers Billy was seeking. Who could tell what life would be like for a couple of dragon kids?

Billy smiled, pressed the button on the tape player, and leaned back, closing his eyes. "Maybe I'm not too tired after all."

For more information on *Raising Dragons* and other titles in the *Dragons in Our Midst* series, go to the series website, www.dragonsinourmidst.com. There you will be able to contact the author and participate in discussions with other readers about these exciting books.

Excerpt from volume two

This excerpt taken from The Candlestone

Published by AMG Publishers
6815 Shallowford Rd.
Chattanooga, Tennessee 37421

Merlin's Prophecy

When hybrid meets the fallen seed
The virgin seedling flies
An orphaned waif shall call to me
When blossom meets the skies

The child of doubt will find his rest
And meet his virgin bride
A dragon shorn will live again
Rejecting Eden's pride

A slayer comes and with his host
He fights the last of thee
But faith alone shall win the war
The test of those set free

A king shall rise of Arthur's mold
The prophet's book in hand
He takes the sword from mountain stone
To rescue captive bands

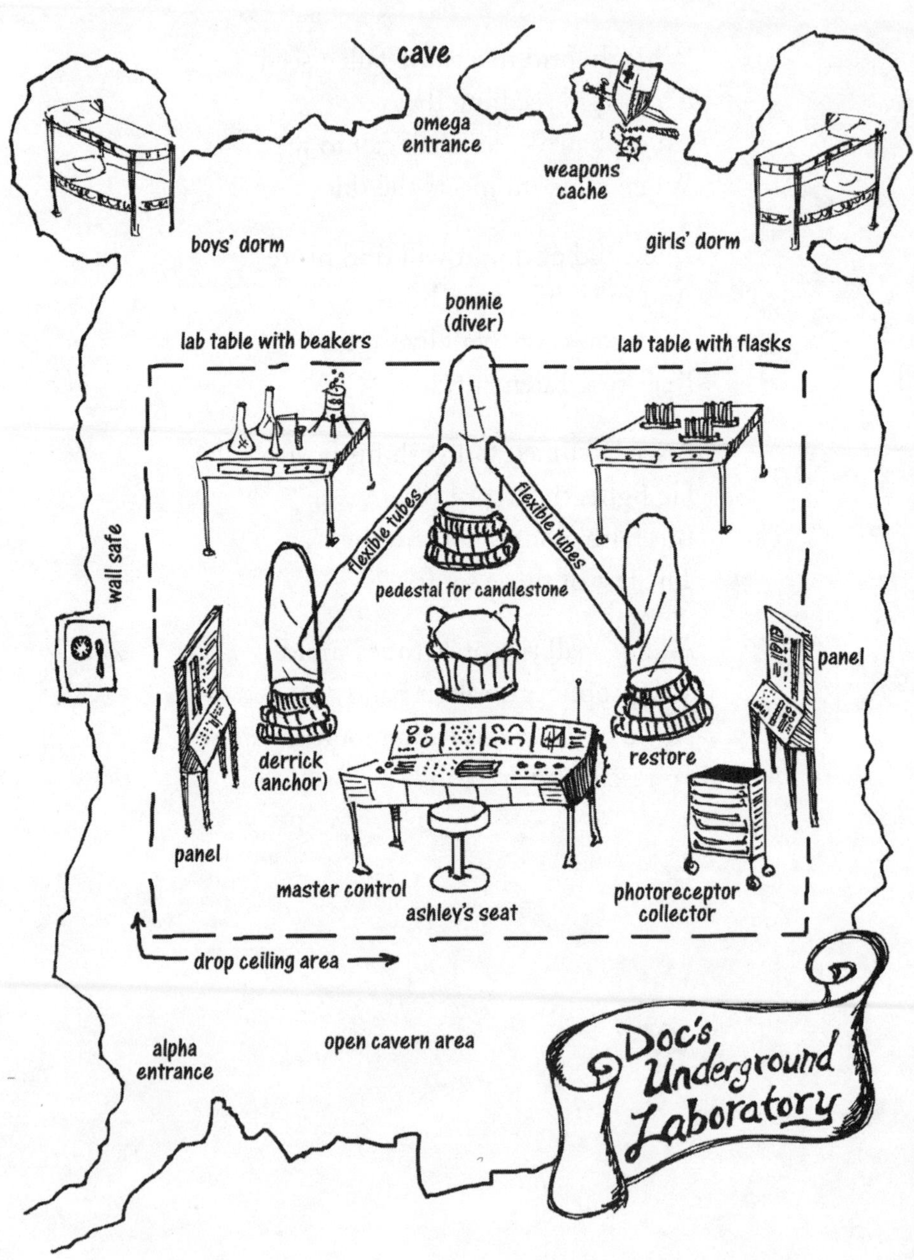

cave
omega entrance
weapons cache
boys' dorm
girls' dorm
bonnie (diver)
lab table with beakers
lab table with flasks
flexible tubes
flexible tubes
wall safe
pedestal for candlestone
panel
panel
derrick (anchor)
restore
master control
ashley's seat
photoreceptor collector
drop ceiling area
alpha entrance
open cavern area
Doc's Underground Laboratory

CHAPTER 1

THE ART OF WAR

With sword and stone, the holy knight,
Darkness as his bane,
Will gather warriors in the light
Cast in heaven's flame

Out of the blackness a growling voice rumbled, "She will come." The rough words reverberated, bouncing off shrouded walls that echoed dying replies.

A solitary man listened in the dark room, lit only by flickers of soft light coming from his hand, a dozen fireflies in a jar. They danced with hopeless wings in stale air, waiting for death to arrive, their distress signals only serving to guide the scientist as he paced the stone floor. "And what makes you so sure she'll come?" his voice replied, tiny and squeaking by comparison. "She won't trust me. Why should she?"

The rumbling voice responded. "You don't understand her; you never did. She listens to a call that rises beyond your senses. . . . she has faith." The growl changed to a deep sigh. "But, alas! What would you know about faith?"

"More than you think." The scientist held up the jar and watched the dimming flashes. "I do know this; it was by her faith that you're in this predicament. I hear she was quite handy with that sword."

The growl deepened, its bass tones making the ground tremble. "If you really think she knew I would end up in this prison, then you're a bigger fool than I thought." After a few seconds, the echoes died away again, and the voice became soft and melancholy, like the lowest notes of a mournful cello. "You have no worries. She will come. She is driven by forces you cannot possibly understand."

The last flicker of light blinked out. The scientist picked up the jar and opened the lid. With a quick shake he dumped the dead fireflies onto the floor. "Very well." His voice stretched out into a foreboding snarl. "We shall see."

Swish! The gleaming sword swiped by Billy's face, its razor point slashing the air and its deadly edge humming a threatening tune in his ear. He jumped back, his cheeks turning red hot. *What an idiot I am! Another mistake like that and this fight will be over in a hurry!* He planted his feet on the tile floor and raised his sword, careful to keep it from stabbing the low ceiling. Eyeing his opponent warily, he slowly counted to ten. *Gotta keep my cool. I'm never going to win if my brain's fried. Besides, this sword weighs a ton. No use wasting energy.* Drops of sweat pooled on his brow and streamed down, stinging his eyes and blurring the light from the ceiling fan's globe. The fan's whirling blades blew a cooling breeze through his hair, a welcome relief in the spacious but stuffy rec room.

His opponent charged, his sword raised to strike. Billy dodged, swiping at the attacking weapon from the side as it passed, and the clank of metal on metal rattled his brain. His opponent twirled and set his feet, bending his knees to brace himself. With his sword held out in defense, he waited.

Billy puffed a loud, weary sigh as he readied his sword for an attack of his own. Heavy, sweat-drenched clothes clung to his body, and the weight of the hefty blade dragged his tired arms downward. He dared not let it fall.

His opponent, a tall, lanky man of considerable years, was quick and agile at the start of the battle but now slower and deliberate. He had spunk, though, a real kick start in his old engine, and that last charge proved his stellar swordsmanship.

Billy lifted his sword, pointing it at his mentor and remembering what he had taught. *"A knight opposes his enemy face-to-face. A stab in the back is the way of the coward; a pre-emptive strike of death is a strike of fear. If you must fight, attack your enemy head on. That is the way of valor."* Billy took a deep breath and charged, pulling his sword back. His opponent met the blow, and the swords clashed once again. This time Billy pushed downward, then back up in full circle, wrenching his opponent's sword from his grasp and flinging it away. He dashed to where the ringing blade fell and stamped both feet on its polished steel. He lifted his own sword, and with a pretend scowl, dared his opponent to approach.

"Way to go, Billy!" a young male voice shouted.

A female voice joined in. "Yay, Billy! You were awesome!"

A surge of heat prickled Billy's face, and he drew in a deep, satisfying breath while nodding toward his friends, Walter Foley and Bonnie Silver. Walter slapped Billy on the back and helped him remove his helmet. "I told you you'd win if you used my helmet. Hambone licked it for good luck."

Billy accepted a towel from Bonnie and wiped his forehead, pushing his short wet hair to the side. Bonnie pressed her thumbs behind the front straps of her ever-present backpack, as locks of her straight blonde-streaked hair caressed her navy polo shirt. Her blue eyes sparkled, greeting Billy with silent messages of congratulations.

Billy smiled. His training was paying off. He felt stronger than ever, certainly not like he did on the mountain, the last time he wielded a sword in a real fight. He had nearly lost his life battling Sir Devin, the dragon slayer. Next time, if there were to be a next time, he would be ready.

A hearty voice boomed from nearby. "Well done, William!" The heavy British accent made its owner easy to identify, his teacher, his mentor, his friend, and now, his conquered opponent, Professor Hamilton. The professor approached with deliberate, stiff steps and his tall form cast a shadow across Billy's face. "William? You seem rather pensive. Are you all right?"

Billy wanted to say, "I'm fine," but his muscles ached, a good, satisfying ache.

He lifted his wet shirt, peeling it away from his shoulder. "I'm sore, but I'll be all right. I was just thinking about the fight on the mountain." He laid the sword on the floor and pulled off his protective gloves. "Do you think I'm ready? I mean, we've still never fought all out. And we're not really using the same equipment those guys had, you know, the authentic battle armor and stuff."

"No, we're not." The professor picked up his vanquished sword and slid it into a scabbard on his back. "We battled 'all out,' as you say, with foam swords early in your training. Just now we did restrain our thrusts with our metal replicas, but it was still a strenuous workout. Yet, until we can combine the weight of authentic swords and armor with the passion of unrestrained zeal, we'll not be sure you're ready." He unfastened the scabbard and tossed it onto a nearby sofa. "You see, I have no true armored helmets, and my fencing guards are inadequate for mortal combat, so I'm afraid it's not safe to attempt an unrestrained match."

Billy ran his thumb along the edge of his blade, leaving a shallow slice in his skin. "Is it 'safe' if we don't prepare for real?"

The professor slid off his headgear, a modified Washington Redskins helmet, his white matted hair pulling up with it, creating a frenzy of wet strings. "Your point is well taken, William, but we would have to find a better sparring partner for you. Your potential opponent will not likely be a creaking old man such as myself." He ran his hand through his tangled hair and examined the logo on his helmet. "And I'll have to find suitable armor. The authentic helmets I've seen don't have an American Indian on the side."

Walter took Billy's sword from his hand. "This sword is so cool!" He rubbed the etchings on the blade. "This looks like a picture of two dragons fighting, but what do the other marks mean?"

The professor stroked the blade with his index finger. "There's quite a story behind these runes." He gave a tired sigh and gestured with his head toward the hallway. "Walter, I trust that your father won't mind if we build a fire and sit in the den while I tell the story. Although our swordplay generated considerable body heat, we will cool off quickly. But first, I must visit the water clo—I mean, the restroom, and clean up a bit."

Billy tugged at his plastered shirt again. "And I have to change these sweaty clothes."

Walter ran ahead. "I'll start the fire!"

Bonnie joined Walter in the den. He was already holding a lit match next to a rolled up newspaper stuffed under a pile of logs in the fireplace. The end of the paper flared, but the flame soon died away.

Bonnie adjusted the left strap on her backpack and peeked over Walter's shoulder. She had been wondering what Walter had seen on the mountain after he kept the dragon slayer from following her that day back in November. Now was her chance to probe her friend for the truth. Had he discovered her dragon wings? She gently cleared her throat. "I was just thinking, Walter. When I was watching Billy fight just now, it reminded me of when you hit Devin with the tree limb."

Walter tore a second match from a matchbook. "Yeah? It wasn't much. It's not so brave to bash someone's head when he's not looking." He struck the match and set the end of the paper on fire again.

Bonnie watched the struggling flame and shifted her weight to her heels. "I . . . I was wondering, though, about how you showed up in the field to help us, right when we ran into the search party. Did you follow us down the slope?"

Walter struck a third match and held it against the newspaper, waiting for it to catch. He shrugged his shoulders. "I saw your tracks in the snow. It wasn't hard."

Bonnie crouched next to the hearth. "What I mean is, did you see us on the way down? Or did you just follow the tracks?"

"Ouch!" Walter shook his hand and sucked his scorched finger. "I was super pumped after whacking Devin, so everything's sort of jumbled in my memory. I don't remember all the details." He stood up, still sucking his finger. "What difference does it make?"

Bonnie straightened her body and folded her hands behind her. "When you met us at the bottom of the trail, did you see . . . anything peculiar? I mean, it seems like you're Johnny-on-the-spot all the time, so—"

"So you're wondering if I 'spotted' anything?" Walter dried his finger on his jeans and flashed a grin. "Maybe I'm like an angel. Maybe God puts me in the right place at the right time."

Bonnie smiled back, reading Walter's playful tone. "You think so?"

"Why not?" He pointed toward his back. "Except I don't have any wings. That would be cool." He stuffed the empty matchbook into his pocket and rushed toward the doorway. "I think Dad just bought some starter logs. I'll go get them and another matchbook." He almost slammed into Billy as he dashed from the room, deftly spinning around his friend. "Back in a minute. Gotta get something to start the fire."

Billy, now wearing a fresh long-sleeved shirt and his favorite cargo pants, pushed his moistened hair back. He spied the blackened matches at the front of the fireplace and then winked at Bonnie while nodding toward the door. Crouching at the hearth, he leaned toward the stubborn logs and waited for Bonnie to block the room's entrance. She stepped into the doorway, using her body as a shield to hide Billy's deepest secret, the dragon trait handed down to him by his father. Walter was a great friend, but Billy didn't want to let him know about his dragon heritage. Not yet.

Billy took in a deep breath and blew a stream of fire at the pile of oak, spreading it evenly across the wood. Within seconds, the logs ignited, shooting flames and smoke into the flue above.

"Knock, knock."

Bonnie spun around. "Walter!"

"Mind if I come in?"

Billy jerked himself up to his feet, and Bonnie jumped away from the door. Walter sauntered in carrying a bag of paraffin kindling and set it next to the hearth. He nodded toward the blazing logs and smiled. "Nice job. You got better matches than I do?"

Bonnie put her hand over her mouth, apparently holding back a snicker, and Billy folded his arms across his chest. "I guess you could say that."

The professor entered, his face washed and his white hair plastered and parted down the middle. He carried the sword at his side and sat in an easy chair next to the fire. His face beamed. "William, I must reiterate my pride in your effort. You were outstanding with the sword."

"Yeah," Walter agreed. "You rocked!"

Billy bowed his head, his face burning. "Thanks."

The professor's eyes narrowed at Walter. "Rocked?"

"Yeah . . . rocked. You know; he was awesome. He really kicked . . . uh . . . gluteus maximus."

"Is that similar to being the cat's pajamas?" the professor asked.

"The cat's pajamas?" Walter repeated. "What's that?"

"It's an American idiom. It refers to someone who is well liked because of his accomplishments. I see, however, that it has passed out of common usage." The professor gestured for his three students to gather around. "Shall we discuss the sword?" He placed the blade on his lap and pointed at the etched writing.

"Some of these lines are inscriptions in an ancient dialect," he explained. He rubbed his finger along one face of the blade. "This one says, roughly speaking, 'May the Lady's purity never depart from the one found worthy to draw the sword.' "

"The lady?" Bonnie asked. "Who's the lady?"

"The Lady of the Lake. The legends say that she gave Excalibur to King Arthur."

Bonnie rubbed her finger along the raised pattern on the wooden hilt. "A lady gave it to him? Can a lady be strong enough to battle with a sword like this?"

"I think a sturdy woman could wield it," the professor replied, handing it to her. "Give it a try."

Bonnie grasped the hilt with both hands and held the blade up, her feet spread apart as if bracing for an attack. She waved the sword through a series of pretend maneuvers, and the professor's eyes followed the blade's swings and parries. "You seem to have no trouble carrying it," he noted.

Bonnie returned the sword to the professor's lap. "I guess it's not as heavy as I thought it would be."

The professor slid the sword back into its scabbard. "It's probably not as heavy as the real Excalibur, but its mass is substantial."

"It seemed heavy to me," Billy said.

"As it should, William; you worked with it for nearly an hour today, nonstop. But I perceive that Miss Silver is considerably stronger than her frame would suggest."

Bonnie's face flushed. "I'm sorry, Billy. I didn't mean to say—"

Billy waved his hand. "It's all right. I know what you meant."

Walter picked up the scabbard and examined its ornate designs, an embossed angelic creature with knights on each side bending a knee in respect. "Do you think those Arthur stories are true, Professor?"

A dreamy expression floated across Professor Hamilton's face, the dancing fire reflecting in his eyes. "Arthur is the stuff of legends, the search for the Holy Grail, the splendor of Camelot. It's hard to decipher truth within the myriad tales." His scholarly air returned as he took the scabbard from Walter. "It seems that each new storyteller tried to outdo the previous one, not really caring whether or not his tale was true. Legends are, after all, not meant to be historical fact. For example, I certainly doubt the existence of a goddess in a lake, but I have no doubts that Arthur once wielded the great and mysterious Excalibur."

He caressed the scabbard again, his finger pausing on one of the worshipful knights. "This is a replica handed down through many generations; its shape and details are based on legends and descriptions in journals. Many tried to copy Excalibur's image, but no one could reproduce its power."

Bonnie's eyebrows arched up. "It had power?"

The professor placed his fingers around the hilt and drew the blade out a few inches. "Power incomprehensible. Whosoever held the sword in battle could not be defeated, as long as the wielder was pure of heart. And the offensive powers in the hands of the holy were a terrible sight to behold."

Bonnie put her hands behind her back and shifted her weight toward her toes. "Does the real Excalibur still exist?"

The professor glanced from Billy to Walter to Bonnie, as if searching for something in each set of eyes. "I have no doubt about it, Miss Silver. I have hunted for it throughout the world, following many rumors and obscure tales. Finding it would make my life complete. You could say that it's something of a Holy Grail for me."

"What about the sword that guy took from Whittier's office?" Walter asked. "Didn't it have some kind of marks on it?"

Billy bit his lip to keep from laughing. He remembered Walter's story of his adventure with Professor Hamilton when they searched for clues in the principal's office. One of the slayer's cronies had come in and picked up a sword from its hiding place while Walter and the professor watched in secret. When Walter told the story again just a few days ago, he acted out every event, using a baseball bat for the sword and coaxing Hambone to play the part of the professor.

The professor slid the sword into the scabbard. "Your memory is accurate, Walter. That sword had many similar characteristics, but I couldn't be sure of its identity. I would like to pursue that lead at the appropriate time." His eyes fell on Billy and Bonnie, and his gaze lingered, making Billy feel uneasy. The professor went on. "And I suspect that there are some people I know who might be able to enlighten me concerning its whereabouts."

Billy twisted his shoe on the carpet like he was squishing a cockroach. How could the professor guess what was going on? He wasn't there when Bonnie battled the slayer in the mountain forest, and no one told him that Bonnie dropped the sword while flying away from the battle scene.

"In any case," the professor continued, "my sword is adequate for young William's training. While this replica is valuable, its symbolism is paramount for his development. His skill in swordplay will become necessary before long. And there is no concern for the replica's safety; it is practically indestructible."

Billy stepped away from the dying fire. Its flames had toasted his backside, and his hair had dried. "When are you going to explain all that to me—I mean, the stuff I'm training for?"

"In due time, William. I'm just putting the pieces together myself." The professor rose to his feet and strolled around the room, holding the sword casually across his shoulder. "Since you were expected to be out of commission for quite a while, I sent our mystery book to a friend of mine, an expert in antiquities. He has completed his analysis and will return the book in time for class Monday. I assume that when we decipher it we will learn a great deal."

Billy folded his arms across his chest and rubbed his aching biceps. Thinking about that book and how it had come into their hands made him feel sore all over. During his ordeal on the mountain with the powerful dragon slayer, Billy sat against the trunk of a tree, his hands and feet bound. The slayer opened a book and claimed that reading from it would summon a dragon, whom the slayer wished to kill. The poem sounded sort of like English, but Billy couldn't understand it. The words seemed archaic and symbolic; they just didn't make any sense. Clefspeare, Billy's father in dragon form, showed up before the poem ended, so it was unclear whether the words actually summoned him or he had sensed his son was in danger and flew to his rescue.

Since Billy was severely wounded in the fierce battle that followed, his memories of the details were fuzzy, but he recalled the professor's amazing crossbow expertise that saved his life that day. How could this wrinkled old guy be so daring, so agile? He could handle a crossbow and a battle sword with great strength and endurance, yet excel even more in his intellectual pursuits. This affable professor was becoming more and more of a puzzle.

The professor stopped his pacing and gazed at the fireplace, sighing before turning to face his students again. "William, I hope you and Miss Silver will carefully consider telling me what you know." He fingered the designs on the replica's scabbard. "I have discerned that you're confused and frightened, and I understand completely. I believe I would be, too. Both of you were severely wounded, yet you have mended at a miraculous rate. These are among the many perplexing mysteries to be solved." He straightened his whole body, his head held high. "I hope you will decide that you can trust me with your secrets. To be quite frank, I think I have earned your trust." A smile appeared on his wrinkled face, though a hint of sadness crept into his eyes. "Good night, students." He turned and stepped quickly out of the room. Seconds later, the front door clicked open, then closed with a muffled clap.

Billy flopped into the easy chair and slapped his hands on the chair's arms. Bonnie sank onto the sofa with a sigh, her brow knitting into three deep furrows. Walter sat on the far side of the sofa, his feet propped up on the coffee table, one shoe on top of the other. He picked at his fingernails, then retied his shoes, his eyes wandering toward Billy and Bonnie every few seconds. He finally jumped up. "I'd better make sure Hambone's warm." With a graceful bound, he dashed from the room.

Billy put his hand to his ear. "Bonnie, was Hambone whining?"

She smiled and shook her head. "Not a whine or a woof."

A sparkling gleam shone in Bonnie's eyes, though only the fading light from outside and a few dying embers in the fireplace illuminated the room. Billy sighed. "Either Walter has mind-to-mind connection with that dog or he knows more than we think."

"Uh-huh, I think he knows something."

"You do? Why?"

"Just some things he said to me today. And you know the professor's going to put all the pieces together before long."

"Yep. He'll figure it out sooner or later." Billy walked over to the small den window, and his thoughts traveled to the distant horizon, hills stretching into tree-covered mountains. He pictured the leaf-strewn battle scene and the dark, breezy cave. Bonnie joined him, and together they gazed at the deepening winter—thick gray clouds, cold, leafy breezes bending naked trees, tiny snowflakes threatening to bring millions of their friends later that night.

Bonnie's phantom reflection appeared in the window, smiling and peaceful. Billy kept his eye on the transparent image and pushed his hands into his pockets. "I think I'd better talk to Dad. I've only seen him once since I got hurt, and I was still pretty bad off then. I didn't ask him about a bunch of stuff that doesn't make any sense."

She leaned against the windowsill, bending forward to make room for her backpack. "A bunch of stuff? Like what?"

"Like, what's the deal with the sword you used on the mountain? And what happened to the slayer and that crazy candlestone? Stuff like that. And if I'm going to tell the professor everything, Dad should give his permission. Don't you think? I mean, I know the professor's going to ask lots of questions, so I'd better have a few more answers ready." Billy placed his hand on his stomach, and, with his lips forming a circle, he created a perfect ring of smoke and pushed it into the air. "Besides," he added as the ring expanded, "I've been practicing fire breathing, and I want to show Dad how I'm doing."

Bonnie put her hand through the ring, scattering the remaining smoke. "You're going to ask your mom to fly with you back to the mountain?"

"Uh-huh. Tomorrow if we can. We have a primitive airstrip up there now, so it's easy to get in and out."

She placed both palms on the windowsill and pushed herself up. "Then can I go with you?"

"That would be great, but isn't tomorrow the big day, you know, the thirty-day deadline?"

Bonnie put her hands on her hips. "How could I forget? Mr. Foley wants to finish the adoption paperwork as soon as possible. The judge said he would sign it for us even though tomorrow's Sunday."

"Mr. Foley? Aren't you going to start calling him 'Dad'? That's what Walter calls him, except when he's acting crazy and calls him 'Pop.' "

She ran her fingers through her hair and then hitched up her backpack, her eyes toward the floor. "Not yet. That's going to be hard to get used to. I called my real father 'Daddy' for so long . . . until he betrayed me."

Tears welled in Bonnie's eyes, and her pain drilled a hole in Billy's heart. How could anyone, especially a father, give an awesome girl like Bonnie over to a dragon slayer? And now she was on the verge of being adopted by Walter's parents, two really cool adults who still had no clue about her dragon heritage. Still, everything might work out great. If her real father didn't make contact in time, the judge would declare abandonment and let the adoption go through. The tension must have been terrible for Bonnie, like waiting for William Tell to shoot an arrow at the apple on her head.

Billy cocked his head and playfully tapped on the window. "I know what you mean. I'm going to a cave in the mountains tomorrow, and I'll be calling a huge dragon 'Dad'!" He placed his hand on Bonnie's shoulder and pointed, as though he were showing her something in the distance. "Can you see it? I'll be going, 'Dad! Dad!' and then I'll hear a roar, and a huge rush of flame will come flying out of the cave. And then I'll go, 'Dad! There you are!' "

Billy and Bonnie laughed together, and Billy noticed his hand resting on her shoulder, his fingers crossing the strap of her backpack. When their eyes met, her smiling countenance melted into a sincere, searching gaze. Billy pulled his hand away and cleared his throat. "Anyway, since it's your big day, I think you'd better stick around here. I should be back the same day or early the next."

They sat down on the sofa, and Bonnie placed her hands in her lap, nervously rubbing her thumbs together. "But what if we do hear from my real father? I don't know what I'd do without you here to talk to, I mean, if he wants me back and stops the adoption."

Billy glanced out the window toward the mailbox at the street. "There's no mail tomorrow, so the only way he could contact you would be by phone, right?"

"I guess so. Why?"

Billy kept his eyes on the street while rubbing his chin. "I don't know. Maybe you should come with me then. Maybe it doesn't make much difference whether you're here or not. I mean, even if your father called, Mr. Foley would be the one to talk to him." He turned back to Bonnie and sighed. "But I'm not even sure if Mom'll have time to go or what the weather's supposed to be like tomorrow. Since they finally started rebuilding our house, she's always busy with that, too."

"When will she be back?"

He glanced at a clock on the wall, an old cuckoo with dangling, weighted cones. "It'll be a while. She spent all day training a new pilot to carry skydivers, so she has to catch up on paperwork. She was pretty worried about the training. Dad used to do that kind of stuff."

Bonnie stood and stepped toward the window again. Billy joined her and pushed the window up, letting in a cold, fresh breeze. Walter was playing "fetch" with Hambone in the leaf-covered grass. The old hound wore a thick doggy sweater, so he probably didn't mind a little romp on this blustery January day. The dog's owner, Arlo Hatfield, a hunter who lived in the mountains, never dressed his tracking hounds in anything so spiffy. Hambone yipped and raced through the leaves, grabbing a ragged ball and rushing it back to Walter.

Billy leaned out the window. "Hey, Walter! Give the old dog a break!"

Walter and Hambone stopped. The hound sat on his haunches with his long tongue hanging out. "He's posing for you," Walter shouted back. "He knows you're doing a portrait of him."

Bonnie shivered and rubbed her hands over her arms. "You're doing a portrait?"

Billy slid the window closed. "Yeah. You want to see it?"

"Sure!"

Billy led Bonnie to a small utility room that Walter's father had converted into a serviceable art studio. He stepped over to the far corner where he kept his easel, dodging several rolled up posters and an empty frame. Gandalf, Billy's cat, lay curled up on the stool under the heating vent, so Billy remained standing. He lifted the cover of the sketchpad and flipped several pages over to find his drawing.

Bonnie let out a chuckle. "That's Hambone, all right. Those big sad eyes and long ears are perfect!"

"Thanks. You think Mr. Hatfield will like it?"

"He has to. It's beautiful! With all those shades of gray it looks almost like a black and white photo. It's so real!"

Billy reached into the deep, side pocket of his cargo pants where he always kept paper and something to draw with. He pulled out a pencil and signed the bottom of the portrait, including his trademark—two letter B's, the first one reversed, sitting back to back with the second. "Well, it's the least I could do. He didn't have to lend me his favorite dog."

"Are you going to give him the drawing when you visit your dad?"

"If I can. Mr. Hatfield doesn't have a phone, so I can't call him to see if he's home."

Walter ambled in, holding a pretend phone and talking in a high-pitched hillbilly twang. "Hallow? Do yew have a number fer Arlo Hatfield? The city? Nowheresville. You know, rait over dere next ta Boondocks? Yeah, I got a drawin' fer him. He caint read, so I drawed a pitcher fer him."

Billy roared with laughter. Bonnie held her fingers over her lips and turned crimson. Following her lead, Billy tried to stifle his own laugh, letting out a snort through his puffed out cheeks.

Walter continued, exaggerating the accent even more. "Naw, he don't have no phone. Why in tarnation wood I want to go and tawk to that critter on the phone? Yew caint send no pickshures over the phone. What kine of fool do yew take me fer?"

Billy snatched the pretend phone from Walter's hand and held it to his ear. "I'm sorry, ma'am. He's a bit loony. We're sending him back to the electric shock room now."

Bonnie folded her hands in front of her and feigned a snobbish air, her eyes closed and her nose raised. Her lips trembled between a frown and a smile. "Well, while you two, ahem, gentlemen decide who's the more loony, I shall be in my room writing my English essay. I suggest that you do the same. Evening is at hand, and it is due on Monday." She started walking out, maintaining her stern librarian frown, but she burst out laughing and hurried down the hall.

Bonnie flipped on her desk lamp. With Billy's mother out late, the Foley household had opted for an a la carte dinner. Bonnie had brought in a sandwich and salad from the kitchen and placed them on her desk blotter along with a tall glass of water. Although it was time to relax, she kept her wings hidden in her backpack, choosing to endure the discomfort rather than risk someone popping in on her while she perched on her chair like a freakish bat.

After kicking off her shoes and socks and changing into a comfortable set of sweat clothes, she sat at the desk and chose a felt-tipped pen from her collection of markers in the middle drawer, pausing a moment to read the calendar hanging on the wall directly in front of her. She leaned forward and carefully drew a dark "X" on today's date, the second Saturday in January. The box for Sunday was already filled, a happy face surrounded by pink and yellow flower stickers. At the bottom of the box a caption read, "Adoption Day!"

Bonnie deposited the felt pen in the drawer and pulled out a three-ring binder, a fat notebook stuffed with paper. The first hundred or so pages were filled with flowing script—her journals, a number of writing assignments, and a sizable collection of stories and poetry. Although Billy and Walter shared a computer for their written work, Bonnie preferred the feel of setting pen to paper and letting her words pour out from mind to hand. Her script revealed her moods—the weightiness of the day exposed in dark, heavy strokes, or happiness riding the page on sweeping loops and roller-coaster m's. The blank pages summoned her eloquence more than any word processor ever could. And clacking on keys just wasn't the same. Computers produced too many distracting beeps and pop-up windows to get any thoughtful work done. No, this way was much better, the soothing slide of her lovely silver Papermate on the crisp, white sheet.

Tonight, as she wrote her essay entitled, "Counting the Cost," her uneven script meandered, frequently slipping below the rule line. Dark ink blotches told of her weariness, and her supper remained barely touched. Through bleary eyes she stared out the window at the thickening fog. The clear, breezy evening had given way, and a cooling blanket of rich mountain air had seeped into the valley in thick soupy layers. The short days of winter had brought once again an early sunset, and mist shrouded the last remnant of twilight. Darkness had fallen, and even the porch lights were swallowed by the engulfing gloom.

With her eyelids drooping like heavy curtains, she jerked her head up. Her eyes flashed open at the sound of a call, her name whispered in a long, dying echo. It was soft, yet urgent, as though a loving hand had rung the dinner bell to signal suppertime while she was playing in a field far away, or the wind had picked up the call and carried the syllables to her ears, lengthened and distorted, but still distinct and familiar—Mama's voice.

Bonnie looked around. No one else was in the room.

She had heard that same voice several times over the last few weeks and had assumed her mind was playing tricks on her. She missed her mother so badly that part of her brain thought she was still around, in the next room making the bed, or in the kitchen cooking dinner, or in the rocking chair ready to read her a story. Although the voice sounded sort of like her mother's, it wasn't exactly the same—somehow it carried the chill of a haunted house.

With no hope of staying awake at her desk, Bonnie got up and slid her window open. The breezeless air outside allowed the mist to seep into her room in wet creeping fingers, caressing her face with damp coolness and sending shivers across her arms. A faint trace of wood smoke tinged the air, a sure sign that the mountains had lent their freshness to the valley.

What a great way to shake off her sleepiness! Although darkness had fallen, it was a little early to go for a fly. She usually waited until late at night when everyone was asleep, but the fog would surely keep her hidden. She climbed out the window and onto the roof, a trick she had perfected over the last few weeks. Since her second-floor bedroom was the only one that faced the rear of the house, it was perfectly placed for her covert escape.

Bonnie took a deep breath of the wet, cool air, and, glancing all around to verify her privacy, she unzipped her backpack, letting it dangle until her nimble wings pushed it off. Once freed, her dragon wings unfurled and spread out behind her body, the span extending more than twice her body's length.

Her roof escapes were times for solitude, unhurried respites for introspection and prayer. She sat just above the eaves, pulling her knees up and admiring her surroundings. She loved how the upper branches of the trees drank from the gray, hovering mist.

She marveled at how birds flitted so differently in a night fog, with rapid wing beats and without chirp or song.

As darkness wrapped her body, she threaded memorized verses through her mind, allowing them to come out in whispered song. She especially enjoyed singing a passage from a psalm of David, having set it to a tune herself during one of her many rooftop visits.

Whither shall I go from thy spirit? Or whither shall I flee from thy presence?
If I ascend up into heaven, thou art there: If I make my bed in hell, behold, thou art there.
If I take the wings of the morning, and dwell in the uttermost parts of the sea;
Even there shall thy hand lead me, and thy right hand shall hold me.
If I say, Surely the darkness shall cover me; even the night shall be light about me.
Yea, the darkness hideth not from thee; but the night shineth as the day:
The darkness and the light are both alike to thee.

With a long, satisfied sigh, Bonnie rose to her feet and climbed to the apex of the roof. Her flying experience told her that fog layers are often shallow. She hoped to be able to cruise above them, finding light in the moon and stars. With a mighty flap and jump, she was off! Propelling herself nearly straight upward, she catapulted into the mist, her hair and face dampening as she flew. She pushed onward, beating her wings against the cool air and watching, but the wet vapor persisted, thinner as she flew upward, but still too murky to be safe.

Not wanting to get too high and fearing she wouldn't be able to find her way home, she leveled off and began flying in a small circle, peering downward for any hint of light. She felt she was swimming rather than flying, streams of water soaking her hair and dripping into her eyes.

Bonnie had no doubt that she was higher than the trees; her only concern was how to land. After a few more seconds, she spotted a light down below. It was small, but bright enough to pierce the fog. She let her wings extend fully and glided toward the steady beam. As she approached, she thought she recognized the glow as a neighbor's halogen yard lamp. She would have to act quickly, land on the run, stuff her wings into her sweatshirt, and sprint about one block home. She folded in her wings and went into freefall, planning to unfurl them again just in time to parachute to a soft landing.

When she came within fifty feet of the light, it moved! It wasn't a yard lamp at all; it was the glow of a car's headlights! What should she do? It was too late to abort her landing. She was falling too rapidly.

Bonnie spread out her wings and pulled against the air, flexing her mighty canopy in the dark gray mist. She drew one wing in slightly and swerved, zipping just in front of the moving car's windshield and angling toward the curb. The car brakes squealed. With her legs already running, Bonnie's bare feet hit the ground, but she toppled forward, rolling into the roadside grass. Before she could get up, she heard the car door slam, and footsteps pounded on the pavement. She was stunned, feeling stark naked with her wings exposed and no hope of hiding them in time. Should she run? Should she wait, hoping the fog would mask her presence?

Then, from the dark shadows of a hundred nightmares, a tall specter strolled out of the soupy mist. Bonnie's eyes shot open, and she gulped.

"Daddy!"

About the Author

Bryan Davis, after working in the computer field for twenty years, quit his job to pursue his passion—writing for the glory of God and teaching his children.

Over the years Bryan has demonstrated a passion for writing in many disciplines and genres, including theology, fiction, devotionals, poetry, youth fiction, and humor.

Bryan sold his portion in an investment business and is now a fulltime author. He lives in Apopka, Florida, with his lovely wife, Susie, and their seven children. Bryan and Susie homeschool their children, several of whom have graduated and are now in college.

Bryan is the author of *The Image of a Father, Spit and Polish for Husbands, The Story of Jesus' Baptism and Temptation, The Day Jesus Died, The Story of the Empty Tomb* (over 100,000 sold), and *Jacob's Dream.*

DRAGONS IN OUR MIDST

Trapped in a crystalline dungeon, Bonnie Silver is stalked by a crazed murderer, a phantom who wields the deadliest of weapons. Billy Bannister, following cryptic messages in a mysterious book, is captured by the dragon slayers. Their courage and ingenuity, and the loyalty of their friends, are their only hope.

ISBN 0-89957-171-9 MSRP $12.99 (US)

Billy Bannister and Bonnie Silver enter a strange new world, a land of utter despair. Their mission? To rescue prisoners held there by the domain's evil mistress. After fighting battles in seven terrifying realms, Billy discovers the origin of evil at the depths of the seventh circle. Now he must choose; keep the evil force in captivity or save Bonnie's life.

ISBN 0-89957-172-9 MSRP $12.99 (US)

Available in April, 2005

TEARS OF A DRAGON

A vicious evil has been unleashed on the earth, and only the dragons can defeat it. With all of life hanging in the balance, Billy Bannister and Bonnie Silver lead the dragons into war. With heart-stopping action, the final battle between dragons and their enemies comes to a climax. But in order to win the war, one of the great dragons must die.

ISBN 0-89957-173-5 MSRP $12.99 (US)

Available in September, 2005